CITY OF BASTARDS

ANDREW SHVARTS

HYPERION
Los Angeles   New York

Copyright © 2018 by Andrew Shvarts

All rights reserved. Published by Hyperion, an imprint of Disney Book Group. No part of this book may be reproduced or transmitted in any form or by any means, electronic or mechanical, including photocopying, recording, or by any information storage and retrieval system, without written permission from the publisher. For information address Hyperion, 125 West End Avenue, New York, New York 10023.

First Edition, June 2018
1 3 5 7 9 10 8 6 4 2
FAC-020093-18110
Printed in the United States of America
Map illustration © John S. Dykes

This book is set in 12-point Minion Pro, Avenir/Monotype; Amulet/G-Type Fonts
Designed by Tyler Nevins

Library of Congress Cataloging-in-Publication Data

Names: Shvarts, Andrew, author.
Title: City of bastards / Andrew Shvarts.
Description: First edition. • Los Angeles : Hyperion, 2018. • Series: Royal
    bastards ; 2 • Summary: Under the protection of the king in the capital of
    Lightspire, Tilla believes she is safe from the treasonous machinations of
    her father Lord Kent, but when her University roommate is murdered, Tilla
    finds herself deep in a plot involving religious cultists, bloodmages, and
    Western insurgents.
Identifiers: LCCN 2017061415 (print) • LCCN 2017048611 (ebook) • ISBN
    9781368002363 (ebook) • ISBN 9781484767634 (hardcover : alk. paper)
Subjects: • CYAC: Revolutions—Fiction. • Conspiracies—Fiction. •
    Magic—Fiction. • Fantasy.
Classification: LCC PZ7.1.S5185 (print) • LCC PZ7.1.S5185 Cit 2018 (ebook) •
    DDC [Fic]—dc23
LC record available at https://lccn.loc.gov/2017061415

Reinforced binding
Visit www.hyperionteens.com

SUSTAINABLE FORESTRY INITIATIVE
Certified Sourcing
www.sfiprogram.org
SFI-00993

THIS LABEL APPLIES TO TEXT STOCK

For Sarah

PROLOGUE:
THE HEARTLANDS

WE FIRST SAW IT WHEN WE WERE MAYBE FIVE DAYS' RIDE away. Night had fallen on the Heartlands, but a single point of white light remained in the distance, a soft, powerful illumination, like the sun had gotten stuck as it slipped behind the horizon. It left an eerie glow across the sprawling wheat fields we'd been riding through for weeks, those long, thin husks swaying around our carriage as it rumbled down the King's Road.

"There it is," Lyriana muttered, her face pressed against the carriage window like a child's at a candy shop. "Home." Her golden eyes sparkled with tears.

The sun rose, and that white light faded. We kept riding. During the day, I slumped on the carriage's fancy pillows and drank too much brandywine and lay back in Zell's arms, which never, ever got old.

You know what did get old, though?

Wheat fields. Wheat fields after wheat fields after wheat

fields. Like, I get it. People need wheat. People like bread. But did our staple crop have to be something so incredibly boring? Couldn't we just eat meyberries or ice blossoms or peaches?

Peaches made me think of Jax. And thinking of Jax made my chest tighten and my eyes burn.

I drank more wine. I slept. Zell held me without a word, his fingertips running so gently up and down the length of my bare arms.

The next night, we could make out the light more clearly, and it made even less sense. Closer up, it was a column of light, a tower, like someone had driven a massive glowing nail into the earth.

"Oh," I said dumbly, "*Lightspire.* I get it now."

Lyriana snickered.

I slid over to the side of the carriage and popped open the latticed window, craning my head out for a better view. A warm wind blew into my face, way too warm for this time of year. I tried to force my eyes to understand what they were looking at. In the darkness illuminated below the pillar, I could make out the rough shape of a city: high stone walls, billowing smokestacks, the occasional golden temple spire. The pillar of light pulsed ever so faintly, and at times, if I squinted just right, it looked less like a single glowing column and more like hundreds of small lights, stacked tight like the hexagons in a honeycomb. For a second I felt relieved that I understood it, before realizing, no, that made even less sense.

"It's impossible," Zell said. He'd pushed out of his window too, jet-black hair fluttering in the wind; it had been growing back since he'd shaved it in that grove near the Markson, a lifetime ago.

"What is?" Ellarion asked. Lyriana's older cousin, the son of the late Archmagus Rolan, was the fourth member in our fancy little ride. I hadn't wanted him to come with us because I hadn't want to look at anyone who wasn't Zell or the Princess, but he'd insisted he had to, as Lyriana's bodyguard. Over the last few days, I'd actually grown to appreciate his company; he was funny, in a relaxed, lazy, don't-give-a-shit sort of way.

"The light," Zell replied, staring off into the distance. "It's like a tower, with hundreds of windows lit up with candles, but . . . it's too big. Too bright. No man could've built something like that."

"Now you're getting it, friend." Ellarion grinned. He leaned back against the soft cushions of the carriage bench, his vivid red eyes glowing vibrantly against his black skin. When I'd first met him, they'd reminded me of the roses in Lady Evelyn's garden, but now I decided that wasn't right. They were hotter than roses, more dangerous, like the flickering embers lying at the very bottom of a fire pit. Whenever he smiled, the Rings on his hands pulsed crimson.

As we rode, when I wasn't sipping (okay, chugging) brandywine and burrowing as deeply as I could into Zell's chest, I glanced out the window and tried to get a feeling for the Heartlands. The wheat stalks stirred with laborers, shirtless men and boys, sweating in the hot sun and gazing at our carriage in wonder. We passed merchant caravans and marching bands of soldiers and, once, a whole troupe of vagabonds on tour from the Eastern Baronies. Now and again, I spotted animals in the fields, hulking bull-like creatures with thick limbs and tiny shrunken heads barely bigger than my fist. According to Lyriana, they were Pullers, created by the Brotherhood of Lo to serve the farmers. I called them ugly-ass cow monsters.

On a bridge over a gentle river, we rode by the blackened ruins of a castle, just a few lone pillars of stone standing on a hilltop. "All that's left of the Kingdom of Jakar," Ellarion said, with a slightly uncomfortable pride. "My ancestors conquered them six hundred years ago."

"Oh. Nice. Good for them?" I replied, and took another sip. For the first sixteen years of my life, I'd dreamed daily of leaving the Western Province and seeing the rest of the world, Lightspire and the Heartlands in particular. But I was here now, and it was just . . . so weird? It wasn't that it was different, because I knew it'd be different; I knew the people looked different and dressed different and ate spicy food and took their religion way more seriously. But there were other ways it was different, ways that I couldn't put my finger on but felt more profound. Everything here felt older, more rigid, like the way of life had been decided centuries ago and no one had questioned it since.

I thought of towering redwoods and black-sand beaches and wide, muddy rivers and dancing bands of emerald light. My breath choked in my throat, and I felt such intense homesickness that it took every ounce of willpower I had not to burst into tears.

We rode on.

For the first half of our journey, Lyriana had seemed the most herself, as if the familiar sights of her home Province were lifting her spirits. She chirped away from her seat, telling us about the history of the region, the different types of crops, and sometimes completely random things like a story about how Ellarion had fallen down a well when he was seven (he swore he'd climbed down there on a dare). But as we drew closer and closer to Lightspire, her good mood seemed to evaporate. She became quieter, more withdrawn, spending most of the day gazing out the window pensively. Was she nervous? Afraid?

More than once, I caught her idly rubbing at the inside of her wrist, at the scarred patch of burned skin where her tattooed sigil used to be. When she'd last left Lightspire, she'd been a Sister of Kaia, an order of mages dedicated to helping the people of Noveris. But she'd broken their sacred vow of pacifism and had killed, to protect and to avenge. Now she was coming home an apostate, a mage without an order.

I figured it would be insensitive to pry, so I decided to keep my questions to myself. I made it about a day.

"So what exactly is an apostate?" I asked as our carriage bumped along a dusty stretch. "Like, what does that actually mean?"

Ellarion and Lyriana shared an uneasy glance. "True apostates are rare," Ellarion explained, "because the penalty for violating your order's views is often death. For Lyriana, there will be a trial. And then a verdict."

"A punishment," Lyriana said, her voice flat, her face turned away.

"Don't worry, cousin," Ellarion soothed. "The only reason you broke your vows was to save the Kingdom, and you're the Princess, the future Queen. They'll let you off with a slap on the wrist." His eyes flitted down to the scarred patch of flesh. "Okay. I'll admit, that was a poor choice of words."

"I shall ask that they try me as they would any mage who broke their vows, that I get no special consideration from my family name," Lyriana insisted, because of course, why would she ever take an easy out? "If the crown's justice isn't fair to me, then it isn't fair to anyone."

"Classic Lyriana," Ellarion sighed, as if reading my mind. "Never missing a moment to make life harder for yourself." He reached over and patted her on the arm. "Fair trial or not, I'm sure you'll be fine," he said, and was that just the slightest hint of uncertainty in his voice?

Now *I* felt nervous.

We stopped to rest at Penitent Springs, a sleepy town built by a monument of a Titan so worn, the face was a blank slab of crumbling stone. A party of pilgrims, led by a spindly, bearded priest, gathered in its shadow, heads bowed in silent prayer. We all shared a big loft at the inn, because Ellarion insisted it was safer for us all to stay where he could see us. Of course, he wandered off a minute later to get a drink at the tavern, and when I peeked down, he was dazzling the pretty barmaid, holding up his hand to make a spiral of fire circle his fingers like a halo. She stared at him in awe, eyes full of wonder, and yeah, this was gonna be a while.

Lyriana was asleep, so Zell and I snuck out to a wide grassy meadow. We lay on a soft blanket of grass, my head nestled in the crook of his shoulder, his strong, toned arm holding me close. He smelled like the frost, and his touch was warm and comforting. I just wanted to lie there forever, to never have to move again. His deep brown eyes sparkled in the moonlight as he reached up to the sky and pointed out the constellations of the gods the Zitochi worshipped, the Twelve. Those four stars were the Crone's cowl, and those three were the Bride's dress, and those, those five made the Grayfather's shield. . . .

Honestly? I just saw a bunch of stars. But I let him keep going, because I loved listening to him talk.

Afterward, we kissed, and he pulled my shirt off over my head, and I practically tore off his. I tasted his breath, felt his heat against mine, ran my fingers along the scars on his bare chest. The first time we'd made love, back in the baths of the Nest, it had been frantic, blurry, a tangle of limbs and lips and passion. This was different: slow, tender, more kisses than bites, more holding and staring into each other's eyes. For a moment, just one moment, I actually felt happy.

That night I dreamed of my brother, and I woke up sobbing.

We rode on.

The next morning, we were close enough to Lightspire that I could finally, fully, make that pillar out. It was a tower all right, but a tower so tall it made every other tower I'd ever seen look like a crappy chimney. It was as wide as the entire courtyard of Castle Waverly, and it stretched up so far into the sky that the very top vanished into the clouds. It wasn't straight and rectangular, but spiraled with thick rounded curves, like a serpent wrapped around a staff. There were no hard edges, no loose bricks, no blocky parapets. The whole thing was as smooth and slick as glass. More amazing than anything else, though, were the colors. This wasn't a tower of cold, gray stone; hell, I don't think it was made of stone at all. Instead it shimmered and pulsed, dancing green and blue and yellow, like the scales of a fish in the sunlight.

I'd seen metal like that once before. Years and years ago,

when I'd still been the bastard daughter who stared at her father with stars in her eyes, the two of us had visited the castle of Lord Collinwood. In his garish, cluttered chambers, the walls lined with the snarling heads of bears he swore he'd killed, he'd shown us his prize possession. It was a scepter, a staff the length of my arm with a round, spinning ball at the end. It was made of a metal as slick as glass, shimmering green and blue even in the flickering candlelight. "Shimmersteel!" Lord Collinwood had wheezed. "Made by the Titans themselves!"

That was how the tower stood so impossibly tall, how it sparkled so impossibly bright, because the whole damn thing was made of shimmersteel. *No man could've built something like that*, Zell had said, and he'd been absolutely right. I'd known that Lightspire was built on Titan ruins. I'd known that the Volaris family had discovered the powerful Rings that gave them magic in the crypts of the Titans, that their priests all worshipped those departed gods, that all the power of the King came from the remnants of the ancient race that had once ruled over all men.

But it was one thing to plunder a ruin. It was another to straight-up live in it.

"The Godsblade," Ellarion said, an uncharacteristic sincerity in his voice. "Seat of the Throne. Heart of the Kingdom."

"Home," Lyriana added, and the two of them quickly made a gesture of reverence in unison, tapping themselves with two fingers between the eyes, on the throat, and at the base of the sternum.

Zell and I shared a skeptical glance.

As we rode closer, I could see more of the city around the

tower, or at the very least the parts of the city that peeked out over the looming stone wall that surrounded it. It was big, so much bigger than I'd ever imagined, sprawling out along the horizon as far as I could see. The biggest village I'd ever been in was Bridgetown, which had seemed enormous at the time, but this made Bridgetown seem like a cluster of thatch-roofed swamp huts. All around the tower were the rooftops of what I guessed were the nice parts of town: high stone parapets, painted steeples, and the occasional golden obelisk or Titan monument. I couldn't see the smaller buildings below the wall, but I could see dozens of columns of smoke, which meant there were probably hundreds and hundred of houses. In Lyriana's stories, she'd casually mentioned the city's neighborhoods: the prosperous Golden Circle, the docks of Moldmarrow, the derelict Ragtown. I'd figured, you know, neighborhoods. But now I was realizing that every one of those was probably a city *by itself.*

And that was just the buildings inside the walls. Now that we were within a day's ride, I could make out a second city *outside* the city. The great Adelphus River entered the city from the northeast, a constant flow of trade vessels lined up to pass inspection at the gates, but the other borders were covered in a mess of rickety shacks that had grown along the walls like barnacles. This was the Rusted Circle, Lyriana explained. Because getting approval to enter Lightspire could take days, even weeks, a whole second ring of a city had formed around its walls, offering inns and brothels and taverns to occupy weary travelers. "It's a den of crime and impropriety," she said.

"Yeah," Ellarion added with a grin. "It's a lot of fun." He

was sprawled back in his seat with a goblet of yarvo, that cinammon-spiced liquor they liked so much here, resting in his hand. His loose silk shirt hung open at the collar, and I could make out a half dozen fresh hickeys on his smooth, hairless chest.

He caught me staring. The tips of his mouth curled into a smile as he raised his eyebrows suggestively at my neck. I blinked, confused, and then I got it and pulled up my own collar.

"Soldiers," Zell said, forehead pressed to the window's glass. "Coming fast."

I slid over behind him and pressed myself against his back, resting my chin on his shoulder. There, coming up the road, were soldiers all right, dozens and dozens of Lightspire men. They marched in lockstep toward us, spears and banners raised high, their polished silver armor reflecting so much sun that I had to cover my eyes. A sudden dread tightened in my stomach. What was this? Why did they need soldiers?

Ellarion sensed my worry, because he stifled a laugh. "Relax, rebel. It's just our escort."

"We need an escort?"

"I'm the Princess. I *always* need an escort," Lyriana said, with the tiniest hint of bitterness. She turned around abruptly and leaned over to Ellarion. "Give me that goblet. I need a drink."

Ellarion blinked. "But . . . you don't drink."

Lyriana held up her wrist. "Sisters of Kaia don't drink. I'm not a Sister anymore, am I? So give me the goblet."

"I . . . I mean . . . I'm just not sure it . . ." Ellarion tried, then gave up.

I kind of wanted to say something, because as fun as Lyriana was tipsy, maybe this wasn't the best time. Then I saw the determined look in her eyes and knew there'd be no point. She snatched the goblet out of Ellarion's hands and took a long, deep swig. Then she dropped it and hunched over, coughing and gasping.

"Yarvo." Ellarion shrugged. "It's not for everyone."

We rode on.

The escort met us just as we entered the Rusted Circle. The commander, a tall man in a horned helmet, barked some orders, and then his men flanked out, forming two thick columns that marched on either side of us. As we crossed into the town, I understood why. Huge crowds had formed, lining the road to gawk. The marching soldiers pushed them back, keeping the way clear, but there were still so many of them, jostling and shoving to try to get a good look.

They stared at us, and I stared back, kind of in awe. There were Heartlanders of course, many, many Heartlanders, but there were also Southlanders with glistening bald heads, and Easterners with thick eyeshadow and brightly dyed hair. And then there were the people who I didn't recognize: tall men in white cowls with red rings painted around their eyes, children with tattooed faces and hands, women with their faces hidden behind blank white masks. And all of them, all of them, were staring at *us*.

Multicolored streaks lit up the sky overhead, as dozens of Whispers flew home. The carriage was hot, sweltering even, but a cold chill ran down my spine. This all felt so weird, so wrong. Two months ago, I'd been the girl on the parapet, gazing down, watching the royal procession roll in. I'd been the face in the crowd, the gawker, the person staring from afar. That's who I was, not the girl in the fancy carriage, not the girl by the Princess's side, not the person that strangers clambered over each other to see. This wasn't me.

And yet . . . here I was.

"I don't understand," Zell said softly. I'd gotten good at reading him during the ride to Lightspire, or at least, I'd gotten better. I could tell when his pensive stare meant he was concerned and when it just meant he was deep in thought, and I could start to see the tiny smiles he sometimes tried to hide, like when I'd lean over and give him a little kiss on the side of the neck. But there were times, like now, when he was still a mystery, the same quiet, distant boy who'd kept me safe on our journey through the West. "Why are they looking at us like that?"

"You're in a carriage with the Princess," Ellarion said.

"No," Zell replied. "That's not what I meant."

Few things in the world made me feel more scared than fear in Zell's eyes. More and more soldiers were coming out now, flanking our carriage as we rolled through the rickety wooden houses of the Rusted Circle. I looked at Lyriana and Ellarion and tried to find comfort in their calm expressions, but the comfort didn't come. Instead, there was a new voice in my head, a voice of trembling panic, a voice growing louder and louder. What if this was all a horrible mistake? I was the daughter of Lord Elric Kent, the greatest traitor Noveris had ever known, the man who'd killed the King's own brother. And instead of running or hiding or anything remotely sensible, I was riding in a carriage right into the heart of the Kingdom.

Lyriana had promised me I'd be safe . . . but what if she was wrong?

The carriage came to a stop, jerking so hard I almost fell out of my seat. Ellarion fixed his shirt, smoothed out his curly hair, and checked his breath in his cupped hand. Then with a big, beaming grin that made all his perfectly white teeth sparkle, he threw open the door. "Time to meet the King."

I turned to Zell for guidance, but he looked as lost as I felt. What could we even do at this point? We were at the city gates, surrounded by what appeared to be an army's worth of Volaris soldiers. One way or another, our fates were sealed.

So I climbed out, followed by Lyriana, who stumbled, and Zell, who caught her. The sun overhead was incredibly hot and bright. We were right at the gates of the city, built into those walls I'd seen from a distance. And if they'd looked big from far away, they were enormous now, looming thick slabs of tan stone that stretched up so high I had to crane my head to see the very top.

An old children's rhyme popped into my head: *Lightspire, Lightspire, shall never fall / for no army's as great as the great city's wall.*

The gate in front of me was maybe even more impressive than the wall itself. I knew from Lyriana's account that this was the King's Gate, a special entrance that only opened for royalty; no waiting in line for us. Two massive curved slabs, like the world's biggest tablets, stood shut before me, looking like they'd take a thousand men to crack open even an inch. These slabs weren't plain like the walls, though. They had a mural carved into them showing the Titans as they founded the city. I fought back a shudder. Sure, the level of detail was incredible, and the craftsmanship was better than any carving I'd ever seen, but in the end, it was still a carving of the Titans, and the Titans were creepy as hell. I'd only ever seen them in statues or tapestries before, but seeing them here as giants, their identical, forever-smiling faces bigger than the carriage I'd come in, felt less like a sign of devotion and more a monument to terrify invaders.

A horn blew, then another, five thundering blasts. The ground rumbled, and the air crackled, and I felt that electric tickle, that palpable stirring in my bones that meant magic was happening. It was kind of weird how familiar that feeling had become. I looked up to see a half dozen mages at the top of the wall, all men, all shirtless, their torsos slick with sweat, and their hair hanging down their backs in long braids. Lyriana had told me about these guys, the Hands of Servo, the school of engineer mages that powered the city. They chanted as one, their voices a deep, undulating rumble, and they raised their hands up to the sky and turned them, around and around, as if they were waving invisible lanterns.

The air surged and thickened. My ears rang with a dull buzzing roar, and I tasted brittle dust and wet sand. The cobblestones shook underfoot, and dust motes spun around us in unnatural spirals. Inside the walls, I could hear the sound of metal grinding and gears whirring, some kind of massive hidden mechanism. The gates trembled and then, with a deafening rumble, creaked open.

I actually gasped. So that was how they did it, how they kept up a wall this big and opened gates this thick. In that moment, it finally hit me just how powerful Lightspire, how powerful the Volaris, really were. It wasn't just the magic, though sure, the magic was a big part of it. It was all of it. The magic, the city, the Titan ruins, this vast citizenry, bringing with them knowledge and strength from every corner of Noveris.

My father had thought he could defeat *this*? That he'd even stand a chance?

My fate hadn't been sealed when I'd ridden into the city. It had been sealed all the way back in Castle Waverly, sealed the minute my father had invited the Archmagus down to that beach. Because there was no winning this war, no defeating the Volaris, no chance of victory, no hope for Western independence. The only option we had was the only option we'd *ever* had: to bend the knee to the Volaris and hope for their mercy.

The gates swung all the way open, revealing the sprawling, colorful city behind them. At least, what little I could see of the city, beyond the huge crowd of soldiers. These weren't just royal footmen like the ones that had escorted us. They wore lighter armor, thin leather, and while they each had a flat, curved sword on their left hip, their right hands were free at their sides, adorned with Rings. And their eyes . . . a sea of glowing colors, some red, some orange, a few icy shivering blue.

Knights of Lazan.

Battle mages.

Their faces remained hard and unblinking, even as they stepped to the side to make room for a man striding toward us. I expected the King, but the man that walked out was old, his face weathered, and his skin was a light brown, not the rich black of the Volaris family. A long white beard framed his narrow mouth, and his gray eyes beamed with a quiet kindness. A narrow silver chain lay across his collarbone, with an iron medallion in the middle, a wide eye. No Rings, so he wasn't a mage. But there was still something powerful about him, something that radiated authority. Maybe it was the way the crowds went silent when his eyes flicked their way. Or maybe it was the way he walked past the mages, storming by the most elite warriors in the Kingdom as if they were a common crowd.

"Who's that?" I whispered.

"Inquisitor Harkness," Lyriana whispered back. "Keeper of the peace. My father's right hand."

"The spymaster," Ellarion added, and for once his voice was flat and respectful.

Inquisitor Harkness strode out through the opened gates and into the plaza where we waited. The whole world seemed to hold its breath as he sized us up and down. Were we being . . . judged? Evaluated?

Sentenced?

After an eternity he nodded to himself, and turned back, satisfied. "It's her!" he called. "I can confirm, Your Majesty. It truly is your daughter. Princess Lyriana has come home!"

The mages behind him parted again, and the heavy silence hanging over the plaza gave way to the chatter of a thousand whispers. A man strode out, and with every step he took toward us, the crowd got more and more excited, a mutter that turned into a rumble that turned into a roar. I took a single glance at the man, and yeah, no question, *this* was King Leopold Volaris. He was wearing ridiculously ornate clothes, an embroidered frock coat with frilled lace cuffs, tight breeches adorned along the leg with glistening pearls, a long billowing cape with a gold trim and a garishly bright floral pattern. His crown was a delicate circlet of shimmer-steel that danced multicolored in the light, throwing rainbow shadows on every surface he passed. He had a glowing lavender Ring, set with the biggest gem I'd ever seen. And his features could not have been more Volaris. He had Lyriana's full lips and Ellarion's curly hair, but more than anything else he looked like his brother, the former Archmagus Rolan, with the same graying hair and glowing turquoise eyes. But where Rolan had been hard as nails, there was a softness to King Leopold, a roundness to his features, a bulge in his belly. He looked like he'd seen a lot fewer battles, and a lot more buffets.

"The King approaches!" a soldier bellowed in the loudest, deepest voice I'd ever heard.

The reaction was instantaneous. In a single motion, the entire crowd behind us dropped down to one knee, bowing with their heads lowered and their hands folded behind their backs. All of the soldiers around us did the same, and even Ellarion and Lyriana followed suit. Before I could think, my body moved, seized by some primal instinct to follow the herd, and I dropped down into a bow myself.

I stared down at the cobblestones. This was normal, right? He was the King. You bowed to the King. Everyone bowed to the King.

Except Zell.

I heard a whisper pass through the crowd, a rumble of tension, before I realized to look over my shoulder. There was Zell, still standing, the only upright person before a sea of kneeling figures. Every head was turned to him, every eye staring, some with surprise, but many with what looked an awful lot like anger. In front of me, King Leopold blinked, confused. Inquisitor Harkness cocked a questioning eyebrow.

I sucked in my breath and felt my chest tighten. How had I not seen this coming? Zell was a warrior champion of the only people on Noveris who hadn't been conquered. While everyone else lived in awe, terror, or silent subordination to the King, the Zitochi wore their independence as a badge of pride, and spat on those who would bend the knee. Even after everything Zell's father had done, Zell was still a Zitochi, still loyal to his heritage and his culture. To bow now, to join the rest of us, would be to betray the values that most profoundly defined him.

But if he didn't bow . . . if he didn't do it . . .

No. I couldn't lose him. Not him too.

"Please," I mouthed, staring into his deep brown eyes. "Do it."

He closed his eyes and breathed deep, his nostrils flaring.

Then he dropped to one knee and bent his head and folded his arms behind his back.

The crowd let out a palpable sigh of relief. "Thank the Titans," Ellarion hissed, and Lyriana nodded. I was still holding my breath. How long was I going to hold my breath?

Thankfully, Lyriana spared me from any further tension. "Father!" she yelled, and rushed toward him, her dress billowing out behind her, her arms outstretched. She made it four steps, and then stumbled, an obvious drunken lurch that brought her down on her hands onto the stone.

"My baby!" King Leopold gasped back, and rushed to her across the plaza. She looked up, embarrassed, but then he was there, crouching down by her side, helping her up and grabbing her in a hug. In that second, they weren't the King and the Princess, the most powerful people in the world. They weren't two mages, capable of raining down death and destruction. They were just a father and daughter, reunited after thinking they'd lost each other forever, hugging and crying in the warm sun.

Tears stung my eyes. It was sweet, so damn sweet, but there was something else, a tight, nasty feeling that I hated to believe could still be jealousy.

I shoved that feeling down, shoved those tears away. I'd promised myself I wasn't going to do that. I wasn't going to dwell on the past. I wasn't going to fixate on Father and my home. I wasn't going to think about Jax. I couldn't.

Then the King looked up, looked my way, and all I felt was dread. He let go of Lyriana and paced toward me, slowly, cautiously, the way you'd approach a hissing snake. A dozen Knights of Lazan followed him like a shadow, their hands on the hilts of their swords. The crowd behind me pushed away instinctively, and if they were afraid, I was terrified. I looked up at him, met his gaze, and then looked back down, immediately, like I'd just glanced into the sun. The sheer enormity of the moment weighed down on me. This was the King of Noveris, King Leopold Volaris himself, and he was standing there, right in front of me.

"Are you her?" he asked, his voice still choked with emotion. "Lord Kent's bastard?"

"I am," I said, and it's a good thing I was bowed because

otherwise he'd see how badly my knees were trembling. "I was."

"Father," Lyriana said softly, and pressed one hand to the King's arm. "She saved my life. I owe her everything."

King Leopold looked at her, then at the Inquisitor, who just gave a little nod. Then the King sprang forward and seized me, pulling me up into a hug, clutching me in his arms. I let out the weirdest sound ever, somewhere between a yelp and a squawk, and I think my brain actually exploded in my skull, because if it could barely handle kneeling before the King, it sure as hell couldn't handle being hugged by him. He smelled of spiced perfumes and his belly was soft as a pillow, but none of that mattered because I was *being hugged by the King*. "I owe you the greatest of debts!" he bellowed. "I name you bastard no more, Tillandra, and welcome you to our great city!"

Behind us the crowd roared. My heart thundered. Lyriana smiled, tears in her eyes, and even Ellarion gave a little smirk. Zell alone remained unmoved, still bowed, knee bent, head lowered, eyes shut. I called out to him, but I don't think he could hear me over the cheers of the crowd. The Knights of Lazan moved to close around us, to usher me into the city, to protect *me*. This was actually happening. We were finally, truly, safe.

Weren't we?

one

I'd like to say I got used to Lightspire pretty quick.

It took me only a week to get used to the food. Sure, some of it was so spicy it made my mouth burn and sent me gagging for a glass of milk. But so long as you knew what to order, it could be so incredibly good. I quickly discovered I liked any food whose name ended with *rellia*, which as far as I could tell meant *baked in a perfect flaky crust*. There was *chen rellia*, which was a chicken pastry, and *marr rellia*, which was a beef pastry, and *porro rellia*, which I couldn't really explain, but it involved cherries and yogurt and just a tiny hint of cinnamon, and it tasted like heaven and sunshine.

It took a little longer, maybe a month, before I got used to the clothes. Oh, they were gorgeous, sure; that I knew before I even wore them. Even as a little girl, I'd dreamed of wearing Lightspire dresses, with their glossy swishing trails and their intricate floral patterns and their slim elegant sleeves that tied together with a ribbon between your fingers. But it was one thing to dream of wearing their clothes and another to actually wear them, not just to some fancy masquerade but out on the street. Lyriana had a crack team of seamstresses fit me up, personally commissioning a full wardrobe of gowns, and while I smiled and nodded and gaped, for the longest time I felt like an impostor wearing them, like a little girl who'd snuck into her stepmother's closet.

Getting used to the noise was harder. Back at Castle Waverly, unless there was a feast or a fight in the courtyard, the nights were still and quiet. If you leaned your head out your window, you'd hear the chirping of crickets, the whistling of the wind, maybe the mournful cry of an owl. But Lightspire was loud, deafeningly loud. My first two nights there, I couldn't sleep because the sounds outside my window were too overpowering: the shouts of hagglers in the night-bazaars, the neighing of horses, the grinding of carriages, the whistle of the Whispers and the caws of the Sentinels, the distant rushing of the Adelphus River, and above it all that constant hum of magic that was part noise in your ears and part rumble in your bones.

You know what I never got used to, even after being in Lightspire for six months?

Alarm clocks.

Stupid, terrible, demon-spawn alarm clocks.

I awoke with a grunt to that awful buzzing, flailing my arm ineffectually at the noise. But of course, the Artificed monstrosity that was my alarm clock wouldn't be deterred by simple swatting. It was an expensive little gadget, hand-crafted by the Gazala Guild, a big glass jar attached to a tiny mechanical clock. When the hands on the clock struck seven in the morning, a little lump of charmed stone at the bottom of the jar let out a spark of magical energy, a translucent blue orb that hovered around the inside of the jar, bouncing off the glass surface over and over again with an infuriating buzz. Lyriana bought it for me after I slept through our morning classes for the fourth day in a row.

With a grumble, I rolled out of bed and padded my bare feet across the cold stone floor of my dormitory room toward my dresser. Barely bothering to brush the tangled auburn hair out of my eyes, I reached out and jammed my hand onto the glass jar, feeling that burning tingle as the blue orb stuck to the underside of the glass, flickering and dissipating. "Shut up," I groaned. "Just. Shut. Up."

"Tillandra, my dear, you truly are such a delight in the mornings," a husky accented voice said.

I turned around to see my roommate, Markiska San Der Vlain IV, sitting in front of her vanity, a makeup brush in one hand and a stem of grapes in the other. I looked like, well, like a person who'd just staggered out of bed, messy and unwashed and disoriented. Markiska's lustrous blond hair circled her forehead in a neat crown-like plait and hung down her back in three elegant braids, each one ending in a silver ring that hung just above her waist. She was wearing a traditional Sparran outfit today, which meant a tight knee-length skirt, a loose silk shirt, and a half dozen necklaces. Her skin was pale, paler even than mine, but adorned with dozens of purple and pink tattoos: dancing fish on her wrists, bands of ivy around her calves, a sparkling horned eel along her collarbone. One night she'd drunkenly told me she had another, a blossoming sea-rose, but only her lovers got to see that.

"How in the frozen hell do you manage to look so good at seven in the morning?" I grumbled.

"By waking up at five." She smiled, her white teeth framed by painted purple lips.

"Lies." I poured myself a glass of water from a crystalline carafe and spilled a good third of it. "There is no five in the morning. That's just something the priests made up to scare children."

Markiska laughed loudly, though to be fair, she did everything loudly. "Some of us still have boys to impress. We don't all have a gorgeous Zitochi warrior to ravage us every night."

"It's not . . . He's not . . . I mean, not *every* night. . . ." I blushed and stared at my feet. I don't know why talking about sleeping with Zell still made me so self-conscious. It's not like it was a secret to anyone, and certainly not to Markiska, who'd taught me to tie a purple ribbon around the door handle when I needed a night to myself. Zell and I were together, and everyone knew it. And still here I was, blushing.

Markiska turned back to her mirror, applying a sparkling gold liner underneath her eyes. She was from Sparra, one of the Eastern Baronies, and the first day we'd met, she taught me two important things. One: the Eastern Baronies were not a single homogenous region but seven distinct city-states, each with its own rich culture, history, and traditions, and to bunch them all together as if they were a single region was to marginalize all of their individual identities, which was hurtful, offensive, and rude. And two: Sparra was totally the best one.

I liked her immediately.

"Speaking of impressing boys," she said, finishing her left

eye and moving on to her right. "Are you coming with me to Darryn Vale's party tonight?"

"Oh, is that tonight?" I asked, even though I totally knew it was tonight. "I don't think so. I have plans."

"Liar."

I considered keeping it up, and thought better of it. Markiska could read me like an open book. "Fine. You know I just feel awkward at those things. Everyone knows each other, and they're all fancy and hoity-toity. . . ."

"Tillandra. How many times do I have to explain this to you? You are a student at the most prestigious university in the Kingdom. You're living with the daughter of the Baron of Sparra. And you're best friends with, oh, that's right, *the Princess*." She clapped her hands together. "Get it through your head! You *are* hoity-toity now!"

I shook my messy hair around. "Sure don't feel it."

"Nothing a good bath can't fix." She cracked open her wooden jewelry box and took out her favorite bracelet, a thin string lined with glowing purple pearls. Apparently, they were only found in Sparra's bay, in the mouths of something called bloodclams. "Please come? This is the last big party before Ascendance Day, and I have so much more fun at these things when you're there," she said. "You can even bring your beautiful, brooding warrior boy."

"Zell can come?" Now she had my interest. I mean, a fancy party at the estate of Lightspire's richest family probably wouldn't be his first pick for what to do tonight. But it would also be a nice change of pace from our usual nights, drinking at the Mewling Serpent or walking along the high wall that enclosed the Golden Circle. Both of those activities usually led to hooking up, but hey, so could a party, right? Wasn't that the whole point of parties to begin with?

"Oh, please." Markiska beamed. "I want to see the faces of all those skinny, weak-legged Lightspire boys when they see a real man walk in."

I cocked an eyebrow. "For someone who claims to be obsessed with boys, you spend a lot of time shit-talking them."

"What can I say?" Markiska grinned, that wry shark's grin that first told me she was way more cunning than she let on. "I'm a girl of boundless mystery."

A dip in the baths and a rummage through my stupidly big closet later, I was strolling through the wide grassy sprawl that lay at the heart of the University. It was still morning, the looming spire of the Godsblade a shimmering emerald in the sunlight, but already, the Quad was packed. Some students hurried along the paths beside me, while others lounged under the dense canopies of the forever-flowering cherry blossoms, reading books or just taking a nap. Vendors lined the cobblestone paths, hawking steaming pastries and cold glasses of beer. A group of students lounged in a circle on the grass, clapping in rhythm as a tall, pretty girl with her hair in tight ropes played a four-pronged flute. Nearby, a bespectacled professor was holding class with a trio of Gazala Guild novices, twirling his hands in delicate circles as dancing pink orbs fluttered around his fingers.

This was the University in a nutshell, amazing and overwhelming, familiar but totally alien. You knew it was a big deal because it didn't even have a real name; everyone just called it the University. As I learned in my extensive orientation, it was almost as old as Lightspire itself, the greatest center of scholarship in all of Noveris, the big juicy brain that informed the Kingdom. For centuries, it had been exclusively for mages, a walled sanctuary for new generations of Beastmasters and Mesmers and Knights to hone their skills. But with the fall of the West and the end of the Great War, it had opened up to everyone. Well, everyone who could afford to go there. Which was actually not that many people at all. These days, in addition to anyone who'd shown the gift of magic, the University was home to the children of Lightspire's noble families, visiting diplomats, and most powerful merchants.

And me, of course. The bastard daughter of Lord Elric Kent, the man who'd committed the gravest act of treason in recent history and was currently waging a war against the crown. Whose men were, even as we speak, fighting and killing the brothers and sisters of many of the very students hanging out around me.

Yeah. I fit *right* in.

After I'd arrived in Lightspire, the King and his council had debated what to do with me for days. A few of the nobles had wanted to see me put on trial for treason, an example to all who'd consider it. But King Leopold had stood up for me, refusing to punish the girl who'd saved his daughter's life, and so this was the compromise they'd reached. I would stay in Lightspire as a ward of the Volaris, a prisoner in the most technical sense. But I would also be allowed to attend the University, to get the same opportunity to learn and grow and party as any other rich-ass Lightspire kid. And when I graduated, and when my father's rebellion was put down, I'd be given the opportunity to swear my vows to the King and be free, a true citizen of Lightspire.

And that was what I'd always wanted, wasn't it? What I'd dreamed about maybe every single day of my childhood? To wear gorgeous Lightspire dresses, to bask in the city of wonder, to live the dazzling life of the noblest of nobles. That was my life now. That's what my life would be.

I squinted up through the sky, pressing a hand over my eyes to block out the light. According to the great golden clock nestled within the twisting scales of the Godsblade, it was nine forty-five. I had a class at ten, History, and we were covering something interesting like the Conquest of the Southlands. Not enough time to grab a bite to eat, even though my stomach was rumbling, but enough to grab a friend.

I hustled across the Quad and took a left toward a pretty redbrick building. The University had six main dormitories, but Bremmer's Cottage was no doubt the nicest, reserved only for the wealthiest and most privileged. Or, in this case, most royal. I threw a quick cursory nod at the two City Watchmen by the door and hurried inside.

Lyriana's room was on the first floor, a spacious apartment with its own kitchen and bathroom. Its name was, no joke, the Princess Chamber. I rapped my knuckles on the heavy, ornate door. "Lyriana! It's me! You coming to class?"

Silence.

I knocked again. "Hey! Seriously! You coming?"

More silence. That wasn't like her. Lyriana was usually ready to go before I even got there, with a sheet full of questions to ask during the lecture. Unless . . .

The door opened a crack, and I could see a Heartlander boy's face through the slit, his features slender and handsome. His brown eyes met mine with surprise.

"It's cool," I said. "I'm Lyriana's friend. Just here to walk her to class."

"Oh, okay," he said, with the stunned cadence of someone who still couldn't quite believe what was happening to him. Given that he'd probably woken up in bed with the Princess, I didn't blame him. Peeking over his shoulder, I could see into Lyriana's room: a messy bed, scattered clothes, and an empty wine bottle lying on its side on the dresser. I could hear running water from behind the bathroom's closed door; she was getting ready.

The boy stepped out of her room in a hurry, still glancing around like he was sure he was about to get caught. He was cute, really cute, with deep dark eyes and full black hair cropped short around his head. He was still buttoning his shirt up, and he had abs you could forge a sword on. I vaguely recognized him from one of my classes, a younger son from some powerful family or another.

"Relax." I smiled. "You're not in trouble." *And you're certainly not the first,* I thought but didn't say.

"Heh. Thanks." He smiled back. "I just . . . I mean, she's . . . you know . . . so I thought . . ."

And all at once, the friendly smile melted off his face as he realized exactly who I was. His eyes widened, then narrowed into angry slits. His mouth tightened in a cold, hard line. I put on a stoic front, but inside, I sighed.

"I should go," he said.

"You probably should."

He pushed past me, still buttoning his shirt, and actually jostled me aside. And just when I thought that maybe this awkward-as-hell encounter was over, he muttered something under his breath, just barely loud enough for me to hear.

"Traitor bitch."

Then he was gone, and I was all alone in the hall, watching him go with my mouth hanging open and no words coming out. I wanted to call him out. I wanted to punch him in the kidneys. But I just stood there, staring. Because on the one hand, who did he think he was, that he could talk to me like that? Did he seriously think he could get away with being a dick to *me*? I had dinner with the King once a month! I was the Princess's best friend! If I told her, if I told the King, the boy would have hell to pay. . . .

Unless I was wrong. And that was the other hand, the kicker, the thought that was always lurking at the back of my mind, the gnawing doubt I'd had since I'd walked through the city gates. Because what if he wasn't being a dick at all? What if he was just saying what everyone was thinking? What if all of them, the students, the professors, the nobles and the commoners, what if they all actually saw me that way? The traitor, the foreigner, the girl who only got to live because the King was a weak, sentimental softie? Was this guy actually an asshole?

Or was he just the only person in this city bold enough to tell me the truth?

TWO

A FEW MINUTES LATER, LYRIANA AND I WALKED TOGETHER side by side, toward the round, domed building called the Hall of History. Lyriana looked great, of course, because she always looked great; my memories of our journey through the West were hazy with emotion, but I vaguely recalled her looking gorgeous with seawater-soaked hair and a sand-crusted dress. Now, she looked like the very model of a Princess at university, in a slim blue gown with billowing sleeves and ornate elderblooms embroidered along the neckline. Her raven hair hung in neat braids down her back, and her golden eyes glowed against her smooth black skin.

That wet fart of a boy didn't come close to deserving her.

"Is everything all right, Tillandra?" Lyriana asked. "You seem distracted."

I hated how easy I was to read. "I'm fine. Just a lot on my mind."

She stared at me hard, one eyebrow cocked, then sighed. "You saw him leaving my room, didn't you? Jerrald, I mean."

"If that was the name of the cute, disheveled guy trying to sneak out, yes," I said. I thought about telling her the other part, what he'd whispered to me, but decided against it. If I told her, she'd confront him, and then it would be a whole thing. I didn't need that drama.

Clearly, Lyriana didn't either. She clasped a hand to her forehead and let out a despairing moan. "I should not have done that," she said. "We were just going to talk. But then . . . he was being so nice . . . and the wine . . . and he looked so good. . . ." She shook her head. "Last one. No more. I promise."

She'd said the same thing after her last hookup, and the one before that. Honestly, I didn't know how to feel about this new side of her. I mean, on the one hand, good for her for getting what she wanted; she'd spent her life so repressed, it was hard to blame her for having a little no-strings-attached fun. But on the other, something about the way it had all gone down rubbed me the wrong way, and set off some weird alarms of protective concern I didn't know I had.

It's not that I was worried about her reputation or that I cared about Lightspire's whole "a woman's value is her purity" bullshit. I'd been to enough parties at the University to see exactly what Lightspire's allegedly chaste nobility did behind closed doors. But what bothered me was that *she* cared, or at least, she *had* cared, for most of her life. The Lyriana that I'd met in the West, hell, the Lyriana I had known for our entire journey, was someone who'd followed the rules, not just because she was afraid of breaking them, but because she genuinely, deeply believed in them. That belief had guided her. It had made her who she was. And now it was gone, bled out with Jax on the cold stone floor of a Western tower.

I sucked in my breath. I was safe. I was good. I was happy.

We reached the Hall of History's carved wooden doors, and Lyriana pushed them open with her shoulder. "There's a party tonight," she said, her voice echoing off the marble floors of the Hall's central chamber. "Darryn Vale is throwing it at his father's manor. I imagine it'll be one of the biggest social events of the year."

"Markiska mentioned that to me."

"You should come!" Lyriana said as we turned down the hallway. "The Vale estate is incredible."

I was pretty sure that if I went to this party it wouldn't be for the estate, but I didn't bother correcting her. "Zell might come, too."

Lyriana's eyes lit up. "Really? That's so exciting! I feel like I haven't seen him in weeks!"

That was because she hadn't, but these days, Zell wasn't exactly the most social person in the world. "No promises," I said. "I'll talk to him today and see."

"Oh, please do, because I . . . I . . ." Lyriana froze in place, and trailed off mid-sentence. I turned around and followed her gaze. There, at the far end of the hallway, were three young women, all wearing long green robes with fine gossamer veils over their faces. Their Rings flickered emerald.

Sisters of Kaia. And formerly, sisters of Lyriana.

Shit.

Probably without even realizing it, Lyriana rubbed at the

inside of her left wrist. The burn there had healed, leaving only a faint white scar where her tattoo had been. Her slender fingers were bare, not a Ring in sight.

I'd been there for Lyriana's trial, watching from the stands of the courthouse on the tenth floor of the Godsblade. I'd sat next to Ellarion, and he'd been his usual cocky self when the trial started: "Relax. She'll be fine. She's the Princess." But as speaker after speaker came forward, his mood had darkened, and his Rings had pulsed a hotter and hotter crimson. The trial turned out to barely be about Lyriana. Instead, all anyone wanted to talk about was the politics of the situation. Inquisitor Harkness spoke bleakly of unrest within the Kingdom, of protests in all the Provinces about inequality and injustice. Molari Vale, the wealthiest merchant in the land, gave a grandiose speech about the sanctity of the Titans' law and how no one should be allowed to break it, Princess or not. Captain Welarus of the City Watch spoke about the growing ranks of the Ragged Disciples, Lightspire's home-grown anti-magic cult. And even Archmatron Marlena, whose life Lyriana had saved, spoke about the need for a fair, impartial sentence, to preserve the image of the Sisterhood in the public's eye.

By the time King Leopold strode into the circle, there was no question the verdict was going to be bad. "My daughter, Lyriana Ellaria Volaris, has sinned in the eyes of the Titans, and broken the deepest covenant between a mage and her order," he said, his voice trembling just a little. "And yet she did so to protect the Kingdom and to save the lives of so many of our mages. She must be punished, and yet she must also be served." He inhaled deeply. I could see his hands shaking. "Lyriana will not be executed, and she will not be stripped of her title. But as an apostate mage, she will be banned from joining another order, or from ever doing magic again, on penalty of death. Lyriana, my daughter . . . you are a mage no more."

It didn't make sense to me, but Lyriana had explained it to me that night in my room, as she'd cried in my arms. Tensions between commoners and mages were high in Noveris, maybe even near a boiling point. The nobles, even the Volaris, were terrified that my father's rebellion in the West would be the match that set the whole Kingdom ablaze. Punishing Lyriana showed the people that the Volaris still had to uphold the laws; having a non-magical Queen might pacify a generation. It was for the good of the Kingdom. For peace.

Maybe the logic made sense to a politician. But looking at Lyriana now, at the sadness in her eyes as she stared at the Sisters, it seemed like a whole lot of bullshit to me. Lyriana had grown up with magic, had been using it her whole life. And all she'd done was use it to avenge Jax and kill Razz, arguably the worst person who'd ever lived. If it weren't for her, my father's armies would be in the Heartlands now, setting it *literally* ablaze. The King should've called her a hero, not stripped her of her identity.

"Hey," I said, stepping in front of her line of sight. "I'll go to the party tonight. With Zell."

She dabbed at her eyes with the side of her hand. "Really?"

"Really." And I guess I was committed now, to keep an eye on her if nothing else. "Now come on. We're late enough for class already."

THREE

History class, as it turned out, wasn't interesting at all. We sat in the round lecture hall, crammed together along the uncomfortable wooden benches, while the tremble-voiced professor droned on about the conquest of the Southlands. Learning about war was pretty much the only thing I'd enjoyed back in my lessons at Castle Waverly, but it turned out every single Lightspire history lecture went exactly the same way: the Volaris wanted to conquer Some Place; Some Place had some great defenses that everyone thought were impregnable; yeah, okay, but mages were better. The absolute worst had been the lectures on the Great War, which had gone on and on about the total superiority of the Lightspire armies, the pathetic weakness of the Western rebels, and a whole bunch of bullshit on the "inherent inferiority" of Western leadership. It'd taken every ounce of restraint in my body not to stand up and yell, "Then why'd it take you so long to beat us, assholes?"

Today was nowhere near as bad, though a lot more boring. I quickly drifted out of the lesson and just let my eyes wander across the ring of students. Lyriana sat next to me, writing down every word the professor said like it was a decree from the heavens. She was pretty much the only one; the two girls on the other side of me were whispering, another one was asleep, and the guy in front of me was doodling what appeared to be a bear with enormous breasts and a broadsword. At the far end of the room opposite me, in the very back row, were three guys not even bothering to pretend to pay attention. They talked loudly, with booming laughs, and one even got up to go get a big hunk of bread for them to share. I recognized the guy in the middle, the one with the hair in glistening beaded ropes: Darryn Vale, son of Molari Vale, richest man in Lightspire. No wonder the professor didn't dare shut him up.

Mercifully soon, the clock in the Godsblade chimed noon, and class was out. Lyriana wanted to go read (which I'm pretty sure meant "sleep off her hangover"), and that was fine because I had the afternoon free, and I had someone I was dying to see. But first, I had a quick errand to run.

The Whisper Roost was one of the University's most trafficked locations, a round brick building just along the campus's edge. It was one of the most modern structures here, with a sleek red facade and semitransparent windows. Two enormous wire cylinders jutted out of its flat roof, and they rustled with movement as Whispers flew in and out of them, the sky overhead alight with silver streaks as they swooped by. Inside, a long wooden counter cut the room in half. On one side were students and teachers, waiting in long lines to get their mail. On the other were the Roost's workers, each with his own window, hustling about to rifle through envelopes and pass along letters.

Back West, Whispers were rare and expensive, used only by the most powerful Lords to relay vital messages. The only kind I'd ever seen had been Talkers, tiny glowing owls with galaxy eyes who would actually remember your exact words and repeat them to whoever you wanted. Talkers were pricey, even here, but your average student could afford a Carrier, round little pheasants with enormous talons, sculpted by the Brotherhood of Lo for carrying letters and scrolls.

I scanned the workers' windows now, and smiled when I found a familiar face. Marlo Todarian was, no doubt, my favorite worker on campus. A short chubby man in his mid-twenties, he had the curly black hair of a Heartlander, the bronze skin of a Southlander, and the sparkling green eyes you only saw out West. He wore big wooden necklaces, pearl earrings, and sometimes sold me meat pies that his boyfriend baked. I'd asked him once where he was from, and he answered with a shrug that he was a true Noverian, because he had a little bit of every part of the Kingdom in him.

"Tilla! My favorite Westerner!" He beamed as I slid up to his window.

"I'm the only Westerner you know." I grinned right back. "Any mail for me?"

He spun around, his fingers rifling with incredible precision through the massive shelves behind him. "Just one letter," he said, drawing out a small square piece of paper. "Looks like a flyer from Madame Coravant's Boutique, inviting you to shop there for an Ascendance Day dress."

I let out a groan. If I had to go to that masquerade, I'd at least make Lyriana buy me an outfit. "Just throw it away, would you?"

"My pleasure." Marlo hurled it over his shoulder, where it arced perfectly into a trash bin. "Anything else I can help you with?"

I leaned against the window, my voice barely above a whisper. "Any news from the West?"

As a worker at the Whisper Roost, Marlo was, of course, strictly forbidden from reading anyone's mail. But he still had his finger on the pulse of everything that was going on in the Kingdom, or at least everything important enough to pass his way. Ever since I'd befriended him, he'd been my best source for gossip about what was happening in my home Province, which was useful since the city newspapers only printed stories like *Glorious Lightspire Army Triumphs Again!* Marlo had told me about the reinforcements the King had sent out, about the brutal battles that had been fought in the foothills of the Frostkiss Mountains, about the slow steady march of Lightspire's forces. I asked because I *had* to ask, because I *had* to know, even as I was bracing myself for the inevitable, for the day he told me that Lord Kent had been defeated, that my father was dead.

Today, Marlo just shrugged. "No news, I'm afraid."

I blinked. "Huh? What do you mean, no news? How does that happen?"

"Well, I—" he started, but before he could finish, a burly student with bushy hair and thick sideburns shoved past me.

"Hey! Worker!" he boomed. "They pay you to sort mail, not chat it up." He crossed his arms over his chest, gold bracelets jangling. He had a heavy Ring on each pointer finger, their gems glowing a dull brown. "Got any mail for Tevus Tane?"

Marlo's lips twisted into a polite smile. "Deepest apologies, sir. One moment, please." He turned and searched through the shelves again, coming back with a heavy yellowed envelope. "Here you go."

The student grabbed it out of Marlo's hands, still scowling. "Hope you weren't expecting a tip," he said, and stomped off.

Marlo let out a weary sigh, and I reached over the counter to pat him on the shoulder. "I think my roommate hooked up with that guy," I offered. "Well, she tried to, but then he got drunk and cried about how his mom didn't love him."

Marlo chuckled. "And that's why you're my favorite student here, Tilla." He reached under the counter and took out a meat pastry, wrapped in fine tissue paper. "Here. Garrus baked it this morning. On the house."

Normally it would've cost five reds, those striped papers with a picture of the King, but I wasn't about to turn a free pastry down. I held it up to my nose, breathing in the smell of that rich herby crust, the savory spiced meat. "That smells so good. . . ."

"Damn right." Marlo grinned. "Listen, if you like, Garrus and I hang out down at this tavern in Rooksbin, the Suckling Duckling. If you stop by, I'm sure he could teach you how to make them. . . ."

If I didn't know Marlo favored men, I would have thought he was hitting on me. "I'll see if I'm free," I said, though I had my doubts. Rooksbin was halfway across the city, with a reputation for being pretty sketchy. Besides, the one time Lyriana had tried to teach me to bake, I'd set the dorm kitchen on fire; I didn't feel like repeating *that* experience.

"Sure," Marlo said, and his eyes told me he knew I wasn't coming. "I mean it, though. You ever need a friend, just stop by."

"Thanks, Marlo. You're the best." I tucked the pastry into my bag and headed out, through the tall arched gate in the thatched iron fence that surrounded the University. Lightspire was a city of fences and walls, rings within rings within rings, and living in it meant forever learning to navigate not just the maze of streets but all the various gates and passages, knowing which Circles your passport would grant you access to and which you were forbidden from. The Godsblade was at the center, massive and glowing, home to the royal family and the Court. Around the Godsblade was the Golden Circle, which contained fancy estates, luxurious gardens, and high-end markets. Beyond the stone wall that closed off the Golden Circle was the Iron Circle, three times as big, with neighborhoods ranging in quality from not bad to genuinely unsafe. Then came the city walls themselves, so massive they blotted out the sun by five every night, and outside of them was the Rusted Circle and the world beyond.

The University sat near the border of the Golden Circle, with the campus's farthest buildings actually resting against the Circle's wall. I left through the gate, where the bored sentry didn't even bother checking my passport; no one cared who left the Golden Circle, just who came in. My destination was the City Watch Barracks, a bland stone structure about fifteen minutes' walk away, just close enough that it wasn't worth it to hail a carriage.

I'd spent my first few weeks in Lightspire getting constantly lost and bothering passersby for directions, but now I knew my way around pretty well, at least when it came to this part of the city. It's embarrassing how much pride I took in that. Navigating the maze of streets, ducking through alleys, having a fruit vendor greet me as a regular when I walked by . . . it made me feel confident and cosmopolitan, like an insider, like I belonged here, or at least, like I could maybe belong here, someday. Most of the city was still foreign to me, a gigantic sprawl of unfamiliar neighborhoods and tangled pathways, but this little six-block stretch from the University to the Barracks? This was *mine*.

Which is why I noticed the beggar immediately. He was in an alley I used as a shortcut, sprawled on the ground against a tan brick wall. He was old, maybe in his sixties, his head bald, his features sunken and wrinkled, his clothes little more than tattered rags exposing gaunt, emaciated ribs underneath. I stared at him, surprised, because you never saw beggars this close to the Golden Circle.

"Miss?" he called out, craning his head my way. He looked even more ragged head-on; his left eye was just a hollow socket, and he reached out to passersby with a trembling, bony hand. "Please . . . I'm so cold and hungry . . . Spare a coin for an old, starving man?"

"I . . . I . . ." I stammered, way more flustered than I should've been. What in the frozen hell was wrong with me? This was a starving old man, and I was wealthy as hell. Of course I could help him out. "Sure. Just give me a second."

I opened my bag, fumbling through the stack of books to find my coin purse, and as I did, the beggar leaned back with a smile. "Thank you, miss. You have truly saved me."

"Sure," I said, and I looked back up at him, and froze. If I'd been surprised before, now I was downright rattled. As he'd leaned back, his shirt had shifted, falling open at his left shoulder. There, on the leathery skin, was a tattoo, its black ink faded but still legible: a mage's ring, but instead of a glowing gem there was just a hollow-eyed skull. I'd seen that symbol before, of course, because it was unavoidable: in the newspapers, in lectures, and most of all, on Wanted posters. The sigil of the Ragged Disciples.

This man, this harmless-looking beggar, was a cultist. And not just any cultist, but a member of the city's most outlawed and dangerous sect, a group that only got spoken of in whispered breaths, a group so forbidden that the penalty for membership was death. The Ragged Disciples didn't just question the politics of the Lightspire priests, like the Westerners did, or worship the Titans with their own rituals, like the Southland heretics; they rejected the religion of the Kingdom altogether. The central tenet of the Titan faith was the Heavenly Mandate, the belief that the Titans had ascended to the heavens and deliberately blessed the city of Lightspire with the gift of magic, that its people would rule the continent and bring mankind to greatness. But the Ragged Disciples called that mandate a lie. Their leader, a mysterious figure called the Gray Priestess, preached that the Titans had never meant for man to have magic, that they'd trusted the Volaris to keep guard over it, not plunder it for themselves; she preached that mages were immoral, that the Volaris would face divine retribution.

And the Ragged Disciples didn't just passively believe this. They acted on it. The cultists smashed statues of mages and burned temples, robbed religious caravans and plundered shrines. A month ago they'd set a pilgrimage ship on fire in the harbor, forcing everyone on it to flee as it sank. They hadn't killed anyone, not yet, but most people in the Golden Circle thought it was only a matter of time. As far as I could tell, they were the only group in the Kingdom more hated than Westerners.

I had that creeping feeling, the kind you get when you know someone's watching you. I glanced over my shoulder and saw a pair of noblewomen in the street, staring at me suspiciously. I realized all at once how shady this looked: a Western girl crouched in an alley, about to offer money to a beggar with a Ragged Disciples tattoo. Would they report that they saw me talking to him, giving him money? Would they doubt for a second that I was in league with him? Or would this just confirm what they, what everyone, secretly believed: that I was a traitor's daughter, that I was plotting against them, that I would never, could never, be loyal? Would they look at *me* the way I was looking at *him*?

"Miss?" he asked, voice wavering, and in that second, the tattoo barely mattered; he was just an old man, sick, weak, hungry. An old man who needed help.

But still, I closed my bag and jerked aside, pacing down the alley, away from him, even as he called out in confusion. The women nodded, turning back to their gossip, maybe even a little satisfied to see that I hadn't helped him. That should've pissed me off. It *did* piss me off. But I closed my eyes and kept walking. I wasn't in Lightspire to feed the beggars or solve injustice. I wasn't a rebel or an activist. I was just a girl trying to live her life as quietly and peacefully as possible, a girl who kept her head low, who made the smart choice, the safe choice. That's who I *had* to be.

A few minutes later, I was three blocks away, approaching the Barracks' bulky facade. The sentry at the gate glanced up to check my passport, but only as a formality. He knew me well enough. "Your boy's in the courtyard," he said, jerking a thumb over his shoulder.

I could hear Zell's voice as I entered, and I ducked into the shadows to watch him at work. Zell stood at the edge of the field in front of a wooden sparring dummy, watched by a small line of young recruits. I didn't recognize four of them, but the one on the right, the one with the smooth face and the big sweet eyes, was Jonah Welarus, fifteen-year-old son of the Captain and Zell's number one fan. The recruits were shirtless, their torsos slick with sweat, but Zell was wearing his full uniform. The blue silk shirt hugged his frame tightly, the top two buttons undone so it hung open to his collarbone. His dark pants were tucked into tall leather boots that stopped just below his knee. He wasn't wearing any gloves, not out here, so his nightglass knuckle-blades sparkled darkly in the light. His hair was cut short, the regulation Watchman's cut, shaved close to the skull along the sides with a narrow jet-black line along the top. A plain scabbard hung off his belt, but it was empty. The sword, a flat, curved blade, was in his hands.

The five young men stared in rapt attention as Zell moved in front of them. He was showing them the *khel zhan*, his flowing Zitochi fighting style. He moved elegantly, softly, as if he were just dancing on the balls of his feet, weaving back and forth in front of the training dummy with infinite patience and precision. He held the sword up in front of him, its polished surface shining bright. Then, all at once, he pounced, ducking low and popping up, his sword a dazzling series of horizontal slits, cutting through the air so fast that all you could see was a bright metallic blur. He slashed, once, twice, three times, then spun around to his feet and stood up, sheathing his blade at his hip with a quick twirl.

Behind him, the dummy wobbled. Its left arm fell off. Then its right. Then the head toppled off its perfectly sliced wooden neck and rolled into the dirt.

The other recruits stared in awe, and Jonah Welarus actually burst into applause. "It seems difficult, but once your body finds the rhythm of khel zhan, a form like that is effortless," Zell explained, using the smooth, formal, highly enunciated voice he always adopted when he was on duty. "Practice the basics today. Ten drills of footwork, ten drills from blocking to thrust. We'll follow up tomorrow."

The young men nodded. Zell turned away from them, wiping sweat off his brow with the back of his hand, and for the first time noticed me. The corners of his mouth twitched to a slight smile, and I melted inside, the way I always did.

Even after the King had decided to let me stay as a ward at the University, he'd had no idea what to do with Zell. Westerners were uncommon in Lightspire, but Zitochi were unheard of, so there was no community for him to join. The

University was out; they wouldn't take him, and the last thing Zell wanted was to sit in stuffy classrooms all day. It had been Lyriana who'd come through for him. She boasted about Zell's incredible fighting skill, so the Captain of the City Watch, Balen Welarus, had demanded he prove it in a fight against his three best Watchmen. After Zell effortlessly dropped their asses, Captain Welarus had offered him a deal: Zell could lodge at the Barracks and work as a City Watchman, and in exchange, he'd teach the other recruits the khel zhan.

As far as I could tell, it was the best possible outcome. Zell had a place to sleep and a job where he could use his skills while still being, for the most part, safe and free.

And he looked good in the uniform.

Like . . . really, really good.

He strode across the dusty field to me, his dark eyes burrowing into mine. "Tilla," he said. With no one around, he spoke in his own voice, lower, huskier, his Zitochi accent clear and unmasked. "I wasn't expecting you this early."

"Just thought I'd stop by." I reached into my bag and pulled out the pastry. "Marlo says hi."

Zell took the pastry, and as he did he leaned in and kissed me, full and deep. My heart thundered and I slipped my arms around him and held him close. How could he still feel so good, every single time? We stood there like that a minute, intertwined, then he pulled away. "Is that the standard cost of a pastry these days?" I asked. "One kiss?"

"One really good kiss," Zell clarified.

I grinned. "You still off duty tonight?"

"No night shift for three days." He smiled, and popped

the pastry into his mouth. "Are we still going to meet up here and practice?"

Shit. Shit! I knew I'd been forgetting something. I'd promised Zell a few days ago that on our next night together, I'd come by the Barracks to continue my training in the khel zhan. And I'd totally forgotten about that promise when I agreed to go to this party. Shit!

The worst part? This wasn't even the first time. I'd flaked on him the last time we'd agreed to practice (had to cram for a mathematics test) and the time before that (hungover from going out with Markiska). It wasn't that I didn't want to practice my khel zhan. It's just that . . . it didn't really feel that important anymore. When we'd been out in the woods, pursued by Razz and his mercenaries, learning to defend myself had felt like the most vital thing in the world. But here, in the city, surrounded by guards and walls and mages . . .

I still wanted to learn how to fight. I did. But I wanted it in theory, the way I wanted good sleep and a healthy diet, the way of wanting something you're not actually going to bother to get. And if I was being totally honest, I mostly wanted it because of how badly Zell wanted to teach me.

He read right through my silence. "You've made other plans."

"Sorry." I winced. "Really, really sorry."

A flicker of disappointment danced across his face. "It's fine. What are your other plans?"

"Well. Um. See." I'd been enthusiastic about asking him earlier, but now I just felt like a huge asshole. "Darryn Vale is throwing this big party, and I kind of thought we could go. . . ."

"A party?" Zell asked, and something in his expression changed instantly. All at once, he wasn't this new Zell, the charming City Watch recruit who greeted me with kisses. He was the old Zell, the one from our journey, the one who'd lost Kalia, the one with the tempest of pain and rage trapped behind his cold front. He was the Zell I'd first fallen in love with, and at the same time, the Zell who worried me. I couldn't read this Zell or understand him, just guess at what he might be thinking by the faintest of clues, like a scholar trying to imagine a castle from its ruins.

"Zell, I'm so sorry," I stammered. "We don't have to go. I wasn't even really planning on going, but Markiska and Lyriana both keep asking me to, and they said you could come, and I just thought, I don't know, it might be fun, but we don't have to if you don't want to, we can totally practice, and—"

Zell cut me off with a kiss, and then he was back, the new Zell, the one who smiled. "We'll go to your party," he said. "I've heard of the Vales. According to the quartermaster here, they have an enormous collection of weapons, going back to the age of the Titans. Do you think we'll be able to sneak off and look at them?"

I grinned. "Well, that depends. How do you feel about making out in front of a bunch of swords and spears?"

"Surprisingly interested."

"That's my boy." I kissed him again. "Meet me at the Nobles' gate at six? I'll get us a carriage."

"Zell!" a grizzled voice shouted from the other side of the courtyard. Balen Welarus, Zell's boss, the Captain of the City Watch. I don't know where his son got his sweet looks from, because it definitely wasn't from his father, a barrel-chested man with a wide ruddy face, messy hair, and breath that always reeked just a tiny bit of liquor.

"Captain!" Zell stiffened into a curt salute.

Captain Welarus scowled at me like I was a mangy dog walking on his pristine marble floor. "You're on duty, Zitochi. That means training these recruits, not gabbing with your tart."

I didn't like being called a tart, and I *really* didn't like the way he spat the word *Zitochi*, but it was hard to get offended by a man whose entire face looked like an angry tomato. "Yes, Captain!" Zell barked. "Be right there, Captain!" He looked to me with an apologetic shrug. "Duty calls. I'll see you at six?"

"See you there."

I turned away from him and started walking back to the University. He was going to the party, so that was good, but that moment we'd had back there bothered me, that second where it felt like his mask slipped to show me the real Zell within. We'd been having more and more moments like that the last few weeks. Was something bothering him? What wasn't he telling me?

Without meaning to, I stepped back into the alley, the one I'd used as a shortcut. I froze, realizing I'd have to deal with the beggar again, but he was already gone, just a rumpled cloth where he'd been sitting. Had he wandered back down to the Iron Circle, knowing there was only so long he could remain here before someone reported him? Or had he already been arrested, dragged off to some cell to be interrogated or whatever it was they did to cultists? I remembered the confusion in his voice as I'd walked by him, the way his hand had trembled, his gaunt bony ribs. Cultist or not, he'd been a hungry old man, and I'd just ignored him. The old Tilla, the Tilla of Castle Waverly, the headstrong girl who snuck through tunnels and took no shit, would've helped him, consequences be damned. But that Tilla hadn't been through what I'd been through. That Tilla hadn't lost what I'd lost. That Tilla still had Ja—

I pushed the thought away, shoved it down into the dark depths of my mind where it had to stay. I couldn't think about that, couldn't think about *him*, couldn't reopen that wound again. Not here, not now, not like this. My knees felt weak, and my vision clouded at the edges, and I could feel it starting again, the panic, the terror, that body-rending attack of anxiety that could reduce me in a moment to a sobbing wreck. No. No no no. I breathed in deep. I counted to ten. I thought of Zell's lips, of my bed, of the party, of that happy little second where I'd felt confident. I counted to ten again, this time backward, and somehow managed to pull myself off the brink, to force that demon back into its bottle, to trap that pain where it had to stay.

"I'm okay," I told myself. "I'm okay."

And I almost believed it.

FOUR

I GOT BACK TO MY DORM ROOM AS THE CLOCK IN THE Godsblade chimed two, which gave me maybe ten minutes to get to my class on classical Lightspire poetry. The responsible thing would've been to get going right away, so instead I kicked off my shoes and flopped onto my bed, sinking deep into that soft fluffy mattress. I told myself it was going to be for just a minute, but even as I did, I knew that was a lie; there was no way in hell I was getting up for at least an hour.

"That kind of a day, hmm?" a voice asked. I craned my head up to see Markiska sitting in her chair, legs delicately folded. She had a book in her lap, one of those thin, paper romances she imported from Sparra; I'd tried to read one and had to put it down after ten pages because I was blushing too much.

"It's not been great," I admitted, torn between my desire to be left alone and my equally powerful desire to be comforted. "I just . . . It's . . . I don't know."

Markiska set her book down and crossed the room, sitting

down next to me on the foot of my bed. "Tilla, my love," she said, and clearly we were going down the comforted path. "What is it?"

I let out a sigh. "It's just . . . I'm deeply grateful for the Volaris. They saved me from my father, let me stay in their city, gave me this life and this school and this future and all that."

Markiska arched an eyebrow. "But . . . ?"

"But it just gets so exhausting to have to pretend all the time," I said. "I just feel everyone's eyes on me constantly, waiting for me to slip up. And so I have to act proper and lie low and avoid generating any suspicion and just . . . it's so draining. I know everything about this city is so much better than my home, but . . . sometimes I miss just being me." I rolled onto my side. "Sorry. I know that sounds weird and selfish. It's probably hard for you to relate."

"Hard for me to relate?" Markiska laughed. "Tilla, do you think I *want* to go to that party tonight?"

"Don't you?" I blinked. I mean, it was all she'd talked about for the past week.

"No!" she exclaimed, and I swear it seemed like her voice was a little more husky, her accent a little thicker, like she was finally dropping the mask, or at least maybe lifting it a little. "Oh, by the Titans, no. What I want, more badly than anything else, is to put on my loosest, most comfortable nightgown, open a bottle of wine, and lie in bed reading novels all night."

"Then . . . why are you going?"

"Because I have to," she said, like this was the most obvious thing in the world. "Molari Vale is the most powerful merchant in Lightspire, which makes him my father's direct competitor. This party isn't just a party; it's a gathering of the most influential people in the city, the nobles and the merchants and the artists, the people who shape the balance of the Kingdom. I need to be there, mingling with them, laughing, flirting, charming the likes of Molari and his oaf of a son. It's my purpose, Tillandra. It's why my father sent me to this place."

I sat up, intrigued. I'd always known Markiska had a cunning side, that there was an element of artifice to her, even with me. But I'd never heard her state it so openly. "So you're . . . like . . . a spy?"

"No. Just the brightest and most beautiful daughter of the Baron of Sparra, humbly serving my people in the way I best can." I clearly wasn't getting it, because she let out a little sigh and shook her head. "Think of it this way. Imagine you're a Lightspire noble, some trumped-up Lord with a fancy name and a fancier manor. You're planning a new business venture, and you need to purchase three wagonloads of Eastern silks. Where do you buy them from? Well, the silks from Orles are of the finest quality. And the silks from Malthusia come at the best prices. You'll probably go with one of them . . . and then you remember that girl. The one from Sparra, who you met at the party. The beautiful one with the radiant laugh, the one who flirted with you as you shared a glass of wine, the one you still think about, all the time. The girl in your dreams." She cocked her head to the side, and I'll admit, in that moment, she looked truly stunning, a goddess. "So you order the silks from Sparra. And you pour yourself a drink as you think of her, while your wife snores at your side."

I leaned back against the wall, humbled and a little

awed. Was this really what it was like being Markiska, what constantly went through her head? Was all of it, her entire persona, an act to represent her Barony? It was hard enough for me to keep up the appearance of the "grateful loyal Westerner"; I couldn't imagine the pressure of having to always be the perfect face of your entire people. "How do you do it? How do you keep it up all the time without losing your mind?"

"I just do, I suppose," Markiska said. "It's something I learned long ago, as a child. You can complain about the unfairness and lament your fate, or you can embrace the absurdity. Make a game of it. Enjoy being young and beautiful and having noblemen throw themselves at your feet, and then laugh about their stupid faces behind their backs."

"You're kind of my hero, you know that?"

Markiska shrugged. "Someday, we will be two rich old women, sitting side by side in a villa by the beach, drinking all the wine, petting all the dogs, and looking back on all of this with a smile. Until then, I say we stick together and take this town for all it's worth." She laced her hands together and stretched them out over her head. "Now, then. Shall we get ready for the party?"

"It's not for another four hours."

She grinned. "Exactly."

• • •

We showed up at the Nobles' gate at eight, a solid two hours later than I'd told Zell. But he was still there waiting, and he greeted me with a smile as we pulled up, like we were right on time. That was one of the things I really loved about him;

just waiting in line for ten minutes made me twitchy, but Zell never seemed to get bored, like he always had something interesting to mull over and was grateful for being given some time to think. He was waiting for us now under a lamppost adorned with a Luminae, an Artificed lantern with a bright blue flame dancing inside. I actually gasped when he looked up at us. He'd changed from his street uniform to his formal wear, a perfectly fitted blue jacket that hugged his lean frame like a second skin, with a high collar that went up to just under his jaw. A fine gold trim lined the sleeves, just above his black leather gloves.

I'm not saying for sure that he was the best-looking guy in the entire Kingdom. I'm just saying it was a real possibility.

"Titans have mercy." Markiska whistled in the seat opposite me, and next to her, Lyriana just smiled. Our carriage jostled to a stop next to him, and he opened the door and hopped in, sliding into the seat right next to me. "Lyriana," he said, and then with a hint of awkwardness, "Markiska."

"Hiya, Zell," Markiska cooed, and I knew she enjoyed how uncomfortable she made him. She was dressed in her finest Sparra gown, a sparkling pink dress that looked almost sheer in the light, with a slit that ran up all the way to her hip, and a low, open chest that showed off a good 80 percent of her ample breasts. Her purple pearl bracelet glittered on her arm; she never left home without it. I couldn't begin to understand the intricacies of Easterner makeup culture, but I'd describe the look she had going tonight as Seductive Cannibal, with bloody-red lips, dark rings under her eyes, purple and pink sparkles on her cheeks, and streaks of hot red through her hair.

I looked a lot plainer, but it was impossible to not feel plain in a carriage with Markiska and Lyriana. I'd put on my nicest dress, a beautiful blue gown with a trail of embroidered roses and flowering gold vines along the waist and hem. It had an opening at the spine that showed off my lower back, and the front hung lower and cleavagier than I was used to. I felt a little exposed, honestly, but then I saw the look in Zell's eyes as he took me in, that flicker of desire.

Oh, we'd be doing a lot more than making out tonight.

Up front, the coachman barked a few orders, and the carriage took off with a jostle.

"So," Markiska said. "Zell. You must satisfy my curiosity."

"I must . . . ?" Zell asked.

"Is it true what they say about Zitochi men?" She batted her eyelids. "You know. In the bedroom."

Zell blinked. "What do they say?"

"And on that note, we're changing the topic!" I clapped my hands together. "Lyriana! Please tell us about . . . anything. Politics. I don't care."

Lyriana stared at me. "Do you *actually* want me to talk about politics?"

"No. Titans, no." I started rummaging through the carriage's trays. "Tell me there's something to drink in here. . . ."

Ten only mildly awkward minutes later, we came to another stop. I peeked out through the latticed window, then let out a long, slow whistle. We were at the northernmost part of the Golden Circle, a wide stretch of luxurious estates. Some people called this district the Gem, and others called it Rich Assholeville, but either way, it was home to the wealthiest noble families. And I could already tell the Vales were the wealthiest of them all.

The gates in front of us were made of shimmersteel, glowing iridescent even in the moonlight. Thick brick walls enclosed the estate beyond, but through the bars, I could make out enough: a luxurious garden lit up by rotating Luminae, an enormous fountain adorned with statues, and a palatial manor the size of a small castle. A house guard, wearing an ornate frilled shirt and shoes with nonsensically large buckles, greeted each carriage, verifying that they were on the guest list. I assumed we'd get waved through because, you know, the Princess, but when we got up he inspected us same as anyone else, even going so far as to request Lyriana's passport. I suddenly remembered an old riddle:

Who's more powerful than the most powerful man?

The man who pays him.

Our carriage parked inside, and we disembarked. I got my first real look at the actual estate grounds, and Titans above, if the party looked nice from the outside, it was absolutely unbelievable once I got in. The garden was packed with guests who stood around laughing and flirting and drinking yarvo out of ornate golden goblets. A full band, twenty-five musicians with all kinds of instruments, played a beautiful song from a raised stage. Around the stage were six Maids of Alleja, their faces painted white, their eyes shimmering purple. They raised their Ringed hands to the sky and twirled them in delicate patterns, while overhead, dozens of blue and white and red orbs danced perfectly in tune with the music. Keflings, magically created forever-kittens with luminescent pink fur and enormous eyes, wandered the grounds, jumping at capes and purring as guests petted them. Servants circled in dazzling outfits, carrying silver trays lined with sizzling strips of meat and seasoned crumbles of spiced cheese and some glistening jelly on a leaf I didn't dare ask about.

"Wow," I whispered. I mean, I'd been to some Lightspire parties before, but those had been smaller affairs, late-night get-togethers in the Observatory or a bunch of people playing drinking games at the campus tavern. But this, this was decadent beyond belief. This made my father's massive feasts in the Great Hall look like a messy rager in the Servants' Quarters.

Honestly? It kind of made me uncomfortable. I could handle the dresses and the University and riding in carriages. This . . . This was too much.

But I didn't want to show that. Not in front of Lyriana and Markiska, who looked thrilled, and sure as hell not in front of Zell, who looked ready to impale himself on his own knuckle-blades. I forced a smile, as best I could, and took his hand. "Pretty amazing, huh?"

His face was a hard block of stone. "It's something," he said quietly. "If I ever went home, if I ever told them of sights like this, they'd never believe me."

"There's nothing in the world quite like it," Markiska said. "Come! You absolutely must see the aviary!"

"But first . . ." Lyriana flagged down a passing servant. "Drinks? Drinks." The servant was an older Heartlander man, one who looked like he'd spent more than his share of years in the rusty fringes of the Iron Circle. His face was worn with deep creases, his eyes weary and bloodshot. He wore the same ridiculous outfit all the other servants were wearing, with the frilled frock and the purple tights. He rushed toward us at Lyriana's beckoning, his head humbly bent, and he spoke in a hoarse, humble voice. "Your Majesty. Esteemed guests. However might I serve you?"

"We'd like to order some drinks, please," Lyriana said.

"And some food," Markiska added. "Oysters. I'd kill for an oyster."

"It is my greatest pleasure to serve you." He reached into his pocket to take out a folded, warm towel. "May I do the honor of washing your hands?"

This was a thing? I guess this was a thing. Lyriana extended her hands delicately, and the servant massaged them with the wet towel. She thanked him with a light curtsy, but when he turned to Zell with the same offer, Zell just stared at the towel incredulously. "No. No thank you."

"The gentleman declines a hand-washing?" the servant asked, confused, as if this were a script he lacked a good response to. "I hope I did not offend."

"No," Zell said. "You didn't. I just . . . I don't need someone to wash my hands. I can wash my own hands. This whole thing feels strange."

I winced. He wasn't wrong. But it wasn't the kind of thing you could just say out loud.

The servant blinked, and I couldn't quite read his expression, some mixture of righteous indignation and deferent self-preservation. "I apologize profusely for making you feel strange," he said.

"Don't apologize," Zell replied, and now *he* sounded flummoxed. "You've done nothing wrong. It's this situation that's wrong."

A few heads turned our way. Anxiety curled like a knot

in my stomach. Zell was my boyfriend, which meant I really ought to take his side. But this also felt like a really small thing to make a fuss about, and I didn't see any outcome where making this a bigger deal would actually result in anything better.

Markiska obviously was on the same page. "Zell, my darling, you're making a bit of a scene," she said, her face smiling but her tone sharp.

"I'm not trying to make a scene," he growled back. "I'm just trying to—"

And mercifully, he was cut off, because a huge ringing bell sounded from the musicians' stage. All heads spun that way, where two men, Darryn Vale and his father, were approaching the edge. The servant in front us of jerked back, abruptly remembering his place, and Lyriana leaned over to him. "Yarvo. Four glasses. Get a strong vintage."

He nodded and took off. I reached down and squeezed Zell's hand, trying to go for comforting, but he didn't squeeze back. His face was hard, a mask hiding back anger. Why had that bothered him so much? What was really going on with him?

Before I could worry how badly I'd screwed up bringing him here, a hush fell over the crowd. Darryn Vale strode to the front of the dais. He was average-looking, okay, I guess, with small, brown eyes and a soft, round face that looked like it had never seen a single hard day. What he lacked in looks, he made up for in showiness: his raven-black hair hung down around his shoulders in ropes beaded with sparkling gems, and the buttons on his perfectly fitted maroon tunic were sparkling rubies. The crowd around us burst into applause as he stepped up, and I found myself joining, if only to fit in. Zell alone refrained, arms crossed.

"Wow," Darryn said, a slight wobble in his step that told me he'd started partying early. The Maids of Alleja closed their eyes, and pressed their hands forward, middle and Ring fingers up, forcing the sound of Darryn's voice to carry effortlessly over the whole garden. "It is so, so amazing to see so many people here. I won't bore you all with some dumb speech," Darryn said, "but House Vale does have something pretty important to announce. So . . . the man who made this all possible . . . my father!"

A big cheer went up, and Darryn stepped back with a grin as his father took the stage. Molari was a big man, with a thick gray beard around his heavy jowls and neatly trimmed salt-and-pepper hair. He spoke with the easy, booming cadence of a man used to giving speeches. "Friends, neighbors, rivals, and guests. I welcome you all to my humble home." A murmur of polite amusement rippled through the crowd.

Molari smiled, broad and friendly, but his deep voice took on a grave timbre. "The truth is . . . these are trying times. A band of low-born cultists riots in our streets, desecrating our temples and terrifying our hardworking citizens. Commoners, young and old, are turning against the godly ways that have guided our civilization for centuries, indulging in blasphemy and vice. And an entire Province of traitors has decided to spit in the face of our great Kingdom and declare war on our way of life!"

A chorus of angry boos rang out, and I stared at my feet aggressively, suddenly feeling very, very exposed.

"In the days of old, a strong fist would have crushed the

foreign threats," Molari continued. "But alas, we do not live in such times. Our leaders have grown soft, weak, cowardly. They have failed the people of this city." Another angry murmur rippled through the crowd, and this one had me looking around in genuine confusion. Were these people . . . booing the King? Was that a common sentiment that I just didn't know about? Or were they just going along with it because that was the vibe? What in the frozen hell did anyone here actually *believe*?

"In times like this, it is important for the righteous, for the prosperous, for the strong, to stick together," Molari went on. I glanced to Lyriana to gauge her mood, and her expression was pinched, impassive. "The Barony of Orles has long been a great friend to House Vale. They're not merely a partner in trade, but a partner in values, a proud state of loyal, hardworking, and pious people." Markiska next to me let out a derisive snort; I guess even her perfect mask didn't extend to praising rival Baronies. "Which is why the time has come to unite our dominion with theirs, to forge an alliance that stretches from the halls of this great house to the beautiful cities of the Eastern shore." His white teeth sparkled as he smiled. "It is my great pleasure to announce the betrothal of my son, Darryn Vale, to Celeste D'Antonia, the Baroness of Orles!"

Now the reaction of the crowd was genuine, equal parts cheers and gasps. I was still a total outsider, but even I knew this was a big deal; nobles as powerful as the Vales never married out of the city, and certainly never to anyone other than a pure-blooded Heartlander. This broke all the social rules, rules that probably existed to keep men like Molari in check.

Next to me, Markiska wore a hardened scowl, and I could see the calculations whirring behind her eyes. Orles was Sparra's greatest rival in the Baronies, and the Vales their greatest competitor in the city; an alliance between the two couldn't be a good thing.

Darryn Vale, on the other hand, seemed totally oblivious. "That's right, ladies! I'm off the market!" He beamed, with a swagger that suggested he had absolutely no intention of being off the market.

Molari didn't even acknowledge him. "I ask you all to raise a glass and toast with me, to this blessed union and to the prosperity of our great people!" He raised his jewel-adorned goblet to the sky. "For the Titans! For the people! For Lightspire!"

The crowd roared, and I tried my hardest to be invisible. The guy gave a hell of a speech, sure. But this whole thing had left me incredibly uneasy. Between the Westerner-bashing, the backhanded digs at the King, and the elevation of Orles (which, okay, I only cared about because of Markiska), this party was feeling decidedly unwelcoming. I glanced back at the others. "Maybe . . . we should go. . . ."

"It's fine," Lyriana said, and it seemed like she was convincing herself as much as me. "Honestly. Molari's always gotten his digs in at my father, and it's never meant anything. It's just city politics."

"*Bad* politics," Markiska said, and that hard scowl was gone, replaced by her usual canny radiance. "I mean, I never thought I'd say this, but I genuinely pity poor Celeste of Orles. Do you think she has any idea what she's gotten herself into?" She jerked her head at the stage, where Darryn was already somehow doing a shot. "No trade alliance could possibly be worth marrying *him*."

"Exactly!" Lyriana grinned, despite herself, and leaned down to squeeze my hand. "Seriously, Tilla. It's just a speech. After a few drinks, everyone'll forget about it and just want to dance."

"And don't worry about that Westerner stuff. It's not about you and Zell," Markiska added. "Everyone knows you two are welcome here."

"Right," I said, wishing I'd sounded more convincing. I forced a smile, but my eyes were still scanning the crowd, still wondering if I should just take Zell and go, still wondering just how safe we could ever really be. *Everyone knows you two are welcome here.*

Except, apparently, us.

FIVE

I'll give Lyriana this much: everyone did pretty much forget about Molari's speech after a few drinks. Me included.

I'm not sure how much time passed. An hour? Two? Something like that. All I know is that I drank a gigantic glass of wine, laid claim to the dessert table, and somehow managed to convince Zell to twirl me around on the dance floor for a whole two songs. My skin was tingly warm and my head was that perfect floaty drunk, and I somehow found myself on a third-floor balcony in the manor. Zell had wandered off to use a bathroom, leaving me all alone, so I leaned over the railing and took in the gorgeous view. The band was back on their dais, now playing a melodic waltz, as their Maids made dazzling light serpents twirl around them. All around them, guests were tipsy and getting playful; I could see four separate couples making out on the dance floor, and a trio of guys chasing a topless giggling girl through the hedge maze.

"Truly, the height of godly tradition," a voice said from right next to me.

I startled, and then saw who it was and smiled. "Ellarion."

He grinned back. I hadn't seen him in months, not since Lyriana's trial. At twenty he was already a graduate of the University and, rumor held, one of the most powerful young mages in the whole kingdom; he spent his days in the Godsblade, studying to become the next Archmagus, and his nights, doing . . . well, I didn't really want to know what he spent his nights doing. It certainly looked liked he'd relaxed back into city life: his hair was wild and messy, big around his head, and a neat goatee framed his lips. His ruby eyes glowed, even in the bright light of the lanterns hanging around us. "I can't say I expected to see you here tonight," he said. "You don't strike me as the dancing-waltzes-in-a-fancy-ball-gown type."

"And what type do I strike you as?"

"Liquor with the servants, making fun of nobles, passing out in a bale of hay?"

"Yeah, okay, that's pretty accurate."

He gestured toward a passing servant for another goblet and turned so he was leaning against the railing with his back. "That's not a knock on your gown, by the way. You look stunning."

The first time Ellarion had been flirty with me I'd been flattered, confused, and a little alarmed. But now I knew this is just how he was all the time, a sleek, bemused tomcat. Once you got to know him, it was actually kind of charming. Especially if you knew how to give him shit back. "And how many girls have you said that to tonight? Twenty? Thirty?"

"If you're not guessing triple digits, you don't know me at all."

I fought back a smile. Lyriana was embarrassed by Ellarion, and Zell was a little edgy around him, but I'd come to like him, the same way I'd come to like Markiska. I just felt so uncertain these days, like such an impostor, it was nice to be around people who were so confident, so at ease in their own skins.

"Can I ask you a question?" he asked, glancing down at his hands. The red Rings pulsed, and a tiny little orb of flame rolled across his fingers like a coin. "A serious one?"

"Oh boy."

For once, he didn't smile. "It's about my cousin. Lyriana. I know you two are close, closer than she and I, and I just . . . wanted to make sure she was okay."

I cocked my head to the side as I stared at him, because I was definitely a little too tipsy to meet Serious Ellarion. "She's good. I mean, she's Lyriana. She studies hard and worries a lot and tries to act like everything's fine all the time, even when it's not." I paused. "That last one might've revealed too much."

"Right," he said. "It's just . . . I think of her as a little sister. I want to protect her, to keep her safe. And I've heard some rumors about her and what she's been up to. . . ."

"I swear, if you of all people are judging her sex life, I'll throw you over this balcony—"

"Oh, no, not at all!" He threw up his hands defensively, and the little ball of flame vanished in a puff of gray smoke. "She can sleep with whomever she likes, and Titans know that if anyone ever needed to rebel a little, it's her. All I care is that she's happy."

"Oh," I said, feeling both guilty and a little surprised. Ellarion had never struck me as the sensitive type. "Look, what she went through out there in the West was hard. I don't know how much you know, but she lost someone. *We* lost someone. And yeah, okay, she's acting out a little now, and maybe some of that is because, well, it keeps the pain away. But she's just coping."

A chill wind blew over the balcony, making the Luminae rattle with a twinkling metallic chime. We stood there together in their dancing light, silent for a long, contemplative moment. "We all are," Ellarion said at last, so softly I could barely hear him. Right. Ellarion was the son of Archmagus Rolan, whom my father had so brutally murdered. Just because Ellarion hadn't been with us on the journey didn't mean he hadn't lost someone, too.

"Ellarion . . ."

He reached over and patted my arm, and his hand felt impossibly smooth and warm. "Take care of her, Tilla," he said, and wandered off. I watched him round a corner, and then a minute later, heard that husky laugh and the tittering of whoever he was flirting with now.

I turned back to the railing because maybe another night I'd have wanted to ponder Ellarion's hidden depths, but now I increasingly just wanted to go pass out somewhere soft. I scanned the garden for any sign of Markiska or Lyriana.

And then I saw *him*.

The man stood on the far end of the plaza by the wading pool, almost hidden in the shadow of the guest house. Unlike everyone else here, he was wearing only a thick brown robe, plain and unadorned, with the hood pulled low over his forehead so I couldn't see his face. And for some weird reason, he wasn't moving. Around him, people danced and laughed and twirled, but this man just stood there, in the shadows, as still as a statue, the looming darkness of his hidden face craned up at me.

All the hairs on my neck stood on end, and I could feel my stomach twist into a knot of fear. There was something off about him, something fundamentally wrong. A part of me knew I should turn and go now, head back into the safety of the house, but instead I leaned in to try to get a better look. . . .

And in the darkness under his hood his eyes flickered, bright and glowing, a mage's eyes. They weren't crimson or turquoise or gold, but a color I'd never seen before, a pulsing seething gray, like the smoke billowing off a campfire. His eyes burned with that gray light all the way across the party, and I could see them clearly because *he was looking right at me.*

I jerked back with a gasp and slammed right into someone, and I would've screamed if I hadn't already recognized that firm torso and that smell of frost. I spun around and pressed myself into Zell's arms.

"Tilla?" he asked, bewildered. "What is it? What's wrong?"

I pointed off the railing with a shaking hand. "I saw a . . . a . . ." But the man was gone, the spot he was standing in completely empty. Already, a million plausible explanations flooded my head: it was just a guardsman; it was someone playing a prank; it was my own drunk eyes playing a trick on me. "I saw this guy," I explained. "He looked . . . I don't know. Creepy. But it was probably nothing."

"You sure?"

I glanced back again at the empty spot by the guest house. "Yeah. Forget it."

"Okay, if you're sure," Zell said, and I realized he actually looked excited, genuinely excited, not just humoring-me excited. "Because I have something I want to show you." Zell took me by the hand and pulled me into the house, where the hallways were lined with multicolored rugs and the walls with lush paintings of Rich Old Heartlanders. I had no idea where we were going, but he confidently led me down a stairway, around a corner, and toward a heavy wooden door lined with an elaborate golden filigree.

"I thought you went to the bathroom," I asked.

"I may have gone looking for the weapons," he said with an adorable hint of sheepishness, then shoved open the door. "I found something even better."

I don't know what I expected Zell's mysterious surprise to be, but I certainly didn't expect it to be a study. Overflowing bookshelves towered around me, so tall you needed a ladder to reach the high tomes. A redwood desk sat covered in piles of papers with complicated formulas. The biggest map I've ever seen, taller than Zell, hung on the wall, showing the entire continent of Noveris, covered in dotted lines that I'm guessing were trade routes. My eyes flitted involuntarily to the Western coast and a surprisingly accurate drawing of Castle Waverly.

Was it even still standing?

Zell had another focus. He crossed the room to an enormous book on a wooden pedestal, thick as a brick and as long as my arm. The leather cover was simple, no drawings, just big block letters: *An Illustrated History of My Travels Through Noveris,* by Markellus Volaris III.

Zell pulled open the book and leafed through the pages, so quickly I could only catch snippets of drawings: a ruined castle, some kind of barbed whip, what appeared to be a winged snake covered in fur. Finally, he hit the page he was looking for and stepped back, smiling. "Look."

I leaned forward. The whole page was a drawing, vividly colored, and it took me a second to understand what I was looking at. At the center was a mountain, tall and snowcapped, but while one side was rocky and jagged, the other looked like it had been smoothed out, like a polished pebble on the shore. And growing out of this smooth side, like moss on a trunk, was a city made of stone, levels and levels of buildings leading up the mountainside like stairs. Some were covered in tiny houses, with little chimneys and columns of smoke, while others had buildings far bigger, like the huge domed palace at the very top. Above the city, massive faces had been carved into the mountainside, their watchful eyes turned toward the buildings with a protective gaze. I recognized a few as Zell's gods: Rhikura the crone queen, Ellizar the blind warrior, and the bearded old man known only as the Grayfather.

"This is Zhal Korso," I said softly. "Your home."

"It's a beautiful drawing." Zell's voice was quiet, reverent, like a schoolboy in a temple. "It really captures the city."

"It looks gorgeous."

Zell turned the page, and this next one had several smaller drawings. "That's the Hall of the Gods," he said, pointing to an enormous chamber lined with looming statues. "And that room right there, with the big stone chair, that's where the Chief of Clans sits. Where my father *used* to sit, before . . ."

Zell didn't finish that sentence, and I didn't blame him. The last time we'd seen his father, we'd left him paralyzed and dishonored on the floor of the Nest . . . which I'd then accidentally blown up. We didn't know who ruled the Zitochi now, because it's not like Whispers flew out to the tundra, but whoever it was had allied with my father; the Zitochi fought alongside the Westerners, making the war just that much more difficult for the Volaris.

Zell turned the page, and then his fingers stopped. This was a full-page drawing of three women standing on some kind of circular stage. They wore heavy fur cloaks that draped down behind them like capes, two the soft white of snow-bears and one the dull brown of elk. At first I thought they were wearing masks, but then I realized their faces were just painted, like Zell had painted mine way back by Bridgetown. One was done up like Rhikura, her skin gray and mottled, while another had blue skin and tiny icicles in her hair. The third had her face painted completely black, except for her eyes, which were totally white, like they'd rolled up into her head. I didn't want to know which goddess she was.

"They're *zhantaren*," Zell said. "The vessels of the gods. Performing *The Rebirth of Terrala*. The caption says it's a harvest holiday, but that's not right at all. It's about the death and rebirth of the world, the exodus of my people. It's one of my favorite holidays. I remember sitting there in the halls as a boy, watching my mother perform. . . ."

His voice choked up, and when I turned to look up at him, his eyes glistened with restrained tears. Oh no. I'd only seen him cry once before, when he'd told me about his first love and how his brother had killed her. To see him like this now, just looking at pictures of Zhal Korso . . . I suddenly felt terrible as I realized just how homesick he was. Did he feel like this all the time? Was this what he was constantly fighting back?

"Do you think . . ." he asked, hesitantly, like he was afraid to even give voice to the question. "When this war is over. When the West has settled. Do you think someday, we could travel back up there? Do you think I could see it again? To show it to you?"

"Oh, Zell." I reached around his waist and pulled him close, pressing my body against his. I just wanted him to feel better. I just wanted him to be happy. "Of course. I would love to see your home." I glanced back at the drawing. "To meet your mother."

A silence hung over us, tense and unbearable. Had I overstepped? Should I have just hugged him and kept my mouth shut? I tried to balance looking at him for a reply but also looking away so I didn't pressure.

Then he cleared his throat and rubbed his eyes with the back of his hand, and the face that looked back at me was his normal face, the calm and reasonable face that I was starting to realize still hid so much. "Sorry," he said. "Maybe I had a little too much to drink. Forget it."

I doubted that, because the only thing I'd seen him drink was a single glass of wine. "Zell, it's okay. You can talk to me."

He smiled, and I know he was going through a lot, but that smile actually pissed me off, because I knew, *knew*, it was bullshit. He was in pain, and he was hiding it from me because, why? Because he didn't like talking about it? Because he couldn't trust me? I know it was unfair of me to judge, and okay, I was still a little drunk, but still! After everything we'd been through, everything we'd done together, every night we'd spent in each other's arms? He still couldn't just open up to me about this?

I could help him, damn it. I could soothe his pain. I could say the right words. But I couldn't do any of that if he didn't just open up!

"Seriously," I said, my voice harder. "Please. Just talk to me."

"Tilla . . ."

Maybe he would've talked to me. Maybe it would've just been another deflection. But I never got an answer because we were both interrupted by the sound of a distant thud and muffled shouting. Zell tensed up instantly, instinctively, the muscles in his neck tightening and his fingers twitching. But I could see over his shoulder, through the study's enormous rounded window, which looked out over a wide grassy patch on the far side of the manor. There were three figures there, rapidly stumbling away from the house while gesturing wildly, and in a way that seemed distinctly unfriendly. I could make out two guys, one dressed in a fine crimson suit and the other in a servant's robe. The noble appeared to be menacing the hell out of the servant, and there was a third figure yelling at both of them, a girl in an ornate teal dress with braided hair, a girl who looked an awful lot like . . .

Shit.

Lyriana.

"Come on." I grabbed Zell's hand and jerked him along. Whatever *thing* we were having could wait; I'd seen Lyriana down three whole goblets, which meant she was in very real danger of embarrassing herself in front of everyone. Before Zell could even ask what was happening, I pulled him out of the study and down the corridor toward a door leading outside.

The night air hit us with a bracing bite. I shivered and rushed forward, pulling Zell behind me as I rushed out onto the grass. This lawn was behind the manor, at the opposite end from the garden, and it was luckily empty, save a passed-out guy with his shirt off and the three figures I'd spotted through the window. The girl was definitely Lyriana, and as we ran toward her, I could make out the rest of the scene. The servant, a thin, middle-aged man, lay on his back, hands thrown up defensively. The noble, who I realized now was Jerrald, that scumbag from this morning, was kicking him in the side.

"You think you can check out my girlfriend, you lowborn piece of shit?" Jerrald slurred, punctuating the sentence with a kick.

"I am *not* your girlfriend!" Lyriana shouted, trying (and failing) to pull Jerrald away. Given the wobbly way she moved, she was lucky to be standing at all.

"Something the matter here?" Zell asked, his voice flat and professional. A tiny part of me was proud, even then. He was a damn good City Watchman.

Jerrald spun, ready to tell us to go to hell, and then he saw whom he was talking to. "You," he sneered. "The traitor bitch and the snowsucker. *Now* it's a party."

Lyriana grabbed her head in her hands. "Titans above, you are *such* a prick! Why did I ever think you were cute?"

"Please help," the servant said. A thick bruise was

blossoming on his left cheek, and his lower lip was split and bleeding. "This man . . . He's attacked me for no reason."

"No reason?" Jerrald laughed, that cocky, cruel laugh that all bullies seemed to share. "You were following us around for half an hour! You were ogling the Princess!" He turned back to Zell and shrugged. "I was just defending her honor."

"My honor doesn't need defending!" Lyriana yelled.

Jerrald hissed, his nostrils flaring, and I could tell it was taking every ounce of restraint he had not to talk back to the Princess. He sucked in his breath, then turned around and kicked the servant again, right in the face, splitting open the man's cheek. Because if you can't hit who you want to hit, why not beat on some poor sap who can't fight back?

"That's enough!" Zell barked, and stepped forward.

"Or what?" Jerrald replied. "What are you gonna do, huh? What are you gonna do?" He swiveled around and strode across the grass toward us, fists clenching. "I'm Jerrald Blayne!"

"You're an asshole," I said, because come on, someone had to.

That was the last straw. Howling with fury, Jerrald turned to me and threw a slow, lazy punch at my head—

That Zell neatly intercepted. He stepped in front of me, caught Jerrald's wrist in one hand to twist him aside, then delivered a hard, open-palm jab to the outside of Jerrald's elbow. There was a sickening wet crack, like someone snapping apart a twig full of chunky soup. Jerrald shrieked and his elbow exploded, and his arm inverted at a horrible, impossible angle. Blood sprayed out over the lawn, and white bone tore out through the skin.

"Oh shit!" I yelled, and Lyriana clasped a hand over her mouth to trap in a gasp.

Zell let go of Jerrald, and the noble collapsed to his knees, his limp hand flopping uselessly in the grass in front of him. He stared at his shattered arm in disbelief, opening and closing his mouth like a stupid fish, not even able to muster up a scream. Then his eyes rolled back into his head and he passed out.

"You just broke his arm," I said quietly.

"He tried to hit you," Zell replied, as if that was the most natural response in the world. "I made him regret it."

"He's a noble," I said, and my brain was trapped between staring in sick fascination at Jerrald's mangled arm and desperately wanting to look away. "You just broke a noble's arm." Any last remnant of pleasant buzz I had vanished with the cold grip of sober panic. Zell's status in the Watch had been controversial from the start, with many of Lightspire's more conservative nobles speaking out in protest. I could already see the rumors flying: Zitochi brute maims innocent noble in drunken party brawl. "This is bad, Zell. This is really bad."

"He was brutally beating a defenseless man," Zell replied, like he almost couldn't believe what I was saying. "And he was about to hit you. Who knows what he would have done if I hadn't intervened?"

"I know, but . . ."

"Oh, Titans' blessings," the servant moaned, scooting back up onto his elbows. His face was still bleeding, but he seemed way more concerned about the scene in front of him. "I swear, I didn't want any part of this. I didn't want that man to be hurt. I was just trying to do my job. . . ."

"Relax." Lyriana swooped down toward him. "I'll handle this. You just get out of here and go home. You didn't see anything. You didn't hear anything. If anyone asks about your face, you tripped and fell down a flight of stairs. Understand?" He stared at her, blinking, and then nodded. "Yes. I understand, Your Majesty. Th . . . thank you."

He pulled himself to his feet and took off running. Lyriana turned back around and hunkered down over Jerrald's unconscious form, carefully examining the fractured bones jutting like bloodied spears through his skin. I fought back the urge to gag, but she seemed totally unfazed, like a cook handling a plucked goose. I guess all that training she'd done as a Sister had numbed her to gore. "Oof," she muttered. "This is a bad break. You really did a number on him, Zell."

"I'm not apologizing," Zell muttered, but Lyriana ignored him. Instead, she straightened out Jerrald's arm, crimson oozing from the cut like sauce from a pie, and placed the shattered bones together as closely as she could. "Okay," she said to herself. "Okay. I can do this."

"Do what?" I asked, but I already had a nervous feeling I knew where this was going. Lyriana reached into her purse and took something out, something small and metal, with an unmistakable shine.

"How?" I whispered. "They took away your Rings."

"I'm the Princess of Noveris. Do you honestly think I can't get my hands on a Ring?"

"Lyriana, they banned you from using magic. They said on penalty *of death*."

"Yeah, well, what do you think is going to happen to Zell if I don't fix this?" She stretched out her long, elegant hand

and slid the Ring onto her right pointer finger. The second it touched her skin, the gem sparked to life, glowing the rich warm green of thick forest moss. The Rings were conduits and amplifiers, Lyriana had explained to me. Most mages needed them to do magic at all, but for the most powerful, the Volaris, they were just tools: helpful, but not necessary unless they were doing something exceptionally difficult. Which made me very, very nervous about whatever Lyriana was about to do.

But before I could say anything, she sucked in her breath and closed her eyes, and there it was, that crackle in the air, that prickling of the skin, that taste of grass, the faint sickly sweet smell. Lyriana wove her hands through the air over Jerrald's arm in intricate patterns, fingers furling and unfurling as she traced invisible bands and spirals. The jagged bones twitched like fingers, grasping for each other, and the skin around the edge of the wound curled and uncurled like paper in a flame. Jerrald moaned, and now it was my turn to fight back a gasp.

"Come on, come on." Lyriana strained, a bead of sweat streaking down her furrowed brow. The bones twitched again, but they were misaligned, scraping at each other with an awful brittle sound. I glanced to Zell for comfort, but he looked as horrified as I did, and I remembered with a dull horror that, oh yeah, she was doing this *drunk*. For breaking Jerrald's arm, Zell would probably get flogged and fired. For making him lose an arm, well, I couldn't think about that . . .

Or what would happen to Lyriana if she got caught.

"Come on!" she hissed again, and a wind swirled, blowing loose leaves in a spiral around her. The world seemed to throb, pulsing in and out like a heartbeat, and then the bones in his arm slid together like puzzle pieces. Very slowly, they clicked back into place, reunified, and a thin webbing of unnatural gray bone grew out of their rift, binding them back together like a spiderweb. Once the bones were fused, the tattered skin was next, stitching itself over the wound like a shroud.

"There," Lyriana said, and slumped back onto the grass with her eyes shut. "All better. Or at least, as good as I can make him. Given how drunk he was, I bet all he'll remember is getting into a fight."

I stared in awe at Jerrald's mended arm. If it weren't for the little white band of scar tissue where the skin had come together, you wouldn't have known it had been broken at all. That, and all the blood everywhere. Whatever Lyriana had done was powerful magic, way more sophisticated than the simple arts she'd done back on our journey. "You've been practicing," I said.

Lyriana exhaled. She looked drained, her face slick with sweat, her hair tangled, her dress mud-stained and rumpled. "I'm not going to give up my magic just because my father told me to," she replied coldly. "I might not be a Sister of Kaia, but I'm still a mage. I still help people. And I always will."

"But—"

"I'm not going to let anyone else die!" she yelled, a booming, unearthly roar that rumbled the ground and hit me like a blast of wind. Her eyes were open now, and there they were, two orbs of pure golden light. My heart thundered, and my breath caught in my chest. The last time I had seen her eyes like that had been in the tower, in *that* tower, and the world spun around me and I felt dizzy and sick and weak, and when

I looked down in the grass it wasn't Jerrald lying there but Jax, it was Jax, his chest ragged red, his eyes white and empty, because he was dead, dead, my brother was dead.

The box was unsealed, the wound reopened, the pain unearthed. There was no bottling it up now.

I sucked back a scream as my eyes burned, and I stumbled to the ground. Zell caught me as I fell. "Tilla! Are you okay?" he asked, but I didn't need him right now, didn't need to worry about something happening to him, didn't even remotely have the strength to deal with his secrets and his pain.

"Leave me alone!" I choked out, and pushed him away, because I couldn't be near them, couldn't be near anyone. "I just need to be alone. I just need to go."

Lyriana blinked, her eyes dulling instantly to their normal golden glow. "Tilla. Wait. I didn't mean to . . ."

"Just leave me alone!" I said, and my feet were already carrying me, away from them, away from this party, from this house, away from the sprawled boy lying limp, the boy who I knew was Jerrald but who I couldn't dare look at again. Before Zell could follow, before Lyriana could explain, I turned and took off, running toward the gate, running into the night.

SIX

THERE WAS A PLACE I WENT TO WHEN I FELT LIKE THIS, A secret place that even Zell and Lyriana didn't know about. I'd found it just a few weeks after moving into the University, on one of those long cold nights where I was too restless to sleep. On the first floor of my dormitory, in a hallway that led mostly to supply closets, there was a creaky old door that opened onto a flight of stairs descending into an ancient, forgotten basement. See, my dorm, Workman Hall, was one of the oldest on campus, but most of it had been renovated to keep up with the other, more modern buildings. Down in that basement, though, covered in cobwebs and shadows, were the old building's bones. The walls down here were worn, crumbling brick, the paint long since faded. The floors were so dusty you could leave a trail of footprints to find your way out, and the basement itself was a labyrinth of narrow tunnels, most leading to locked doors and dead ends, some stretching into unknowable darkness.

I know, it was a really weird place to hang out alone, and also probably horrifically unsafe. But I liked it down here. Lightspire was so modern and loud, so overwhelming with its technology and its magic and its bustle. But this basement was old, and it was quiet, and it was still. When I felt totally overwhelmed, when I just needed to get away, I would go down here and slump against a wall and enjoy that silence, that musty old smell, the fact that I was probably the only person in the world who even knew this place existed.

If I closed my eyes, I could almost convince myself I was back in Castle Waverly. Back in the tunnels.

I sat in that basement now, my back against the hard brick at the foot of the stairs, until my heart stopped thundering and my chest stopped feeling like it was collapsing in on itself. I don't know how long I sat like that. Maybe an hour, maybe two.

What was wrong with me? Why was I like this? I had so much good here, so much to be thankful for. I had great friends and endless comforts and a shot at a future so much more exciting than I could have ever imagined. Why the hell couldn't I just appreciate that? Why did I have to feel so broken inside?

I sniffled, rubbing at my eyes, and that was when I heard a footstep.

I stiffened instantly, pulled my breath into my chest. I hoped for a second that it was just the building creaking, but then I heard another footstep, and then another, the unmistakable *thud* of leather on stone. And the thing is, they weren't coming from the stairs next to me, where someone else coming down would be, but from deeper into the basement itself, from those long dark passages even I hadn't been brave enough to explore.

I opened my eyes and pressed myself hard against the wall, hiding in the shadow of the stairs. I'd left the door at the top open, and the Luminae in the hallway cast just enough light to illuminate the stairway itself. Beyond that, I could just make out the contours of the rest of the room, the hard shadows of the edges of doorways, the pitch blackness beyond.

In a heartbeat, the basement had gone from safe to very, very scary. Why the hell was I even down here again? How stupid *was* I?

The footsteps approached, closer, closer, faster, faster. I wanted to get up and run for it, up the stairs and into the big, well-lit dorm lobby, but I couldn't quite will my legs to move. Maybe this person wouldn't see me. Maybe this person wouldn't care. Maybe there was nothing to be scared of.

Then the person stepped into a doorway and oh no, there was *plenty* to be scared of.

It was him, the man from the party, the one who'd stared at me across the garden. I still couldn't see his face in the shadow of his hood, especially not in the dark room, but I could make out his tall, thin silhouette, his long gray cloak. The air crackled, a strange, sickly rasp. I felt the pulse of magic, that surge of invisible energy, but there was something off about it now, something that made my stomach roil and my eyes water. The smell of sulfur and ash flooded my nose. The air around the man rippled, and wisps of gray smoke billowed off his hands, like there was a fire burning within his skin.

Then his eyes lit up, shining from the darkness of the hood, and I saw just what was so wrong about them. Mages' eyes glowed, but they glowed a single bright color, like lanterns in their skull. This man's eyes glowed too, but they weren't eyes at all, just two ovals of spiraling gray and black light, twisting and writhing. It was like someone had trapped smoke in a glass ball, and that smoke was alive and angry, desperate to break out. In that flickering, throbbing gray light I could almost make out his face, but there was something wrong with it, something twisted and misshapen.

"Tiiiillllllllaaaaa," he sang.

And okay, yup, that was enough of that right there. I lunged to my feet and spun around, sprinting up the stairs faster than I'd ever moved in my life. I couldn't see the man anymore, but I could still hear him. I heard a hiss of rushing air, the sizzle of steam, and I heard something else too, a harsh wet popping like a dozen knuckles cracking at once. I didn't dare look back and see what was happening, didn't dare stop. I hurtled through the basement's doorway and into the hallway, nearly tripping as I crossed the last step. I was moving off pure instinct at this point, running not to get anywhere but just to get away.

I raced around the corner, through the dorm's empty lobby, and up the big flight of stairs leading up to my floor. I couldn't see if he was following me, and I didn't care. My feet thundered as I ran down the hall to my door. It was unlocked, thank the Old Kings, so I threw it open, rushed in, and slammed it shut behind me, my trembling hands pulling the dead bolt shut. I didn't think it would keep him out, but it might slow him down.

I spun around the other way. My room was pitch-dark, the shades drawn to keep even the moonlight out, so I couldn't see a thing. "Markiska!" I whispered urgently. "Are you here? Wake up!"

Silence greeted me. She was almost certainly still back at the party. I fumbled through the dark room, feeling my way along the bedpost toward my dresser. Something brushed against my face, something clammy and cold, and I shoved it away. My hands found my dresser and I grabbed the little Luminae there and pressed the knob. Soft pink light flooded the room.

Markiska wasn't at the party at all. She was in our room, hanging from a rafter with a thick rope around her throat. Her face was blue, veins bulging through her skin, her mouth open. Her white dead eyes stared down at me.

I screamed.

seven

THE NEXT FEW HOURS PASSED IN A HAZE. WHEN I TRY TO think back on them, it's like I'm looking at the memories through a pane of frosted glass.

Zell and Lyriana were the first ones to find me. I guess they'd come to the dorm looking for me, had been just down the hall in the bathroom when they heard my scream. They smashed into my room and found me there, on the floor, with Markiska hanging from the rafter.

Lyriana held me in her arms as I shook, and fought back her own tears as she tried to keep me calm. Zell, after a second of stunned silence, climbed onto a chair to cut Markiska down, then gently laid her body on her bed and covered it with a sheet. Her left hand hung off the edge, dangling from under the sheet, and I could see the blue skin on her bare wrist and the cracked colored nails on her fingertips. I wanted to throw up. I wanted to scream.

I didn't know what had happened here, or why, or how.

All I knew was that Markiska—sweet, funny, brilliant Markiska—was dead. Markiska, my first friend in Lightspire, who'd once kicked a drunken sailor in the balls for grabbing my ass, who couldn't wait to go home to Sparra and her family and her half dozen dogs. Markiska was dead.

And that creepy son of a bitch with the smoky eyes had killed her.

I tried to say that, to tell Zell and Lyriana. But the words didn't come, not yet. So I just sat there with them, in silence, with Lyriana's arms around me and Zell hovering protectively nearby.

Provost Kendrin, the head of our dorm, burst in, took one look at the covered form under the sheet, then took off running with a high-pitched shriek. And maybe an hour later, the door shook with a heavy knock that could only mean an actual authority had arrived.

I'd expected a City Watchman, maybe even Captain Welarus, but when Zell threw open the door, we were greeted by the deeply concerned face of Inquisitor Harkness himself. He shoved past Zell without a word, walked over to Markiska's bed, and lifted the sheet covering her. He took one look, then set it back down with a sigh. "Terrible," he said, shaking his head. "What an awful thing."

He turned back around, his thoughtful gray eyes looking over the three of us. In my months at Lightspire, I'd only interacted with him a few times, but he'd always struck me as incredibly smart and thoughtful, like a kindly grandfather who was also a brilliant tactician. "You three found the body?"

"Tilla did," Zell said, his voice flat and professional. The

Inquisitor wasn't just the King's spymaster and right hand, but was also the person to whom the Captain of the City Watch deferred. Which made him Zell's boss's boss. "She came back from a party tonight, and found her like this."

"My condolences," Harkness said softly. "I'll need to talk to each of you alone, to hear your stories."

Lyriana blinked, surprised. "I hardly think that's necessary. I mean, you don't think . . ."

She trailed off, unable to finish the sentence, so Harkness took over. "Your Majesty, my job isn't to think," he explained. "My job is to *know*. That means getting full statements from the three of you so I can figure out precisely what happened here tonight."

"Are we under suspicion?" Zell asked. "There's no cause for that."

"With all due respect, Novice City Watchman, why don't you let me be the judge?" Harkness said. "The fact is, that poor young woman there is the daughter of the Baron of Sparra. And she was discovered in this state by the daughter of the traitor Kent." He glanced at me, as if sensing my immediate discomfort. "I do not accuse you of anything, dear Tillandra. I merely point out the obvious. This, if I may be frank, does not look ideal. And all I want to do is ensure that your name is not wrongfully dragged through the mud."

"Why would her name be dragged through the mud?" Lyriana cut in, maybe a little too forcefully. "Markiska was her friend. *Our* friend. People wouldn't think . . . I mean . . . would they?"

Harkness sighed a weary sigh. "I cannot promise you what the people will or won't think. In truth, I'd be lying if I said I wasn't often disappointed by them." The corners of his mouth twitched, and I wondered, not for the first time, what it was he really did. "I don't suspect any one of you of a crime. But the fact is, her father is a very powerful man who's going to want to know what happened. Right or wrong, he's going to blame us for her suicide. And the last thing this city needs now is—"

"She didn't commit suicide," I cut in. They were the first words I'd spoken since I found her, and they scraped hard against my raw, parched throat.

Everyone in the room turned to stare at me. Zell looked alarmed, Lyriana looked confused, and Inquisitor Harkness's white eyebrows arched in befuddlement. "Excuse me?" he said.

"She was murdered," I replied, and it was like I'd sucked all the air out of the room. "By a man who'd been stalking me all night. I saw him in the basement here, just a minute before I found Markiska. He . . . had eyes . . ." I breathed deeply, realizing just how implausible my words might sound if I didn't choose them right. "I think he was a mage."

We all sat there in silence for another moment. Lyriana's grip on my arm tightened, and I could see the creases of worry tighten in Zell's forehead, his mind whirring through every possibility. Inquisitor Harkness let out a long, slow sigh. "Well, then. To the Watchtower we go."

We were escorted out of the dormitory by the Inquisitor and a small group of Watchmen. I could see heads poking out of doors and eyes staring from behind windows, could hear the other students as they gossiped and whispered. For a second, I wished I could have left the dorm more discreetly, maybe snuck out the back before the Inquisitor arrived. Then we stepped out into the cold night air, and I decided no, I was happier traveling with a bunch of armed soldiers. Markiska's killer was still out there, but whatever he was, he wouldn't dare attack a dozen armed men.

I hoped.

The Watchtower was a narrow, unmarked building three blocks from the University, tall and thin like a spear thrust into the earth. I must have passed it a dozen times and never really looked at it, but now, its dull, unadorned facade took on a sinister tone. A few birds flew overhead, flapping thick leathery wings as they swooped into the building's highest windows. They were Sentinels, birds created by the Beastmasters, with the stringy, featherless bodies of vultures, and three bloodred eyes set in their skull, two on the sides of their head and a third right above the beak. The Inquisitor used them to keep watch over the city, but no one seemed to really understand how they worked. I just knew they creeped me the hell out.

Harkness led us into the Watchtower and upstairs, to a floor with five identical unmarked doors. "Interrogation rooms," he said. "I'd like you to each wait inside one. Alone."

Zell stepped in front of me. "I'm staying with Tilla."

Harkness's eyebrow twitched, the barest suggestion of emotion. "I know you wish to be with your beloved, Novice City Watchman. But I assure you, having separate interviews is the fastest and easiest way to resolve this. And I do believe that's what we all want tonight."

I knew Zell wouldn't back down, and the absolute last thing I needed tonight was him destroying his career for me.

"It's fine, Inquisitor. We'll do whatever you say," I said, and shot Zell a look that said I meant it. He backed down, silently. And I felt something, a flicker of . . . annoyance? It was wrong, I know, to be mad at him for trying to protect me. But why did I always have to be the one who ended up looking out for him, the one who kept him from making these dumb mistakes? At this point, after everything, couldn't he just *know*?

Without another word, we split off into the rooms. Mine was basically empty, a tiny unfurnished stone cell with only a hard wooden table and two chairs. There wasn't a clock or anything, so I have no idea how long I was in there. I spent that time pacing around, crying, fuming, worrying, and over and over again, closing my eyes and counting to ten.

At last, the door swung open, and the Inquisitor walked in. There was another man with him, one I hadn't seen before. He was thin and lanky, his face a gaunt skull, his smooth head shaved bald, his skin a sickly brown that bordered on gray. He wore a plain gray cloak, and his hands sparkled with Rings, three on each, with gemstones as black as nightglass. He sat down at the table opposite me, and laid his hands flat on the table. I squinted, trying to figure out who he was, and then I saw the tattoo on his left wrist, a plain black square.

Oh *shit*.

The Shadows of Fel were the smallest and most secret order of mages, so rare I'd never actually even seen one before. Like the Inquisitor, they were handpicked for their solitude and dedication, men with no wives or children or living parents, men who couldn't be bribed or blackmailed, men who were loyal to the death. They served the King and the Inquisitor directly, as interrogators and assassins. And they and they alone learned what Lyriana called "dark magic," arts with names like "Mind Rending" and "Blood Scrying."

Before the Shadow had walked in, I'd been mostly swept up in exhausting emotion about Markiska. But now, all of a sudden, I was terrified. "Listen," I said to Harkness. "I . . . I don't think we need him here to . . ."

"Relax, Tillandra," Harkness soothed. "This is just a formality, nothing more. I believe you're innocent, I just want to find who hurt your friend. Tell me the truth, and you'll have nothing to fear." He turned to the Shadow. "Begin."

The Shadow nodded, his face blank and expressionless, and then, very slowly, began to drum his fingers on the table, pointer, middle, ring, pinkie, in a steady pat-pat-pat-pat, like playing an invisible piano. I stared at his hands, not comprehending, and then I saw his Rings begin to glow, a pulsing, throbbing black so dark it seemed to suck in the light around them. The room dimmed, and a gray haze crept in at the edges of my vision. I'd gotten used to the electric tingle of magic, but this was something else, a crawling in my skin, a nauseating tickle at the back of my throat. I tasted rotting meat and heard the buzzing of insects. But worst of all was the feeling in my head, a horrible creeping, gnawing sensation, like there was a spider in there, not just in my skull but *in my mind*, scraping my memories with its fangs and prodding my thoughts with bristled legs.

I gasped for air, but the air had curdled around me. "What . . . what . . ."

"Tell me everything," Inquisitor Harkness said, "about this 'mage' you saw."

And I did, because I had no idea what this Shadow was

doing to me, but I was pretty damn sure I shouldn't lie. I told him about going to the party, about seeing the man near the guest house, about how Zell and I had snuck off to look at maps. When I got to the part about the confrontation in the back lawn, I just said that Zell hit Jerrald; it was true, technically, but even as I said it, the Shadow's rings pulsed and that gnawing feeling got so painful my vision blurred. I rushed on, telling him about the basement, about seeing the man there again, about his terrifying eyes and his smoky aura, and then finally, about finding Markiska in our room.

When I finished, the Shadow nodded, and his drumming slowed. "She speaks truth," he said impassively, "or at least what she thinks is the truth."

"Hmmm," Harkness said, and it was clear that wasn't quite the answer he was looking for. "Did you consume any mind-altering substances this evening? Grief-weed? Dream mushrooms? Glitter dust?"

"No," I said. I hadn't even heard of glitter dust.

"But you were drinking. How much?"

"One drink." The Shadow's Rings pulsed again, and it felt like whatever the hell was in my head took a deep bite. I hissed, gritting my teeth. "Three drinks, I think. Maybe four."

"So you were drunk," Harkness said, without judgment. "And given the atmosphere of decadence at that party, it wouldn't surprise me if you'd been slipped something stronger without even knowing it."

I blinked. Even through the pain and nausea, I could tell where this was going. "The man was real," I insisted.

Harkness merely nodded. "Your roommate, Markiska

San Der Vlain IV. Would you describe her as spirited? Passionate?"

"I . . . I mean, yes . . ."

His eyes narrowed, and the Shadow kept drumming, pat-pat-pat-pat. "Impulsive, even?"

"I . . ." I remembered us sneaking out of the dorm once because the moon was so full and pretty she had to see it from a rooftop, remembered the time she'd smashed a professor's window because the professor had called her obnoxious. "Yes. She was impulsive. But that doesn't mean she—"

"Did you know that she was flirting with several members of Lightspire's rising nobility at the party tonight? That she snuck off toward the bedrooms with a young man?"

I blinked, because, uh, how did *he* know that? "I didn't. But I lost track of her at the party pretty early. . . ."

"Several guests saw her and a gentleman head that way. They heard sounds of an argument. And one reports seeing her leave the manor with tears in her eyes." Harkness shook his head sadly. "It seems she was quite heartbroken."

If he thought that, he *really* didn't know Markiska. "I'm sure she was flirting," I admitted. "That was kind of her thing. But I don't know what you're getting at."

"Perhaps a boy rejected her. She was upset. Emotional. Drunk, maybe worse," Harkness said. "You yourself said she was passionate and impulsive. Do you really think it's so implausible that a girl like that might, in the heat of the moment, do something foolish?"

I really didn't like how he emphasized the word *girl*. "No. I'm telling you. This was murder." But even as I said it, I realized it didn't matter. Harkness could claim that what he cared about was the truth, but all he really wanted was his narrative. That's why he didn't press me for more details on Zell's fight, even though I was obviously hiding something. He didn't believe me, straight up, and it would be a hell of a lot easier to tell the Baron of Sparra that his daughter had killed herself after a tiff with a boy than to even suggest she'd been murdered. So putting me through this interrogation, subjecting me to whatever the hell the Shadow was doing, wasn't just unpleasant, it was *pointless*. A formality.

"She didn't kill herself," I said, with so much anger I hope the Shadow felt it in my brain.

He didn't react, but I think his drumming skipped a beat. "Are we done here, Inquisitor?" he asked.

"Just one last question," the Inquisitor said, and with a swiftness that was surprising for a man his age, he swooped toward me, leaning over the table. I jerked back, startled. His eyes pierced into mine, and it was like he was an entirely different man. Any trace of kindness, sympathy, understanding was gone, and all that was left was a vicious vulture's scowl. The kindly grandfather thing was an act, I realized, a facade to make people trust him and lower their guard. This was the *real* Inquisitor, the ruthless enforcer, the spymaster behind the Sentinels and the Shadows. "Are you still in contact with your father, Lord Elric Kent?" he demanded. "Are you his spy?"

"Wh-what?" I stuttered, genuinely caught off guard. The Shadow drummed intensely, and that tightening, gnawing pain got worse. "No! No, of course not!"

"Do you know what he's plotting?" Harkness pressed, leaning so close his face was just a few inches from mine. He was intense, too intense. I could smell his sour breath, and see a sweat drop streak down his brow. "Do you know what he's going to do next?"

"I haven't talked to my father since he tried to kill me six months ago!" I yelled back, and slid away from the table instinctively. "I swear!"

The Shadow nodded. "She speaks truth. Or at least, what she thinks is the truth."

The Inquisitor stared at him, and for just one second, I could see surprise on his face. Then he stood up and spun around, hiding his expression. "I see," he said, mostly to himself, his voice again calm and gentle. Bullshit. He wasn't fooling me twice. "You can release her now."

The Shadow stopped drumming, at last, and that horrible feeling faded alongside the glow in his Rings. As my breath rushed back into my lungs, I realized how hard my heart was thundering, how my body was soaked with sweat. But more than that, I realized just what the Inquisitor's moment of surprise had meant.

This wasn't a formality at all. This was a trap. All that setup, all that interrogation, had just been to get me softened up for that final attack. And he'd been genuinely confident that it would work, that I was about to give myself away as a Western spy.

I felt anger, because what the hell? And deeper than that, I felt fear. The Inquisitor was one of the most powerful men in the Kingdom, and certainly the most well-informed. And despite all the evidence, he was sure, absolutely sure, that I was still loyal to my father. If the King hadn't vouched for me, if Lyriana hadn't been so adamant in my defense, what would he have done to me? What would he do now if he managed to get the right excuse?

And there was something else worrying me, something it took me a minute to put my finger on. It was the way he'd asked his question about my father's plans, that hint of passion in a man who'd otherwise been cold as a corpse. That wasn't the confident, capable demeanor of a man who thinks he's got everything under control. There'd been fear in his voice, real honest fear.

The Inquisitor, right hand of the King, master of the Shadows of Fel, was afraid of my father.

That was scarier than anything else.

He let me out shortly after, and I staggered into the warm night air. Lyriana and Zell were waiting for me outside the tower; I guess their interrogations had been a lot quicker, but that's probably because they weren't accused of being Western spies. Zell wrapped me up in a hug, my face buried in the crook of his neck, and Lyriana gently patted my back. "Let's go to the Godsblade," she said. "You can stay there for the night. I don't think either of us wants to go back to the dorms."

Zell could sense something was wrong, though. He cocked his head to the side, staring at me, then glanced back at the Inquisitor's tower. "Are you okay?" he asked. "What took so long?"

"It was . . . I . . ." I started, but my words trailed off as they left my lips. Because what would happen if I told them the truth, if I told them how the Inquisitor had treated me? Lyriana would storm into the throne room, demand an explanation, make a huge scene with her father, and just blow the whole thing up. And Zell? I don't even know *what* he would do at this point. Would he quit his job? Would he tear into that tower and attack the Inquisitor himself? I thought of the way Zell had glowered at the Vale estate, that anger I sometimes saw simmering behind his eyes. And I know it was wrong to doubt him, even as I enveloped myself in his arms, but I couldn't help it. I trusted him to do what he thought was the right thing. But I didn't trust him to do the right thing *for me*.

And tonight? I just didn't want to deal with it. I didn't want to deal with defending myself before the King. I didn't want to deal with calming down Zell. I just wanted to go and lie down and curl up under a blanket in the dark, to cry myself to sleep, to have all of this be over. I wanted to be somewhere safe and quiet, with the people I loved, and no one in danger, and no one dead. Why couldn't I just have that?

"It was fine," I said, refusing to meet Zell's gaze. "Can we go? Please?"

I could tell Zell wanted to know more, wanted to pry, and I could see the exact moment when he decided not to. He leaned down and gave me a kiss on the forehead, his lips warm and gentle. That kiss said more than any words could. *Keep your secrets*, it said. *I trust you.*

Which just made me feel so much worse.

EIGHT

THE NEXT MORNING, I JERKED AWAKE WITH A START, BECAUSE my bed was so comfortable it was kind of alarming. It was like the mattress was actually a gigantic pillow that I'd sunk into, covered in smaller pillows and soft, fur sheets. For one confused second, I didn't realize where I was, and then I saw the sleek shimmering blue of the ceiling overhead, the creeping golden filigree along the edges of the ceiling, the slim brass pipes that ran along the walls toward the sprawling personal bathroom.

Right. I was in the Godsblade.

I'd been in the great tower before, and even in the top floors where the royal family lived; before the semester at the University had started, I'd had to come here to visit Lyriana, which meant trying to not freak out over the fact that I was, you know, in the bedroom of the Princess herself. But it was one thing to visit the place, and another to wake up in it. I sat up in my bed, rubbing at my eyes with the back of my hand, and tried to adjust to my surroundings.

The Godsblade was unlike anything else in the Kingdom, unlike anything else in the world. Because the whole thing was made out of shimmersteel, every single wall, floor, and ceiling was constantly shining, the sleek metallic surfaces dancing with colors, like an oil spill in the sun. There wasn't a brick or a stone in sight, and while the furniture was man-made, it was all ornately carved wood: towering cabinets with intricately carved flowers, tables with lions' paws for feet, and bedposts inlaid with jewels. The smoothest, clearest mirrors hung in the bathrooms, their surfaces as slick as the water of a still pond, and if you pushed a little silver lever over the sinks, you could get hot or cold water to come out.

As a little girl, I'd spent days imagining how wonderful the lives of the Volaris were, but I'd mostly focused on "really pretty dresses" and "cakes stuffed with other cakes?" Knowing the truth would've made my little head explode.

I pulled myself out of bed, noticing briefly that I'd changed into a gold-colored nightgown, and padded my way across the room's metal floor. Tiny halos of light appeared around my bare feet, and the floor warmed instantly at their touch, because what royal could possibly live with the unimaginable cruelty of their feet being cold for a second? I crossed the room, toward the framed square of wall near the bed, and pressed my palm against the cool metal.

My skin tingled, and then the stretch of wall in the frame shimmered away, turning as clear as glass. My wall became a window, from which I gazed out from impossibly high above on the sprawling Circles of Lightspire. The King and his immediate family lived on the fiftieth floor of the Godsblade, and the view never ceased to amaze me. It was like looking down on the world's most intricate dollhouse, like seeing all of humanity in one glance. From up here, I could see all the sprawling manors of the Golden Circle, the markets, the parks. I could see the houses and shops of the Iron Circle, the ships sailing down the Adelphus as it snaked its way through the city. And if I squinted just right, I could make out the people, tiny as gnats, running along the streets, living their lives.

I tried to fight it, but my eyes wandered to the domed lecture halls and tall clocktowers of the University.

I wondered if Markiska's body was still there.

I slumped back down in my bed, sinking into those soft, warm sheets. The Godsblade had this odd hum, always present, like the walls were vibrating just a tiny bit. I closed my eyes and focused on that noise and let it drown out the thoughts running through my head.

The distinct whistle of a Godsblade door sliding open startled me. I peeked my head out from the sheet to see Lyriana, already dressed in a resplendent gown, standing in my doorway. "Tilla," she said softly, like she was struggling to say even that much. "Hello."

"Hey," I said.

I heard her cross over to sit by the foot of the bed, and felt her hand squeeze my calf, warm and assuring. "Last night was awful."

"Mmm," I muttered, though I honestly had some doubts if she even remembered all of last night. Especially the part where she drunkenly fused a guy's bones back together.

"I hope it's okay that I took us up here," she said. "I just couldn't bear the thought of going back to the University."

"No, it was the right call." I sat up, angling my head toward the window. "I'm not ready to go back out there. I don't feel safe."

A tense pause hung in the air. "Because of the man," Lyriana said at last. "The one you saw in the basement. With the eyes." I nodded. "Did Inquisitor Harkness have any idea who he was?"

I snorted. "No. I don't think he even believed me." Another silence, so I glanced back. "Do you?"

"Yes. Of course," Lyriana said quickly. "After everything we've been through, I know better than to doubt your word. I just . . . I just can't make sense of it. Who do you think he is? Why would he hurt Markiska?"

"No idea." I turned back to the window and stared out at the sprawling city, full of dark alleys and sinister hiding places. I knew the politics of the Eastern Baronies were complicated, that they all kind of hated each other and were always feuding, but as far as I knew, they mostly just stuck to trade wars and spreading scandalous gossip. And that wouldn't explain why the mage had been staring at me, why he'd followed me into the basement, why he'd known my name.

It didn't make sense. None of it.

"I'm going to take a few days off and just recover up here," Lyriana said. "You're free to stay as long as you want. I'm sure our professors would understand." I nodded again, and Lyriana rose to her feet, clearing her throat. "My family will be having breakfast in the private parlor. My father has invited you to join us."

"Oh . . . I . . . I mean, well . . ." I tried, and failed, to come up with an excuse. The absolute last thing I wanted right now was to sit in that fancy hall, to force myself to make polite small talk with King Leopold, to pretend I wasn't terrified of doing something wrong and offending him. I barely even wanted to be with my close friends, much less the most powerful strangers on the continent. But no matter how badly I wanted to go back to sleep, I couldn't say no. The King was the one who'd saved me after the disaster in the West. The King was the one who gave me shelter in this city of wonders, who offered me this chance at a great life. The King was the only reason I was safe. And also? The King was *the King*.

So I took a long soothing soak in my private bath. I tossed on one of the dresses in the closet, the simplest one I could find, and brushed my hair until it looked moderately presentable. And I headed down to the forty-ninth floor, to the gorgeous sprawling dining room they laughably called "the private parlor." A long redwood table, big enough for a dozen, stretched out across the polished shimmersteel floor. Lavishly detailed oil portraits of the great kings of yore lined the walls. At the far end, by the door, stood a marble statue of Leopold himself, looking a whole lot more impressive than he did in real life, with a massive sword in one hand and a flowering elderbloom in the other. But really, it was impossible to focus on any of that, because my attention immediately went to the food.

The table was covered, end to end, with a spread of every conceivable breakfast item. There were crispy fried cakes shaped like blossoming flowers, folded crepes oozing blackberry jam, sizzling strips of bacon and fluffy hunks of bread topped with a glaze of honey. At one end was a tray covered in at least a dozen different cheeses, and two dozen different olives; at the other was a plate piled high with *marr rellia*, fist-sized balls of flaky dough stuffed with spiced beef. And the fruit, everywhere the fruit, massive glass bowls overflowing with huge ripe peaches, juicy meyberries, prickly pears from the Southlands, and cocoaberries all the way from the K'olali Isles.

It was jaw-dropping, mouthwatering, and it made my stomach growl way louder than was acceptable. But it made me a little uneasy all the same, the way the party at Vale Manor had me uneasy. How much did this *cost*? How many people could they feed with this? Did they even eat most of the food, or did they throw it all out?

The rich, delicious smells hit me like a wave, so overpowering I had to slide into a chair just to keep my balance. The royal family was already gathered there. Lyriana sat next to me. Opposite her was her mother, Queen Augusta. King Leopold was at the head of the table, and the brawny statue of himself he was sitting under didn't do him any favors. He was wearing what I think passed for casual clothes: a loose purple shirt with billowing sleeves, a gold necklace with a sparkling black gem, and of course, his shimmersteel crown. He also had jam in his beard, but I don't think anyone was going to tell him that.

Servants bustled up to the table, pouring hot coffee, wiping away crumbs, and yes, ugh, washing hands. The Palace Priest, a withered husk of a man who looked, generously, five hundred years old, came forward, and we all bowed our heads in prayer. "We thank the Titans for the gift of this meal, as we thank them for all the gifts they have bestowed," he wheezed, the golden beads in his beard jangling as he spoke. "May it strengthen our bodies, and nourish our minds, and bring us all closer to joining the Titans in Ascendance."

"Blessed were the Titans," we all said in unison, even me. It's not like I'd suddenly got religious. If anything, the constant exposure to priests and prayer was making me more skeptical than ever. But I knew better than to stand out. If the King was praying, I was praying, too.

The Palace Priest stepped back, and the meal began. I grabbed one of those *marr rellias* and took one bite, and okay, you know what, it was good enough that I could stand behind thanking the Titans. They might have been giant terrifying gods who vanished one day into thin air, but their legacy gave us these meat pies.

"Tillandra," Queen Augusta said, and I craned my head her way. She was, by my reckoning, in her early fifties, but a combination of incredible genetics and the best Mesmer Arts left her looking like she was maybe thirty. High cheekbones and a slender jaw framed her elegant face, and her black hair was braided around her head in triple-bands, a symbolic crown under her actual shimmersteel circlet. Her eyes burned a vibrant gold, like Lyriana's, and her voice had a soft melodic undercurrent, like a tiny pulse of magic was always running underneath it. "I'm so terribly sorry for your loss."

"Oh. Um. Thank you," I mumbled, staring down at my plate. Whenever I was around the royal family, especially the Queen, I somehow reverted to being a timid five-year-old, hiding behind the tablecloth while my father met with his Lords. "I, um, appreciate it."

"A terrible thing," King Leopold said, sawing through a massive steak with a pearl-handled knife. "Whenever a young person takes their life, it's so tragic, so inexplicable. I had a cousin who did that when we were teenagers. Gregor, I believe his name was. Beautiful boy, full of promise. And one day, he just drowned himself in the river. None of us ever knew why."

I had no idea how to respond to that, or really, how to respond to anything the King ever said. I'd spent my first few visits with him in total awe, trying to comprehend the majesty, to understand the brilliance. What was he really thinking? Why was he so keen on protecting me? What was his master plan? But the more time I spent with him, the more I realized there wasn't really any brilliance, or honestly any majesty. The King was just . . . sort of a guy. He liked good food and fancy wine, he listened to his priests and his advisors, and he loved the hell out of his daughters. In a city full of snakes trying to get ahead, he was just a soft old bear who wanted to hang out. He didn't shelter me because of some master plan; he sheltered me because Lyriana liked me, and he loved Lyriana. It was vaguely comforting to know that I wasn't a pawn, but in its own way, that truth was even more nerve-racking. It meant my safety, my life, my well-being, was entirely contingent on *being liked.*

"Why would anyone drown theirself?" a soft little voice cut in, sparing me from having to reply. It was Princess Aurelia, Lyriana's little sister, and I hadn't seen her because she was sitting on the far side of the table, hidden behind a tower of pancakes she'd stacked on her plate.

"Drown *themselves,*" Queen Augusta corrected.

"I really don't feel like this is the most appropriate breakfast conversation," Lyriana cut in. "And for the sake of the Titans, Aurelia, move that ridiculous pancake tower. We can't even see you."

"I was trying to make the Godsblade," she grumbled, and slid it aside. Aurelia was gorgeous, with straight black hair hanging down her back, and the high cheekbones and sharp chin of the Volaris. At the same time, there was something a little quirky about her, a gawkiness that made her all the cuter. Her nose was a little big, and her skin was lighter than Lyriana's. Most noticeable, though, were her eyes, which were a soft brown, not a glowing gold or a shimmering red or a pulsing turquoise. Even though she was nine years old, Aurelia hadn't Awoken as a mage yet, which meant she still had her natural eyes. Her *baby eyes*, they called them. Which, let's agree, is pretty creepy.

"In any case, you have my deepest condolences, Tillandra," King Leopold said, and really, I just wanted everyone to stop talking to me so I could actually eat. "You may stay with us here for as long as you desire. Though I do imagine it will get a bit hectic as we approach the Ascendance Day Masquerade...."

"Any excuse to discuss the masquerade," Queen Augusta said with a smirk.

"You know me too well, queen of my heart." King Leopold grinned back, waggling his fingers at her like the world's dorkiest husband.

"I actually do have a thought on this year's masquerade," Lyriana interjected. "I'd like to propose an idea. A new tradition that I think could make a really positive impact on the city, one that would be celebrated for decades."

"I'm listening," King Leopold said, not without a hint of skepticism. I got the impression Lyriana suggested new traditions a lot.

"Well, the whole point of Ascendance Day is remembering when the Titans left us, and honoring the great responsibility they left House Volaris," the Princess went on, with the unmistakable cadence of someone who's rehearsed a speech in front of the bathroom mirror a dozen times. "The responsibility that we dedicate ourselves to serving the people of Noveris, to bringing prosperity, peace, and enlightenment to all."

"Yes? And?"

"And . . . don't you think it's a bit odd that we celebrate that responsibility by cloistering all the nobles in the Godsblade, far from the people we're meant to serve?"

The Queen let out a barely muffled sigh, and King Leopold shifted uncomfortably in his seat. "The tradition of the masquerade is almost as old as the Dynasty itself!" the priest chimed in. "To question it . . . to suggest that it's unjust . . . nears blasphemy!"

"I'm not saying it's unjust," Lyriana replied. "I'm just saying, I think we could do more. What if, the day after the masquerade, we declared a day of service? All of the nobles and their retinues could travel to the Iron Circle to meet with the smallfolk, to lend their gold and their strength? They could build houses and bake bread and treat the sick and so much more! If for just one day, all of the nobility worked together, just think what we could accomplish!"

"My dear daughter," Queen Augusta said, and her voice sounded melodic even when she was clearly annoyed. "The masquerade is the most important holiday of the year. Lords and Ladies will travel from all over the continent to come here, to be merry, to spend just one fleeting night in the company of their King. Do you really think they'll want to do that if they have to spend the next day shoveling manure and shaking hands with paupers?"

King Leopold nodded. "I agree, it's all a bit too much. I don't know where you get these ideas." His gaze narrowed. "Is this more nonsense from the Sisters?"

"I'm not a member of the Sisters anymore, and you know it!" Lyriana yelled, shaking the table, and suddenly the whole mood was less mildly-awkward-breakfast and more incredibly-awkward-family-fight. "I'm just trying to serve the people of this Kingdom!"

"And you're implying that I don't?" the King rebutted.

Queen Augusta just shook her head. "Our family's alliances are fragile as is. Do you want to drive even more Houses away?"

"I'm just saying that we need to try to hel—"

"There's a tradition in the West!" I blurted out, and every head swiveled toward me. I don't know why I spoke. I really shouldn't have. But now I'd started down that road and there was no turning back. "During all the great feasts, the Old Kings would have the cooks make extra food. Nothing fancy, just meat and porridge and bread. And they'd send all their knights out into the towns nearby to give it to the people who needed it most. You know, the poorhouses, hospitals, that kind of thing. It always kept the people happy, and it actually didn't cost them much at all."

"Now that is an interesting idea." King Leopold stroked his beard, which just rubbed the jam in more. "The nobles would remain unbothered . . . but the smallfolk could still feel as though they are benefiting from the kindness of the crown."

"The priesthood could help," the Palace Priest offered. "We could even distribute the food from our temples."

Lyriana let out a little sigh. "It's not quite what I'd intended . . . but I suppose it's better than nothing."

"Well, I hate to be the one who spoils the mood," Queen Augusta said, and her gaze flicked to me. Her face was still smiling, but her eyes sure as hell weren't. I was starting to realize, maybe too late, that she was the real brains behind the throne. "Given what's happening out there, do we really think now is the best time to be adopting *Western* customs?"

The room went silent. Everyone, even Lyriana, looked away. And I stared into my coffee as intently as I could, because maybe if I stared hard enough I'd melt into it. Why the hell had I spoken? Why had I just painted a target on myself? All I had to do was stuff my mouth with pies and I'd be fine, but no, I had to offer my stupid suggestion, and now they were all acting like I was some kind of Western infiltrator. I needed these people to like me, *damn it.* What was I thinking?

"But why did the man drown himself?" Aurelia asked, and I've never been more grateful for a child's self-absorption.

Breakfast ended, mercifully. The day dragged on. In the afternoon, I mustered up enough strength to head to the Glass Gardens on the forty-eighth floor, where I paced silently among the multicolored roses and the towering orchids and the sweet, ever-flowering elderblooms. Zell came by as soon as his shift ended, and we hung out on the Garden's balcony together, his firm arm around me, as the soft summer winds blew over us.

• • •

That night, just before midnight, I was back in my room alone, unable to sleep, when my door hummed with a soft little melody. I had a visitor. "Lyriana, I'm sorry, but now's not the best t—" I started, and then the door slid open and I saw the man standing there. "Oh."

The last time I'd seen Galen Reza, Lord of the Nest, had been six months ago, as we'd ridden away from the makeshift army camp in Pioneer's Pass. We didn't actually talk then, not unless you consider a knowing nod through a carriage window talking, and I kind of assumed that'd be the last I'd ever see of him. It wasn't that I liked him; I didn't. In our brief time together, he'd been cynical and cold and more focused on defeating my father than saving innocent lives. But I still felt an attachment to him, and felt an odd sense of comfort from the sight of his lanky figure in my doorway. I guess once you've fought back-to-back with someone against a room full of mercenaries, you always have a bit of a bond.

"Lord Reza." I sat up in my bed and straightened my gown. "What are you doing here?"

"I'm visiting the city for the Ascendance Day Masquerade, hoping to get an audience with the King." He strolled into my room and let the door slide shut behind him. "And Princess Lyriana suggested it might be nice for me to pay you a visit." Lord Reza was a Heartlander in his late twenties, with dark skin, sharp cheekbones, and curly black hair. His narrow feline eyes were as alert and intelligent as ever, but heavy bags hung underneath them; the last six months must have been rough. "She told me what happened with your friend. I'm sorry."

I closed my eyes because as nice as his words were,

I didn't want to rehash this with yet another person. "Thanks."

"Are you doing okay?"

I was too tired to lie. "No. Not really."

"Me neither." Galen turned toward a small cabinet and idly rifled through it. "You'd think after everything we went through, we deserve a break. But no, that's not how it works. I think some people are just followed by death, like a shadow at their heels, striking every time they dare relax." He found what he was looking for, a crystal decanter of brandy. "You and I? We have that in common."

"What do you mean?"

Galen uncorked the brandy and poured himself a glass. "My mother died when I was eight, my father when I was twenty. My only sister died of frostkiss fever, and the first boy I ever loved died in a house fire." He raised the glass and took a long, slow sip. "I'd kind of figured I'd gotten used to it. So of course, the Titans threw me headfirst into a damned war."

I hesitated, mulling over how coyly to ask my next question. Then I decided to screw being coy. "How's the war? Who's winning?"

"Who knows?" Galen shrugged. "For a while, we were. The mages pushed your father's men back to the Markson in a month, and it looked like it was all over save the beheadings. Then the tide seemed to change. Your father's men got more cunning, more ruthless."

A dread swirled within me. "Is he using mage-killers?"

"On occasion, but not many. Even without them, he's got the knowledge of the land on his side. He's got a ruthless guerrilla army poisoning our supplies and burning the forests around us. And that rat, Hampstedt, has proven to be a surprisingly capable general."

I blinked. "Hold on. Miles? *Miles* is a general?"

Galen shook his head. "I don't understand it either, but it seems to be the truth. They call him the Bloodhawk now. His tactics led to the defeat of the royal scouts at the Gurgling Brook, and to the capture of an entire company of mages."

In a world that increasingly felt like it made no sense, this was the hardest stretch. Miles . . . dorky, cowardly Miles . . . Miles who ran when a fight broke out, who always hid behind his mother's dress, was some kind of brilliant general? Brilliant enough that *other* people called him a cool name like the Bloodhawk? He probably loved that, thought it made him sound so tough and intimidating. Just thinking about his existence made me furious, but knowing that he was doing well out West, building a reputation, earning respect? After what he did to me? To Jax?

The only thing Miles deserved was a swift punch to the face.

"It's not just your father's men that vex us," Galen went on, either not noticing or willfully ignoring the fact that I'd balled my hands into fists. "It's the Western smallfolk, too. They sing praises for the Volaris when we march into town, but when night falls, three out of four are willing to drive a knife into our backs." He finished the glass and set it down, a little too hard. "These days, we gain a yard one day, lose it the next, and start all over again. That's why I'm here, to beg our esteemed King to send more men."

"And will he?"

Galen snorted. "Doesn't seem likely. Between the chaos of the Ragged Disciples, the tensions with the Southlands, and now the death of an Eastern Baron's daughter, he wants every man he has protecting this city. I tried to reason with him, but he seemed more invested in talking with his steward about the decorations for the masquerade."

His tone was so bitter, it was halfway to treason. It set me on edge. "Galen . . . what are you doing in my room? Why are you telling me this?"

"Well, I suppose I thought I was currying favor with a good friend of the Queen-to-Be, but that's just an excuse." He poured himself another glass, then turned to me, and I saw his eyes weren't the same at all. There was a pain in them now that hadn't been there before, a desperation. "I might be a Heartlander, but I grew up in the West. And it breaks my heart to see it so devastated. The rivers run with blood. The forests are smoldering husks. Whole villages have been razed. And the men I'm fighting with, the mages I'm feeding and sheltering, couldn't even begin to care less. Half of them *want* to burn the whole Province to ash." He let out a long, slow sigh. "I suppose if I'm being honest with myself, I mostly just wanted to talk to another Westerner. To someone who understood."

"I do," I said, and crossed over to him. I took the decanter out of his hands and gently clinked it against the edge of his glass. I thought of grassy cliffs by the surging ocean, of fog-shrouded forests with redwood trees that reached up into the sky, of faded murals on ancient tunnel walls, and buried shrines in mossy hidden glades. "Here's to the West we love."

"To the West we love," Galen replied, and we both drank.

He left shortly after that, and I sat in my bed, mulling over what he'd said. So the war was still going. So my father actually had a chance. His men were holding back the armies of the King and the Knights of Lazan, enough so that the Lord of the Nest himself was here begging for help. Part of me didn't understand how that was possible. Part of me was terrified at even the remote possibility he could win.

And a different part of me, an ember buried deep, burned with Western pride.

nine

I stayed with Lyriana in the Godsblade for another three days, three slow, languid days that passed with the hazy boredom of a hangover. There was no reason to leave; this place had all the food and clothes and drinks I could ever want, and while I knew, logically, that I should probably get back to the University and resume my studies, I also knew that I never actually *wanted* to set foot there again. So I sent a Whisper to my friend Marlo at the Roost, asking him to hold on to my mail, and settled into my room up here. As long as Lyriana let me crash here, I'd take her up on it.

It was afternoon on the third day when that plan fell through. I was in the royal foyer with Lyriana, Aurelia, and Queen Augusta. The three of them sat around a small marble table while I sprawled on a long fluffy couch, idly popping big, juicy grapes into my mouth.

"Come on, Aurelia," Lyriana said, leaning over her little sister. "You can do this! Just visualize them moving!"

"I'm trying!" Aurelia replied. The table had a bunch of little iron rods lying on it, and Aurelia was hunched over them intently, her little brow creased into the deepest furrow I'd ever seen on a child. She had Rings on, big translucent gems set in simple gold bands that were meant to help magically inclined children Awaken their inner powers; training Rings, Lyriana had called them. They sat on Aurelia's fingers, dull as plain stones, while the iron rods stubbornly refused to move.

"You should be able to see the beams of power around them," Queen Augusta coaxed.

"I don't see the stupid beams!" Aurelia yelled, and swept the rods off the table with one wild swing of her arm. Augusta gasped, and Lyriana frowned, but I smiled. I liked the kid.

"Aurelia Relaria Volaris!" Augusta said. "Collect those rods and try again at once!"

"Ah, go easy on the child," a voice said from behind me. I spun around to see Inquisitor Harkness in the doorway, smiling at the girl like a kindly uncle. My skin prickled into goose bumps. *Liar.* "She's only nine. There's plenty of time for her magic to Awaken."

"Nine is late for a Volaris to Awaken, and you know it, Landon," Queen Augusta replied.

"Not always," Lyriana chimed in, and why was it that everyone was at their brattiest when talking to their parents? "Sheldoni Volaris III didn't Awaken until he was thirteen, and he conquered the Southlands."

Queen Augusta shot her the angriest mom-glare I've ever seen, then swiveled back to the Inquisitor. "I imagine you're not here for a conversation on the finer points of parenting."

"Not at all, Your Majesty," Harkness replied with a delicate bow. "I'm here for our esteemed guest, Tillandra."

My goose bumps got goose bumps, but I had to play it cool in front of the royals. "What can I help you with?"

"Just a word." His beady eyes narrowed. "In private."

I thought about telling him to take a long dive down a short well, but bit my tongue. Creepy or not, he still had the power to have me jailed or exiled or worse. That meant I had to play along.

I put on a smile and followed him out, through a pair of sliding translucent doors, onto the foyer's balcony. We stood on that platform, the wind whistling around us, as the whole sprawl of the city stretched out before us. "What do you want?" I asked.

"Tomorrow, Baron Kelvin San Der Vlain and his family arrive to claim his daughter's body," the Inquisitor said. "She'd written to him of you, and he'd like you to be there. Maybe he'll ask you some questions, I don't know." He stepped forward and gripped the railing tight with both hands. "If he does . . . I'd ask that you don't bring up your little story about the mystery mage in the basement. Stick with the official report."

"That she killed herself," I said. "You want me to lie?"

"One thing you learn when you torture enough people is that truth is a remarkably subjective idea. You *think* you saw that mage. *I* think you were drunk, possibly drugged, and imagined it. Neither of us can ever really know what happened. What I'm doing right now is giving you the generous offer to choose the right truth, the one in the interests of the Kingdom."

"And if I don't take your offer? If I tell Markiska's father what really happened to her?"

"Then you'll sound like a madwoman," the Inquisitor said, casually. "And even the King won't be able to protect you this time. We have some special places in this city where we put women who've lost their minds. I suspect you really wouldn't like them."

I imagined what it'd feel like to shove him over the balcony. "You're a real piece of shit, you know that?"

He let out a brittle laugh. "There aren't many people who have the moxie to say that to my face. You really are your father's daughter." He turned back around, the setting sun a bloody red disk framing his gaunt silhouette. "You may have everyone else fooled. But I see through you, Tillandra. I know exactly what you are."

"You still think . . . what? That I'm working for my father? That I'm some sort of master spy?"

"Nothing that simple," Harkness replied. "Your story could be true. You might well be innocent. But no matter how many parties you go to with the Princess, no matter how much you doll yourself up in Lightspire silks, I can see your true nature in your eyes. You're a Westerner. A rebel. A traitor. And one day or another, the moment will come when you're forced to choose between your real home and the one that has taken you in." He reached down and rested a hand on the hilt of the dagger at his waist. "And when that day comes . . . I'll be waiting."

"You're evil," I said, sounding more scared than I wanted to. "A monster."

"Perhaps," he replied, almost amused. "The funny thing

about power is that the more you get, the harder you have to work to keep it. The King and the Queen give their speeches and hold their parties. The priests prattle on, the soldiers march, and the nobles play their silly games. And yet for all of that, I'm still the man who holds this Kingdom together, who keeps the cultists in the shadows and the rebels outside the walls. I'm the knife in the dark, Tillandra, the last step against chaos. Monster or not, this city needs me." He strode into the building, his gray robes billowing behind him like a hungry shadow. "Show up to the memorial tomorrow. Keep your mouth shut. And you just might live to call me a piece of shit another day."

Then he was gone, stalking off back into the foyer and down a side hallway. I watched him go, breath still tight in my chest, then wandered back inside.

"Do you want to join us?" Lyriana called from across the room. "Aurelia's almost got the rods figured out. I'm pretty sure the next try is going to be the one."

Aurelia's agonized face told me that was absolutely not the case.

"Thanks, but I'm good," I said, my knees still shaking. "I think I need to go my room now."

• • •

Sitting in my room alone was only marginally better than watching Aurelia struggle to move some rods, but luckily, Zell came by that night. I'd planned to tell him about the Inquisitor, but he greeted me with a kiss, long and passionate, his hands undoing the clasps of my dress, and well, suddenly it seemed a whole lot less important. We made love for the first time in a week, and there was a hunger to it. I needed to feel him now, feel him in every way, feel his warmth and his breath and his firm, calloused hands. We lay together afterward on a fur blanket sprawled over the floor, our bodies entangled like a pair of laced hands, the flickering orange light of the fireplace the only illumination.

"Can I ask you something?" I whispered. My cheek was pressed against his bare chest, and I could hear his heart thumping steadily. "But you have to be totally honest with me."

"Of course."

I hesitated, afraid not because I thought he'd lie, but because I knew he wouldn't. "Do you believe me? About the man I saw? Because everyone else thinks I just imagined it, and I'm starting to think, I mean, what if they're right? Even Lyriana. She says she believes me, but I see the doubt in her eyes . . . and—"

Zell cut me off with a kiss, long and tender, then pulled away. The tips of our noses touched, just barely, and he looked into my eyes from just an inch away. "I believe you," he said, and his words were like diving into the ocean after days spent in the tormenting heat.

"Thank you. By the Old Kings, by the Twelve, whatever, thank you."

He kissed me again. "I love you, Tilla."

"I love you too," I whispered, and I melted into him. I knew we still had issues. I knew he was still hiding things from me, that I was still hiding things from him. But I didn't care. I needed *that* moment, that feeling.

The next morning, when we woke up, we dressed together for the meeting with Markiska's father. Zell wore his formal blue uniform, which somehow looked a lot less hot and a lot more somber. Lyriana had gotten an appropriate outfit for me, a conservative dark dress with latticed black gloves. We didn't say anything. We didn't have to.

Lyriana and her mother met us in the foyer, and we walked together toward the aravin. Its great metal doors slid open at our approach, and we stepped into the slim glass tube, one of several that ran alongside the Godsblade. A mage was waiting inside, a brawny Hand of Servo, and he began doing his thing once we'd stepped in, turning his big hands in wide circles. I could hear gears rumbling, somewhere nearby, and the wispy howl of wind in a funnel. The wide flat platform we were standing on wobbled a little, then began its graceful descent down the tube, like a leaf floating down a drainpipe.

I shut my eyes tight and fought back the roiling sickness turning in my stomach. I *hated* this. Really, really, hated it. I'd asked Lyriana once how it worked, and she'd gone on about air currents and pressure and levitation arts, all of which just made me more nervous. She swore up and down aravins were safe, but nothing in this world could convince me I wasn't going to die every time I set foot in one.

After maybe a minute or maybe an eternity, the platform came to a lurching stop. I opened my eyes to see a gathering through the tube's glass frame, waiting in the courtyard below the long steps of the Godsblade. Soldiers surrounded the outskirts, keeping away the public. Squinting, I could make out the squat figure of the King, his black, somber attire still dazzling in the light, and the tall gray figure of the Inquisitor next to him. Beyond them were a group of huddled people in vibrant clothes who I guessed were Markiska's family. And in front of them, resting on the painted pavilion, was a slick redwood casket, its lid propped open.

I hesitated. No. *No.*

Zell's hand found mine. I breathed. We went on.

Markiska would be laid to rest at her home in Sparra, cast out to sea in a boat loaded with all of her beloved possessions. So this was the closest I'd get to a funeral for her, the last chance I'd have to say good-bye to my friend. I steeled myself and walked forward, through the aravin's doors and down those long steps, closer and closer to the coffin.

I knew that when Markiska would be sent to sea, she'd be resplendent, wearing a dazzling dress of red and gold, her makeup done by her family's best artists. But now, in that box, she was unadorned, plainer than I'd ever seen her. They'd put her in a simple gray dress, and her face was completely unpainted. Most noticeable of all was her hair. It had been cleaned, the dyes that Markiska constantly treated it with washed away, and that lustrous impossible blond was now a plain, dull brown. This was the real Markiska, the face behind the mask, the vulnerable girl behind the goddess she pretended to be. She looked small and gentle and unbearably human.

I stood there by the coffin, silent, as one by one her family members cried over her. Her mother and sisters were first, then a wizened woman with a white-painted face who I'm guessing was her grandmother. Her father was last. I don't know what I expected him to look like, but it certainly wasn't this, a short, red-cheeked man with enormous bushy eyebrows, like caterpillars stuck to his forehead. His face was painted a dusty gray, with thin black lips and glistening jeweled teardrops stuck on below his eyes. He clutched my hand in his, his skin slick and sweaty.

"You were my daughter's friend," he said, his voice cracking.

"I was," I replied, unable to keep eye contact. "She was great. Amazing."

"I know," he said, and his choking gasp made me want to cry all over again. "I just . . . I can't believe she would do this. I just don't understand it. I don't." He grabbed at my wrist, my arm. I couldn't deal with this. Not today. Not ever. "Was she unhappy? Did someone wrong her? Why would she do this?"

"She . . . she . . ." I stammered, but the words didn't come. I could feel Lyriana tense up next to me. My eyes wandered to the Inquisitor, who was staring at me intensely, his lip curled up just enough so that I could see his clenched teeth. I knew I had to lie. I knew I had to say what they all wanted to hear. But no matter how hard I tried, the words just wouldn't come. "I'm sorry, I . . ."

Then I saw him. The man at the edge of the crowd, lurking at the back. His face hidden in the shadows of a hood.

For a second, my heart leaped into my throat, and I thought it was *him*, the mage from the basement, the one who'd killed Markiska. But then the hood fell back and I saw his face. Round cheeks. Soft eyes. Hair pulled back in ornate ropes.

Darryn Vale.

His eyes caught mine, across the crowd, and they opened wide with surprise. And . . . fear? Guilt?

Then he turned around and ran away, vanishing into the streets.

A thought sprouted in my mind, a seed that instantly tangled into a vine. What had the Inquisitor told me, back in the Watchtower? That Markiska had snuck off to the bedchambers with some boy during the party, that they'd fought and she'd left in tears? I'd dismissed it as him trying to create a narrative for why she'd commit suicide, but maybe that story was the key all along. Because what if that boy hadn't been any random boy, but a very specific one? A boy who absolutely under no circumstances should have been hooking up with Markiska, not at the party announcing his betrothal? A boy with a very powerful family who had everything to lose?

Every theory I'd had about Markiska had involved some grand plot, some intricate scheme between powerful nobles. But what if it was all something so much simpler? What if this whole thing was about her and Darryn?

"I'm sorry," I repeated to Markiska's father, who was still staring at me with those terrible watery eyes. "But I have to go. I have to go."

I turned away, rushing up the stairs back toward the Godsblade. I could feel all their eyes on me. I'm sure I looked like some distraught girl, unable to handle her grief. Fine. Whatever. Let them think that. I didn't care. So long as it got the Inquisitor off my back.

I wasn't going to give up. I was going to find out exactly what happened to Markiska. I was going to bring whoever killed her to justice.

And I had my first good lead.

TEN

WE GATHERED IN A FOYER LATER THAT AFTERNOON. I PACED across the floor, my mind buzzing with ideas. Zell stood alert against a wall, his eyes tracking my every movement, while Lyriana watched from a couch. She'd come later, having waited below until Markiska's family had left, and it took a good ten minutes of my agitated rambling to catch her up to speed.

"You really think this?" she said, and I could tell she was balancing her natural skepticism with a desire to believe me. "You think Darryn had Markiska killed?"

"Tell me it doesn't make sense," I replied. "Darryn just got betrothed to the Baroness of Orles. That's a huge deal for the Vale family, right? Like warehouses-of-gold huge? And Markiska hears about this at the party. She's smart. She knows that an alliance between two of her family's biggest trade enemies would be a disaster. So she sabotages it the way she does best, by seducing Darryn."

"You think she planned to blackmail him?" Zell asked.

"Maybe. Or maybe just expose him as the cheating sleazebag that he is."

Lyriana nodded. "If word got out that Darryn was being unfaithful to his betrothed, with the daughter of a rival Baron no less, it would've brought tremendous shame on House Vale."

"And on Darryn specifically."

"The marriage would've been called off," Lyriana said. "And Darryn would've caught most of the blame. Knowing Molari, he would've been disowned, cast out on the streets."

"Exactly!" I said, and it made so much sense I can't believe I didn't think of it earlier. "But Markiska underestimated Darryn. She didn't know what he was capable of. That man I saw, with the smoky eyes . . . he was hanging around the party at the Vale estate. What if he works for them? For Darryn? What if Darryn ordered him to kill Markiska?"

Zell shifted uneasily. "Is that a possibility? Are there mages who would murder for hire?"

"There shouldn't be. Mages are held to the highest standards of conduct by their order. To kill an innocent would be an unspeakable crime, punishable by the most painful death." Lyriana hesitated, as if revealing something she shouldn't. "But . . . there are always rumors. Of rogue apostates, mages brought up outside of the Orders, loyal only to the highest bidder."

"And what higher bidder is there than the richest family in the Kingdom?"

Zell let out a long exhale. "So. Let's say this is all true. What then? What do we do now?"

"We call Darryn out," I said. "We tell the King what he did, and we have him put on trial."

"It's not that simple, Tillandra," Lyriana said. "What you're talking about is the gravest of accusations, the sort of thing that starts blood feuds. If it isn't true . . . or if it is true, but we can't prove it . . . it could be catastrophic for all of us. The Vales would see you tried for slander . . . or worse."

"Then we'll get proof first," Zell said. "The question is how."

"I might have an idea," a low, sly voice said from the back of the room.

We all spun around. Ellarion rested against a pillar, arms folded across his chest.

"Ellarion!" Lyriana jumped in surprise. "What are you doing here?"

"Eavesdropping, obviously." He paced toward us and plucked a big green apple out of a bowl, dusting it against his tunic. "And you'd better thank the Titans I was. Because if you're going to prove Darryn had Markiska killed, you're going to need my help."

I turned to Lyriana, who looked concerned, and at Zell, who looked alarmed. I liked Ellarion, but I had no idea how much I could trust him. "You believe us? You think she was killed?"

"I knew Markiska. We were . . . friends," Ellarion said, and the slight pause told me they'd been more than that, at least once. "I talked to her at the party. We laughed, we drank, we caught up on old times. She left me to go flirt with Darryn, and I saw the two of them sneaking down a hallway later. She looked sober, cunning, in control. I don't believe the girl I saw then would have killed herself that night." He shook his head. "I came here to share my suspicions with Lyriana. It turns out you've already beaten me to it. You lot never cease to impress me."

"You said you could get proof," Zell said bluntly. "How?"

Ellarion glanced around, like he was making sure there wasn't a *second* charming rogue eavesdropping from the shadows. "What I'm about to tell you is a secret of the highest order. Can I trust you to keep it within this room?" His eyes passed over Lyriana and me, and bored straight into Zell.

"Of course," Lyriana said, and Zell just nodded.

Ellarion hesitated, then shrugged. Apparently, that was good enough. "Training to be the Archmagus comes with its perks. But the best of them is that I get to study with the heads of all the Orders, to learn any arts I want. Even the ones that come from the Shadows of Fel."

Lyriana's eyes went wide, so clearly I was missing something. "No . . . you're kidding. . . ."

Ellarion grinned. "I can Echo-Scry."

Still missing something. "What's Echo-Scrying?"

"According to the rumors, it's a difficult and incredibly complicated spycraft art," Lyriana said. "I've never seen it done. I mean . . . I wasn't even sure it was real."

Ellarion kept grinning. "Oh, it's real. I'm no master, mind you, but I've got the basics down. If I focus, I can see Echoes going back a few days, maybe even a week."

"Is this supposed to be making sense?" I asked. "Because everything you say just makes me more confused."

Ellarion sat down in a chair opposite me, taking a hearty bite from his apple. "You have to understand. Part of being a mage is seeing things that normal people cannot. You look around this room, and you see the *reality* of it. The furniture. The walls. The people. But when I look around, I see so much more. I see strands of possibility, like beams of light, that connect everything. I see a tapestry of hidden energies, red and gold and white, all around us like a great invisible loom." His crimson eyes sparkled, dancing flame, and I could almost see it, almost imagine what he meant. Mages were always so secretive about how it all worked, but Ellarion's words actually made sense.

"A great loom," Zell muttered. "Our shamans speak of the same thing. What's your point?"

I couldn't tell if Ellarion looked intrigued or annoyed. "When you pass through life, you brush against this loom, and you leave small traces of yourself in your wake, like footprints in the sand. They fade and vanish over time, but if you look in the right place, in the right moment, you can see them. Does that make sense?"

"No."

Ellarion sighed. "Get me in Darryn's room, and I should be able to see exactly what he did that night."

"You're serious," Lyriana said. "Ellarion, using an art like Echo-Scrying without the consent of the Inquisitor is a major crime, much less Scrying on a noble family with the clout of the Vales. What if you get caught? What if it goes wrong? You'd lose everything." She shook her head. "I want to know what happened to Markiska too, but . . . I can't ask you to do this."

"Look. It's about Markiska. But it's also much bigger than that," Ellarion said. "There have been rumors about the Vale family for years. That they're involved in criminal practices. That they hire apostates to do their dirty work. That they want to seize the power of the crown." His gaze narrowed. "Don't forget, dear cousin. It was Molari Vale who spoke out so strongly against you at your hearing."

"So that's what this is really about," Zell said. "A chance for you to get dirt on some rivals."

Ellarion's gaze flicked to him, and now *that* was definitely annoyance. "Look. Do you want proof or not?"

"Even if we said yes, we'd still have to somehow get you into Darryn's room," I cut in, because I was really not in the mood to watch these two fight. "How are we going to do that?"

"Actually, I might have an idea," Lyriana said. "But I don't think anyone's going to like it."

ELEVEN

We spent the rest of the day refining Lyriana's plan until it felt foolproof, and the next morning made the call to really go through with it. A part of me wanted to wait, to think more about it, to find a reason to hesitate before, you know, breaking into the manor of the city's wealthiest merchant. But I knew that was just cowardice talking. Besides, Ellarion said that he could only Scry a few days back, so every day that went by was a day the proof of Markiska's killer faded away. We had to act now.

So that afternoon, the four of us rode an aravin down to the ground floor in silence, trying our hardest not to act like we were totally up to something. My stomach was a mess of butterflies, and my hands tingled from worry. Next to me, Lyriana pleated her dress over and over again, while Ellarion snapped his fingers idly, each one sparking a tiny burst of flame, like striking a flint. Only Zell looked normal, standing calm and resolute with a distant expression. I couldn't tell if he was just that good at keeping it together, or if he wasn't as nervous because his part involved the least risk.

See, our plan needed three of us to get into Darryn's room and find the proof: Lyriana to distract Molari, Ellarion to do the Echo-Scrying, and me to keep a lookout and make sure Ellarion was okay. We'd do it on a school day, when Darryn was in class, but that didn't cover the entirely plausible scenario where he'd decide to ditch and come home early. That's where Zell came in. His job was to head to the University, keep a close eye on Darryn, and stall him if he looked like he was heading our way.

I'd tried to think of a way to keep us all together, because I hated the idea of doing something risky without Zell by my side. But there was just no way to make it work. So I parted ways with him at the base of the Godsblade, in that massive marble-floored ballroom on the first floor. While Lyriana and Ellarion got us a carriage, I held him close, and he gave me a gentle kiss on the forehead.

"Tilla," he said quietly. "You're sure about this?"

I nodded. "If Darryn had Markiska killed, he has to pay. And this is the only way we'll ever know."

Zell looked down at me. "Look. I . . . I know things have been a little off with us lately. Soon, we need to sit and talk. But for now, I just . . . I . . ." He shook his head. "Forget it. Good luck. I'll see you on the other side of this."

I kissed him, long and slow and tender. "I'll catch up with you soon," I said, hugged him one more time, and then walked out to join Lyriana and Ellarion in their carriage. I hopped in and slumped down into my seat, my cheeks still a little flushed.

Ellarion shot me a look of wry amusement. "You two are absolutely adorable."

Lyriana grinned. "Right? Aren't they just too much?"

"Shut up, you guys," I said, and turned away, hiding my smile.

Soon enough, our carriage rolled into the Gem, and dropped us off at the ornate gate of Vale Manor. We weren't scheduled to come by, so we waited outside the estate's tall brick walls, tapping our feet in the hot sun for what felt like an eternity. The street around us was mostly empty, but one bit of motion did catch my eye. Just around the corner from us, toward the far side of Molari's land, a shirtless young man with a bucket was busily scrubbing away on his hands and knees. A statue stood above him, a big marble figure of a mage with outstretched hands, the kind you saw all over the city. Except this one didn't have a head anymore, just a ragged neck, and its arms ended in jagged stone stumps. Below the statue was a message, scrawled in messy red paint: *The Titans Return. The Usurpers Burn. All Hail the Gray Priestess.*

It was a sweltering day, but I felt a cold chill. I'd known the Ragged Disciples were growing in boldness, but it was one thing to know it and another to see it. This was the very heart of the Gem, the safest neighborhood in the city. And yet here it was, the vandalism of the Ragged Disciples, a statue defaced not twenty feet from the home of Molari Vale himself.

The guard came back a few minutes later and ushered us along a path toward the manor's main door. I wondered if we'd have to wait long, but it swung open even before we got to the steps. Molari Vale, his bulky frame pushing the limits on his tight silk tunic, stood in the frame. His gray eyebrows arched in curiosity at the sight of us. "Princess Lyriana."

Behind him, the servants in the manor's foyer all bowed, dropping to one knee and folding their hands behind their back. But Molari didn't bow, which felt like it maybe should've been a pretty big warning sign. He just bent his head a little, the absolute bare minimum to count as a gesture of respect.

"I wanted to talk to you about Ascendance Day," Lyriana said, with that slightly stiff cadence of someone who's rehearsed the words a million times. "I had this idea for the masquerade, a surprise dedication to my father to celebrate his twenty years as King, but I'll need fine goods from the Southlands, and I know you have connections to their merchants."

Molari let out a rumbling sigh, and I could practically see the gears in his head spinning as he tried to find a way out of this. "I have quite a bit of business to take care of today, but . . . I suppose I could spare a few minutes." His gaze flitted to Ellarion and then, for the first time, to me. "Are you two a part of this conversation?"

I took a deep breath. The plan we came up with required three of us in the house. Getting Lyriana in was easy enough, because, you know, Princess. Getting me in would be a lot harder.

Ellarion stepped forward with an enormous grin. "Actually, Molari, I couldn't care less about the masquerade. But when I heard my dear cousin was visiting you today, well, I had to tag along."

Lyriana rolled her eyes in over-the-top embarrassment. "I tried to stop him. Really."

Ellarion threw his arm around my shoulders and

pulled me close against him. His skin was warm again, that impossible tingling warmth, but I could also feel his body, surprisingly firm. "See, Tillandra here is a good friend of mine. And I promised her I'd show her your collection of Titan-era tapestries."

I let out a giggle and rested my head on his shoulder. "I've never seen anything that old. I can't even imagine!"

Look, I'm not proud of it, either. But it was the best plan we could come up with, and it played to all of Molari's prejudices: Lyriana the obnoxious princess, Ellarion the dimwitted playboy, me the Western gold digger. Just once though, just once, it would've been nice to have a disguise other than *girlfriend*.

I will admit one thing. Ellarion's arm felt a hell of a lot better than Miles's had back in Bridgetown.

Molari's lip curled into a disgusted frown, and I realized we might well have overplayed it. "You're going to be the Archmagus of the entire Kingdom, Ellarion. Is this really the company you chose to keep? Some Western whore?"

Would our plan fall apart if I punched Molari in the face? I mean, probably, but wouldn't it be worth it?

Ellarion spared me by stepping forward. His grin vanished instantly, replaced by a furrowed brow and eyes that glowed with anger. "You're right, Molari. I'm going to be the Archmagus. Which means you should really think twice before taking that tone with me or my friends."

Molari's face barely moved, except for a single twitching vein just above his right eye. "My apologies," he said at last, then gestured behind his back to one of the servants. "Arkanos. Show them to the hall of tapestries." His gaze flicked back to me. "The *public* one."

And then we were off, striding through the entryway and down the halls behind the unlucky servant we'd been forced onto. Lyriana stayed with Molari, veering off toward the gardens, but I shot her a pointed glance over my shoulder. She nodded. So far, so good.

Arkanos was a Southlander, with narrow eyes, thick eyebrows, and a gleaming bald head. He was also, I'm guessing, the servant who got the shit jobs around here, a nervous, spindly young man constantly muttering to himself. "Now, we're coming up on the south wing," he said, as we rounded a corner to a long empty hallway. "The tapestries should be he—"

"Quick question," Ellarion cut in. "Do you know where Darryn Vale's room is?"

Arkanos turned, blinking in confusion. "Why, yes. It's just back around the corner, the third door on the left. But why do you—"

He was cut off again, this time because Ellarion reached out and ran his hand down along the man's face "Sleep," Ellarion said, his Rings pulsing black, and Arkanos's eyes rolled back into his head. He crumpled like a puppet with its strings cut, and Ellarion slid forward to catch him, gently easing him down to the floor.

"Whoa," I said, stepping back. "I didn't know that was a thing mages could do."

"It's a rare art. Difficult to master. Do it wrong and you end up permanently scrambling the victim's brain." Ellarion opened a door to an adjacent storage closet, and slid the servant's slumbering body in among the brooms and buckets. "Don't worry. I did it right. He'll wake up an hour from now with a bad hangover." He closed the closet door and turned back to me with a concerned look. "Listen. About what Molari called you . . . my apologies. The man's arrogance overwhelms his sense. He should never have felt like he could say that out loud."

Ellarion was trying to be nice, but his apology revealed the most cutting truth. Molari's faux pas was just speaking what everyone else already thought. "It's fine. Let's get to Darryn's room."

We hurried through the halls, back where Arkanos had instructed us. Darryn's door was locked, but Ellarion rested his hand on the knob and closed his eyes. His Rings flickered a dull brown, and I actually heard the tumblers click into place as the door creaked open.

By the Titans, how many different arts did Ellarion know? Just how powerful was he?

We stepped into Darryn's room and closed the door after us. Amazingly, this room was even bigger than Lyriana's in the Godsblade, making Darryn officially more pampered than the Princess. Sunlight streamed in through a curved skylight overhead, lighting up the round chamber's marble walls. Thick fur rugs stretched out across the floor. Bowls of fruit, bread, and dried meat rested on a wide table. Darryn's canopied bed looked big enough for four people to sleep in, and a half dozen empty wine bottles littered the floor around it. For some inexplicable reason, the walls were covered in pretty paintings of horses.

"So, what now?" I asked Ellarion. "Because I'm kind of tempted to go grab one of those pears."

He bowed his head and laced his fingers together. "I'll

need a bit of Darryn's body to start. Go check his pillow for hair."

"Seriously?"

"Yes, seriously." His mouth flirted with a smirk. "Magic isn't all flashy lights and pretty baubles. Sometimes, it can be downright messy."

"Fine. But you owe me a drink afterward." I walked over to Darryn's bed, stepping over his strewn, soiled clothes, and shoved aside the canopy. The sheets smelled like sweat. This was so gross. With a wince, I flipped over the pillow and plucked a strand of curled black hair. "Here," I said, bringing it to Ellarion. "There's also probably some spit in those bottles."

"Don't be disgusting," he said, and took the hair. He rubbed it between the thumb and forefinger of his left hand, and closed his eyes in deep concentration. His breaths came fast and shallow, and his nostrils flared. His Rings flickered a deep black, then went dull. "Damn it," he said.

"Is it not working? Do you need more hair?"

"Just . . . give me a second," Ellarion hissed. He swallowed hard and tried again. His eyes fluttered back and forth between his closed eyelids, and a sweat drop streaked down his cheek. "This isn't . . . easy magic. . . ."

"Don't talk. Just focus."

"I. Am." Ellarion winced like he was actually in pain, and sucked in his breath through gritted teeth. The veins in his arms strained out against the muscle, and the air around him wavered and sizzled. Even though the sun was bright overhead, the room dimmed, a shroud of darkness billowing out from Ellarion's taut form. My stomach roiled, and I tasted bile and something else, like chalk or ash.

"I am!" Ellarion repeated, and now his words were a thunderous roar, reverberating not just around the walls of the room but somehow inside my head. His eyes fluttered open, and I fought back a scream, because the irises and pupils were gone altogether, replaced only by a sea of the purest black, dotted with specks of blue and gray.

"Is it working?"

"Yes," he gasped. "I can see the Echoes. I just have to . . ." He crinkled his forehead, his right hand clenching and unclenching. "Find the time . . . find the party . . . there! There he is!"

I looked around. "Should I be seeing anything?"

Ellarion's hand shot out and grabbed my shoulder. His skin crackled with energy, like touching a lightning bolt, and I felt that tingling heat race all through me. I gasped, and then his hand slid down along my arm, slipping into mine. He gripped my hand, and his fingers laced with mine, and then I saw *it*, the world as he saw it, the world of a mage.

The room was the same shape and layout, but it was so much richer than it had been before. All the colors, of the walls, the floor, the sky, were more vivid, impossibly bright, everything in the room glowing like it was full of stars. And all around us, there but somehow not at the same time, were strands of pulsing light, ribbons of gold and red and blue from floor to ceiling that wavered and twirled and danced, every color of the rainbow at once. It was so beautiful but also just . . . so much. My eyes hurt, and I fought back tears. "Wha . . . what . . ."

"There!" Ellarion pointed at the bed with his other hand. There was a shape moving on it, a person but not a person, like a glowing red shadow wrapped around flesh. One second, it was firm, so vivid, I could reach out and touch it. The next, it was a transparent ghost, a shroud, then a grid of lines, then a skeleton or a labyrinth of veins. I couldn't see a face, but I could make out the basic shape of the body, the ropes of braided hair. It was Darryn, I realized, Darryn's Echo or whatever.

"Whoa . . ." I whispered. "Wait . . . is he . . ."

"Making out? Yeah." Darryn's Echo lay on his back in the bed, his hands wrapped up around some invisible figure on top of him. His mouth opened and shut, his tongue darting in and out like a fish from a burrow. I now got how this whole Echo-Scrying thing worked: we could see what Darryn did that night, but only him, projected over the room like a drawing on a pane of glass. It was amazing, really amazing, ruined only a little by the fact that I was watching him aggressively grind his crotch against empty air.

"This is the night of the party?"

Ellarion nodded, his eyes still that ghostly black sea.

"So is he with . . ." Even saying it felt weird and invasive. "Markiska?"

Ellarion nodded. "I think so, yeah. This was just after I saw the two of them walk off."

Darryn's Echo hoisted his shirt off over his head, though right now, he was just a flickering man-shape of muscles. "Um. How long are we going to watch this?"

"I . . . don't know," Ellarion said. "I mean, I hadn't really thought this far ahead." He waved his hand through the air, and the image flickered, now clearly on top, then back on bottom, then finally seated on his side of the bed, as if talking to someone.

"What's he saying?"

"Echoes don't capture sound, only light," Ellarion said. "But it doesn't look like he's happy."

Darryn said something, finger wagging drunkenly, then jerked back sharply, nearly toppling over. He rubbed at his eyes and tugged at his shirt, as if it had just been soaked.

"I . . . think she just dumped a goblet of wine on him," Ellarion said.

I fought back a smile. "Good."

Darryn's Echo stood up and waved his hands angrily, arguing with the invisible specter of Markiska. A chill ran through me, because I could imagine her so clearly, telling off Darryn, putting him in his place. It was almost like she was still here, still with us, and I was somehow still rooting for her, for this ghost of my friend.

Darryn's Echo abruptly moved toward us, and I jerked back as he crossed the floor. My body braced for an impact as he walked right into me, but I felt nothing at all. He passed through me toward the door and yelled something at it, shaking his fist. For just the barest of seconds, his face appeared, and he looked *pissed*.

"So Markiska dumped the wine on him and left," I said. "Now what?"

"Now we'll see what he did next," Ellarion said. "Let's see if he goes to talk to our rogue apostate."

But Darryn didn't go after him, or anyone for that matter. He stomped around his room like an angry child, at one point kicking the side of his dresser and hopping around in pain. Then he pissed out the window (which, seriously?), drank what I'm guessing was at least half a bottle of wine, and collapsed onto his bed. And then he just lay there.

"That's it?" I asked. "He just got drunk and passed out?"

"That . . . is what it looks like, yes," Ellarion replied. He waved his hand, speeding up the Echo, but Darryn remained infuriatingly still, sprawled out with his legs splayed and his mouth open.

"Maybe he got up later and called the apostate?" I tried.

Ellarion shook his head. "No. He's been out for at least four hours. By now . . ."

By now Markiska was dead.

"Ellarion, we should go. Before any—"

But before I could finish, Darryn's Echo shot up, jerking up in one motion from slumbering to almost sitting upright. It looked like he was flying, and then I realized that someone, someone I couldn't see, had grabbed him by the shirt and yanked him up.

"What the . . . Who is it?"

"I don't know," Ellarion whispered. "But they're not happy."

Darryn's Echo stammered something, and then whoever was holding him shoved him aside, sending him toppling out of the bed and onto the floor. He was talking with the person, blubbering something, but of course I couldn't hear a damn thing.

"This is the morning after the party, right?" I asked. "So who's so mad at him?"

"No idea," Ellarion replied, and now in front of him, Darryn's Echo reached out an open hand. Whoever he was talking to dropped something into it, because he stared at it in disbelief. He was practically trembling. "What in the frozen hell . . ."

Darryn's Echo rose to his feet, hands trembling, then walked over to his desk and hid whatever he was holding in a lower drawer. Then he turned and rushed toward us, through us, and out the door.

Ellarion let out a low exhale, and ended whatever trance we were in. The blackness bled out of his Rings, and the dimness over the room faded, the sunlight once again streaming in as the ribbons of magic vanished. That bitter taste left my mouth, but so did that warm pleasant tingle, that rush going through me. I stood there for a second, letting the world become itself once more.

I realized I was still holding Ellarion's hand, and I jerked mine away. "You saw that he had something, right?" he asked. "Something he put in the drawer?"

"Something secret," I said. "Something important."

Ellarion crossed the room to Darryn's desk and pulled it open. He reached in, fumbling through some papers and coins, and then he stopped, frozen in place.

"What is it?" I asked.

Ellarion turned around slowly. He held in his hands a small yellow envelope, the kind Carrier Whispers would sometimes use to deliver coins or other small goods. On the front, written in a crude scrawl, was a name: *Molari Vale*. But Ellarion wasn't looking at the front. He was looking inside it, and his face was hard and somber. "What *is* it?" I demanded again, and then Ellarion turned the envelope over and let something fall into the palm of his hand.

A pearl, small and shiny, glowing a vivid purple. I'd only ever seen pearls like that in one place.

"Markiska's bracelet," I said, and now I was scared again,

not at the possibility that we were wrong, but at the crushing, terrifying reality that we were right. I hadn't realized just how much I'd secretly doubted myself until that doubt was gone. Markiska hadn't killed herself. She'd been murdered. She'd actually been murdered.

The emotions came in a rush. There was fear, yeah, but there was also anger and sadness and underneath it all, a drive, a sense of purpose, a desperate need to *act*. I hadn't felt this way since back in the Nest, when I'd picked up a dagger and charged into a room of mercenaries, ready to fight or die. Lyriana called it being *willstruck*.

"We were right," Ellarion said quietly. "I mean. We were almost right."

"We were just going after the wrong Vale."

We stared at each other, the weight of the truth hanging over us like a shroud. Ellarion, for once, looked stunned. My hands were actually trembling. Holy shit. *Holy shit.*

Then the door to the room swung open, and Arkanos stepped in.

Time froze. Ellarion's eyes went wide. Arkanos's jaw started to drop. And I knew that this was going to be it, this was the moment where we lost it all, where we got caught and tried and punished, so so so close to the truth.

I couldn't let that happen.

So I reached up and grabbed Ellarion's shirt by the collar and pulled him into me, pressing my lips to his in a long, hot, passionate kiss. And if touching his hand had been a surge of feeling, it was nothing compared to what kissing him was like. The magic was like a rush of fire, passing through my lips and then scorching through my face, down my neck, my chest, through every part of my body. It was like kissing a smoldering star, like he was full of this light and power and I was siphoning just the tiniest drop. The world around me throbbed and pulsed, and my skin didn't tingle, it straight-up sizzled. And it hurt, yeah, it hurt, but it also felt good, too good, too much, too overwhelming, and I wanted to gasp and cry all at once.

"You shouldn't be here," Arkanos stammered, his voice a million miles away.

Ellarion jerked away from me, and it all went with him, all that feeling and energy and whatever-it-was, and it felt like someone pulling a flask of water away from my lips as I was dying of thirst. I could barely breathe. If this was kissing a mage, what was sex like?

I fell back, flushed, but Ellarion was already handling the situation. "Ah, well this is awkward," he said to Arkanos, his head bowed sheepishly. "You appear to have caught us in a delicate moment."

"Did you sneak away from me?" Arkanos asked, his forehead a landscape of crinkles. "I was supposed to show you the tapestries. . . ."

"Yeah, and then you wandered off, talking to yourself, and we decided to make the most of it," I said impulsively. If I'd been more committed to the act, I would've reached out to stroke Ellarion's cheek, but I didn't think I could handle any more of him.

Arkanos seemed to buy it. "You two shouldn't be here," he repeated, more annoyed than suspicious.

"And you shouldn't wander off and lose sight of guests," Ellarion chided. "So I guess that means we're all doing something we're not supposed to."

"I suppose . . . I don't have to tell Master Molari . . . if you don't."

"That's the spirit, friend." Ellarion walked forward and patted Arkanos twice on the arm, then glanced over his shoulder back at me. His outward demeanor was still cool and unflappable, but his eyes were grateful.

I'd kissed Ellarion.

That was a thing I'd done.

"Come on, Tilla," he said, and was that the slightest hint of uncertainty in his voice? "I do believe we have some very important business to discuss."

TWELVE

"I don't understand," Lyriana said softly, staring down at the tiny purple pearl in the palm of her hand. "Why would someone send this to Molari?"

"As proof," Ellarion replied. We were in the rear of a carriage as it bustled its way back toward the Godsblade. Lyriana and I sat on one side while Ellarion sat on the other, unusually tense. "When Molari learned what had happened with Markiska and Darryn, he knew he couldn't let word get out and shame his family. He sent his pet apostate to take care of her. And that apostate sent him back the pearl to show the job was done."

"Titans' Breath," Lyriana whispered. "I know Molari has a reputation for ruthlessness. But to have a Baron's daughter killed in cold blood . . ."

"Do you doubt he'd do it?"

Lyriana thought for a moment, then shook her head. "No."

"Me neither."

"So he did it. He really did it." I slumped back in my seat, trying my hardest not to show how overwhelmed I felt. Because I felt angry and I felt vindicated and I felt guilty as hell over that kiss, but more than anything else I just felt sad. Poor Markiska. All she'd wanted was to serve her Barony and her father, to inhabit the role she'd been trained for her whole life. She'd played the game, the same game of cunning and deception every half-assed noble in this city was always playing, but just this once she'd overshot, gone too far, underestimated her opponent. And just like that, she was dead. She'd never see her dogs again, never see her father's smile, never bask on a beach with a bottle of wine and a romance novel.

All to protect Molari Vale's precious reputation.

"So what do we do now?" I asked.

"We play this very safe and very quiet," Ellarion replied. "We know Molari is willing to kill to protect his secrets, which means none of us are safe. If we act too soon, we risk losing everything. If we're going to go after Molari, we need undeniable proof."

"The pearl?"

"It's a start, but I'm sure he could come up with an excuse that got him off the hook." He glanced out the window at the crowds passing by, the dozens of faces glancing our way as the carriage rolled past. "We need that mage. The apostate. If we can track him down and get him to testify, there won't be a damn thing Molari can do."

"Yeah, but do we—" I began, and then the carriage hit a bump in the cobblestone and jolted, just a little, sending me sliding forward. My knee brushed against Ellarion's, and for a second I felt it again, that all-encompassing surge, that

151

electric rush, that feeling I'd had when, oh, right, *I'd kissed him.* He jerked back and looked away, his eyes avoiding mine. Was he actually feeling bashful? Was that even a thing he was capable of?

My stomach twisted, and my chest felt tight. I was going to tell Zell, of course. I had to. And I was almost certain he'd understand. In all the time we'd been together, he'd never once been controlling or possessive. He trusted me, trusted me even when I was wrong. He would understand why I had to do it and probably just nod and say some proverb about the masks we wear to serve a greater good. He'd absolutely understand.

So why did I feel so nervous? Why did I still feel so guilty?

I banged on the wall of the carriage, and felt it jolt to a stop. I needed to talk to him now, to rip this bandage off before my thoughts spiraled out of control. "I'm going to stop by the Barracks," I explained to a confused Lyriana and a not-at-all confused Ellarion. "They're just a few blocks away. I'll walk."

"Are you sure?" Lyriana asked. "I mean, if you want, we can all go together and—"

"I imagine she wants to go alone," Ellarion said firmly, and *now* his eyes met mine. I could swear they were redder than usual.

I hopped out of the carriage and hustled along the cobblestone. Above me, the Luminae flickered to life, tiny balls of magical fire twirling in crystal cases on long, curved iron posts. Night was falling fast. I hurried to the Barracks, glancing over my shoulder every step, but when I got there, the front gate was barred. I rapped my knuckles on the small shack by the gate where the guardsman usually sat, and jolted back when it swung open to reveal none other than Captain Welarus.

"What do you want?" he snarled at me. He looked like more of a mess than usual, his hair ruffled and the top of his shirt unbuttoned, revealing a broad chest covered in curly black hair.

"I, uh, sorry," I said, and okay, did I really have to tell him why I was here? Like, was it actually a question? "I'm here for Zell. Is he in?"

Welarus scowled harder, which I wouldn't have thought possible. "None of your business," he said, and slammed his door shut in my face.

Well, screw *that* guy.

I turned away from the office and slumped down onto the curb. A cold wind whistled down the street, blowing a handful of crumpled papers in the gutter by me. I hated feeling this lost, this needy. I should have been able to handle it, to keep going, to keep fighting and searching. But by the Old Kings, I just didn't want to. I wanted to curl up in Zell's arms. I wanted to sleep and drink and rest. I wanted to not have to worry about my father or magical killers or having to explain why I'd kissed another guy. I just wanted things to be easy. Couldn't they just be easy for once?

If Jax was here, he would've cheered me up. He would've known exactly what to say, exactly how to tease me and give me hope and fix me. I'd have given anything to have him with me again. To hear his voice. To be called *sis*, just one more time.

I wiped my eyes and pulled myself to my feet. I didn't want to go back to the Godsblade, with Lyriana's helpful, prying words, and Ellarion's . . . whole . . . person. And Zell wasn't around, and Jax and Markiska were gone. So what option did I have except just huddling in the street, crying and feeling bad for myself?

I blinked. Wait. I did have one other option, didn't I? Someone who'd told me to come by and see him and his friends. Someone friendly and supportive and safe. Someone from the Roost who worked with Whispers all day. Who might know how to track down whoever sent Molari that envelope.

I hopped to my feet and flagged down a carriage.

Time to take Marlo up on his offer.

THIRTEEN

I TOLD THE DRIVER TO TAKE ME TO THE SUCKLING DUCKLING in the Rooksbin neighborhood, which I remembered because, uh, that's a really memorable name. The carriage driver cocked his eyebrow, then shrugged and spurred his horse. I didn't understand why he'd looked so surprised until the ride got bumpy, and I cracked the window, taking in the sight of Rooksbin for the first time.

The first difference I really noticed was the lights. In the Golden Circle and the districts around it, the streets were lit up with mounted Luminae that bathed everything in softly glowing blue and green. But here, the lanterns were the plain old fire kind, candles ensconced in glass bulbs, half of them extinguished or broken. The nice, lined cobblestone had given way to an uneven dirt road. In the Golden Circle, the buildings had some space to them, with yards and fences and little courtyards. Here, the rickety, unpainted structures were all pressed together, leaning on one another wall-to-wall like wobbling drunks, with each story its own cramped little apartment.

And then there was the noise! The Golden Circle could be loud, but loud in a timid way, the loudness of young students debating philosophy, or violin strings twanging from a garden soiree. But Rooksbin was unabashedly loud, loud like Bridgetown or the Servants' Quarters back at Castle Waverly. Leaning out the carriage window, I could hear the rumble of a packed tavern, the jangling strings of a street band, the clatter of dice in alleyways, the shouts of staggering drunks. I closed my eyes and took in that noise, and it was honestly surprising how familiar it was, how *missed*.

There were other differences too, less comforting but familiar all the same. I saw laborers in tattered clothes with soot-stained faces, wearily trudging to another shift. I saw buildings held together by loose boards and graffiti-stained tarps, stray dogs as lean as skeletons eating trash in alleys. I saw beggars huddled in clusters around fires, men and women and even a few children, their clothes ragged, their faces dirty with sweat and mud. It was jarring, so jarring, to come here from the Golden Circle, with its perfect streets and elegant citizens, to know these two worlds were just a stone wall apart. I'd spent too much time there, too much time isolated and sheltered, like a beetle trapped in amber. Spend enough time in warm, coddled safety, and you forgot what the rest of the world was like. You forgot what it meant to be cold.

The carriage came to a stop by a packed little tavern with swinging doors and a rowdy crowd on the steps. The swinging sign over the door said THE SUCKLING DUCKLING, and had a drawing of what looked like a topless woman with a duck pressed to her heaving breast, which made me wonder why taverns always seemed to let thirteen-year-old boys with weird fetishes design their signage. Either way, I headed inside. Marlo wasn't there, because why would anything go easily for me, but the barkeep pointed me to his apartment, on the second story of the building across the street.

I made my way there, up the rickety iron staircase, and rapped my knuckles on the door. "Come in!" Marlo's voice shouted. That seemed clear enough, so I pushed open the door and stepped into his house.

Though honestly, calling it a house was being generous. The place had two rooms, by the look of it. Through an ajar door to my left, I could make out a bedroom, so narrow the bed touched all four walls, lit up only by the moonlight streaming in through the smudged window. The room I was in was some combination of a dining room and a kitchen, with a narrow wooden table, a basin for washing produce, and a few shelves of crusty bread and smoked meat.

Marlo sat hunched over the table, a tall glass of beer at his side. He was wearing just a thin undershirt, sweaty in the heat, and his curly hair hung messy around his shoulders. A Heartlander I didn't know sat opposite him, burly, tattooed, and bearded, with a dimpled chin and big calloused hands the size of my head; I'm guessing this was the baker boyfriend, Garrus. But it wasn't either of the men that caught my eye. It was what was lying on the table.

Envelopes. Dozens of them. Big ones, small ones, all different sizes, spread out neatly as if they were being sorted. A letter opener lay on one side, and a jar of thick, white adhesive, presumably to reseal them, lay on the other. And all of them, every last envelope, bore a stamp of a chain of hands, linked together around a book. The sigil of the University.

Son of a bitch.

Marlo was stealing our mail.

"Took you long enough, Niels," Marlo muttered, and then he looked up and saw me and realized that I was very much not Niels. His big green eyes went wide with surprise. We stood there like that, two goggling idiots, staring at each other in silence.

Garrus, however, acted fast. He lunged to his feet, throwing a protective arm in front of Marlo. "Who the hell are you?" he demanded.

"I . . . I . . ." I stammered, and I couldn't help but notice how enormous his biceps were. Was I in danger here? What exactly had I walked in on? Should I run and scream? Close the door behind me and come in? Act like I hadn't seen anything?

How did things like this keep happening to me?

Marlo snapped out of his daze and sprang into action. "It's Tilla!" he yelled, and the way he pulled Garrus back told me I wasn't wrong to be worried. "The girl I told you about! Lord Kent's daughter! The one who's always chatting with me at the Roost?"

"What's she doing here?"

"I . . . I just came by to see Marlo," I tried. "I mean, I needed some help, and he said to stop by the bar . . ."

"Yeah." Marlo nodded. "Stop by *the bar*. Not barge into my home."

"You said come in," I said quietly, and my cheeks burned. "Look, I can just go. I'm sorry."

"No, wait, look, it's not what you think." Marlo stepped in front of Garrus, toward me, looking genuinely embarrassed. "I'm not some common thief, okay? That's not what this is. This is . . . I am . . . It's . . ." He stopped and let out a long, slow exhale, like he was steeling himself for something unpleasant. Then he lifted up his shirt, and there it was, tattooed on his lower back, just above his waist. A mage's Ring with a skull for a gem.

Holy flaming shit.

Marlo was a Ragged Disciple.

"What are you doing?" Garrus bellowed. "Now she knows who we are!"

"I won't tell anyone," I blurted out, but was that even true? I mean, I'm pretty sure I had an obligation to the King and Lyriana to report the cultists who were causing chaos in their city . . . but that was a lot easier when the cultists were an abstract and not, you know, the nice guy I joked around with when getting my mail.

"She's lying," Garrus said. "Look at her."

"So what do you want to do? Kill her?" Marlo barked back, and the way his tone implied it was a ridiculous idea gave me a little comfort. "She's my friend, okay? And I trust her. I think . . . I think we can trust her."

Could they? I didn't know. But I nodded, because that seemed like the best bet.

"I'll handle this, Garrus," Marlo said. "Just go for a walk. Find Niels and yell at him for being late. Don't tell anyone anything. Tilla and I are gonna have a little talk. And when we're done, we'll figure out what to do next."

Garrus looked me up and down, then sighed. "All right.

If you're sure. I'll be back in fifteen." He walked past Marlo, giving him a little kiss on the shoulder, then looked up to me with a burning glare. "Don't try anything."

"I don't even know what I'd try," I said, exasperated, and he stomped out into the night.

That just left Marlo and me alone. He shuffled the envelopes on the table into neat little piles. "So. Looks like the cat's out of the bag," he said, with an apologetic smile.

"You can say that," I replied. I was still trying to wrap my mind around this whole thing. Marlo—goofy, cheerful, pastry-loving Marlo—was a cultist. "So, stealing students' mail, that's part of your faith?"

"Exposing the lies of the nobles and ending the tyranny of the mages is a part of my faith," Marlo said, his voice harder than I'd ever heard it. "That's a lot easier to do if you know what they're up to."

"Look, I'm not going to judge you for your beliefs. This whole thing, it isn't any of my business. . . ."

"Your father is the only noble in this Kingdom brave enough to stand up to the Volaris," Marlo said. "How is it possibly *not* your business?"

I felt an unexpectedly familiar pang of guilt, a flare from an old wound. In the Golden Circle, no one criticized the Volaris, so it was easy to forget how many people hated them, how unjust many believed their reign to be. I remembered talking to Jax by that frozen corpse in the river, when he'd asked if we were on the right side. I remembered my father pleading with me to join him, his voice full of righteousness and pain. "I don't know. I mean, it's complicated. . . ."

"It's not," Marlo scoffed. He got up and paced toward

the window, the big wooden beads on his necklace clacking together as he moved. "The priests teach that the Titans blessed the Volaris with the gift of magic, so that they could build a better, more perfect world. You look out the window, and you tell me what kind of world you see. See the families cramped into tiny, crumbling homes, the fathers working the docks till their backs break and their hearts give out, all so their children can just barely not starve another day. See the homeless huddled in the alleys, and see their bodies stacked like cordwood whenever a plague hits. See the jails packed with anyone who dares speak up in protest." His nostrils flared, and the little gold stud in his nose glinted. "This is not the world the Titans wanted. This is not why they Ascended. This city, this Kingdom, is a perversion of everything they meant for mankind."

I didn't say anything to that, because what could I say? He wasn't wrong. This city was unfair, profoundly, horrifyingly unfair, and there was a part of me, a tiny buried part, that was always writhing with guilt and frustration. But the unfairness was so enormous, so overwhelming, so fundamental to the order of the world, that even indulging that guilt felt like screaming into a thunderstorm. It felt like yelling at the sun for rising, like standing in a river and demanding it stop rushing. Maybe this wasn't how the world should be, but it's how the world *was*, so what use was there in fighting it?

Marlo must have picked up on my uncertainty, because he cocked an eyebrow. "The thing about you, Tilla, is that you *do* see it. Maybe it's because you're a Westerner, or maybe because you're a bastard, I don't know. But I can see it in your eyes, in the way you talk to me, in that little hint of disgust you can't hold back when you look at your peers. You're not like the rest of them. You see the injustice." He took a step toward me. "But still, you choose to do nothing."

"As opposed to what? Joining a cult and reading people's mail? Maybe smashing up a statue or two? As far as I can tell, the Godsblade's still standing. What you're doing isn't some grand revolution, it's just . . . lashing out."

"It's more than that," Marlo defended. "The Gray Priestess guides us toward liberation. She's been blessed by the Titans. She speaks for them. She sees the destiny mankind was meant to achieve, and if we follow her teachings, we can . . ." He stopped because he saw the look on my face, the look I always got when people started talking about blessings and destiny and teachings. "Look. You don't have to believe in the faith. But you can still stand up for what's right."

"This isn't my fight, Marlo," I pleaded. "This isn't my home. I don't want to get involved."

"When it comes to a system of oppression, you're always involved," he replied. "You're either resisting or you're collaborating."

"It's not like that," I said, because who was he to come at me with that dripping judgment? "You have no idea what I went through out West, no idea what I lost to get here. Yeah, it's bullshit that Molari Vale craps in a golden toilet while kids starve in the street. But what am I supposed to do about that? Turn my back on the only people who took me in, the only people who are keeping me safe from my father, the only people who've ever treated me like anything but some worthless parasite bastard?" I yelled, and apparently I was yelling now. "I owe so much to Lyriana and her family. I'm not going to turn on them. I'm not."

Marlo didn't reply right away, just looked at me thoughtfully. Then his face lit up with a wry smile. "Does Molari Vale really crap in a golden toilet?"

"I mean, it's not like the whole thing is golden. But yeah, it's got a gold base. Also the seat was really warm, in a way that was maybe magic? I don't know. It was weird."

The tension was broken, because there's nothing to defuse a situation like discussing the bathroom habits of the rich and decadent. "I'm sorry," Marlo said. "I was too harsh. I know things can't be easy for you, with your father and everything. The fact that you see the truth, that you're kind to others . . . that's enough."

I could tell he didn't really mean it, but I wasn't going to press the point. "I should probably go. Before your boyfriend gets back and decides to take me to your Priestess or whatever."

"You won't tell anyone about us?" Marlo asked.

"No," I said, and this time I meant it. I was still loyal to Lyriana, still loyal to her family, I guess, but I wasn't about to rat Marlo out, not for being a good person fighting for a better world. "Your secret's safe with me." I began turning toward the door when I remembered, oh right, the whole reason I'd come here in the first place. "Listen. This is going to sound kind of weird, but I have this envelope from a Whisper and I was wondering if you could tell me anything about it."

It sounded even more ridiculous out loud, but Marlo didn't seem surprised. "Maybe," he said. "Let me see."

I took the envelope out of my purse and handed it to him. He blinked at the name on the front. "Molari Vale?"

"It's a long story. Any idea who sent it?"

"No, but I might know where they sent it from." Molari turned the envelope over, running his finger along the edge. "Every Whisper Roost has a unique mark on its envelopes, so we can easily find and return lost mail." He held it up to me and now I could see what he meant, a few almost-invisible lines etched into the envelope's corner, forming a symbol like a pair of slanted crosses. Marlo crossed the room to a heavy book and opened it, revealing a page of similar symbols, and skimmed them until he found one that matched. "Huh."

"Huh what? Good huh or bad huh?"

"Odd huh," he replied. "Parsin's Messages, a third-tier independently owned Roost down in the Rustwater, by the docks. The kind of shady Roost that sends a lot of middle-of-the-night Whispers, and is always getting raided by the Watch for running contraband." Marlo arched an eyebrow. "Why would someone be sending messages to Molari Vale through them?"

"That's what I want to figure out," I said, and took the envelope back. I couldn't believe I'd actually gotten a lead, but I wasn't about to question it. "Thank you."

"Of course," he said, eyeing me warily. "You're not going to do anything stupid, are you?"

I glanced at the stacks of papers on his table. "Stupider than risking my life to steal a bunch of mail?"

"Fair point." He nodded. "Take care of yourself, Tilla."

"You too."

I stepped outside. The night air was warm, unusually

warm, and my shirt stuck to my skin. The neighborhood had quieted down a little since I'd arrived. Way down the street, a young couple sat in silence on a stone flight of stairs, her head on his shoulder, his arm around her waist. Somewhere nearby, a horse trotted down the road, its hooves clopping in the dirt.

Don't do anything stupid, I thought.

Then I turned and flagged down a carriage for Rustwater.

FOURTEEN

RUSTWATER WAS A DOCK NEIGHBORHOOD, WITH EVERYTHING that entailed. The Adelphus River was the biggest in the continent, and it wound its way through the eastern part of Lightspire. A few canals ran through the heart of the city, serving nobles who didn't want to be bothered to leave their cushy districts, but most of the city's commerce happened out here, in the boisterous neighborhoods that bordered the hundreds of docks along the riverfront. The air smelled like fresh fish, and you had to talk loudly to be heard over the river's roar. The streets were always busy, bustling with sailors and merchants, and the taverns never shut.

Parsin's Messages wasn't on a main street, so the carriage dropped me off a block away, with instructions how to get there. As I made my way through the narrow alleyways, I did my best to shut up the logical whining of my brain. Because I knew this was stupid. I knew this was reckless. I knew I should go back to the Godsblade, tell the others, play it safe.

But I felt close, so close, and something else, the thrill of validation, of purpose. I'd been right about the Vales, and I'd been right to talk to Marlo, and I knew, I somehow just knew, this next lead would pay off, too. I'd talk to the Roost keeper and find out who sent the envelope, and *then* I'd go back to the Godsblade, with the name of the man we were after, the apostate who'd killed Markiska. That's all I was doing here. Having one quick conversation.

At least, that's all I planned to do. Until I stepped out of an alley and found myself staring right at the gray-eyed son of a bitch himself.

I hurled myself back into the alley with a gasp, pressing myself against a wall and hoping like hell he wouldn't see me in the shadows. The man was on the other side of the street, coming out of a narrow building with a latticed mesh cage on the roof. Parsin's Messages. Even across the way, I could tell it was him. Same brown robe with the hood up. Same lurching walk. And the same smoke-gray eyes, just barely visible below the cowl. He stepped out of the building, and he didn't see me. At least I think he didn't, because he didn't react. He just turned a sharp corner and took off down the street.

I stood there for a minute, catching my breath. Okay, if my brain had been whining before, it was screaming now, saying *Go back, go back, go back.* Just seeing him made my stomach lurch, and I remembered the terrifying way he'd sung my name, the way he'd stared at me across that courtyard.

But there was another fear in me too, the fear of regret, of letting my prey slip out of my grasp. I could come back tomorrow, but maybe the Roost keeper wouldn't cooperate. Maybe the apostate had given him a fake name. Maybe he was right now headed to a ship to sail off, down the Adelphus, escaping forever.

My feet moved without real approval, pulling me around the corner. I could still see the man, hustling intently down the sidewalk, seemingly indifferent to anyone and anything around him. I bowed my head low and paced after him, one step at a time, trying to blend in on the off chance he turned around. But he didn't turn around, or even look around for that matter. He just hurried forward, a man on a mission, striding farther and farther from the main stretch and toward the run-down wooden warehouses on the edge of the docks.

I knew I ought to turn back, but I was close, so close, and honestly, I was doing a lot better at this "tailing a suspect" thing than I would have thought. The man entered a cluster of warehouses, climbed up a rickety staircase, and rounded a building's corner. I crept up after him, wincing at each creak underfoot, but I couldn't lose him now. I just had to see where he went, which door he finally went into. Then I'd know where he lived, and I could be sure I'd get him tomorrow. That would be enough.

But when I rounded that corner, the man was nowhere to be found. There was just a cluster of warehouses, packed tightly together like cobblestones, connected with narrow wooden catwalks. A few still had signs, but most only had peeling paint and shuttered windows, drunken sailors sleeping in the gutters. Abandoned warehouses, then. The perfect place for a nefarious apostate to do his dirty business. Or, you know. Kill a Western girl who'd been following him.

Right around then was when my logical brain won out, and the rest of my body caught up to its panic. What in the frozen hell was I doing here? I turned around to run back to the nice, densely populated streets of the city . . .

Only to find myself staring directly into the mage's eyes, smoldering at me through the shadows of his cowl.

I didn't even have time to scream. He grabbed me by the shoulders and hurled me sideways, through a termite-eaten door into one of the warehouses. I smashed through it and sprawled out on the crumbling wooden floor. Moonlight lit up the place through gaps in the broken ceiling. In a few places, the floor gave way to jagged holes, plunging down to the first floor below. Signs of inhabitance littered the room, dirty rags and frayed blankets and picked-over chicken bones, not to mention a few rolled-up tubes that I'm pretty sure were grief-weed pipes. But despite all that, the room was empty, except for me and the brown-robed killer in the doorway.

I scrambled back on my haunches, trying to get away from him, but the man didn't run or even walk. He just stood there, head cocked to the side, and then he lifted a hand up, a weathered hand with long sharp nails and thick pulsing veins. Tendrils of black smoke spiraled around it like hungry serpents. I'd seen a whole lot of magic in my six months at Lightspire, but I'd never seen that. "Tilla, Tilla, Tilla," he cooed. "You really shouldn't have come here."

"Who are you?" I choked out.

"An old friend," he replied, and there was something odd about his voice, something familiar about his accent that I couldn't quite put my finger on. More and more smoke was billowing out of him now, wisps curling out from his shoulders, strands twisting around his arms. That smell was back, sulfur and ash, so thick it made me gag.

I jerked up to my feet and ran, but the man flicked his hand toward me, almost like throwing an invisible knife. There was a rushing sound, like an intake of wind, and then he disappeared, vanished into nothingness. Only his smoky silhouette remained, hanging in the air where he'd been standing, a wispy ghost that held his shape.

I started to yell, but before I could get a sound out, he reappeared right in front of me, like, *right* in front of me, with a loud *pop*. He threw out a hard sweeping punch that caught the side of my temple. My vision flashed red. Blood streaked down my cheek. I crumpled to my knees, just a few feet away from one of those gaping holes. Pain flared through my whole face as he vanished again, leaving only a reeking cloud of smoke that billowed into my face.

I let out a moan, and he reappeared again, now on the other side of the room. I'd never seen a mage do that. I'd never even *heard* of a mage doing that. I panted through gritted teeth and tried to remember the khel zhan chant to push through pain.

"Impressed?" the man asked, and I could now hear a low wheeze beneath his words. I still couldn't see his face, not quite, but I could almost make out a chin, and smoke billowing out of his lips when he talked. "It's a new art, one no one's ever done before. I call it blinking. Want to see it again?"

"No!" I shouted, but it was too late, because he vanished once more, with another rush of air. I braced for another punch, but this time he appeared behind me, which I only knew because I heard that pop and felt his boot slam into my lower back, sending me toppling even closer to the hole's edge.

It hurt like I'd been stabbed, and this time I full-on screamed as his murky silhouette enveloped me. It hurt, it hurt *so much*. Tears burned my eyes, which I hated, because the last thing I wanted to do was show weakness. "Who are you? Why are you doing this? Why did you kill Markiska?"

He reappeared a few feet in front of me again, and now he stopped, thoughtful. "Oh, I didn't kill the girl. That was Murzur's work. I just kept watch." I had no idea what he was talking about, or who Murzur was. The smoke around him swirled thick and wild. "I actually wanted to kill you, you know. More than anything. But our master forbids it." He said that last word, *master*, with a hint of disgust. "He's got big plans for you, and they made it very clear I was to make sure you were unharmed." He laughed a wheezing laugh. "But now you came here. Into my gods-damned house. *You* did this. And when they ask, I'll just say, well, I didn't have a choice. The castle-rat knew too much. She had to be put down."

Those words . . .

Gods-damned.

Castle-rat.

He was a Zitochi.

"No . . ." I whispered.

"She understands at last," said the man. He reached up with his wispy hands and pulled back his hood, his face lit up by his twisting eyes. His hair was long and black, his skin a light brown, and the right half of his face had soft features, a smooth cheek and a gentle chin. The left side, though, was a ruin. Thick white scars blotted his temples. The whole cheek was sunken in, like it had been crushed, and instead of lips there was just a hole, exposing bloody gums and cracked teeth. And even like that, half his face completely destroyed, I still recognized him.

Pretty Boy.

Razz's mercenary, the one I'd fought back at the Nest.

The one I'd smashed in the face with a heavy, spiked club.

"You did this to me," he hissed, and there was nothing pretty about him, not anymore. "You *ruined* me."

Questions, so many questions, raced through my mind. How had he gotten into the city? Who was he working for? What was his mission? And how in the frozen hell had a third-tier mercenary suddenly become some sort of super-powered mage assassin?

But none of those questions mattered, not now, because there was another thought that overtook them, a powerful certainty that drowned out everything else. There was no talking with this man, no reasoning, no negotiation. He was going to kill me no matter what I did or said.

Which meant I had nothing to lose.

With all my strength, I jerked my body forward, over the lip of the hole in front of me, and plunged down. Pretty Boy let out a gasp of surprise. For one second, I was weightless, free-falling through the darkness, and then I hit the wooden floor hard. My side spasmed with pain, but I pushed past that, because for this one moment, I had a shot at getting out of here. I bolted up and looked around frantically. This was another wide abandoned room, its floor somehow even filthier than the one above, but it had something the other hadn't: a door, ajar, light streaming in, on the far end.

I took off toward it in a sprint. There was that rush of

air from above again, the sound Pretty Boy made when he blinked, and then with that *pop* he appeared right in front of me, so close that I actually ran into his chest. We both stumbled back, surprised, and he threw a left jab square at my face.

Turns out, even when you neglect your khel zhan training, it never really goes away. I lilted to the side, dodged his punch, and caught his wrist with my right hand. This was the part of the form where I should have twisted his arm behind his back, pushing him down into a submission hold, but he vanished, blinking away, leaving me holding only smoke. I lurched forward, and he appeared behind me and smashed the heel of his boot into the back of my right calf. My leg betrayed me, and I fell down onto my hands and knees. Instinctively, I spun back to where he was, hoping to grab him, but he was gone again, and then he was suddenly to my right, enshrouded in a cloud of gray and black, and he kicked me hard in the side of the chest. I felt a brittle crack that was almost certainly a rib breaking, and I fell over, panting, gasping, all the breath rushing out of me.

How was I supposed to fight someone who could just appear and disappear? How could *anyone*?

He kicked me again, knocking me onto my back, and then he was on me, pressing his knee on my chest to hold me down. It hurt, it hurt so much my vision blurred. He grabbed a handful of my hair and jerked my head up and punched me again, right in the face, and again, and again. I felt my nose shatter. My mouth flooded with the taste of metal. The world grew hazier, darker, redder. I couldn't even scream, just gasp, choking on my own blood, my hands uselessly pawing at the cragged craters of his jaw. Maybe it was the smoke or maybe it was the fact that my face was a swollen bloody ruin, but I could barely even see his expression anymore. All I saw was gray smoke, and the whites of his teeth curled into a smile.

He let go of my hair and shoved my head down, smacking the back of my skull onto the hard floor. "Not so tough now, are you?"

He wound up his fist again, probably to bash my head in once and for all. But in that moment, that somehow-protracted instant between when he drew back and when he punched, a memory struck me, so vivid it was like I was almost there again. It was from my journey through the West, sometime after we'd left Bridgetown but before we met Galen, that wonderful week when Jax was still alive and I still had hope. Zell and I were training in a wide forest grove, red and yellow leaves crackling under our feet as we sparred. I threw jab after jab at him, but he dodged each one effortlessly, a bemused smile on his face. After my tenth whiffed punch, I pulled back, frustrated. "How am I supposed to hit you when you're so fast?" And Zell had just smiled. "Stop hitting where I am," he'd said. "Hit where I'm going to be."

I jolted back into the present moment and rolled to the side. Pretty Boy's fist slammed into the floor where my head had been, his knuckles cracking open. He jerked back, hissing with pain, which gave me just enough time to see something lying on the ground: a wooden board, thick and sturdy, with three rusty nails jutting out of the end.

I didn't feel pain anymore, just bloody-eyed rage and the furious, howling need to hurt back. I grabbed the board, spun around with a roar, and smashed it into the side of Pretty Boy's face, right where his jaw met his neck. The rusty nails burrowed deep into his skin and tore clean through, ripping out a wet, red chunk of flesh and sending it sloppily sliding across the floor. He jerked back off me, clutching a hand to his wound. Crimson spilled forth between his fingers, and smoke hissed out, a thick, dark gust stained red with his blood. I kicked up to my feet, driven completely by adrenaline at this point, and now, for one amazing second, Pretty Boy was afraid. He stumbled back, hands weaving wildly, and blinked into nothingness.

Instead of punching or running, I jerked back in a dodge, and sure enough, Pretty Boy appeared in front of me and swung, his fist streaking right past where I'd been. He stumbled past me and I hit him again, swinging the board with both hands and smashing the flat of it into the base of his spine. He staggered and then vanished, but now I was starting to get the hang of his rhythms, see the weaknesses in his one and only attack. I dodged to the right, and again he flew by me, and this time I hit him in the side of his stomach, driving the nails into the flesh and tearing open a long ragged gash through his belly.

He vanished a third time, and now he reappeared far away from me, on the other side of the room, blocking the door. My heart was thundering, my vision was blurred, but a part of me, the terrifying violent beast caged deep within, was howling with vicious triumph. Our eyes locked across the room, mine swollen and bloody and narrowed with the raw rage of a fighter who knew she was going to survive. His were still smoky, swirling like trapped tempests, but there was something else in them now, flares of orange and red, a fire igniting. The scars on the side of his face glowed with an inner light, and the wisps billowing off him sizzled and sparked. He let out a low inhuman growl and charged toward me. I planted my legs in a fighting stance and tightened my grip. He ran, closer, closer, closer . . . then blinked away, right before impact, his smoky silhouette crashing into me like a wave.

Stop hitting where I am. Hit where I'm going to be.

I shoved the board behind me, blindly.

I heard that distinctive *pop* as he appeared at my back, and something else, a warm wet crunch.

And then there was only silence.

I spun around. Pretty Boy stood there, frozen in place. The back half of the wooden board jutted out of his chest like the head of a spear. The front half was embedded deep within him, skewering him clean through. There was no blood on the wound; he'd blinked right onto the board, and it had fused with him, *into* him. I had no idea how that worked, but given the agonized look in his eyes, I didn't think it was pleasant. He reached up and touched it, poking at the board with numb disbelief, then fell to his knees.

Then he craned his head up at me, and any feeling of triumph I had vanished, because something was happening to him, something very, very bad. He trembled and shook, his whole body vibrating. Those orange embers I'd seen in his eyes swirled like lightning, scorching through the smoky gray, and then his eyes actually exploded, hot jets of flame scorching out of the holes in his skull. He jerked back and roared, a bellowing impossible howl that made the walls tremble. His thick veins pulsed with rivulets of red and gold, and little licks of flame sizzled out through the scars on his face.

I turned and ran now, as fast as I could, toward the door.

I couldn't see him anymore, but I heard him roaring, and felt the ground shudder, and heard the sounds of sizzling flesh and thunderous flame. I hit the doorway and the bracing fresh air of the street and then there was a deafening blast behind me. Wood splintered. The earth shook. I felt myself lift off my feet and hurtle through the air like a doll, before slamming onto cold, damp dirt.

The world flickered in and out of the darkness. I tried to move but couldn't even twitch my legs. My body hurt so much, it actually felt numb. I heard people screaming and running all around me. With the last of my strength, I craned my head up. There was nothing left of the building but a smoking crater, and there was nothing left of Pretty Boy at all.

"Who's tough now, you son of a bitch?" I whispered, and then passed out cold.

FIFTEEN

THIS IS WHERE IT GETS HAZY.

I know the facts of what happened next, of course, because people told me. A couple of dockworkers found me lying in an alley a block from the explosion, bloody, unconscious, my face so badly beaten I was unrecognizable. They took me to a nearby hospice in Rustwater, which basically meant a stiff bed in a crowded, dirty tent. I lay there, clinging to life by a thread, for two whole days, before Ellarion found me. They were all out there looking for me, I guess, him and Zell and Lyriana, but Ellarion was the one who made the connection with the unexplained explosion in Rustwater, and decided to check nearby hospices. He took me back to the Golden Circle, to the Kaius Kovernum, temple of the Sisters of Kaia, where the greatest mages of their order nursed me to health.

That's what happened. But that's not what I remember.

I remember the cold, wet dirt of the street as I passed out. I remember a feeling of weightlessness, of floating through a gray void that was somehow at once intangible yet suffocatingly dense, like I was being smothered by a scratchy, cottony nothingness itself. I remember waking up in a rough bed, unable to open my eyes or move my body, unable to shut out the moans and screams around me. I remember hands on my skin, warm and tingling, hands that felt safe and strong. I remember feeling like I'd suddenly been lowered from the freezing cold into a warm, soothing bath, a bath that soaked in through my skin but was also somehow hugging me and telling me I'd be okay. I remember female voices whispering and murmuring, cants in a language I didn't understand but also kind of did.

There are other things I remember too, things I can't explain, images that swam in and out and wouldn't go away, like a nightmare I couldn't shake. I saw a massive tower, charred and broken, lying on its side in a vast red desert. I saw a man with skin of glistening stone, and a beautiful ballroom covered in black ash. And I saw an explosion, hotter than fire, hotter than the sun, billowing out like a raging storm, so vast and unquenchable it swallowed the whole world.

Nine days after I killed Pretty Boy, I woke up for real.

My eyes fluttered open to the pretty, dancing lights of a stained-glass skylight. I was on some kind of weird floating bed-thing, a flat firm mattress suspended by billowing green cloths that swayed back and forth like a bough in a breeze. Looking around, I could make out a small private room, with narrow windows streaming in sunlight, and wooden walls covered in beautiful flowering ivy. I wasn't in much pain, except for a distant dull ache in my side, but my throat was so parched it felt like I'd swallowed a bag of sand. "Water," I croaked.

A figure stirred next to me, a Sister of Kaia on a stool by my bedside. I couldn't quite see her face through the gossamer veil, but I could make out a weathered brow and heavy crow's-feet around her glowing emerald eyes. She smiled, just a little, then brought a small bowl to my lips, and the water that poured from it was maybe the most refreshing thing I'd ever tasted.

"Your friend is awake," the Sister said over her shoulder.

I still couldn't quite sit up, but I heard the commotion of footsteps as several people raced into my room. Two faces appeared over me. Lyriana's lip quivered, cheeks slick with tears. Zell was harder to read, but I could see relief in the tiny upturned corners of his mouth, and something else in his gaze, a pain I hadn't seen since we were back in the West.

"Oh, thank the Titans!" Lyriana dove forward, grabbed my hand and pressed it up to her lips, kissing it again and again. "They said you'd be fine, but I was worried, so so so worried . . ."

"The Sisters know their shit," I rasped out.

"Does it still hurt?" Zell asked. His voice was quiet, barely more than a whisper, and his eyes flitted away from mine. I realized what I saw in them, what I hadn't seen in months: shame. Now I understood. He blamed himself.

I reached up and touched my face. It was still swollen, but other than that it felt fine. "No. I think . . . I think I'm okay now."

"When Ellarion brought you in here, you were more dead than alive," the Sister of Kaia said. Even as she talked, her hands never stopped moving, turning in slow rhythmic circles while her Rings hummed with a soft green light. I hadn't really noticed how warm I felt, enveloped, like I was wrapped up in a thick fur blanket even though I was just wearing a simple nightgown. "Truly, the Titans have bestowed upon you their favor."

"If this is their favor, I'd hate to see their judgment," someone muttered from the corner of the room. I turned to see Ellarion, leaning against the corner with a dark look on his face. There was no smirking amusement for once, no flirty smiles or confident winks. He looked *pissed*. "Who did this to you?"

"I . . . It . . ." I began, and for the first time since I'd turned around on that rickety staircase, I actually had a second to *think* about everything that had happened. The enormity of it all struck me in a wave. I felt like I was drowning, like there was a massive weight on my chest. This wasn't just about Markiska or Molari Vale. This was something so much bigger, so much worse. "This is bad," I whispered. "Really, really bad."

The three stared at me, and even the Sister craned her head up in curiosity. "A moment's privacy, please," Ellarion said, and with a sigh, she excused herself. I took a deep breath and a deeper sip of water, and then started talking.

The tone in the room hadn't exactly been sunshine and rainbows, but the more I talked, the more it darkened. Zell's mouth stiffened into a furious angry line, and his eyes burned with the hottest rage I'd ever seen. Lyriana and Ellarion looked angry too, but there was something else about them, a confused horror, a way they kept looking back and forth at each other with increasing alarm. They knew something I didn't, something even more worrying than my story, which I thought was pretty damn worrying. But when I finished, they didn't say anything. We all just sat there in a suffocating silence, and then Zell stood up, crossed the room, and slammed his fist into the wall, his nightglass knuckles punching four deep holes into the thick wood.

I got his anger. A part of me felt comforted by it. But right now, I needed to know what was up with the others. "Well?" I asked. "What do you think is going on? It's my father, right? It must have to do with my father? I mean, I don't know how, but it must, right?"

Ellarion and Lyriana shared another one of those infuriatingly conspiratorial glances, and then Ellarion walked over and took a seat by my bedside. "Listen closely," he said, his voice dead serious. "Soon, Inquisitor Harkness will come by to ask you what happened. Whatever you do, you *cannot* tell him what you just told us."

"What? Why not?" I mean, I was in absolutely no hurry to tell him anything, but I didn't see the connection.

"Of all the many nations of Noveris, the Titans granted the gift of magic to the people of Lightspire and Lightspire alone," Lyriana said softly. "That's the Heavenly Mandate, the holiest principle of the church, the central basis for why our people should rule this continent."

"Okay? And?"

"And there is no greater threat to the legitimacy of the Volaris Dynasty than the rejection of that mandate, than the idea of magic being granted to the other Provinces," Ellarion explained. "In the last five hundred years, there have been three major rebellions against the crown, three that actually threatened the Kingdom: the Bandits' Revolt, the Southern Heresy, and the Merchants' Uprising. And do you know what all three had in common?"

"They were all led by false mages," Lyriana said, saving me the effort of trying to remember my history classes. "Do you understand, Tillandra? Do you see why we're so alarmed?"

"I get why a Zitochi mage is a big deal, yeah," I said. "But isn't that more reason to tell the Inquisitor? I don't remember exactly what Pretty Boy said, but he mentioned his master, some kind of a mission, a plan. And someone named Murzur, who he said killed Markiska? This is a big deal, right? Shouldn't we be rushing to warn the King?"

Ellarion pinched the bridge of his nose in frustration. "You don't understand. There was no Zitochi mage. The very idea is . . . It's beyond impossible."

I looked to Lyriana for support, but she just nodded. "He's right, Tilla. There has never, ever been a mage who wasn't born in this city. It's just not how magic works." She looked across the room. "Tell her, Zell. Has there ever been a Zitochi who could do what she's describing?"

It looked like it was taking Zell every ounce of restraint he had not to tear the room apart. "No." He glowered. "There hasn't. Our shamans can see the truths of the world, what has been and what will be . . . but nothing like this." He shook his head. "I knew the man you're talking about. The one you call Pretty Boy. He was Ghellus of Clan Rize. Soft-witted, vain, a runt even by the low standards of Razz's men. He's no sha-man. No mage."

"What about Murzur?" I asked. "Were there any Zitochi with that name?"

"No," Zell replied. "It's not even . . . It's not even a Zitochi name."

I looked at the three of them, struggling for words. They

didn't believe me, not a one of them, not even Zell. The only people who'd stood by me, the only people I had left in the world, and they didn't believe me, either. I tried to look tough, to keep it together, but my eyes were burning and there was a tight lump in my throat. "So that's it? You think I'm making it up?"

"No." Ellarion reached out and put his hand on my bare shoulder, and even here, it tingled with impossible warmth. "I think you're being used."

I jerked my shoulder away, maybe because I didn't want his comfort but also because I felt weird about it, especially with Zell just a few feet away. "You're going to have to explain that."

"Imagine it from the Inquisitor's point of view," Lyriana said. "A Western-Zitochi alliance has declared independence. It's the biggest war in two centuries, coming at a point of major domestic unrest, and against all odds, it seems like we're losing. And now you come along. Daughter of the despised rebel leader, already regarded with suspicion and distrust."

"Don't pull any punches, now," I grumbled.

"The fact that your very important roommate died mysteriously doesn't look good," Ellarion cut in. "And now, all of a sudden, with no proof, you're spreading the most dangerous of rumors, and claiming that the very same Province that we're at war with has been blessed with its own mages. And all of this at a time when cultism is at record highs, when the Ragged Disciples undermine our King with their claims that the Heavenly Mandate is a lie. How do you think this is all going to look to the Inquisitor?" Ellarion's eyes flickered like a match being struck in the dark. "I know what I'd think if I were him. I'd think you were a Western spy, working for your father, spreading blasphemous lies and sowing dissent."

"And that you probably killed Markiska, too," Zell said.

"Look," I said, a little too forcefully, "I know what I saw. This wasn't some dark room, hazy silhouette kind of thing. I saw his face. I heard his voice. I *talked* to him."

"There are mages who can change their appearance, make you see things that aren't really there," Zell offered, which I guess was better than *you're making it up* but still a lot worse than *I believe you.* "Maybe this was one of them?"

Lyriana shook her head. "No. The Maids of Alleja can perform Mesmers, acts of illusion, but these are widely known to be the most difficult and limited of all arts. A high-ranking Maid might be able to change her appearance to that of another . . . but to keep it up while fighting? While performing this 'blinking' at the same time? No. It's just not possible."

"There is, however, another explanation," Ellarion said. "There are mages out there who can affect your thoughts, who can creep into your mind like a thief in the night. Some—the highest of their order—can even plant false memories, memories that feel completely and utterly real the next day."

"The apostate is a Shadow of Fel," Lyriana whispered. "Titans protect us."

Ellarion just nodded. "It makes sense, doesn't it? If Tilla was getting too close, the apostate would cover his tracks by planting a false memory in her mind . . . the most damning, dangerous memory he could think of, the one certain to see her imprisoned."

I slumped back into my bed and pressed my hands against

my eyes. A part of me, a big loud part, wanted to yell and protest, to insist that everything they were saying was dismissive bullshit. *I know what I saw. I know what happened. It wasn't an illusion or a false memory or any of that.* But that loud voice was drowned out by the others, the million tiny nagging ones that seemed to hold so much sway these days. *They're your best friends, and even they don't believe you. You'll just be painting a target on your back. Everyone's just looking for an excuse to turn on you.*

I suddenly felt tired, so tired. I just wanted them all to go away, but at the same time, I never wanted to be alone again. "Okay," I said, soaking into the darkness of my palms. "I'll lie to the Inquisitor, as best as I can. If that's what you all think is best. But I don't know if I'll be able to keep it up if he brings one of those Shadows with him."

"He wouldn't do that," Lyriana assured me, and I realized I'd never actually told her about my first interrogation. I'd have to do that. But not now, not here. I couldn't take any more conflict with them right now.

"If the Vales are willing to employ such a man, the situation is far graver than even I'd imagined. This isn't just about an arranged marriage or a trade deal. It's about treason," Ellarion said. "Lie low. Keep your head down. Stay safe. I'll take it from here."

Lyriana reached out and took my hand off my face, holding it tight in hers. "I love you, Tilla. We will get through this. We will make it right." She squeezed it, then stood up and turned to Ellarion. "Come, cousin. Tillandra needs rest."

"And perhaps some time alone with her man, when he's not busy punching holes through temple walls," Ellarion said, shooting an oddly pointed glance at Zell. "We'll see you later."

The two of them left, and when they were gone, Zell closed the door and took a seat by my bedside. He still couldn't meet my gaze. His nostrils flared with rage, and his eyes still burned. I reached out and took his hand, and felt his blood, warm and wet, streaking down in rivulets from his knuckles. "I should have been there," he said quietly, and there it was in him, that anger, that pain, but deepest of all, that shame. Lying on that bed, I was Kalia all over again, his first love whom he'd failed, the one he hadn't and maybe never would let go of. "I should have protected you."

I knew what I was supposed to say to make him feel better, to soothe those bloody bitter wounds inside him. I should have said, *No, you couldn't have known.* I should have said, *You'll be there next time.* I should have said, *You did nothing wrong.* But as badly as I knew I should say all those things, what came bubbling out of my lips was something else, a deeper truth, a deeper question, one I couldn't hold back no matter how much harm I knew it would do.

"Where were you?"

He looked down, this man who'd sworn he'd love and protect me, unable to even look me in the eye. "Captain Welarus sent me out on a special assignment," he said. "There were rumors of glitter-dust smugglers in Moldmarrow, and we had to raid a dozen houses to try to find them. It took all night." He breathed in deep. "I'm sorry, Tilla. I'm so, so sorry."

I could see how badly this hurt him, how raw and consuming his grief was. Zell was a man driven by purpose, by duty, by a need to serve another. That other had been Kalia, and then his Clan, and then me. And all three, he'd failed. Even though I was the one lying in a bed, with bandages around my ribs and a puffy swollen face, it felt like he was the one in pain. "Hey," I whispered. "Hey. It's okay. I'm fine. It's not your fault."

I reached out and put my arms around him and pulled him down, against me, and held him pressed to my chest. His arms slid under me and pulled me against him, and we lay there like that, my nose buried in the crook of his neck, my face enveloped in his soft hair and his smell of frost and rain. It felt good, so good, that all I wanted was to stay here forever, to melt into him, to push away all the worries of the world and just lose myself in his touch. I wanted that, I wanted that so bad.

But even as I did, there was another voice, a new one, lurking relentlessly at the back of my mind, undermining every thought I had with its low, cruel whisper:

He's lying to you.

I forced that thought down, buried it, smothered it. I couldn't think that, couldn't even consider it. If I said that, if I dared even hint at it, we'd be crossing a point of no return. Even with this horrible, gnawing uncertainty, I absolutely could not deal with the possibility of losing Zell. Another day we could talk about it. Another day I'd tell him what happened with Ellarion. But right now, all I could do was hold him, and let him hold me, and for a few seconds forget about everything else in the world.

SIXTEEN

I SPENT TWO MORE DAYS IN THAT ROOM IN THE KAIUS Kovernum, being tended to by the Sisters and hoping they wouldn't notice the dents Zell left in the wall. After that, they told me I was free to go. Lyriana invited me back to the Godsblade, but I declined. As nice as it was, there was something suffocating about that place, a smothering comfort that made you lose all perspective. I knew if I stayed there, I'd lose sight of what happened with Pretty Boy; I'd start to believe everyone's explanation that I was just being manipulated, and give up searching for the truth, for justice, for Murzur. I had to stay focused.

So instead, I moved back into the University. They had a new room for me, thank the Titans, in a new dorm: Makalia Hall, a sprawling structure made of dense gray stone that was home to the Gazala Guild Laboratory and a whole lot of aspiring Artificers. This was actually great for me; the Artificers were, for the most part, shy and nerdy, timidly glancing away when I passed them in the halls. I caught a few whispers behind my back, a few point-and-stares, and the nice guy who was helping me move my stuff in abruptly left when he realized who I was. Whatever. A week ago, it would've bothered me, but after what I'd been through, passive-aggressive bullshit was actually a relief.

I sat through my first class, a guest lecture by a Southlands scholar on the history of their neat-looking ziggurats, and then headed out across the Quad. See, I hadn't just moved back because it was the only place I could go. I actually had an idea, or something close to an idea anyway. Back in the Kaius Kovernum, Ellarion had said that there were three rebellions that had threatened the Kingdom, and all three had been led by "false mages." In theory, they were all frauds. But what if they weren't? If Pretty Boy had really been a mage . . . then maybe the others had all been real, too.

The Library was the oldest building in the University, one of the oldest in the city. At a glance, it looked like a great temple or a small castle, its ancient stone front marked with intricately carved reliefs and dazzling stained-glass windows. Four massive spires jutted out of its roof, towering over the rest of the campus, and a steady line of people flowed in and out, coming from all over the city to borrow and learn. According to Lyriana, it was the largest collection of books anywhere on the continent. Which made it that much more embarrassing that I'd only gone there three times, and once had been to use a bathroom.

The inside was even more impressive than the outside. The entryway led to an absolutely massive chamber, at least four stories high, with stacked, towering bookshelves stretching all the way up to the mural of the Titans' Ascension on the ceiling. Long tables stretched out across the main floor, covered in papers and tomes, while tall wooden platforms with built-in ladders slid around on wheels, granting access to the higher shelves. Visitors paced around, reading, whispering, leafing through books, while white-cloaked librarians shushed and offered assistance.

I was a little nervous asking about the false mages, because maybe it was taboo, but the librarian I nervously mumbled to was more than happy to help. She fluttered about the racks, racing way too spryly up a ladder toward the third level, before coming down with a thick leather-bound tome. *Madmen, Heathens, and Bloody Damned Heretics*, the title read in an intricate golden script. "We have quite a few books on the topic," she said, "but I suspect you'll like this one."

She wasn't kidding. As soon as I flipped it open, I was greeted with a grisly full-page illustration of something called "The Mid-Summer's Massacre," which depicted a dozen Southlander priests nailed high to wooden posts. I spent a while reading about that (I guess the Southlanders tried *really* hard to form their own church), before remembering why I was here, and skimmed ahead to something called the Bandits' Revolt. After three pages of boring details on trade disputes, I hit what I was looking for:

While the bulk of the rebel forces were comprised of Eastern peasants, the revolt is most notably remembered for its tactical leader, the enigmatic false mage known as the Hooded Serpent. A mercenary from the Red Wastes, the Hooded Serpent (real name: Si Too or possibly Si Tay), claimed to have discovered an entirely new school of magic, outside the Heavenly Mandate, and without the use of any Titan Rings. Though the rebellion's Eastern leaders were initially skeptical, the Hooded Serpent proved incredibly popular with the soldiers, and after a series of surprising victories over the Volaris armies, ascended to the role of Grand General. His rise in power (as well as in public opinion) escalated the revolt from a regional quarrel to a full-on crisis and prompted Queen Correllia II to deploy the entirety of Lightspire's armies to quell it. Brilliant tactician though he may have been, the Hooded Serpent was unable to stand against fifteen companies of the Knights of Lazan, and he was killed at the Battle of Blasted Fields, alongside most of the rebel forces.

Historians remain sharply divided on precisely how he was able to deceive so many for so long. Some have maintained that all accounts of his magic are suspect, and the entire character nothing more than rebel propaganda. Others give credence to the accounts, but argue, fairly convincingly, that every act the Hooded Serpent is alleged to have done could be accomplished through clever use of Artificed technology. More recently, Professor Vasilos Von Del Stoor of the University has argued that the Hooded Serpent was likely the alias for one or more apostates who defected from Lightspire during the prior reign of King Gaius.

"Historians remain sharply divided," huh? I'll admit I was biased, but that sounded a whole lot like "We have no idea how this guy did it." Blasphemy or not, I was really starting to think there was something to these so-called false mages.

Also: "Hooded Serpent"? Bad. Ass.

I was about to turn the page to see if there was any more

about him when a hand tapped me on the shoulder. I leaped halfway out of my seat with a yelp, and turned around to see Lyriana grinning at me. "Tilla in the Library? Truly, the world has gone mad."

"I should've known I'd run into you here." I grinned back, and stood up to give her a hug. "Do you have a class in here? Or is this just where you woke up?"

"I'll have you know I woke up in my own bed, alone and sober," she said with a flourish of mock pride, then glanced over my shoulder at the book on the table. "Ah. I see you've developed a sudden interest in Lightspire history."

"This is . . . I . . . I mean, I just . . ." I stammered. "Ellarion mentioned those other rebellions, and I just wanted to see . . ."

"If any of the false mages were real," she finished, shaking her head. "Tilla, I admire your persistence. Really. But you must be careful."

"I'm just looking at a book—"

"And do you think the librarians don't note every person and what books they ask for? Do you think suspicious readings aren't flagged?"

I blinked. "No, actually, I hadn't thought that." I glanced at the librarian who'd helped me, the sweet old lady, with blossoming distrust. "Are you messing with me? Is that really a thing?"

"Let's just say that this probably isn't the best time to be researching the history of rebellions." Lyriana took a seat next to me, and reached out to take my hands in hers. "Listen. I've been thinking. We need to go out."

"What do you mean?"

"I mean, get out on the town. Go have some fun. You were

in the Kovernum for a week, and I've been drowning in boredom without you." She glanced over her shoulder. "There's a really great festival happening at Mercanto Plaza tonight. I was thinking we could go."

"I don't know," I said, and not just because the last time I'd been at Mercanto Plaza, I'd had to sit through three hours of sonnets. "I mean, I want to go . . . but . . . is it safe?"

"Incredibly safe. There's City Watchmen everywhere in case of trouble. Plus everyone wears heavy hoods, so we won't stand out. And I can always cast a Glamour art over us to draw attention away."

I pulled my hands out of hers. "Lyriana. You know you're not supposed to use magic."

"Yeah, and you're not supposed to sneak into Darryn Vale's room and go through his things, but that didn't stop you."

I cocked an eyebrow. "Since when are you so down to disobey rules?"

"Since when are you so afraid to break them?"

That . . . was a fair point. "You're really sure it'll be safe?"

"I am. Really. But look, if it'll make you feel better, you can invite Zell. I don't think the Titans themselves could hurt you if he was around."

That did make me feel better, so I agreed, which of course meant that Zell was nowhere to be found. I swung by the Barracks, but he wasn't there, and the Watchman running the gate had no idea where he was. That was increasingly the norm these days. I knew it was wrong to blame him. He was busy with his duties, just trying his hardest to serve the city. It wasn't fair of me to ask him to risk his job just because I wanted his support.

He's lying to you.

A scared part of me wanted to use Zell's absence as an excuse to back out, but the rest of me said screw that. Zell made me feel safe, but I didn't need him for that. So that's how I ended up meeting Lyriana alone, at the base of the Gods-blade, just as the sun set and the glowing lights of the tower came on.

Mercanto Plaza was a short walk away, so we didn't bother with a carriage. Instead, we strolled side by side down the pristine cobblestone boulevards of the innermost Golden Circle, wearing identical heavy brown robes that Lyriana assured me were normal. "They're called commoncloths, and all patrons wear them," she explained. "That way, we don't distract attention away from the performers. It's a tradition as old as the Festival of Tears."

"Festival of what, now?" I tugged at the scratchy cloth. "What am I walking into here?"

"You'll cry from laughter, or you'll cry from sorrow."

"That explains *nothing*."

"Once every three years, all of the vagabond troupes in the Heartlands come together for a great festival," Lyriana said. "They set up tents and sing beautiful songs, put on the finest plays, and showcase the greatest offerings of the modern theatrical scene."

"And is there drinking?"

Even under her hood, I could see Lyriana smile. "Oh, so much drinking."

Mercanto Plaza was a huge circular area three blocks north of the Godsblade. Normally, it housed an open-air market, but tonight it was cluttered with densely packed tents, each one boasting a different multicolored flag. Jugglers roamed between them, tossing flaming knives in dazzling spirals, while acrobats swung overhead on invisible strands. Magical Illuminations danced above the tents, spirals of lights and floating orbs and ripples of color like waves lapping on a shore. Music swept over me, plucky string jigs and mournful harps, at once cacophonous and weirdly compelling. Wagons circled the plaza's circumference, manned by vendors hawking snacks and drinks. And the smells . . . succulent roast beef, cinnamon and spices, sweet treats and earthy herbs.

"Okay, yeah," I said. "This was a good idea."

"Told you." Lyriana smiled. As we approached, more and more people in commoncloths walked alongside us, until we were part of a surging crowd, pushing onto the crowded plaza floor. Glancing under the hoods, I was surprised to see a mix of faces. Sure, there were the usual slender aristocratic chins and glowing mage eyes. But there were others too, broad stubbly sailors, rough-hewn farmers, painted Easterners, even a few scrawny, unkempt, haunted-eyed men who I'm pretty sure had come up from Ragtown. It was nice to see some diversity in the Golden Circle, but I could tell not everyone was comfortable with it: City Watchmen stood on guard in their blue fitted uniforms, their faces blank, their right hands resting on the pommels of their sheathed swords.

I'd never seen so many of them in one place. Was Zell working here tonight? Why hadn't he mentioned it?

I started to ask Lyriana if she'd seen him, but she was gone, already rushing over to a nearby wagon manned by a heavyset Southlander woman, her head bald save for a long black ponytail. Lyriana paid the woman, took something, and ran back to me with a little brown cloth in her hands. On it were a pair of . . . pastries, I guess, small golden cubes covered in powdered sugar. "Eat it," Lyriana said, before I could even ask what it was. "Trust me on this. Your life will never be the same."

I took one of the warm cubes and popped it into my mouth, and I can say, with no exaggeration, that it was the best thing I had ever tasted, *ever*. The powdered sugar coated my mouth, even as the pastry's shell dissolved in a burst of fluffy bread and cherry jam and cardamom, and then, if that weren't enough, I hit the pastry's center, which had a shot of rosewater liqueur. I must have made a ridiculous face because Lyriana laughed out loud, then swallowed her own, though of course she did it in three dainty bites. "What was that?" I asked, still tasting that sweet flaky bread even as the liqueur settled into a delightful warmth in my stomach. "And where has it been my whole life?"

"They're called Sinners' Secrets, from the city of Tau Lorren in the Southlands," Lyriana said. "Aren't they amazing?"

"Could I have another? Or, you know, a dozen?"

Lyriana grinned and took me by the hand, pulling me deeper into the festival. Each tent had a different performance, and we hopped from one to another, checking them out over the shoulders of the crowds. In one, a trio was performing a scene from Recarton's *Landa and Tristan*, a tragedy so famous even I'd read the script; we came in the middle, but the actor playing Tristan was so convincing as he cradled his wife's body, so real in his howls of anguish, that it made me tear up. The next tent had a group of actors putting on a comedy in Old Orlese, but I didn't need to understand the language to know it was about a king who couldn't stop farting, so that was more my speed. The next tent had a contortionist wrapping herself uncomfortably around a pole, and the one after that had a tamed singing monkey from the K'olali Isles, and the one after that had a trio of fit, tanned men from the Barony of Malthusia, naked save for tiny loincloths, performing a sensual dance that involved oil-slicked abs and a whole lot of pouty eyes and erotic caressing. Let's just say I was *very* interested.

At some point in the night, the tents started to blur together, but that was also possibly because I'd had two more Sinners' Secrets and their sweet, sweet liqueur. Still, if I was trying to run the leisurely marathon of a golden buzz, Lyriana was sprinting hard toward sloppy drunk. Every time I looked away, she had another goblet of yarvo in her hands, and by the time we left the Tent of the Sexy Dancing Guys, she was wobbling on her feet, her cheeks flushed, a dopey grin on her face. "This is so much fun!" she yelled. "Did you see those guys?"

"I did, yeah," I said, forcing a smile. Look, Lyriana's life was her own, and if she wanted to get drunk, who the hell was I to stop her? But honestly? I hated dealing with her like this. It's not just that she was annoying, although yeah, she was pretty annoying. It's that even as much as she acted like she was having fun when she got wasted and danced on a countertop and went home with a turd pocket like Jerrald, there was something else in it, that core of pain she was shutting out, that Ellarion had asked about on the balcony at Vale

Manor. She was trying so hard to show the world how happy she was that it just called attention to the dark pit of whatever-it-was eating her up. It set off every mother hen impulse I had, even as I had to plaster on a smile and join her for another round.

"Look! Look!" she shouted. There was an enormous tent at the center of the plaza, the size of five of the smaller tents put together, with a dozen billowing flags on top. Music spilled out, a loud boisterous jig that had me tapping my toes, and through the canopy flaps, I could see a bunch of people dancing inside, performers and guests alike. "Can we go? I'm gonna go!"

"Maybe we should—" I started, but Lyriana tore off before I could finish, pushing her way into the circle and almost knocking over two of the other guests. With a sigh, I began to follow, when I heard a raspy voice bellow out from behind me, at once unpolished and yet oddly confident: "Praise! Praise! Praise the Titans!"

I turned around. The words hadn't come from a tent, but from a small crowd of guests behind me, where apparently some kind of commotion was taking place. I took one more glance at the big tent, making sure Lyriana was happily dancing, and then went the other way, toward that crowd. At the center of it, in a small circle, was an old Heartlander man in a pleated golden robe, his white beard twisted together with a pair of silver beads. A priest, then, doing some kind of street preacher routine. I'd seen them before, standing on corners, ranting on about the wisdom of the Heavens and the glorious future we'd all ascend to. That didn't make it any weirder seeing one *here*, though.

"For truly, we of all men are most blessed!" he cried, waving his hands wildly. "That we may gather here so freely, to see so many sights and wonders! That we may come together, sheltered by magic, to wonder and marvel! That we are protected by the greatest of Kings, and live in the greatest of cities!"

"Liar!" another voice cried out, and now every head spun. A figure shoved into the center of the circle, and threw back its hood to reveal the face of a young man. He had light brown skin and shaggy black hair, and his left eye was just a milky orb. "Liar," he repeated, practically spitting the word.

"Explain yourself!" the priest demanded. An uneasy murmur passed through the crowd, a ripple of tension. I felt my chest tighten.

The young man paced forward, and I half thought he was going to just slug the priest right there. But instead, he turned and spoke to the crowd, his voice loud, clear, and charismatic. "This man, this priest, would have us all believe we live in the greatest of cities?" he bellowed. "A city where mothers work until their fingers bleed? A city where fathers hang from the gallows? A city where nobles gorge themselves on lavish feasts while children starve in the gutters? You call *this* the greatest city?"

"Mankind is flawed, yes," the priest spoke, and though his voice was calm, his eyes darted around looking for help. "But that's precisely why the Titans have entrusted us with the gift of magic! That we may overcome our flaws, that we may transcend hunger and pain, that we too may Ascend!"

"The greatest lie of all," the young man said, and the crowd was growing more and more agitated. A few people booed, but a surprising number nodded in agreement. And then there were the others, bulky men with their faces hidden under their hoods, coming to the front of the crowd with their arms folded across their chests. There was something about them that set my teeth on edge, something synchronized and meticulous.

The realization hit me like a frigid breeze. These weren't mere onlookers, and this wasn't some random demonstration. This was organized, deliberate.

These were Ragged Disciples.

I instinctively pushed back against the sea of bodies, trying to get away. This wasn't my fight. This wasn't my place. This whole thing felt dangerous, a stack of kindling just waiting for one spark to set it ablaze.

"I'll tell you all the real truth," the young man went on, and now the priest wasn't even trying to argue, just huddling away with a stunned look. "When the Titans Ascended, they trusted mankind to be their world's caretakers, to watch over their cities, to guard their magic. But the Volaris broke that trust. They raided the vaults and plundered the secrets, conspired with the priests to steal the holiest of holies!" He was practically shouting now, with the fiery passion you'd hear from a general rallying his troops. The crowd was getting angrier, pushier, louder. The man next to me, a swaying bearded drunk, rolled up his sleeves. "They have taken the power of the gods, used it to subjugate all other men, and they dare tell us that this is for our own good?"

"That's enough right there," a shaky voice cut in. A young City Watch recruit stepped forward, and all heads turned toward him. I recognized him right away: Jonah Welarus, the

Captain's son, the big-eyed boy with the soft baby cheeks who was always staring at Zell with adoration. A kid who didn't look like he was ready to handle a broken streetlight, much less a possible riot.

Still, he tried. He walked into the circle and grabbed the ranting man by the wrist, jerking him back. "You're preaching blasphemy and causing a disruption," Jonah said. "I need you to come with me."

But the man yanked his wrist free, sending poor Jonah stumbling back, and strode forward, toward the crowd, toward us. "The Gray Priestess has seen beyond the veil! She has felt the true blessing, been gifted the true light!" His eyes were wide and terrifying. "The Titans will return! The righteous will be redeemed! And the usurpers will b—"

I'm pretty sure the next word was *burn*, but I didn't get to hear it because the hulking drunk next to me wound up and threw an empty bottle directly into the side of the young man's head. It shattered with an explosive crack, splitting open the side of his head, and he toppled backward with a choked scream. Another man in the crowd rushed toward him, but before he could get there one of the cloaked Disciples stepped forward and dropped him with a devastating right hook. And then in an instant, as if that were some invisible signal that everyone knew but me, this stopped being a festival and became a full-on brawl. A bunch of the people in the crowd charged forward, yelling and swearing, but even as they did, four other young Disciples threw back their hoods and surged forward to me, wielding clubs and bottles.

They must have known this would happen.

Had they been counting on it?

I didn't have time to think about that because the chaos was spreading like wildfire. In front of me, the brawl was a mess of flailing limbs and bloody faces; I'm pretty sure no one had any idea who they were fighting anymore. I saw Jonah Welarus fumble out a whistle and let out a single blast, but then a hand jerked him back into the fray, out of sight.

Then someone slammed into me, hard, and sent me tumbling to the ground. I tried to get up, but a boot smashed down on my hand, hard. I hissed and jerked back, clutching it to my chest, and only then did I realize just how bad the situation was. The brawl was out of control, but even worse, the guests who weren't brawling were pulling away, shoving out from the fight in a dangerous, bolting mob. People ran in a wild scramble, knocking each other over, tearing over tents, scurrying in all directions. Terrified screams filled the night air: *Fight! Murder! Bomb!* I saw a sword juggler knocked onto his back, his blades plummeting dangerously down, and a panicking man punch an elderly woman in the face. At this point, most of the people running had no idea what was happening, but the riot was too strong to stop, too wild to contain. This was bad. Really bad. People were going to die.

I jerked myself up onto all fours and looked across the chaotic crowd. I saw a wizened face with a beaded beard. The old priest, the one whose preaching had started this. He was backing away from the fight, retreating into the fleeing mob . . . but there was something weird happening with him, something I couldn't quite make sense of. He had a scrunched-up expression, like he was deep in concentration, and the air in front of his face was shimmering, wavering, purple ripples of light flowing like waves in the air. In that strange moving light, his face warped, twisted, refracted, like an image on a broken mirror . . . and then suddenly, he wasn't an old priest at all anymore. There was a woman where he'd been standing, an older Heartlander woman with gray hair and vibrant purple eyes. Her gaze met mine, and her mouth hinted at a smile, and then she stepped back, disappearing into the crowd.

I'd seen a lot of baffling stuff in the past few days, but I think that was the final straw. The priest hadn't been a priest, but a mage? How did that even . . . How could that . . . What . . .

Lyriana. *Shit! Lyriana!*

I pushed myself up to my feet just in time to avoid getting trampled, and shoved back, pushing against the surging mob. Over their heads, I could see the big tent—the one with the dancing—wobble, wobble, and then collapse in on itself, with another wave of screams. *Shit!* "Lyriana!" I shouted. "Lyriana!"

"Tilla!" she shouted back, from somewhere to my right, and thank the Old Kings she wasn't hurt. I pushed toward the sound of her voice, shoving past a group of scrambling teens and a sobbing, bloody-faced Southlander, and then I saw her, her hood down, golden eyes scared and bleary, staggering through the rushing crowd. I reached out, grabbed her wrist, and pulled her toward me, throwing my arm around her in a protective hug. "I got you," I said. "I got you."

"What's happening?" she slurred, and okay, wow, she was *incredibly* drunk. It took all my strength to keep her up on her feet.

"Disciples. Fight. Riot." I shook my head. "I'll tell you later, okay? Right now, we've gotta go."

By now, the shrill piercing whistles of the City Watch were blaring through the night. *There* they were. Knights of Lazan had arrived on the scene and were trying to manage the crowd, casting golden bubbles of light that contained groups of people and kept them from crushing each other. Leather-winged Sentinels swirled around above us. "Everybody stay calm!" a voice boomed, in that mage way where it sounded like someone was talking directly behind your ears. "The situation is under control!" And sure, they were kind of right, in that I didn't see anyone actively trampling anyone anymore. But the Festival was a ruin. Tents lay in tatters all around. Whimpering, wounded people sprawled on the cobblestone. The faces all around me, so joyous and kind just a few minutes ago, were bloodied, tear-streaked, terrified, furious.

"Come on." I slid my arm around Lyriana's waist to keep her on her feet. "Let's go home."

It took us a solid half hour to make it the three blocks to the Godsblade, because Lyriana kept needing breaks to hunker down and take deep breaths. The Hand of Servo who manned the aravin shot us a skeptical glance as we lurched onto the platform, and it turned full-on judgmental when, somewhere around floor thirty-five, Lyriana lurched over, looking bright green, and said, "I do believe I will vomit."

So he let us out on some random floor, one I'd never been to before, which was completely empty except for a half dozen obelisks covered in illegible writing and a pair of bronze planters with flowering sticks growing out of them. I managed to wrangle Lyriana over to one of those planters to puke in, and the big purple flowers let out a shrill whistle that I swear sounded annoyed.

You ever have those moments where you feel like you're out of your body, looking down at yourself from above, where you feel totally aware of the unreality of your circumstances? I had one right then, as I hunkered down in the Godsblade of Lightspire, holding back the Princess's hair as she threw up into a planter. Me, Tilla, the bastard of House Kent, the dirty-haired girl who ran in tunnels and slept in rafters. What a world.

Lyriana pulled away from the planter and collapsed back onto my lap, lying there with her eyes shut and her chest heaving. The Luminae on the walls were off, and I didn't feel like finding the switch, so the only light in the room was the moonlight coming in through the wide, round windows. I'm not sure how long we stayed there, both of us somewhere between asleep and awake. Lyriana moaned and rolled around, restlessly working through the last of her drunk, while I just sat with her, mind racing as it replayed the night again and again.

The priest had been a disguised mage. Had she been in on it all along? Was she helping the Disciples? How did any of it make sense?

Markiska, the Ragged Disciples, Pretty Boy, Murzur, Molari Vale . . . it was like I had all these pieces of a puzzle laid out in front of me, and no idea how to begin assembling it.

We sat there like that for a while, maybe an hour, maybe three, before Lyriana's eyes sleepily blinked awake and took a second to focus on my face. "Tilla," she said, in a voice barely above a whisper. "What happened? Where are we?"

"The Godsblade," I said. "The Ragged Disciples held a demonstration, and the whole thing turned into a riot. You're lucky we made it out okay."

"Oh," Lyriana said. "I don't remember any of that."

I patted her shoulder. "You were very drunk."

"Oh," she said again, now tinged with sadness and embarrassment. She rolled onto her side, her head still resting in my lap but now turned away from me. "I'm sorry. I didn't mean to be. I was planning to not drink so much, really. I just . . . I guess I lost control." She sniffled loudly. "I'm sorry, Tilla. You shouldn't have to deal with that."

"It's fine. What are friends for, right?"

She lay there quietly for a moment, then let out a little concerned sound. "Tilla. Your hand."

"Hmmm?" I glanced down to see a dark purple bruise blossoming on the top of my right hand, right where that guy had stomped on it. With all the adrenaline of the night, I somehow hadn't taken stock of it, but now that I was looking at it, I felt the throb of dull pain.

"Let me see that," Lyriana said, and before I could stop her, she reached out and took my hand in hers. I felt a soft, pulsing warmth, and a delicate green light flickered between her fingers. When she let go, the bruise had almost faded, and the pain was gone. Guess she didn't need even Rings anymore for magic that simple. How often was she practicing?

"Lyriana. You shouldn't have done that. It's too risky."

"You were hurt because you went out with me. It's the least I could do."

"The least you could do is keep yourself safe!" I said, maybe angrier than I'd wanted to, and then it was all pouring out of me, all the pent-up worry and frustration I'd managed to keep bottled up for the last six months. "I know, okay? I know this is about Jax. I know you feel guilty, and I know you feel like

you can't let someone else get hurt. I get it. I feel the same way."
I was crying now, and also yelling, but there was no holding
it back. "But you know what's not going to help anyone? You
getting yourself killed or exiled or whatever. Do you have any
idea how worried we are about you? All of us? But me especially? Do you have any idea what I'd do if I lost you, too?" My
voice felt hoarse, and at this point I was probably loud enough
for someone to come check on us, so I took a deep breath and
closed my eyes. "I know your heart is in the right place. I know
you're in pain. But you have to look out for yourself, too."

We sat there in silence for a long time as Lyriana took
in my words, and I brushed away my tears with the back of
my hand. Finally, she rolled back over to face me. Even in
the dark, her golden eyes sparkled. "It's not just about helping
others," she said quietly. "I mean, that's a lot of it. But it's also
about helping *me*."

"What do you mean?"

She let out a long, slow sigh. "Before I went out West, I
spent fifteen years following every single rule, and believe me,
there were many rules. I believed that I had to, to be a model
Princess, to serve my family and the Kingdom. And there was
so much I gave up, so much I turned down, so much *life* I
didn't live, because the rules said I couldn't. It made me sad,
of course, but it was for the greater good. I believed that.

"But when I met your brother . . . when I met Jax . . . when
I fell in love with him . . . it was different." Her words came
out hard, choked. "I wanted to act. I wanted to just . . . to just
kiss him, so badly. But I knew it wouldn't be proper, so I held
myself back. I dreamed of a day when it might be possible."
She paused, eyes shut. "And then he died."

"Lyriana . . ."

"I don't want to be like that anymore, Tilla," she said. "I don't want to feel that, that loss, that guilt, ever again. I don't want to grow old, haunted by regrets of all the things I didn't do." Tears were flowing down her cheeks now, golden glowing tears. "I just want to live, Tilla. I just want to *live*."

"Hey, it's okay," I said, and hugged her close. "It's okay." Whatever anger I'd had toward her was gone, replaced only by a profound sadness. Losing Jax had wrecked both of us, but at least I'd gotten sixteen good years with him, sixteen years of adventures and laughs and long, late nights on the beach. Lyriana hadn't just lost him; she'd lost the possibility of ever even knowing him, and the pain of that loss was a wound that would never heal. Who the hell was I to ever judge her for that? I cradled her in my arms and kissed her forehead. "We'll live together, okay? No matter what happens. No matter where we end up. We'll both live."

She shot me a weak smile, the kind of smile that said *I'm trying to believe you, but I really don't.* "We should probably go back to our rooms, shouldn't we?"

"Think you can make it up the aravin without puking?"

Now the smile was a little more genuine. "I'll do my best."

The aravin arrived, and we boarded, trying not to meet the Hand of Servo's disapproving gaze. As it rushed up the translucent tube, I looked down at the flickering lights of the city, hundreds of little gleams, each a home, a family, a life. It reminded me of that night on our journey through the West, when we buried that family by the cottage and stood together in the rain, holding hands, while Lyriana's Lights glowed into the sky above us. That night had been one of the worst of my life, the sight of that family forever scarring, but in that moment, I'd felt this profound sense of togetherness, this feeling that the five of us would always be together, helping each other, protecting each other, forever.

Now Miles was the enemy. Lyriana was broken. Zell was off . . . wherever he was.

And Jax was dead.

The aravin roared up, higher and higher, and the lights grew tinier and tinier. I hugged Lyriana close, but even as I did, I felt utterly alone.

SEVENTEEN

THE NEXT DAY, I GOT UP WITH A RENEWED SENSE OF PURPOSE. Well, okay, first I slept in until noon, and then I ate a crispy flatbread with a fried egg on top. But after that? Renewed sense of purpose.

I skipped my morning class and headed off campus. I'd taken a break from trying to figure out what was going on in the city; just thinking about it made me feel flustered and lost. But I did know one thing that would make me feel better, one thing that would make feel strong and confident. One thing that I'd been putting off way too long.

Zell was at the Barracks, thank the Old Kings, and for once he wasn't busy. He was practicing by himself in the courtyard, shirtless in the center, his toned body sweat-slick in the sun. He glanced my way and his eyes lit up, and even now, with everything going on with us, they still made my heart skip a beat. "Tell me you're not just here to chat."

I cracked my knuckles with a grin. I knew we needed

to talk, to catch up on absolutely everything, but there was something else I needed first. "Not on your life."

We started with the basics, because, I'll be real, I was rusty, especially without a terrifying teleporting mage trying to kill me. The two of us squared off in the sand, and Zell had me run my jabs and my dodges, throwing an occasional kick at my shins to make sure I was minding my footwork. We hadn't done this in a month, maybe more, but we fell right back into our old groove, weaving in circles, eyes locked, breath heavy, somewhere between sparring and dancing as we came together and split apart. The faster we moved, the more we fought, the more I lost myself in the haze, that zone where the rest of the world didn't exist, just his body and mine. I wanted to hit him, to conquer him, to pin him down and watch him squirm, but also to kiss him and feel him. How had I blown this off for so long? How had I forgotten how good it felt? How right?

At some point the drills fell away altogether, and we were just fighting. I ran at him with a howl, streaking across the sand, and threw a spinning elbow at his head. He ducked low, impossibly fast as always, so I hit only the air where his head had been, and then his long arm wrapped around my waist, pulling me back down in a grapple. Normally, I'd have gone down, but I kicked up, still carried by my momentum, and my bare feet found purchase in the firm frame of a practice dummy. I kicked off it, sliding out of Zell's grip, and grabbed him by the hair as I hurtled past. I hit the ground hard on my back, but I pulled him down with me, on top of me, instinctively wrapping my legs around his waist to keep him down. We lay there like that, and I could feel every inch of his firm body pressed against me, could feel his heart beating against mine, could feel his warmth burning against me. I stared into his eyes, his beautiful eyes, and there was nothing, nothing I wanted more.

"I've missed this," I whispered.

"I've missed *you*," he replied.

"Ahem," a voice said from the courtyard entrance, and Zell awkwardly rolled off me, dusting himself off as he rose into a salute. Always the golden boy. I craned my head to the side to see a familiar figure in a red tunic gazing at the two of us with an amused smirk. Lord Galen Reza, of all people, flanked by a group of about six burly men.

"Do you need something, Lord Reza?" Zell asked, already slipping into that super-proper Watchman voice.

"I'd heard rumors that you were teaching your fighting technique. I thought I'd bring my personal guard here for a demonstration, just so they know what to expect if we're ambushed by a Zitochi war party." He arched an eyebrow my way. "Unless . . . you're busy."

Oh, we were busy, because I'd been a second away from just saying screw it and kissing him. But now that Galen was here, I was distracted, and not just by his smug little smile. I hadn't thought about talking to him, had forgotten he was in town, to be honest, but maybe he'd know something about what Pretty Boy had been doing in the city, or if this had any-thing to do with my father and his plans. It couldn't hurt to ask, right?

"We're not busy. But I actually need to ask you about something. Privately." I shot Zell a meaningful glance, and he nodded. "Zell can show your men some basics while we talk."

"Of course," Galen said, and his men filed into the court-yard. The two of us found an empty office in the Barracks, and with the door shut, I told him everything. In retrospect, maybe I should have been more guarded, but I couldn't help myself; for some reason, maybe that Western bond, I just felt like I could trust him. I told him about Darryn Vale and Pretty Boy, about the pearl from the bracelet and the mage at the festival.

"Well?" I said when I finished, because he was still just sitting there, fingers steepled together in front of his face. "What do you think?"

"I think what you've described is profoundly blasphemous. Outright treason."

"Oh." My heart sank.

"But it's a familiar treason," he went on, "and that worries me." Galen rose up, pacing around the room with a deeply troubled look. "In the last few months, I've heard a few reports like this from the front. Unexplained acts turning the tides of battles. Western soldiers conjuring flames and ice. A Zitochi commander who controlled the wind. I'd dismissed them as nonsense, the chaos of the battlefield misremembered. But if you're saying that you see the same here . . ."

"What does it mean?"

"I can think of two theories," Galen said. "First, that there is a calculated propaganda operation by your father to spread the idea that the Heavenly Mandate is a lie. He may even have a few apostate mages in his employ who he's using to fake this idea. This is still, far and away, the most likely explanation."

So, the same thing I'd already heard. "What's the other theory?"

"That the cultists are right." Galen lowered his voice, even though we were in a closed room. "That the Titans truly are angry at the King, and that they have chosen to bless his enemies with their gift. That the rebels really do have magic."

"Do you think that's possible?"

"By all accounts, it shouldn't be," Galen said. "But I've come to believe there's no greater danger than underestimating your father."

I slumped back in my seat. I'd gotten so used to being disbelieved, to being told I was imagining things, it was actually jarring to have someone take me seriously. I wish I'd felt relief, but all I felt was a cold, growing dread. My father was terrifying enough with just his cunning and his army. If the Titans had decided to bless him? If he'd gained the power of magic?

Then no one was safe from his reach.

"What do we do?" I asked.

"*You* don't do anything," he said, eyes narrowed. "I'll talk to the King again. Convince him to send those reinforcements. And when I get back West, I'll make sure to look into these rumors. If there's any truth to them, I'll send word right away."

"That's it?"

Galen arched an eyebrow. "What were you expecting? That I would march into the throne room and declare to everyone there that the foundational principle behind the entire Kingdom is a lie?"

"I guess not," I said. And it's not that he was wrong, because yeah, that was a good point, but it still just felt like such a weak response. Everyone seemed to want to take it slow and careful, to make sure they'd sussed out the full truth before actually doing anything, and all the while my father was getting stronger, bolder, more powerful. By the time anyone decided to act, it would be too late.

They just didn't get it, none of them. They couldn't. To them, this was all just an abstraction, an unpleasant "what if," a puzzle to be worked out. They hadn't fought Pretty Boy. They hadn't felt his fists, hadn't seen what he was capable of.

Galen adjusted his collar and paced toward the door. "I should get back to my men," he said. "Stay safe, Tillandra."

"You too," I replied, as if it were remotely under my control.

I walked back out into the courtyard a few minutes later. Galen was standing to the side, arms folded across his chest, watching Zell spar with three of his guards. I tried to play it cool. I really did. But I couldn't stop thinking about what Galen had told me, couldn't stop imagining my father with mages at his disposal, his armies burning their way toward us even as we spoke. What would they do if they got here? I pictured the city besieged by Western catapults, streets aflame with warfare, assassins slitting throats in the halls of the Godsblade. And if against all odds, he won? I might get spared, maybe, *maybe*. But my friends? Lyriana, Ellarion, Zell? He'd mount their heads on pikes and make me watch.

No. *No.* I hadn't come this far, hadn't fled across the continent, just to see my loved ones die at my father's hand. The others could take their time, but I wasn't going to just stand around twiddling my thumbs until it was too late. I had to act.

So with a quick wave I left the Barracks and hurried over to the Godsblade. The mage at the aravin was the one who'd been there the night before, and he shot me a judgey glance, but took me up all the same, to the forty-seventh floor, to Ellarion's private chamber.

"Tilla," Ellarion said, as I stepped through the sliding doors. He was sitting at his massive desk, poring over a stack of yellowed papers. Also, he was shirtless, and when he stood up, I gave an involuntary swallow. His body was leaner than Zell's, lankier, his muscles taut in a narrow frame. His chest was smooth and hairless, and in the soft sunlight ghosting in through the translucent wall, his rich black skin almost glowed. "We need to talk."

"Yeah, we do." I cleared my throat. "Mind, uh, putting on a shirt?"

"Too much for you, huh?" he said with a bemused smirk, and reached into a drawer to grab one. It was sheer silk, see-through, opened at the center down to beneath his sternum. When it came to modesty, it wasn't much better. "Now, then. Care to tell me what in the frozen hell you were thinking last night? Sneaking to a festival with the Princess where you nearly got killed . . ."

"First of all, that was one hundred percent her choice. And second of all, it's none of your business."

Ellarion kept smiling, but something else flickered in his eyes. Anger? Was he seriously pissed at me? "I thought I told you to lie low and let me investigate things. What part of that translates to 'go out for a night on the town with Lyriana'?"

I *really* did not need his Disappointed Dad voice. "Look. She was going to that festival with or without me. So instead of getting on my ass, maybe you ought to be thanking me for keeping her safe." That was true. True enough, anyway.

"Besides, that doesn't matter because I learned something really important. I told Galen . . . Lord Reza . . . about what happened, and he says he's heard similar things from the West. Soldiers are reporting that my father's men have gained magic, that there are Zitochi mages, that they're turning the tide of battle!" I didn't realize how wound up I was before, but I was almost yelling. "It's real, Ellarion! I'm telling you! It's real!"

"You told Lord Reza what happened," Ellarion said slowly, as if it was taking a lot of restraint to keep calm. "As in, you told him about us breaking into the manor of the city's wealthiest merchant and performing an unauthorized act of Scrying in his son's bedroom."

"I . . . I mean . . . well . . ." I tried, and okay, when he put it like that, it sounded pretty bad. "All right, that might have been a bad call. But you're still not hearing me. The evidence is piling up, Ellarion. There's something going on. Your enemies—this city's enemies—are discovering magic. My father's men are becoming mages. Does no one get how serious that is?"

Ellarion let out a long exhale. "Tilla. Listen to me. It's not happening. Your father's men, the Zitochi, the cultists . . . none of them are discovering magic."

"How do you know?" I yelled. "How can you be so certain?"

Ellarion didn't say anything for a little while. He just stared at me, brow furrowed with thoughtful scrutiny. Before, he'd always looked at me with playful amusement. But now it was like he was actually seeing me for the first time. "You are the most stubborn, bull-headed girl I've ever met," he finally said. "You're not going to give up, are you? You're just going to keep doing this until you get yourself, and maybe the rest of us, jailed."

"I'm trying to keep us all from getting *killed*."

He let out a weary sigh. "Titans stop me, I'm about to do something very foolish, and show you something that I absolutely positively should not."

I arched an eyebrow. "What are you going to show me?"

"Certainty."

He led me back down the hall and into a different aravin. The Hand of Servo, a husky bearded man I'd seen around a few times, bowed his head politely as we entered. "Sixty-fifth floor," Ellarion said to the man. "Take us to the top."

The Hand's demeanor changed instantly. He stiffened, his mouth hardening into a tight line, and his right hand drifted toward his sheathed blade. "Authentication. Now."

Ellarion rolled his eyes, then stretched his hands out in front of him. His Rings pulsed as he twirled his hands in a series of precise gestures, like he was drawing with his fingertips on an invisible canvas. And sure enough, when he was done, he threw open his palms and a shape appeared in the air in front of him, a twirling multicolored flowery thing, with intricate bands of pulsing light and flowering petals, frozen in midair, like we were floating underwater. I just stared at it with my mouth hanging open, but the Hand examined it like it was a priceless painting, squinting both eyes and cocking his head to the side. After a minute, he stepped back and took his hand off the hilt. "You're cleared," he said, then scowled at me. "But I wasn't told anything about *her*."

"She's with me. So she's cleared, too."

The Hand shook his head, visibly uncomfortable. "That's not how it works. She's not on the list."

"Not on the list," Ellarion repeated, with a laugh that didn't sound at all amused. "Listen here, friend. I get that authenticating me is your job. I'll play along with that. But now you've authenticated me. You know exactly who I am and what I can do." His voice had turned hard, scary even, as he stepped toward the man. "So we can play this game where you make me call up the master of your order and tell him that you're being a huge pain in my ass, and then you get chewed out, maybe demoted, and we've all wasted an afternoon. Or you can just take me and my friend to the top." He reached out and clasped the man's shoulder, which made him actually jolt back. "What do you say?"

The Hand looked at Ellarion, then at me, then at the hand on his shoulder. He swallowed deep. "Apologies. I overstepped. Of course I'll take you."

"Good man," Ellarion said, and paced back to me. The Hand closed his eyes and begin doing the motions, lips puckered with rhythmic breaths. Below us, the disk rumbled and began its ascent.

"What was that?" I whispered.

"That was me bluffing our way into the most secure chamber in the Kingdom," Ellarion whispered back. "Act a little impressed."

The aravin sped up, higher, and higher, past the King's Court and the royal lodgings where I usually got off. I'd always thought those *were* the very top floors, which meant we were going up to . . .

"The dome," I said, and Ellarion just smiled. At the very

top of the spire, all of the curved serpentine bands that made up the Godsblade converged into a single enormous dome. It sat on the top of the building like a turtle shell, covered in hundreds of polished shimmersteel panels that glistened like mirrors. I'd always assumed it was just, you know, decorative. I mean, what would possibly be up here?

The aravin slowed to a stop, and the doors slid open. I don't know what I expected, but the room we stepped out into was almost totally dark, lit up by just a few glowing halos on the floor. And the only thing in front of us, maybe a few feet away, was a second shimmersteel shell, curved up to make a dome within the dome, this one blank and dark and unpolished.

"What am I . . ." I began, but Ellarion just waited for the aravin doors to slide shut and the Hand to leave. Then he stepped up to that second dome and pressed his palm against it, eyes shut in concentration. Like frost melting off a window, the darkness of the metal cleared away, creating a translucent window for us to look through, like we were peering into the shell of some enormous egg.

"Holy shit," I whispered.

Inside this second dome, hovering an inch over the ground, was an enormous rock the size of a carriage. No, *rock* doesn't do it justice. More like a boulder, maybe, but one that refused to be one shape for more than a second. And I don't just mean that it was changing shapes, although it was doing that, too. It's more like it somehow *was* different shapes at the same time, in a way that made no sense. One second, it was a craggy gem, but then also a polished pyramid, and then it changed to be a glistening slick diamond while also a menacing spike-encrusted orb. And it wasn't just the shape that was changing, it was the colors. The whole thing pulsed and swirled with every shade I could imagine, spiraling bands that lit up one section a hot pink and another a rich black, blossoming green ribbons that danced through clouds of shimmering gold, streaks of silver lightning and expanding clouds of glittery purple and flowery lavender.

It was the prettiest thing I'd ever seen, and just looking at it gave me a splitting headache. "What is it?" I gasped out.

Ellarion shrugged. "The proof of the Heavenly Mandate. The greatest secret of the Volaris. My certainty."

"So, like a . . ." I held my hand over my eyes to try to block out its blinding, dazzling light, which was making thinking very difficult. "Like a big magic rock?"

"That's not a magic rock. That's *magic*. Period." He ran his hand over the dome again, fogging it just enough that it stopped actively causing me pain. "We call it the Heartstone. All the magic in the world, every single little art, comes from that beautiful monstrosity. It's the engine that drives the Kingdom, the beating heart that pumps magic into our bodies, our hands."

"I don't understand."

"Magic is the art of breaking the world, of turning nothing into something, of violating the rules that govern the earth and the stars." Ellarion raised his hand and unfurled his fingers, and a thin strand of fire danced out from his palm, curling in the air until it formed the shape of a flickering rose. It was a cheap trick, but it still made me gape. "But doing so requires tremendous energy. That force, that power, to break the very laws that keep this planet from plunging into the sun, it has to come from somewhere." He closed his hand into a fist and the rose vanished, leaving only a tendril of smoke. "The Heartstone is the source of that power. The root of all magic."

"The Rings," I said, with a sudden moment of clarity. "You make them from that thing."

Ellarion nodded. "Yes. It's known as the Rite of Mana, and it can only be done twice a year, on the solstices, when the Heartstone is at its tamest. It takes a team of fifteen of the best Hands of Servo, wearing full-body shimmersteel suits, to strip away maybe two dozen shards of the stone, which can then be repurposed into Rings."

"Huh," I said, trying to act cool and not like he'd just exposed the entire foundation of the Kingdom as a lie. The cultists had been right after all, but the truth was even worse than even they'd imagined. "So it's all bullshit. You guys just make the Rings yourselves, and then tell everyone the Titans made them for you. Why? So we think you're special?"

Ellarion smiled again, but there was an odd sadness to it. "Oh, we are special. Just not how everyone thinks." He lifted his hand up, turning it over so his many Rings glistened. Behind him, the Heartstone throbbed a pulsing blue. "The Rings are just conduits, remember? They connect us to the stone, let us funnel its energy and turn it into arts that change the world. If that stone is the heart, then the Rings are the veins that carry its blood to us mages, its many limbs, no matter where we are in the world. But those veins only pump if the limbs are connected. Put a Ring on a Westerner, and nothing happens. Put a Ring on a Volaris, and we can turn over mountains. Why?" A sour look crossed his face. "Because we've been *cultivated*."

"Cultivated?" I asked. "Now I'm confused again."

"See, the Heartstone doesn't just create magical energy. It leaks it. That's why it's behind this dome, why the Hands have to wear shimmersteel suits just to get near it for an hour. If I were to dissolve this wall, we'd die in seconds. We'd burst into flame or melt into goo or rip inside out as our organs turn into shards of glass."

"That's just a thing you made up, right? That doesn't actually happen?"

Ellarion ignored my question, which was not comforting at all. "Maybe in the past, back in the Era of the Titans, the shimmersteel dome was strong enough to contain all the energy. But it's been wearing down for centuries. And that energy has been seeping out from the dome, from the Godsblade, down into the city. It infects our bodies. It pulses under our skin. And it trickles into our mothers' wombs, warping us, changing us. The Blood of the Titans, they call it. Running through our veins from the moment we're born." He breathed deeply and ran his hand along the dome, clearing away the little window so we couldn't see the Heartstone at all anymore. "A child born on the outskirts of the city, in Marrowmold or the Sprawl, has a one in five hundred chance of being a mage. But a child born here, in the Godsblade? A child whose parents were touched by the stone, and their parents before them?"

"You're guaranteed to be magical."

"Not guaranteed. Engineered," he went on. "Did you know that when a Volaris woman is pregnant, she's not allowed to leave the Godsblade, to ensure that she's saturated in the flowing energy? That they make them sit in this chamber for hours, soaking it in? It lingers in the blood, stronger and stronger with each generation, so every son is a little more altered than his father. A little less human." Ellarion's gaze met mine, his red eyes burning, and for the first time, I was actually a little afraid of him. "Do you know what I see when I look at you? I can see your heart beating in your chest. I can hear your blood rushing through veins. I can smell your emotions seeping off you. And all around I see the tendrils of possibility, the beams of power that I can touch, can bend, can shape." I remembered what the world had looked like when we'd Scryed together, but I'd assumed that had just been part of the art. Was that really what he saw all the time? What Lyriana saw?

"What are you saying?" I asked.

"I'm saying that magic isn't something I do. It's something I *am*. The energy of the Heartstone is within me, shaping me, as much a part of me as my blood or my breath. I can't turn it on and off, can't shut out the visions, can't drown out the voices." He actually sounded pained. "I'm not the most powerful mage in the city because I tried the hardest or because I was blessed. I'm this powerful because my parents ensured that I would be. Because they cultivated me. That's it. That's the only thing that makes me *me*."

I stared at him hard in that room's soft light. It felt like he was laying himself bare, showing me this vulnerable side he kept hidden behind a dozen masks, but even now, there was so much I didn't understand, so much I still couldn't see. I wanted to reach out, to comfort him, but I couldn't bring myself to. I was scared of what I'd feel. "Ellarion . . ."

He glanced away, almost a flinch. Could he really sense my feelings? "That's why I'm so certain, Tilla," he said. "The

Heavenly Mandate *is* a lie, but it's a lie to give people hope, to make them feel like there's a good reason why some men can barely lift a plow and others can melt glass with their will. But there is no purpose, no grand plan, no gift. There's just this." Ellarion patted the side of the dome. "Magic can't be discovered, can't be gifted. It doesn't come from the Titans or from the Rings. The only magic in the world comes from being born near this stone."

"Oh," I said, and that was about all I could muster. I mean, how could I possibly argue with that? This wasn't murky ancient history or dubious theology. This was reality, plain and inescapable. I understood his certainty now (and maybe, on some level, understood *him*). And I understood why the only logical explanation, the only explanation, period, was that I hadn't seen what I was so sure I had seen. That I was being manipulated. That I couldn't trust my own mind.

I finally understood the truth. And it was devastating.

"Now come on," Ellarion said, pacing back toward the aravin. "If anyone finds out I showed you this, we're both in serious trouble."

We rode down in silence, watching the ground streak toward us as the aravin descended. When it came to a stop on the ground floor, Ellarion turned to go, but I stopped him, grabbing his hand. I felt that tingle again, that little electric surge, but it felt different now, scarier. *It infects our blood*, Ellarion had said. *It pulses under our skin*.

"Tilla? What is it?"

"Just . . . thank you," I said softly. "For showing me that. For being honest with me. It's not what I wanted to hear, obviously. But it's what I needed."

Ellarion looked at me carefully, one eyebrow cocked. "Can I trust that you won't do something reckless?"

I looked down, and I realized, unexpectedly, that I was crying. "I'll try," I said.

He reached out and wiped away my tear, and as he did, it vanished with a tiny wisp of steam. "We'll get through this. We'll be safe. I promise."

He stepped away, and the heavy doors slid shut behind him. I slumped back against the wall. I didn't *want* to get through this. I didn't *want* to be safe. I didn't *want* to be in this tower, in this city, in this world of lies and schemes and power, this world where parents cultivated children, forged them like tools.

All I wanted was to go home.

EIGHTEEN

"TILLA."

A voice, cutting through the dark. Familiar. Frantic.

"Tilla!"

I shot up out of sleep with a noise that was half yelp and half snore. It took one groggy second to make sense of where I was: in my room in the University, in bed, in the dark. So why was I . . .

"Tilla . . ." the voice said again, and now I spun toward it. Zell. The room was dark, almost pitch-dark, but I could just barely make out his tall figure, leaning against the wall by the door. I couldn't see his face, not quite, but I could see there was something off about him, about the way he was hunched.

"Zell?" I rubbed at my eyes. "What are you doing here?"

"It doesn't matter," he said, and there it was in his voice, an urgency, almost a panic. "Listen. We don't have much time. I just . . . I need to tell you . . . I . . ." He stammered for words. Why was Zell stammering? He *never* stammered. "I'm in trouble, Tilla. We all are."

His tone was like a bucket of ice water dumped on my head, because all at once I wasn't even remotely groggy. He actually sounded scared. And if Zell was scared, that meant things were really, really bad. "What is it?" My hand shot out, finding the button on the little round Luminae by my beside.

"No, don't t—" Zell started, but it was too late. The Luminae flickered on, bathing the room in a soft blue light. I could see Zell now. And I had to clamp both hands over my mouth to choke back a scream.

He was wearing his City Watch uniform, but it was torn at the side, with a big hole that showed the side of his stomach and a long jagged cut running across it. His hair was messy, which it never was, and I'm pretty sure the side of his face was splattered with blood. Worst of all, though, were his eyes. They danced around, wild, terrified, like there were a million thoughts screaming through his head and every single one of them was bad. I'd seen Zell tense, I'd seen him fighting, and I'd seen him cry. But I'd never seen him look so broken.

"Zell, what happened to you?" I lunged out of bed. "Who did this?"

"It doesn't matter." He stepped toward me and took my hands in his. They were cold and wet and I didn't want to look down, but I did anyway. Blood everywhere, not just on his palms and mine, but on his nightglass blades, their jagged points stained crimson. "I don't have time to explain. Not now."

"You show up in my room at three in the morning soaked in blood. You'd better believe you have to explain."

He let out a harsh exhale, the kind that meant he knew I wasn't kidding. "I broke into Captain Welarus's office tonight."

"What? Why?"

"It doesn't matter, okay? What matters is what I found." He dug into the inside pocket of his coat and pulled out a small envelope. "Look familiar?"

My heart leaped into my throat, and a cold chill slithered up my spine. Oh, it was familiar, all right. It was the exact same kind of small yellow envelope we'd found back in Vale Manor, and on it, *Captain Welarus* was written in the same messy, borderline illegible scrawl. I could tell there was something inside too, something small and round. "No . . ." I whispered, but Zell shook the envelope, and it fell out into his open palm.

A bright purple pearl, unmistakably from Markiska's necklace. Just like the one Molari had received.

"I don't get it," I said. None of this made sense, and every time it seemed like maybe we were figuring it out, it fell apart all over again. What connected Molari Vale and Captain Welarus? Why would someone send both of them Markiska's pearls?

Suddenly, Zell's tattered appearance made a lot more sense. He'd been caught in Welarus's office. There'd been a fight with some other members of the Watch. He'd hurt them. Maybe even . . . maybe even . . .

"I had no choice," Zell whispered, as if reading my mind. "You have to believe me. I had no choice."

Oh *shit.*

A horn of distress sounded from somewhere nearby, then another, then another. I spun back to Zell, and now I was in full-on crisis mode, because if I stopped to actually think I'd just collapse in a twitching ball of terror. "Listen. You need to get out of here. Get somewhere safe. Hide until I can explain it all to the King. With Lyriana backing you, you still might be able to go—"

"No," Zell said. "I'm not letting you get dragged down with me. I can face the consequences for what I've done, but you, you still have a whole life to live." His voice choked up, and it was like an instant trigger for tears burning my eyes. My stomach plunged, and I felt that tightness in my chest, closing, closing, making it harder and harder to breathe. Zell wasn't just talking like a man in trouble. He was talking like a man accepting his doom. "I just had to see you one last time, Tilla. Before they take me away. Before they hang me in the street or throw me in some dark cell. I just had to see your face."

I could hear a commotion just outside my building now, voices shouting, footsteps thundering. I wanted to run, to hide, but where could I go? What in the frozen hell was I supposed to do?

Zell reached out and stroked my cheek, his hand shaking just a little. His skin was warm, hot even, but when he pulled away, the nightglass brushed my chin, and it was so cold it made me shudder. "Promise me one thing, Tilla. No matter what you hear about me, no matter what they tell you, remember me the way I was. Back in the West. When we were fighting together, when we were lying together, when you'd make me laugh, and I'd show you how to wield a blade. Remember me then. Before this city. Before its corruption. Before I lost myself."

The floor shook underfoot as those footsteps drew closer,

coming down the hall, closing in. "Zell, please," I begged because the sheer despair in his voice was crushing me. "You can still run. You can still fi—" And then before I could finish, the door behind us flew open, and he jerked away, spun around, and threw his hands up in the air. "I surrender fully and without contest!" he yelled, the way you're trained to when the City Watch makes an arrest.

But these weren't City Watchmen in my doorway. Inquisitor Harkness himself loomed from the darkness, flanked by four Shadows of Fel, their eyes glistening pitch-black. "Take them both," the Inquisitor said.

"No!" Zell yelled. "Not her!" He dove toward them, but before he'd even crossed half the room, the Shadows jerked their hands up in unison, flicking them toward us like they were throwing daggers. Their Rings pulsed black, and a horrible pain flared in my head, throbbing, red, blinding, like someone had put a drill in my skull, and it was boring its way out through my eyes. I screamed and fell to my knees, and Zell dropped in front of me, gritting his teeth and clutching his temples. It hurt, it hurt so bad, I was crying and choking and gagging. My teeth were chattering, and the whole world pulsed and spun. "I'll . . . kill . . . you . . ." Zell rasped in front of me, pulling himself to his knees, and one of the Shadows clenched his fist, and for a moment I could see *something*, a tendril of shimmering darkness, barely visible, stretching from his palm to Zell's temples. Zell howled in agony and collapsed again. I tried to crawl toward him, to will any part of my body to move, but the pain was too much, too terrible, too overwhelming. The floor raced up to meet me, and the darkness that followed was a relief.

nineteen

THE NEXT THING I FELT WAS FABRIC RUSTLING AGAINST my face as someone jerked a bag off my head. Reality blinked into focus, and I let out a gasp as I tried to make sense of my surroundings. I was in a dark stone room without any windows, lit only by a pair of red Luminae. A small group of people was standing in front of me, but with the only lights behind them, I couldn't make out their faces, just their gray hooded silhouettes. It was cold in here, with a dusty smell that reminded me of the crypts below Castle Waverly. Oh, and I was sitting in a stiff iron chair with my hands bound behind my back.

"Tilla," a voice said softly from my right. I craned my head to see Zell, hunched over in a chair next to me. They'd washed the blood off him, but he still looked like hell, his eyes weary, his face haunted. Thick iron chains bound his hands together behind his back. No escape this time. "I'm so sorry."

Memory came back to me in a rush. The Shadows. The

Inquisitor. He was already convinced Zell and I were traitors, spies for my father. I still didn't understand what had happened to Zell tonight, but if he'd been caught in Welarus's office, well, that was all the evidence he needed to convict us, right?

No. No. That was pessimism talking. There was still a way out of this. We just had to tell the King the truth, about the pearls, about the Vales and Welarus and how it was all somehow connected. I know King Leopold wasn't always the most involved ruler, but I still trusted him, trusted him enough to believe he'd hear me out, especially if Lyriana begged him to. He had a soft spot for me, damn it, and that meant I had a chance. And for all his power and daggers-in-the-dark, I was pretty sure Harkness still bent the knee when it came to it. "The King," I croaked out weakly. "I demand to talk to the King."

"Why, of course," a kindly voice replied, and one of the figures pulled back his hood, revealing Harkness's neat beard and gentle smile. "Despite the rumors, I'm not some monster who just disappears people in the night. You will have your chance to plead your case." At the far end of the room, the wall trembled, and a slim crack of light appeared. A door opening. "Ah. What fortuitous timing. I do believe that's the King here now."

The doors swung wide open. Squinting against the light, I could make out three figures entering. Two were tall and armored, swords at their sides. Knights of Lazan. But the man between them was smaller and portly, and he walked with a slow, heavy gait and his head bowed low. King Leopold Volaris.

He stepped into the light, and all of the hooded figures

except the Inquisitor bowed. King Leopold was wearing the most extravagant nightrobe I'd ever seen, with a fur trim and a trailing green cape. The circlet around his head, usually multicolored and sparkling, had only the room's Luminae to reflect, so it glowed a sinister red. As he walked toward us, his face was stony, a forced look of severity, the kind I'd seen him adopt when he gave fiery speeches from the steps of the Godsblade. But when his eyes fell on me, bound, roughed up, I saw something else in them, something I hadn't seen before. They flared a bright burning turquoise, hot with anger.

He looked *pissed.*

"This girl is my ward, Harkness," he growled. "You'd better have a damn good explanation for this."

I would've thought that would trigger a reaction, but the Inquisitor seemed completely unfazed. "The restraints are a necessary precaution, given the severity of the accusations," he said calmly. "Please, Your Majesty. I understand this is deeply distressing, and I, as always, serve only your will and command. When this is over, if you believe I have erred, I will resign at once, and subject myself to whatever punishment you believe appropriate."

"When *what* is over?" I said. "What is going on here?"

Inquisitor Harkness turned back to me, and in his expression I saw no kindness, no mercy, not even a hint of human understanding. He looked at me like I was vermin, a rat carrying a plague into his beloved city. "Your trial," he replied.

I looked to Zell, but his head was still down. Like he'd already accepted his fate.

Inquisitor Harkness stepped forward and spread his arms

wide. When he spoke, his voice was firm and commanding, echoing off the room's walls. "By the powers granted to the Inquisition, I call to order a Shadow Tribunal. Does the King consent?"

King Leopold looked from me to the Inquisitor. He could end this all now. All he had to do was take a stand, refuse the trial. But the King just nodded his head. "I do," he said. "And know that if you're wrong, there *will* be consequences."

Harkness nodded. "I won't waste your time with formality, then, Your Majesty. I call this Tribunal because I have evidence these two youths are guilty of the highest of crimes: of blasphemy, of treason, of conspiracy, of murder. I believe they are acting on behalf of Lord Kent, and were sent here for precisely this purpose: to spy, to spread dissent, to poison our beloved Princess against her own family."

"I know you've long mistrusted the girl, Harkness," King Leopold said, and his rings flared gold. "But do you have any proof?"

The Inquisitor stepped back and cleared his throat. "First witness. Come forward."

The first hooded figure on the left stepped forward, uneasily, like he wasn't sure quite what he was supposed to do. Inquisitor Harkness gestured at him impatiently, and he pulled back his hood, revealing a young man's face, scared and sweat-streaked.

I did a double take. Jerrald Blayne. Lyriana's ill-advised hookup. The boy whose arm Zell had snapped.

"Tell us what happened on the night of Darryn Vale's party," Inquisitor Harkness prompted.

"They attacked me," Jerrald blurted out, aggressively

refusing to actually look at us. "The Princess, the Zitochi, and the Western traitor. They beat me up in the garden and broke my arm. Then the Princess healed me with some magic." He rolled up his sleeve, showing the white scar tissue where his arm had been shattered. "See?"

"Impossible!" King Leopold spun on the boy. "My daughter swore a sacred vow to never use magic! She wouldn't break it! Not for you!"

"Tell him the rest," Harkness said. "What happened the night before."

Jerrald was trembling, his eyes staring firmly at the ground as tears streaked down his cheeks. "The Princess . . . she . . . she invited me to her room . . . and I . . . we . . . I . . . we . . ." He swallowed so deeply his whole throat bobbed. "We slept together."

"Liar!" the King roared, and honestly, it was bullshit that he was angrier about that than the whole broken arm thing. He grabbed Jerrald by the front of his robe and slammed him back against a wall, bellowing in his face. "My daughter is a good girl! Pure! Chaste! She would never compromise herself with the likes of you!"

"Your Majesty," Harkness said softly, his voice tinged with sadness. "I interrogated the boy with a Shadow. He speaks the truth."

King Leopold let Jerrald go and spun back around. He looked stunned, numb, like he'd just been told his whole family was dead. "But . . . Lyriana . . . she wouldn't . . . She's a good girl . . ."

"She *was*," Harkness replied. "Before she went West. Before she fell under Tillandra's influence. You know how the

Westerners are, my Lord. Venal. Blasphemous. Immoral. I believe this was Tillandra's plan all along. To manipulate your daughter. To turn her against Godly ways. To drive her to sin."

King Leopold turned to look at me, and now there was something new in his gaze.

Suspicion.

"It's not like that," I tried. "Lyriana made her own choices. She acted of her own will."

But the King didn't hear me, couldn't hear me. Not when his sense of denial was so strong. "No. No, she wouldn't. That's just not her. You must have influenced . . . manipulated . . ."

"Second witness," Harkness said. "Come forth."

The second man stepped forward, this one bulky and broad. He pulled back his hood, revealing the jowly face of Molari Vale. I was starting to realize how this whole trial was going to go, how bad the case against us looked if you didn't know the real truth. Maybe even if you did.

"Molari Vale," the Inquisitor said. "Tell the Tribunal of the transgression you discovered in your manor."

Molari's stare pierced into me, like he was trying to force himself into my thoughts through sheer will. How much did he suspect? How much did he *know*? "The three of them came to visit me. Princess Lyriana, Ellarion Volaris, and the Westerner." I was getting *real* sick of them not calling me by my name. "The Princess told me that she wanted to discuss a sale of Eastern goods for the Ascendance Day Masquerade, and though I found her request dubious, I humored it." His gaze flitted to me, and his lip curled in disgust. "And then my servant discovered the Westerner and Ellarion having an improper tryst in my son's bedroom!"

"What?" Zell asked quietly, and as horrible as the situation had felt up until that point, it felt *really* crushingly, horrifically, unspeakably awful now, like all the walls were closing in at once. Because of course, I hadn't told him, not yet. I was going to, I really was, and then there'd been the whole thing with Pretty Boy, and my recovery, and the festival, and I just hadn't, okay? But I'd always planned to. And I would've explained what happened, and he would've understood, and we would've laughed it off. It would have been fine. It would've worked out.

But him finding out like this? With the truth only coming out during a literal tribunal in a literal dungeon? It seemed like I was trying to hide it. Like there really *was* something there. Like I was a cheater.

And the worst part is, he didn't look hurt or angry or even betrayed. He just looked blank. Emotionless. Unreadable. Like maybe he couldn't believe it was true.

"You see, Your Majesty, how powerful the Westerner's influence is, how cunning her wiles," Harkness went on. "Even as she professes to be the Zitochi's lover, she seduces the Archmagus himself, bends him to her will!"

"It's not like that," I said. "We were . . . we were . . ."

"When I learned of it, I'd hoped it was merely a foolish tryst," the Inquisitor cut in. "We all know of the Archmagus's reputation. And yet, I believe her goals are far more nefarious." He gestured at the line. "Third witness. Come forward."

The third figured stepped up and pulled back his hood. It took me a second to recognize him. The Hand of Servo. The one from the aravin, who'd taken us up to the Heartstone. "Tell us what happened in your aravin yesterday. With discretion."

"The Archmagus showed up in my aravin," he said, and I'm pretty sure he was in a lot of trouble, too. "With the Western girl. He told me to take him up to the top floor. He said he wanted to show her something."

I saw an odd look of confusion cross Molari's face. The Heartstone really was a deeply guarded secret, if even he didn't know about it.

"He showed her the . . . the . . ." King Leopold began, as if this was too much for him to comprehend. That one wasn't even my fault! Ellarion had *wanted* to show me the stone!

"Our own Archmagus, betraying the Kingdom's most precious secrets to a Western spy." Inquisitor Harkness shook his head. "He will face his own reckoning soon enough. Yet for now, we must deal with the root of this nightmare. With the serpent in our midst."

I almost wanted to laugh, because the idea that I was this brilliant seductress, capable of making even the strongest men do my bidding, was just so absurd. Then I saw the King's face, the way he was looking me. Any protective impulse, any sympathy was gone, replaced with horror, anger, and betrayal. "Your Majesty," I pleaded. "Please. You have to listen to me. I know this looks bad, but it's not what you think. Yes, we made some mistakes. Yes, we probably should have gone straight to you. But Lyriana, Zell, Ellarion and I . . . we're trying to help you. There's something going on in this city, something terrible, and it involves Molari Vale and my father and Markiska and . . . and . . ." And I ran out of words because I could tell it wasn't working, could tell they saw this all as the desperate babbling of a traitor exposed. "Please, just bring Lyriana down here," I begged. "She'll explain everything. I promise you. Just give me this one chance."

King Leopold turned to Inquisitor Harkness, one eyebrow arched, and it was working, it was actually working. His heart was turning against me, but it would never turn against his daughter. And I knew he wanted to give her this chance, give her the benefit of the doubt, give her the opportunity to clear herself and me. . . .

I hoped Inquisitor Harkness would look scared, or at least worried, but his expression was nothing but grim resolution. "Bring out the body," he said.

The what, now?

Two of the Inquisitor's Shadows came forward, carrying something long and limp on a stretcher, covered by a thick cloth. It was so dim in the room, and the cloth was a dark brown, but I could still make out a few stains. What was this? What was happening? Why did my heart feel like it was going to smash through my chest?

One of the Shadows pulled back the cloth. Jerrald Blayne gasped. King Leopold recoiled in horror. And I just sat there, jaw slack, hands numb, as I saw the Inquisitor's trap slam shut.

The cold, bloodless body of City Watch Captain Balen Welarus lay on the stretcher, staring at us with wide, white eyes. His uniform was soaked through with crimson, his beard matted to his face. There was no question what had killed him, because we could all see the four deep stab wounds in the side of his neck. Exactly the kind you'd get if you were punched by someone with razor-sharp nightglass knuckles.

I'd been so caught up in the moment, so distracted by the

Tribunal, I'd completely forgotten how my night had started, with Zell bursting into my room, disheveled, frantic, talking like he was doomed. It all made so much sense now. He hadn't been panicking because he'd been caught in Captain Welarus's office. He'd been panicking because he'd *murdered the Captain of the City Watch*.

Every eye in the room turned to Zell. He didn't say anything. He didn't even react. He just stared ahead, brow furrowed, his mouth a hard narrow line.

"Balen Welarus, Captain of the City Watch, was found murdered in his office," Harkness said. "His son, Jonah, has been missing for two days. This Zitochi . . . this pawn of the Western snake . . . he's responsible."

"Zell . . ." I whispered. "Did you do this?"

"I acted purely of my own accord," Zell said, colder than I'd ever heard him. "Tilla was not involved in any way. Let her go."

"No," I said, "no no no," but it was already too late. There was no getting out of this anymore, no intervention by the Princess that would save us, no chance of mercy or understanding. King Leopold stepped back, staggered, staring at us with quaking outrage, with pulsing fury. I took one look in his eyes, and I knew. I knew. We were done.

"I had hoped it wasn't true," Inquisitor Harkness said, turning his back to us. "I wanted to believe in this girl like you did. But after tonight, there can be no doubt. The Westerner and the Zitochi are spies, bringing poison and treason into our walls . . . and your poor daughter and nephew have been corrupted by them."

"I trusted you," King Leopold hissed. "I *defended* you."

And even in my fear and panic, I was surprised by how much it hurt to see him look at me like that, to see that paternal kindness curdle into hatred. "I'm sorry," I said, and it was all I could muster.

"What do we do now?" King Leopold asked the Inquisitor. "If my daughter's been compromised . . . turned against me . . ." A thought struck him, and he clasped a hand over his mouth. "The Ascendance Day Masquerade is in two days. We have to cancel."

"No," Molari Vale cut in. "The city is on the edge of chaos already. To cancel the holiest of festivals would light it ablaze."

"I agree with the merchant," Inquisitor Harkness said, as if he wasn't happy to be doing so. He reached out a bony hand and took King Leopold's shoulder. "I am sorry, old friend, that this happened. Truly, we live in terrible times. And yet . . . I still believe the situation may be salvageable."

"How?" King Leopold demanded, and I realized for the first time that he was crying.

"We'll discreetly detain the Princess and the Archmagus until we can be certain the influence has been removed. They'll be treated kindly and gently, eased back to loyalty. A story can be spun to explain their sudden absence. An illness, perhaps." He'd thought this all through. How long had he been planning it? "Your daughter may have drunk the Westerner's poison, but I believe, with enough time and the proper influence, her true character can be restored. The Archmagus as well."

"And the others? Tillandra and the Zitochi boy?"

Inquisitor Harkness glanced back over his shoulder, and in his face I saw not scheming or cruelty, but the calm satisfaction of being vindicated. He really believed it, I realized. He really thought he'd cracked the big case. "We'll take them to the Black Cells and torture them for everything they know," he said, "and then we'll mount their heads on the prison walls."

King Leopold looked over at me, one final time. This was the man who'd taken me in. Who'd offered me his home. Who'd defended me and protected me. Who was the closest thing to a loving father I had.

"Good," he told the Inquisitor, then turned and walked away.

TWENTY

THEY DIDN'T KNOCK US OUT OR PUT THE HOODS BACK ON our heads; why bother with secrecy when they were just going to kill us? So they just dragged us through the halls, hands still bound, and loaded us up into a bulky, undecorated Watchmen's carriage, the kind with the heavy doors in the back. If I'd had more energy, more drive, I might have tried to figure out where we were, or if there was an opening to try an escape. But it all just seemed so pointless. We were done. Beaten. Doomed.

Zell and I sat side by side on one bench in the carriage, and a pair of Shadows took up the bench opposite us. One I recognized as the man who'd interrogated me in the Watchtower, gaunt and sickly, staring at me with eyes black as nightglass. The other was an older man, lean and tall, with thickly lashed eyes and an odd asymmetry to his face, like he hadn't quite been assembled right. They stared at us in silence but kept their hands prominently on their laps, their black Rings glowing softly, ready to strike.

After a minute, the carriage took off. The Inquisitor himself took a seat up front, by the driver; I couldn't see him, but I could hear his voice, dispatching orders, calm and casual, as if he wasn't driving us to our deaths. Through the barred window, I could make out more Shadows, maybe a dozen, marching alongside us, many of them armed with swords or staves. Guess the Inquisitor didn't want to take any chances.

Zell sat next to me, and he still hadn't spoken a word. He just stared down with that distant expression, so broken he couldn't feel anymore. As the carriage bumped down the cobblestone streets, bringing us closer and closer to the prison we'd almost certainly die in, I tried to shift closer to Zell, to press my hand to his, feel his warmth, but the iron chains were too tight. "Zell," I whispered. "Zell!"

"I'm sorry," he said, not able to even look at me. "This is all my fault."

There was still so much I didn't understand. "Did you really kill Captain Welarus?"

Zell nodded, eyes shut. "I didn't mean to, but he walked in on me in his office. When he saw me with the envelope, he drew his sword and attacked. I defended myself."

"And Jonah? His son? The one who's missing?"

Zell shook his head. "I don't know anything about that. I had nothing to do with it."

That was a relief, if nothing else. "But why were you in the Captain's office at all?" I asked.

"Because I . . . I was . . ." He exhaled deeply, then turned away. "It all just got so out of hand."

"What did?" I demanded. "Zell, what are you talk—" But I never got to finish the sentence because the carriage suddenly jerked to a stop so hard it jostled all of us around in our seats. The horses snorted as they reared. The chain bit into my wrists as I lurched forward. The two Shadows riding with us glanced at each other uneasily.

"Inquisitor Harkness." It was Ellarion's voice, clear and unmistakable, coming from somewhere outside the carriage. "Release the prisoners."

I jerked around, craning my head against the window to see. The carriage was stopped in a narrow courtyard, surrounded by one-story shops and apartments. The Shadows marching alongside us had taken up defensive stances, weapons drawn, Rings glowing. And at the front of the carriage, blocking the road, were two defiant figures. Ellarion and Lyriana.

My heart surged with the sudden, unexpected rush of hope.

"Archmagus. Princess." I couldn't see Harkness, but I could hear him, and was that, at last, some uncertainty in his voice? "You know I can't do that. These are lawful prisoners of the crown. Your father sentenced them himself."

"Only because you manipulated him!" Lyriana yelled. "Did you honestly think you could pull this off? Sending your goons to detain us while you arrested our friends?"

"Apparently, I should have sent more," Harkness grumbled. The air outside crackled with incipient magic, that buzzing, terrible tension I felt through my bones. "Perhaps we can discuss this later. But right now, I'm ordering both of you to move out of the road."

"I don't give a damn what you're ordering," Ellarion said. I couldn't totally see him through the window, but there was a glow about him, like he was pulling the light clean out of the air. His voice was booming, like bottled thunder, and the earth trembled with each word. "Let them go. Now."

"I operate on orders from the King. If you stand in my way, you defy him. That's an act of treason," Harkness barked back. The surge of magic got louder, stronger. Tendrils of translucent darkness flickered around the Shadows, snakes coiled to strike. "This is your last chance, Archmagus. Get out of the road."

The two Shadows opposite us in the carriage were on the edge of their seat, braced for orders. Zell was alert now, his wrists grinding against the chain. I looked at him for some help, some guidance, but he was just as helpless as I was. I wanted Ellarion and Lyriana to fight and rescue us, but I also wanted them to run away and never look back, to not put themselves in danger for our sakes. I was breathing fast, every hair on my body standing on edge. The smell of sulfur flooded my nose, the buzzing of insects my ears. There were at least twelve Shadows on the street, and two more in the carriage. As good as Ellarion and Lyriana were, did they stand a chance?

Ellarion decided to test it. "The hell with this," he said, and took a step toward the carriage.

I don't know if Harkness gave a signal, or if a Shadow just got overeager. But one of those black tendrils lashed out across the courtyard, plunging toward Ellarion like a spear. He dodged to the side, but it scraped past his shoulder, tearing through his shirt, ripping open the skin with a bloody spray. Ellarion gasped, as much surprised as he was hurt, and then he threw his own hands forward with a roar. A concussive blast of force shot out, striking the carriage and sending it jostling roughly to the side, slamming hard into one of the building's walls. The wooden frame creaked and buckled. Splinters rained down on us. I saw a shape streak by that I'm pretty sure was Inquisitor Harkness, tumbling to the street.

I couldn't see what was happening anymore, not with the carriage smashed into the wall, but I could sure as hell hear it. Mages bellowed and grunted, and the air shuddered with the clash of magic. I could hear the sizzling whistle of streaking fireballs, and the cracking hiss of striking tendrils. I heard a voice that I think was Lyriana's cry out in pain, and felt the ground explode as Ellarion let out another roar. Stonework crumbled somewhere nearby, and hooves thundered as the horses broke free of the carriage and tore off.

I tried to lunge up, to get out, but those stupid chains kept me bound. "You have to let us out!" I shouted. "We need to help them!"

"Sit down!" the younger Shadow in the carriage commanded. He'd been cool as ice back in the interrogation room, but he looked downright terrified now. I tried to get up again, and he stood up and jabbed me in the chest, knocking me back against my seat. "Both of you stay right there! If you even think about moving, I'll—"

I never got to find out what he'd do, because the other Shadow, the older one, stood up behind him and drove a thin little dagger up to the hilt into his ear.

I screamed and jerked away, and even Zell let out a gasp. The younger Shadow stood there, stunned, a trickle of blood streaking down the side of his neck. "Huh," he said to himself, then crumpled, and lay still.

"What . . . what is . . ." I stammered, pulling back now, away from the remaining Shadow, who was just standing there calmly, like he hadn't just brutally murdered his partner. He stared at us with those odd asymmetrical eyes, and then he raised his hand in front of his face, long fingers bent in a complicated contortion. His face shimmered and rippled, like the air above stone on a hot day, but in those ripples it also seemed to fracture and reflect, as if we were seeing him on a dozen invisible mirrors. It hurt to look, like staring into the sun, but I couldn't look away, because in those weird, reflecting ripples, his face was changing, stretching, twisting, becoming something different.

The rippling stopped, and the figure in front of us wasn't a Shadow anymore, or a man for that matter. She was an older Heartlander woman with sharp cheekbones, curly gray hair, and full lips. I recognized her immediately: the woman I'd seen at the Festival, the one with the purple eyes, the one who'd Mesmered herself to look like the priest. She wasn't smiling now, though. She looked pissed. "This was supposed to be a clean rescue. We had it under control." She wiped her hands on her robe and kicked the Shadow's corpse aside. "That death's on you."

All of a sudden, this part of the puzzle, at least, made sense. "You're the Gray Priestess," I said, surprised at how much awe I felt. "The leader of the Ragged Disciples."

"Right now, I'm your one chance at staying out of the Black Cells." She pulled an iron key out of the dead Shadow's pockets and quickly opened the lock keeping Zell and me chained up. "If you want to live, you'll do everything I say."

"Okay, but—" I started, but she had no intention of hearing me out. With a firm slam of her shoulder, the Gray Priestess pushed open the carriage doors and stepped out onto the street. Zell and I fumbled after her, right into the midst of a full-on magical melee. It was a little after dawn, the sun cresting the horizon just enough to light the whole world up in soft gold, which gave the whole scene a surreally beautiful air. Lyriana and Ellarion were down the street, crouched behind a shimmering curtain of purplish light, a Shield. Two of the Shadows were knocked out, and a third was probably dead, his head a charred ruin. But the others were still up and fighting, some lashing at the Shield with those inky tendrils while others lobbed orbs of twisting darkness or sent tremors through the ground. With each hit, the Shield trembled, rippled. It couldn't hold much longer.

"Kill them!" a hoarse voice shrieked. I spun to see Inquisitor Harkness, huddled in the doorway of a nearby shop, clutching his bleeding shoulder. "Kill them all!"

The Gray Priestess was unfazed. She reached into a pocket in her robe and drew out a small silver whistle, shaped like a bull. She put it to her lips and blew, a shrill piercing shriek.

The rooftops all came alive as a dozen cultists appeared on them. Mostly men but a few women, dressed in black robes, their faces hidden behind featureless masks. And every one of them was holding a drawn bow.

Oh shit.

They fired at once, a volley of arrows streaking down into the courtyard. The Shadow closest to me caught one through the throat; the one next to him took two to the chest.

I stumbled back, throwing my hands up, like that would do anything, as the remaining Shadows turned to the rooftops, firing on their new attackers. I saw one cultist skewered on a tendril of darkness, pulled down into the street, while others drew more arrows and fired again. The melee had become a full-out war.

"Over here!" someone shouted from behind me. There, in a narrow alley between two apartments, was a young male cultist frantically waving at us. "Run this way! Now!" He pulled down his mask, revealing his ruddy cheeks, his sparking green eyes. Marlo. "Seriously, Tilla! Run!"

Horns of distress thundered out from nearby. The City Watch would be here soon, and then it would be too late. I glanced to Zell, who nodded, and then at Lyriana and Ellarion, still huddled behind their Shield. In that moment, I think all four of us made the same calculation. The Ragged Disciples were a big dangerous unknown . . . but right now, they were a hell of a lot better than being captured by the Inquisitor.

With the Shadows distracted battling the cultists, Ellarion dropped the Shield, and he and Lyriana sprinted toward us, crossing the courtyard and passing the smashed carriage. A single Shadow tried to stop them, and Ellarion dropped him with a devastating punch, his fist turning, for just a moment, into a ball of stone. The four of us ran, along with the Gray Priestess, into the alley, moving in tight single file over the damp stone. "This way! Follow me!" Marlo yelled. He led us through the alley, around a corner into another one, and then a pair of cultists emerged from where they were waiting, covering our tracks with surprising efficiency by sliding a heavy cart, piled high with hay, into that alley's entrance. I could still hear fighting as we moved, but it was growing fainter, now just the occasional distant scream or crackle.

"Sentinel!" a voice bellowed from above. I looked up to see a Sentinel all right, one of the Inquisitor's spy-birds, streaking over us with its veiny, leathery wings spread wide. Its hideous vulture face stared down at us, and its third eye, the big, bloody red one in the center of its head, pulsed and throbbed like a beating heart. It let out a truly ugly sound, somewhere between a caw and a croak and a gargle.

Then an arrow whistled through the air and caught it right in the center of its chest. With an undignified squawk, it tumbled in the air and dropped like a stone. I turned to the rooftop of the nearest building, where there were even more of the black-clad cultists, running in parallel after us. An exceptionally burly one pulled down his mask for a moment to reveal the face of Garrus, Marlo's boyfriend, and Marlo grinned.

"Here," the Priestess said, and pulled us into a door toward the end of the alley. We were in a small room now, cluttered with dusty boxes and billowing spiderwebs. It looked like a third-rate storage room to me, without anywhere to run, but the Priestess sure seemed to think it was the right place. She hunkered down in the center of the room and slid her long fingers into a crack in the floor. Marlo ran over to join her, and together the two heaved an uneven round tile away, revealing a hole leading down into murky darkness.

"We're going . . . there?" Lyriana asked.

"Oh, you'd prefer to let the Inquisitor capture you?" the Priestess replied, and even now it was shocking to hear someone be so openly sarcastic to the Princess. "By all means, stay if you'd like."

Which of course we weren't going to do, but she didn't have to be a dick about it. Marlo reached behind one of the boxes to reveal a thick, securely tied rope, and tossed it down into the hole. "After you."

I looked at the faces of my friends, who looked equal parts apprehensive and bewildered. But what were we gonna do? As sketchy as this seemed, as politically questionable, we didn't have a choice. The Inquisitor had taken that from us.

Marlo went first, followed by Zell, then Ellarion and Lyriana, and last myself and the Priestess. I hadn't slid down a rope since I was fourteen and sneaking out of my bedroom to drink with Jax, so I was a little worried I'd end up slipping and taking the whole group down with me. Luckily, it was a short climb, maybe twenty feet, and when we hit the stone floor below, a cultist up top slid the stone covering back into place, leaving us in total darkness. Lyriana shuffled around and a ball of Light appeared, floating alongside us like a helpful companion. In its warm white glow, I could make out where we were: an underground tunnel, wide enough for us all to stand in a row and almost double my height. The walls were made of smooth, carved stone, ingrained with strange symbols and lined with rusted brass pipes. It reminded me of the tunnels at Castle Waverly, but where those had been crumbling and rocky, tombs of a lost era, these were in excellent shape, like they'd been built to last for centuries.

"Now, then," the Priestess said, "we're going to want to walk this w—"

But before she could finish, Ellarion sprang forward. He wrapped one hand around her throat, slamming her back into the wall, and made an intricate spiraling motion with the other, which caused it to burst into dazzling red-and-blue fire. Marlo yelled in surprise, but Lyriana held him back, and Ellarion brought his hand so close to the Priestess's face that the licks of the flames were almost kissing her cheek. "A mage leading the Ragged Disciples," he said with disgust. "I thought I'd seen everything, but hey, it's nice to know I can still be surprised." He squeezed tighter. "Give me one good reason I shouldn't kill you here and now."

"My *name* is Lorelia Imarolin," she hissed back, and if there was any fear in her eyes, I didn't see it. "And if I die, you will never, ever see the surface again."

"Ellarion." I reached out to grab his shoulder, gently pulling him back. "You saw how many men she had up there. And now we're down here, in her turf. I think . . . I think we should hear her out."

He glanced back at me, eyes burning. "Hear her out," he repeated. "The woman who started a cult just to attack my family. The woman who preaches that we're thieves and monsters, that we should all be killed."

"The woman who just saved our lives."

Ellarion took that in, and with a deep, nostril-flaring exhale, let her go. His fire extinguished, and the Priestess, Lorelia, slid back down onto her feet, rubbing at her neck with one lean hand. Her arms were thin, bony, with strange round bruises all along her forearms. "I can't say that was the most pleasant greeting, Archmagus, but I suppose I'll give you another chance."

"Why did you save us?" Lyriana asked. "What is this all about?"

"And here I thought you were supposed to be brilliant,"

255

Lorelia said, and I'd swear it sounded like she was kind of enjoying this. "Come, now. I'll tell you all about it, but we have to get moving. The others will need to know the mission was a success." She gestured with one hand toward the dark tunnel stretching before us. "Now, then. Zell, you remember the way?"

"What?" I blinked. "Why would Zell know the way? And how do you know Zell?" I turned to Zell for some kind of explanation, but he just stared away . . . guiltily? Was that guilt?

Lorelia cocked her head to the side. "Why, Zell—you haven't told them?"

No reply.

"Zell," Lorelia repeated, harder, a teacher chastising a tardy student. "Tell them."

"I . . ." Zell started, but he didn't have to finish, because the truth hit me in a rush, like a wave crashing onto a beach and washing away all the pretty little sandcastles that had been built up. I staggered back, and my chest felt tight and my knees felt weak, because of course. Of course. It all made sense now, didn't it? Zell's strange detachment . . . his odd absences . . . his anger at the nobles . . . even the question of what he'd been doing in Welarus's office.

The Inquisitor hadn't been totally off the mark. I wasn't a spy, helping a group that committed treason against the King.

But Zell was.

"You've been helping the Ragged Disciples," Lyriana said quietly, and Ellarion just shook his head in silent anger.

Screw that. There was nothing silent about how I was feeling. "All this time." I stepped toward him, and he still wouldn't look at me, and oh, by the Old Kings, did that piss me off. "All this time, you've been working for them . . . and you didn't think to tell me? You didn't think that little detail was worth sharing?" I poked him in the shoulder. "You didn't think to say, 'Oh, by the way, Tilla, I'm helping the outlaw cult who's trying to overthrow the King, just thought you should know'?" I poked him again, harder. "Look at me, asshole! Talk to me! Tell me it isn't true! Tell me you haven't been lying to me this entire time!"

I started to poke him again, but his hand shot out and caught my wrist. His head swiveled to me, and his eyes met mine, and for the first time in what had to be months, they were totally, openly honest. "Yes," he said. "I've been lying to you. I've been lying to all of you for months. I've been helping the Ragged Disciples. I'm their spy in the City Watch. This is who I am. Who I've become."

He jerked away, turning his back on me sharply, and even though I was the one who was supposed to be angry at him, it still somehow hurt. In all our time together, he'd never treated me like that . . . but how much of it had been a lie? What else was he lying about?

"Well!" Lorelia clapped her hands together, breaking the silence. "I'll admit, this has certainly played out more dramatically than I'd anticipated, but now really isn't the time to work out your romantic squabbles. I must insist we get moving, before our absence causes any alarm."

It took all the willpower I had not to tell her to go screw herself, but I managed to hold it down.

"Sure," I said, swallowing down that rage, that hurt, and gestured to the tunnel before us. "Lead the way, *Zell*."

TWENTY-ONE

THE SHAFT LED ON AT A SLIGHT DOWNWARD TILT, TAKING us deeper and deeper below the city. Zell didn't say another word on our long walk, and in a way, I was grateful. I wanted so badly to hash this out with him, but I wanted to do it in private, away from Lyriana and Ellarion and their worried eyes. So I walked in silence instead, and let the others do the talking.

"So," Ellarion said, his voice low and cautious. "You're a mage. A Maid of Alleja."

"A mage, yes, but not a Maid," Lorelia answered. "I've never been part of any order."

"Bullshit."

"Life's strange, isn't it?" she replied, like that was an answer. "I was born in the Iron Circle, the daughter of a seamstress and a tailor. No one in my family had ever been magical, and sure enough, neither was I. I took the test for it when I turned six, of course, like all the other children, and the mages sent me home, saying I was just a common girl. And, you know, truthfully? It wasn't so bad." She shrugged. "I apprenticed under my mother. I became quite a skilled seamstress. I took over her business when her hands became too frail, and did a damn good job at it. I married a decent man." A wistful smile crossed her face. "And I had a son. Petrello was his name. A beautiful boy, my sun and moon, the light of my life."

I was already not a fan of this past tense.

"I would have been content living like that for the rest of my life. I had a house, a job, a family. But Petrello had big dreams. He wanted to change the world, to bring justice and fairness, to feed the poor and help the oppressed. I thought it was charming, if naive. I assumed he'd grow out of it." She sighed. "But he didn't get the chance. When Petrello was fifteen, he got involved with a group of other young people that believed they could make a difference. They led a protest outside the city gates, demanding that the food stores be distributed to the starving poor in the Rusted Circle. It was meant to be peaceful. I believe that."

"I remember this," Lyriana said. "A riot broke out, didn't it? Several people were killed. . . ."

"They brought in the mages to break it up," Lorelia said, and that wistfulness was gone, replaced by something colder, something harder. "We still don't know who started the fight. They claim the protestors threw a rock, but I doubt it. The mages scorched the crowd with waves of fire. Fifteen protestors, peaceful young people doing no harm, were burned alive."

"Your son . . ."

Lorelia closed her eyes. "They brought him to me, clinging

to the barest vestiges of life. I held him as he died. He cried out for his mother, for me, even though I was right there."

We were all quiet for a moment. "I'm so sorry," Lyriana said at last.

"Oh, many people were sorry," Lorelia said bitterly. "But I didn't need their pity or their support or their assurances that life would go on. I needed my boy back." There was an anger in her voice, a rage simmering below the steady tone. It reminded me of my father, the way he sounded when he'd talked about the injustices done to our family. "Every time I saw a mage, my heart burned with fury. I stopped going to the temple, unable to tolerate the priests singing their prayers. My husband begged me to move on, but I couldn't. I had too much anger. Too much hate."

"You fled," Lyriana said.

"I traveled the world," she replied. "Saw the Southlands, the Baronies, even spent some time in the West." She glanced at me like, what, that gave us a common bond? "But no matter where I went, I could find no peace, no relief. Everywhere I went, I saw only the oppression of the Volaris, the lies of the church. I gave up hope. So I returned here, to my home, to the place where my beautiful boy died. And I swallowed a glass of nightblossom and hurled myself into the river." She said it so calmly, like this was the most common thing in the world. "There, in the depths of the Adelphus, I had a vision. I saw a Titan, a woman, her skin smooth as marble, her face ageless and beautiful. She told me the truth behind the Volaris. That they were thieves and plunderers. That the Heavenly Mandate is a lie. That this entire city is a towering monument to injustice."

At her words, Marlo closed his eyes reverently, pressing a closed fist to his chest as he whispered a prayer.

Ellarion was having none of it. "Nightblossom is known to cause hallucinations. That's probably all that happened."

Lorelia ignored him. "The Titan told me that she'd spare my life if I swore my service to her, to spreading the true gospel, the true word of the Titans. I was to be their prophet, the one who opens the eyes of the deceived, to pave the way for their glorious Return." She nodded, smiling again. "I swore to serve her. And so I lived, waking up miraculously unharmed on the banks just outside the city. But now, now I had a purpose."

The tunnels seemed to be growing wider, more polished. What was this place?

"I gave up my old life, my old name," Lorelia went on. "Instead, I sought out the others like me. The outcasts. The rebels. The downtrodden. The heretics. And there were many, so so many, once I knew where to look. I spread the word to them, and they spread the word to others, and it spread through the gutters and the shelters and the alleys like a raging fire. The kindling had always been there. It just needed my spark to set it alight. Soon, people from all over the city were coming to find me, to hear my gospel, to join my church."

"You make it sound so noble," Ellarion said. "But you didn't just found some benign little prayer circle. Your cultists deface temples. They shatter shrines and burn ships and attack festivals. They wreak anarchy in our streets."

"I do only what I promised the Titans," Lorelia said. "I challenge injustice. I attack the corrupt, the lying, the unjust. My followers strike, yes, but only at the wicked usurpers who loot the Titans' secrets to enrich themselves. At the corpulent nobles who live in decadence while the people of this city starve."

"That's my family you're talking about," Lyriana said, with just a hint of hesitation in her defense. "My father." I knew she often doubted the King's choices, and that she'd joined the Sisters of Kaia as a sort of rebuke to his rule. But he was still her *father*.

"Your father just sentenced your best friend to be tortured to death," Lorelia replied coldly. "They would have flayed every inch of skin off her bones, and torn her mind in half." She let out a long, slow sigh, perhaps realizing she was scaring the shit out of me. "Look. I know you may not approve of my choices. But the truth is, I'm acting to protect you. To save not just your lives, but your very souls."

"Yeah, well, you've got a lot more you need to explain," Ellarion grumbled. "Let's start with that Mesmering."

Lorelia smiled, her face crinkled as her eyes flashed a simmering purple. "For four years, I served the Titans. I heeded their call, spread their word, and built this church. And three months ago, they rewarded me for my service." She waved her hand idly at the wall, and the stone writhed to form a man's grinning face, which was cool because now I'd have nightmares about it for weeks. "One morning, I awoke, and I could simply do this. I never learned or studied. I was simply . . . blessed. This power I have . . . this is the Titans' reward. Their gift to me, that I might see their mission to its end."

Ellarion and Lyriana shared a skeptical glance. "So you're a late Awakener. It happens sometimes," the Archmagus said, but his voice betrayed his uncertainty. "It doesn't mean anything."

Lorelia shrugged. "You can deny the river is surging even when the water is up to your ankles. But when the flood comes, it will sweep you away all the same."

"Can I ask a question?" I said, before realizing there was no good reason to ask permission. "I don't know what Zell's told you, but all kinds of weird things have been happening to us. My friend Markiska was killed, and the pearls of her necklace were sent to Molari Vale and Captain Welarus for some reason. And I was attacked, kidnapped, and beat up by this guy, this Zitochi mercenary who could do this magic where he was, like, blinking around. Which of course, doesn't make sense because everyone tells me Zitochi can't do magic, but you also couldn't do magic, and now you can, so . . ." I took a deep breath. "Do you have any idea what's going on with any of that?"

Lorelia stopped and turned, staring at me like I'd just vomited a swarm of bees. Marlo, standing next to her, seemed equally confused. "No," she said. "I have absolutely no idea what you're talking about."

Phenomenal.

We were nearing the end of the tunnel, which led to a wall with a thick set of stone doors. Lyriana and Ellarion both went quiet as we approached, and I realized they were looking at the carvings on them, which showed massive figures, their broad arms reaching to the sky, their smooth faces smiling placidly. A pair of men stood in front of the doors, holding heavy clubs, and they bowed their heads in deference as we approached, fists clenched to their hearts.

"So, this is what, the secret headquarters of the Ragged Disciples?" Ellarion asked.

"I suppose so," Lorelia said, as the guards threw open the doors. "But I'd like to think it's a little more than that."

"Titans' Breath," Lyriana gasped, and I clasped a hand over my mouth. Because behind those doors was an absolutely massive chamber, a huge circular room as big as Mercanto Plaza, with a domed ceiling towering ten stories above. The whole room was made of the same smooth, clean stone as the tunnel we'd come through, and it was lit up with hundreds of hanging Luminae, dangling from a spiderweb of chains that hung under the ceiling. The door we'd come through was just one of many lining the walls.

And in this massive chamber was a *full-blown compound*. There were at least twenty buildings down here, maybe more, crammed together tightly like fruit in an overstuffed basket. The one at the center was the biggest, a round three-story structure made of sturdy brick that I'm guessing was the heart of this place. The buildings all around it were smaller, flimsier, a few no more than glorified tents, but they all seemed to serve their own purpose. One was a lodging, I figured, based on the rows and rows of beds. Another was a market, a cluster of rickety stands offering fish and textiles and questionable-looking fruit. Carts laden down with goods sat on the outskirts, as black-robed workers distributed them to the crowds. I could smell cooking meat and sizzling vegetables, and hear, just barely above the cacophony of voices, the distant rushing of a canal. People bustled through the streets of this inexplicable little village, just going about their everyday lives: a man hanging out his clothes to dry on the roof of his shack, a trio of women sharing a meal, a pair of young men practicing with wooden swords.

"What?" I gaped. "Where are we?"

Lorelia just smiled. "Welcome to the Undercity."

She kept walking and we followed, staring around with our jaws hanging open in disbelief. The thing I couldn't wrap my head around, what just made no sense, was how normal it all seemed. Here was a one-room schoolhouse with a group of children seated in a circle, taking lessons from a teacher. Here was a long, sturdy building that had to be a tavern. Here was a green-glass dome with a garden inside, the carrots and potatoes growing in the light of those expensive sunlight-capturing lanterns. A trio of armed men passed us, bowing their heads at the sight of Lorelia. Mangy-looking cats stalked the rooftops overhead.

The place was run-down, no doubt about that, rougher than even the roughest districts I'd seen. People's clothes were tattered and stained, the ground was littered with trash, and half of the buildings looked flimsy enough that they'd fall over in a strong breeze. But still, just the existence of this place was amazing. It was a village—a tiny, poor village but a village nonetheless—hidden below the very streets I'd been walking on for months.

"How is this possible?" Ellarion said. "What *is* this place?"

"The Catacomb of the Titans," Lyriana answered, her voice distant. "Don't you remember your scripture, cousin? The Testimony of Mattiato, Passage 36. 'For the great city of the Titans reached up to the heights of the Heavens above . . .'"

"'And into the furthest depths of the earth below,'" Ellarion finished. "I always thought that part was just metaphor."

I had no idea what scripture they were citing, but I could

figure it out. Lightspire had been the city of the Titans, their capital when they'd walked among men, but when they Ascended, all the buildings had collapsed save the Godsblade. But what if they hadn't been built just up, but also *down*? If the architects of Castle Waverly had thought to build the tunnels, why wouldn't the Titans have built their equivalent? And if the Titans' buildings were shimmersteel beauties that dwarfed our tallest towers, how deep did their underground pathways really go?

I wished Jax was with me to see this place, the tunnels to end all tunnels. He would've loved it.

"We call the tunnels here the Great Maze," Lorelia boasted, like she'd been the one who'd built them. "These passageways and chambers run below the whole city and go down, way, way down. Most of them are sealed off, but enough remain to move around unknown, to shelter those in need. In truth, I suspect we've only seen the very tip of what lies below."

"Trust me, it's better that way," Marlo chimed in. "I've got a few buddies who've gone exploring. They say there's all kinds of scary shit that lives down here."

Lorelia shot him an annoyed glance, but kept her tone civil. "It's one of the ways we've managed to keep this place a secret for so long. The Maze is massive, confounding, and full of dangers. Exploring even a fraction of it would take all the Inquisitor's men."

"How many people live down here?" Lyriana asked, staring at a mother with a baby pressed to her breast.

"Just under a hundred," Lorelia answered.

"And no one knows about it?"

"Oh, people know about it." Marlo grinned. "Just not you

fancy-pantses in the Golden Circle. For those of us in the Iron Circle, it's a legend, a rumor, a dream . . . till someone shows you the way in."

"This is a home for outcasts," Lorelia continued. "For rebels and fugitives, for free-thinkers and exiles, for wanderers and bastards. For all those who have no place in the Kingdom, nowhere to hide under the Volaris' rule . . . we offer shelter."

"So long as they worship you," Ellarion said.

"So long as they accept the truth," Lorelia replied.

We were nearing the tall, round structure at the center. This was definitely the most important building; guards stood around the entrance, holding massive spears, and murals of the Titans adorned the walls. "My inner sanctum," Lorelia explained. "My home, my temple, my war room. This is where I live. And where you'll stay for the time being." She gestured up toward the top of the builidng. "We have a few spare rooms on the top floor. I'll arrange for you four to stay in them, and make sure any needs you have are met."

"How exactly do you see this playing out?" Ellarion asked, his fist clenching and unclenching at his side. "You put us up in a nice room, send us wine and cheese, we all get along, and decide hey, maybe we oughta join the cult that's trying to kill our family and burn down our Kingdom? You really think that's gonna work?"

Lorelia turned back. Her lips were smiling, but her eyes were ice. "You cut to the point. I appreciate that. So let me cut to the point as well." She gestured with a hand behind her back, and the guards outside leveled their spears at us. "You are welcome to stay in the sanctum. But you are not free to leave."

"We're hostages. A bargaining chip to use with the King."

Lorelia laughed. "It's true. There are many down here who would prefer to see you killed, your heads left on the Godsblade steps as an example. But I don't think that's what the Titans would want." She looked out at the city around her. "You are nobles. Powerful. Influential. And I believe, in your hearts, still reachable. I'd love to see you join my church, to embrace the truth. So I offer you my hospitality, or as much hospitality as I reasonably can. But don't test me." Her eyes narrowed, and in that moment, it was like she was a different woman, one far harder, colder, meaner. "A company of my best men will be stationed with you at all times. If you try to leave, or pass along a message, or do anything else in any way suspicious . . . If I so much as see a spark of magic from any of you . . . my generosity will be revoked. And you will quickly discover that the dungeon here is far less hospitable. Do we have an understanding?"

"Crystal clear," Ellarion muttered, with more defeat than defiance.

"Good." Then she spun and walked away, her robe billowing behind her like a cape, leaving us with just Marlo and the armed guards to show us to our rooms. I turned back to Lyriana and Ellarion and Zell, who all had the same stunned, am-I-dreaming look that I'm sure I did.

"So," I said. "Here we are."

TWENTY-TWO

TRUE TO LORELIA'S WORD, MY ROOM WAS PRETTY DAMN NICE. I mean, not as nice as my room in the Godsblade, obviously, or even my room back at Castle Waverly, but it had a bed and a pillow and a blanket, and really, that was all I needed. I sat there for a while, fuming and then forced myself up. There was no way around this. No more stalling. I had to talk to Zell.

Marlo was waiting outside my door in a chair, which had to be the most boring job ever. "Hey," he said at the sight of me, giving an awkward little wave. "I, uh, hope there's no hard feelings."

"About the whole 'your cult took me hostage' thing?" I replied. "Let's say between that and saving my life, we're even."

"Seems like a fair deal."

Even if I'd wanted to, I couldn't stay mad at Marlo. "Any idea where my friends are?"

"The Princess and the Archmagus are in their rooms.

Your Zitochi boy is on the roof." He cleared his throat nervously. "I imagine you have some questions for him."

"That I do," I said, and made my way down the hall and up a narrow flight of stairs, toward a door that led out onto the inner sanctum's roof. There was something profoundly disorienting about being on a roof but still inside, but here we were. I glanced up at the chamber's massive domed ceiling above me, and from up here I could make out the details on it more clearly, distant inlaid carvings in that blocky Titan style. What was the point of this place, anyway? What did the Titans do down here? Castle Waverly's tunnels were for sneaking around undetected, for flanking intruders and laying ambushes, but the Titans wouldn't have had any need of that . . . would they?

Those thoughts left my head the second I looked down and saw Zell. He was sitting on the edge of the roof, his feet dangling over, gazing out at the cluster of shacks before him. He was wearing just a pair of cloth pants and a thin white undershirt, the low collar revealing the taut muscles of his back. His broad hands rested on the roof's lip, clenching tight, the nightglass blades on his knuckles sparkling in the flickering light of the Luminae overhead.

I took one step, and his head perked up. "Tilla."

"Yup. It's me," I said, and all at once, words failed me. How was I this nervous, this awkward? This scared? "We need to talk."

His voice was choked, like he was forcing the words out through a cage. "I don't even know what to say."

I paced over and took a seat by his side, and we stared out at the Undercity together. Eye contact was just too much.

"Why don't you start by telling me the whole truth? When did you start working for the Ragged Disciples?"

"Two months ago."

"Two months . . ." I repeated. Two months he'd been lying to me. All that time we'd spent together, talking, cuddling, worrying, he'd had this massive secret and hidden it. It made me angry, but so much deeper than that, it hurt, that he could have looked me in the eyes, said the things he said, and just been lying all the while. Did he not trust me? Could I ever trust him? "How?" I finally got out. "Why?"

"I didn't plan on it," Zell said, and there it was, the tiniest hint of a tremble. "I never wanted to hide anything from you. I never wanted to lie. It just . . . It all got out of hand."

"What did?" I repeated, maybe angrier than I would have liked. "Would you just tell me the whole story? Please?"

Before I throw you off this roof?

Zell closed his eyes and arched back his head with a deep inhale. "I never wanted to be in the City Watch. You know that. But it was my only way to stay here, to be with you. So I accepted the duty. And for a few months, it wasn't bad. Training the recruits, rounding up drunks, helping with the occasional raid on a glitter-dust den . . . It wasn't the most challenging work, but it was still honorable. I was helping people. Keeping the peace. The Twelve would have smiled on that." His eyes flitted to me, for just a second. "And I had you."

"What changed?"

"After a few months, Captain Welarus called me into his office. He'd seen me do enough good work that he wanted my help on a special assignment. One he needed my 'unique skills' for. At first, I thought this might be my chance to do some real good. Then I discovered exactly what sort of man Welarus was." Zell's face darkened, his brow furrowing as he stared out across the city. "He took me to a warehouse in Moldmarrow where he met with three local criminal leaders. They were to pay him a weekly sum, and in exchange, he would permit their activities to continue. One of them had been refusing to pay up." He paused, like the words were causing him literal pain. "Welarus had me break his arm."

I'll admit, this is not where I thought the conversation would go. I mean, it wasn't a total surprise; Welarus had been a surly scumbag, so it wasn't that much of a stretch to also imagine him as corrupt. But I couldn't wrap my mind around the idea of Zell being a willing accomplice. "Why didn't you report him?"

"He told me that if I talked, no one would believe me. That no one would take the word of a Zitochi exile over a decorated Captain. That he'd make sure you and I were both implicated, our reputations ruined. We'd be exiled . . . or worse."

Given how quickly everything fell apart for us, I could believe that. "Fine. I get that. But why didn't you tell *me*?"

"I was going to. I had it all planned out. And then . . . do you remember the night of the Harvest Parade?"

I remembered dancing my ass off on a float shaped like a seahorse, but I didn't think that's what he was getting at. "What about it?"

"That was the day after Welarus dragged me into his dealings. I went to your room to tell you. And then . . ." He paused, and an unexpected expression crossed his face, wistful and longing and achingly sad. "And then you came out to see me. You were wearing that dress Lyriana got you, the violet one with the ribbons on the back and the buttons shaped like butterflies. She'd done your hair too, like a Heartlander, with those three overlapping braids. You looked so beautiful, for a second I couldn't even breathe, like I was looking at a goddess made flesh." He shook his head. "I was still going to tell you. But then I looked at you at the parade. You were with Lyriana and Markiska, and the three of you were dancing by a band. You were all laughing and smiling, and you just looked so happy, so radiant." His eyes glistened, just barely. "I'd never seen you like that before. Like you were in the place where you wanted to be. Like you were actually content and relaxed and safe. Like you had the life you deserved. After everything you've been through, I couldn't bear to take that from you. I couldn't shatter your happiness. So I decided this was my burden to bear alone."

"Zell," I said, and oh, were my feelings a mess. Because I could see the pain in him, pain that made my heart hurt, and I felt guilt and sadness that I'd missed it, that I'd let him suffer it alone, that I'd been so swept up in my own life I hadn't seen what he was hiding from me. But I also felt anger, real anger, at his stoic masculine bullshit, at his need to protect me, at the idea that my happiness was some fragile little snowflake that had to be shielded at all cost.

"For a while, I just did whatever odd jobs Welarus asked of me. Sometimes it meant picking up shipments late at night, or looking tough at his side. A few times, I had to rough some-one up." He closed his eyes. "I tried to soothe my conscience. I donated my money to the needy, and prayed daily for Rhikura's forgiveness. It was almost enough."

"You could have told me. I would have understood."

"Then it all fell apart," Zell went on. "Welarus caught a member of the Ragged Disciples preaching his gospel. The man wouldn't talk, but Welarus had this idea that if he could get the man to give up the Gray Priestess, he'd impress the Inquisitor and earn a promotion. So he told me to torture him." Zell paused, swallowing his breath, forcing the words out. "And I did. I broke every bone in the man's hand, while he screamed and begged. I forced his head into a bucket of water, and only let him out when he gasped and gagged. And still . . . he wouldn't talk."

I looked away. I felt sick. And I didn't want to judge him, I didn't want to loathe him, but I also couldn't accept it, couldn't believe Zell, my Zell, would do a thing like that.

"That night . . . as I tortured that man who'd done nothing worse than pray to the wrong church . . . I was no better than my brother. No better than Razz." A silence hung over us, and I almost wanted him to stop there, because I couldn't bear to hear any more.

But still, Zell went on. "The guilt was overwhelming. I couldn't live with myself. I hated myself so much, Tilla, hated everything I'd become. So I broke into the barracks, and I let that man out. Made it look like he'd escaped. Welarus blamed the night watchman, and didn't think to question me," he said. "A few days later, a Whisper arrived. Inside the envelope there was an address for a warehouse in Rooksbin, and the symbol of the Disciples. And even though I knew I shouldn't, I went there. I felt like . . . like I had to. Like if I didn't, I'd be damned."

"And you joined them," I said. "Became . . . what? A Disciple?"

"I don't share their faith," Zell clarified. "The Titans, mages, the Priestess, none of that is for me. The Twelve teach that all Southborn magic is corruption, and I see no reason to doubt that."

"So you just work for them."

Zell nodded. "I was their spy inside the Watch. I gave them our patrol routes, and tipped them off to our raids. I protected their people from harm."

"You're a traitor, Zell. A double agent." It was just still so hard to wrap my mind around. Zell had his flaws, sure, like we all did. But I never would've thought him capable of deception or disloyalty. Not like this.

"I see the good these Disciples do, Tilla. Sheltering the poor. Feeding the hungry. Challenging corruption, corruption I'd been a part of. I didn't have to worship their Priestess to believe they do the right thing." Now he looked at me, right at me. "I thought I could have both worlds. I could keep you happy and safe, let you live the life you'd dreamed of. And I could serve the Twelve by undoing the works of Welarus from within, by dedicating myself to fighting for something greater, something better."

"You could have told me, Zell. You could have brought me in. You could have shared this burden with me . . . and I would have helped you carry it."

He turned away, gazing down at the city. "I couldn't risk it. This whole world was too dangerous. If I pulled you in and we got caught, you'd be killed. I couldn't risk it."

"No. *No.* Don't give me that bullshit," I said, and I'd never talked to him like this, but I didn't care. "You were scared, Zell. You were scared I'd judge you. Scared of what I'd think.

Scared I'd leave you. And that's fine. I get why you'd be scared. But don't you try to play this as protecting me." The words were spilling out now, a burst dam that could never be mended. "You could have told me. You could have brought me into your life. You could have trusted me like I always trusted you. But you didn't, Zell. You went through this whole profound crisis of faith, this whole big personal journey, and you kept me totally in the dark. You lied *to my face*, Zell. You lied while you held me in your arms."

"You kissed Ellarion. You never told me about that," he rebutted, which sucked the words right out of my throat. His voice wasn't angry, just flat, calm, like he'd already armored himself up past the point of pain. "You've kept secrets from me too. I know that much."

"I . . . I didn't . . . That was different!" I stammered, and yes, it was different in a way, but I knew I was feeling so pissed because it *was* kind of the same, wasn't it? I'd hid the truth because I didn't want to deal with the conversations, because I put my own care ahead of honesty. I hadn't told him about Ellarion, just like I hadn't told him about my first interrogation with the Shadow, like I hadn't told him about my constant anxiety and fear, about how I was terrified of losing him, of losing everyone. Even as I'd fumed at Zell's walls, I'd built up my own.

"Look." I took a deep breath. "I kissed Ellarion to distract Molari's servant. That's it, I swear. And I didn't tell you about it . . . or about other things . . . because I was afraid. That was wrong of me. I'll . . . I'll admit that." So why didn't I feel better? Why didn't it feel the same? "But those things all happened recently. In all this chaos and horror. You lied to me *for months*, Zell."

"I wanted you to be happy."

"But I *wasn't* happy," I replied, and that was the truth, wasn't it, the truth I'd been denying myself for months, the truth behind every single anxious moment I'd had since I'd set foot in this city. I wasn't happy pretending to be someone else. I wasn't happy without my brother. And I wasn't happy with Zell, not with this chasm between us, not with his secrecy, not with his lies. "I'm not even sure I *can* be happy anymore. But I could have stood by you. I could have figured this out with you. I could've joined you in your cause." I shook my head. "But you lied to me. You closed that door before I could even consider going through it. You didn't trust me, Zell, and in your whole big quest for fairness and equality, you didn't think to treat *me* fairly. To treat me like an equal." Now my eyes were burning with tears, and my voice was ragged in my throat. "And that fucking hurts."

He didn't say anything for a while, just stared out, his eyes wet, his breathing hard. "So what happens now?" he asked.

"I don't know," I said, and by the Old Kings, how could I feel so much? I wanted to hurt him and to hold him, to kiss him and kill him, to forgive him and never look at him again. It was too much, just too much, and I couldn't deal with it. "I need to go. I need to get away. I can't do this now."

I stood up, and even as I did, all I really wanted was for him to reach out and grab me, to make this better, to say the words, whatever they were, that I needed to hear. But he didn't grab me, and he didn't say anything. He just sat there, looking out, looking broken, like a man swallowed by the pain he couldn't stop raging inside. And maybe it made me a bad person, but I couldn't take it, not now, not anymore. He was drowning, and if I stayed, I'd just drown with him.

"I'm going to go," I said, and I turned away and walked off, using every ounce of willpower I had to force myself not to look back.

TWENTY-THREE

I STORMED BACK DOWN THE HALL, THOUGHTS RACING SO fast it felt like my head would burst. Was this seriously it? Had I just ended things with Zell? I mean, I couldn't have. I loved him, loved him so much. The idea that we were just done was inconceivable. But so was the idea of going back to him, of being with him again, of somehow finding the love behind this aching wound.

I practically slammed into my door, throwing it wide open. Ellarion was there, inexplicably, and he jumped backward with a fumble. "Titans' Breath!" he barked. "You scared the hell out of me."

"I . . . I just . . . I . . ." I tried, but the words weren't coming. I realized that I probably looked terrible: unwashed, my hair a mess, my eyes red and puffy. I also realized that I didn't care. "What are you doing here?"

"I came by to see if you wanted to grab a drink." He cocked his head to the side to get a good long look at me.

"But I'm pretty sure the answer to that is going to be a resounding yes."

I wiped my eyes with the back of my hand. "Please. Now. All the drinks."

Lyriana was napping, so that left the two of us. Marlo led us down the stairs to the back room on the first floor of the sanctum, its canteen. Honestly, even calling it a canteen was a stretch: it was a half dozen empty tables arranged around a long bar, manned by a single bored-looking man and offering a choice of "yarvo" or "good yarvo." Still, it seemed to fit the bill, because the three of us slumped over to a table. "Three goblets of the good yarvo," Ellarion called out.

"Oh, I probably shouldn't drink," Marlo said, in the tone of someone who actually really wants to drink.

But Ellarion wasn't biting. "I was ordering for me."

The goblets came out (and one more for me), and Ellarion took a long, gulping draught. "So," he said, turning my way, "I take it you and Zell had a talk."

"Mmmm," I said. I'd come out here because the idea of getting a drink beat sitting alone in my room, but it turns out I really didn't feel ready to talk about it. Or anything for that matter.

"Guessing it didn't go well."

I lifted my goblet and took a drink. It tasted flat and a little over-spiced, but it was still getting me buzzed, and right now, I needed that. "You could say that."

"He lied to us. To our faces. I have half a mind to beat him senseless." Ellarion raised the goblet to his lips and took another big swig. "But what does it matter?" He gestured around angrily. "Looks like we're all cultists now."

He slammed his goblet down, and I noticed it was empty. That was not a small amount of yarvo. "You, uh, you doing all right, Ellarion?"

"Am I doing all right?" he repeated, lifting the second goblet to his lips. "Let's see. Yesterday morning, I was training to be the Archmagus, living the height of luxury, and genuinely believed I was about to uncover a conspiracy against the King. Today, I got attacked in the street by the Inquisitor, I'm hiding in an underground village, and the only people willing to protect me just so happen to be the cultists who see me as the embodiment of all evil. Does that cover everything?"

"It's pretty thorough, yeah."

Ellarion turned to Marlo, and he had a slight lilt, a clumsy wobble that told me the yarvo was already hitting. When was the last time we'd eaten, anyway? What *time* was it? "Hey. You. Cultist."

Marlo shifted back uneasily in his seat. There was a weird tension in there, the shifting frictions of an uneasy power dynamic. We were the hostages, and Marlo was our guard, which put him in charge—but Ellarion was still the Archmagus. And I was pretty sure that even without his Rings, he could level half this block before anyone stopped him. "Yes?"

Ellarion squinted. "Lorelia. Your Gray Priestess. You actually believe everything she has to say?"

"She has been blessed by the Titans and seen through the veil," Marlo said, as if it were inconceivable that anyone would *not* believe her. "She is our mother, our savior, our blessed light. She's given us, all of us, a real chance."

"A real chance at *what*?" Ellarion growled, and there was

the second goblet emptied on the table. "At seeing all the royal mages strung up in the streets? At seeing the Godsblade toppled, the temples burned, the Kingdom shattered? What, pray tell, is the endgame your church hopes to achieve?"

"All we do is show people the truth," Marlo replied. "We expose the lies of the priests and the King. We bring the true gospel of the Titans to everyone in this city, in this continent, and let them know there is a better way, a better world." Ellarion rolled his eyes, but Marlo kept going. "There are still a thousand people in this Kingdom for every one mage. If they all stood up in defiance, the King would have to yield. We could return the Rings to their vaults, end the rule of magic. And maybe then the Titans would return to us and bless us with their forgiveness."

Ellarion scoffed and reached for his third goblet. I had an instinct to stop him, but didn't; it was annoying enough having to manage one Volaris's drinking problem. I really didn't want to be responsible for two. "And you really believe that's what's going to happen?"

"I do."

"Well, I think you and all your friends here are hopelessly naive," Ellarion said. "You want to know what would happen if your little cult really caught on, if the people of the Kingdom rose up in defiance? Civil war. Blood in the streets and fire in the sky. Purges and executions, brother killing brother, whole families put to the sword. You'd die, your friends would die, and probably every last person in this underground village would die. And do you know why I'm certain that would happen?" He took a long sip. "Because it's what *always* happens."

A sharp pain throbbed in my skull. Maybe it was the alcohol or the sleep deprivation or the stress or all of it combined. But there was just too much to deal with, too much going on. I wanted to tone down this conversation, but I also kind of wanted to leave, and I also wanted to know what Zell was doing, and I wanted to go home, and I wanted Jax to be here, to make me laugh, to tell me it was all going to be okay. More than anything else, I wanted Jax.

"You think this is the first rebellion we've had in this city?" Ellarion went on. "The first cult that questioned the priests? This happens again and again, always the same rhetoric, the same speeches, the same grand promises. And it always ends in the same bloodshed."

"I disagree." Marlo chose his words carefully. "Just because all the other rebellions failed doesn't mean ours will. There's never been a movement like us before. There's never been a place like the Undercity before, or a prophet like the Gray Priestess. This is *different*. I can feel it." He gestured around at the bar, as if daring Ellarion to take it in. "Look at what's happening outside the city, what's happening in the West, the Baronies, the Southlands. The world is changing, Ellarion. This is our moment. Our chance at something better."

"Something better." Ellarion reached for the goblet, tipped it over so it spilled on the floor, then shrugged. "Let me tell you something. I love Lyriana. Love her like a sister. But she was always the naive one. She thought everything was perfect and wonderful in the world, believed every little word the priests told her, and then she got one good look at Ragtown and off she went to the Sisters of Kaia!" He made a sound that was mostly a laugh but also a little bit of a cry. "But me? I always knew. I knew this world was cruel and cold and mean. My father made sure of that."

I remembered Archmagus Rolan's piercing eyes, his terse gaze, the casual way he'd frozen a man's hand in a ball of ice. He didn't strike me as the gently paternal type.

"But here's the thing," Ellarion went on. "I still believe. You understand? Not in the priests or the Heavenly Mandate or the King's pompous speeches." I caught a hint of sarcasm when he said *Heavenly Mandate,* but I doubt Marlo noticed it. "But I still believe in the Volaris. I believe in the mages. I believe in *order.*"

"Order?"

"'The Volaris are the light against the darkness, the nails in the wood, the ship keeping mankind afloat in the raging sea,'" Ellarion said, and even I knew that was from the scripture. "Say what you will about the rest of the holy scrolls, but there's truth there. There's truth, damn it. There is so much cruelty in the world, so much senseless violence and chaos, that you need a strong hand to keep it together. Our dynasty, our mages, might be a cage, but it's a cage that keeps the monsters out, a cage that holds society together, a cage that makes the world better, bit by bit by bit. Without the Volaris, you wouldn't have this great city. You wouldn't have Luminae or cures for the redpox or a hundred years without war. Without us, it would all be bloodshed and madness, a world so much darker and more terrifying. Our fist might be harsh, even cruel, but it's still the clenched fist keeping the world from breaking apart."

"You sound like the Inquisitor," I said quietly. "The knife in the dark."

Ellarion swiveled toward me. "Don't tell me you're buying it, too."

"No. I just mean . . ." I struggled for words, struggled with the weight of all the thoughts I'd had about this. "I've been where you are now, right? I saw the violence and horror that my family was capable of, and I had to make a choice not to be a part of that. It's not that . . . It's not like I wanted to be on *your* side. I mean, the more time I spend here, the more I see this city, the more it's clear that everyone rebelling against you has a pretty good point. The Volaris *are* oppressive. This Kingdom *is* unjust."

"So what if it is?" Ellarion replied. "We just join the cultists? Or maybe we go out West, take up arms alongside your father's men?"

"No!" I slammed my hand down, a little harder than I meant to. "That's what I'm trying to say. What if *all* the sides are wrong? What if the whole idea of sides is the problem?" I shook my head. It was all in there, churning around, my father, the Volaris, the Disciples, all these endlessly feuding groups, each convinced that they alone had the answers. "It's like someone drew these lines centuries ago, and now we're all shackled to them, forced to endlessly pick and repeat history. My father fights for Western freedom because *his* father made him swear to do it, because *his* father did the same thing. You've spent your life convinced your family is the only order holding this Kingdom together because of a scripture that's been passed down for centuries. Even the people down here are just sticking to the same old story, playing out the same rebellions that have happened dozens of times before, hoping this time it'll be different."

"So what do we do?"

"Let's throw it all out," I said. "Forget all the sides. Forget your family, forget my family, forget all the baggage we carry on our shoulders. You're not your father, and I'm not mine. We've seen their failures. We can do better. We can make our own side, our new side, that's not a slave to anything. We're a whole new generation, and we've got a chance, right now, to stop going down the same roads that everyone before us went down. You, me, Lyriana, Zell, all of us." I looked earnestly at Ellarion, at Marlo. "History doesn't have to repeat itself. Not if we don't let it."

Ellarion stared at me for a while, then reached up and brushed the side of his hand across his face. "It might just be the yarvo talking," he said, his voice a little wobbly. "But I think that might've been the most beautiful thing I've ever heard."

"I'm kinda proud of it, yeah," I said, then reached out to pat his shoulder, but before I could reach him, the door to the inn swung open and three men walked in and my whole world fell apart.

The first man was Garrus, Marlo's boyfriend, looking big and handsome in his robes, sleeves rolled up to show his thick tattooed biceps. Next to him was another rebel, a woman with thick-lidded eyes and a gap-toothed scowl. But it was the man behind them that caught my eye. He was a Westerner, a pale older man, with gray streaks through his short red hair, a thick ruddy beard, and a smattering of brown freckles across the bridge of his nose. He wore black leather armor with thick, fur-lined gloves, and tall boots caked in mud.

My heart stopped in my chest. My breath froze with a gasp. I clenched the table so tight, the wood buckled.

"Tilla?" Marlo asked. "What's wrong?"

I didn't kill the girl. That was Murzur's work. That's what Pretty Boy had said. At least, what I thought he'd said. But with his accent, I'd misheard him. He hadn't said *Murzur* at all.

"I know that man," I whispered. "His name is Mercer. Mercer Stone. He was a sergeant at Castle Waverly. One of my father's top men." I knew I should maybe run or hide or fight, do anything but sit there, staring. It was like I'd swallowed an anchor, like my body was rooted. "He's the one who worked with Pretty Boy. Who killed Markiska."

"What?" Ellarion gaped. "What's he doing here?"

"I don't know," I said, but I *did* know, because even as I said it I saw it, the truth that made all the pieces come together. Marlo talked of rebellions all over the Kingdom like they were separate movements, a bunch of seeds coincidentally sprouting at the same time. But what if they weren't? What if one man was orchestrating all of it, sending his best agents all around the continent, coordinating with rebel groups and stoking insurgencies, all as part of a grander plan to break the yoke of his mightiest enemy, the Volaris King? What if his men had been in the city all along, hiding in the ranks of the Ragged Disciples, spying on me, torturing me, killing those whom I was close to?

What if everything that had happened here was my father's revenge?

"You're absolutely certain?" Ellarion whispered back, and

all at once he seemed stone-cold sober, like the flare of his eyes had burned all the drink right out of him. "There's no chance you're mistaken?"

"No," I said, my gaze still frozen on Mercer. He strolled to the bar and drummed his fingers as he waited for the bartender, apparently having not noticed me. "It's him. I'd know that face anywhere. He was a mean old prick. Liked to train new recruits by making them run laps around the courtyard until they vomited, then beat them with a wooden sword."

And he was here. Here. In Lightspire. In the Undercity. In the inner sanctum. In this very canteen.

"Whoa, hey, let's all calm down," Marlo said, his voice an urgent whisper. "Lots of people wind up in the Undercity. We don't have to leap to conclusions."

But I'd already leaped. "It was my father," I said. "All along. He's infiltrated the Disciples. He sent Pretty Boy and Mercer. He had Markiska killed. All this time, Ellarion, everything that's happened, it's been my father's plot."

Ellarion sucked in his breath, his fingers flexing. The air crackled the tiniest bit, and a little current of wind whistled around the table, billowing the dust motes around us in a distinct spiral. "I can take them," he said. "One hard gust, knock them all back, then we grab him and run. Find a quiet place to interrogate him. And get the damned truth."

"Whoa, no, no no no." Marlo threw up his hands. "Seriously, no. This is a terrible idea. This is going to get us all killed. Please, don't do any—"

Before he could finish, Mercer turned his head toward the commotion and saw us. Saw me. His eyes went wide with surprise, even as he mouth curled into a scowl. "Tilla," he growled.

Ellarion moved fast, incredibly fast. In one swoop, he spun out of his chair, dropped into an offensive crouch, and flared out his right hand. A torrent of wind rushed out of him, blasting toward Mercer and his guards like a screaming demon. . . .

But Mercer threw up his own hand, palm wide and outstretched, and the air in front of him flickered with a hundred lightning bolts. A Shield blinked up in front of him, and as Ellarion's rush of wind hit it, it buckled but didn't break. The wind instead shot out in all other directions, shattering the canteen's windows, flipping over tables, and hurling the bartender clear into a wall.

The room was silent. The moment hung for an eternity as we all stared, stunned, at what had just happened. Because there was no denying it anymore, no questioning it, no uncertainty.

Mercer Stone, a man who'd been born in the West and spent fifty years without ever leaving its borders, had just performed magic.

I was right.

I'd been right all along.

But Mercer, of course, wasn't stunned. He knew exactly what he was doing. He whipped his other hand forward, pointer and middle finger outstretched, and a lash of sizzling yellow lightning scorched out of it like a whip, curling through the air to strike Ellarion across the arm. He screamed as it hit him, and plunged to the ground, writhing and twisting in pain as the electricity coursed through him. "No!" I screamed and rushed toward him, but now Mercer was coming at me. His lips parted in a cruel yellow-toothed grin as a gauntlet of lightning formed around his left hand, sparking in all directions.

"Stop this at once!" a woman's voice bellowed, and it was enough to freeze even Mercer in his tracks. I spun to see Lorelia in the doorway, flanked by guards of her own, arms folded across her chest in stern disapproval. "What is this madness?"

I bolted toward her, tripping over myself and scrambling back up. "That man!" I yelled, pointing over my shoulder. "He works for my father! He's infiltrated your church, infiltrated your village! He's . . . he's . . ."

The words died in my throat. Because as I rushed toward Lorelia, I could see her expression as she looked at me and at Mercer. She wasn't surprised or alarmed or even confused. She just looked angry, annoyed, like someone whose carefully constructed plan had fallen apart.

Lorelia's cult hadn't been infiltrated by my father's allies. *She* was my father's ally.

I dropped to my knees and threw up my hands, because I knew there was no way out of this. Behind me, Ellarion had stopped writhing but was still lying on his back, eyes squeezed shut, gasping for air. I reached out to him, but a hand grabbed my collar from behind and jerked me up to my feet. Mercer. He pulled me up against his bulky frame, and I could feel his rotten breath on the side of my face. Up close, I could see his eyes, and there was something deeply wrong with them: jagged veins, as yellow as a sunflower, ran out from his irises, twitching in the whites like wounded snakes. He raised his other hand up in front of my face, the one encased in sizzling bursts of yellow lightning, and I twisted and pulled to get away from it. It was hot, so hot, little wisps licking my face with painful stinging strands.

"Markiska," I whispered, because even now, I had to know. "Did you . . . Was it you?"

"Your little Eastern friend died nice and quick." He grinned. "But don't worry. For you, I'll take my time."

"Let her go," Lorelia said, but Mercer's grip tightened.

"This little bitch betrayed us to the Volaris," he said. "She got a thousand good men killed. Let me pay her back for each one."

"I said no," Lorelia repeated, and this was the real Lorelia, a woman as hard as a nightglass blade and twice as sharp, a woman who'd do anything, say anything, to get her way, the woman who'd driven a dagger into a man's ear without a second's hesitation. "Her father demanded she be kept safe. We'll honor our word."

With a snarl, Mercer shoved me forward, back down onto the floor. Lorelia gestured to the guards behind her, who strode over and helped me up. "It appears our little experiment in hospitality has come to an end. Take them up to their rooms. Bind their hands. Lock the doors."

The guards held me tight, but I thrashed against them, my vision red, my teeth clenched. Right now, I didn't care about the Kingdom, didn't care about my friends, didn't care about my own life. I'd throw it all away just for the chance to rip out Mercer's throat. "I'll kill you," I growled. "I swear by the Old Kings, by the Titans, by the Twelve. I will end you."

"Come and try it, little girl," Mercer teased.

"Um . . . excuse me . . . Gray . . . Gray Priestess . . ." a wavering voice said. It was Marlo, peeking up from the table he'd hidden behind once the fighting had broken out. He rose up, hands held high.

"Marlo," Garrus said, his tone at once worried and pitying. He'd known. Of course he'd known. He'd been Mercer's private guard. Only poor Marlo, the true believer, had been left in the dark.

"I just . . . I'm . . . I'm a little confused right now," he said. "Is what Tilla said true? Is that man . . . Are we working with the Westerners?"

"Yes. It's true," Lorelia replied, and her voice was ice. "This is a war, Marlo. Wars aren't won through rousing speeches or vandalized statues. They're won through allies. Through weapons. Through blood."

"But . . . I thought we just wanted to spread the word of the Titans. I thought we wanted to inspire the people to rise up, to boost their voices and give them hope," Marlo said, and I could see him realize how ridiculous his words sounded, even as he spoke them. "Was this . . . Is this really what the Titans want?"

"The Titans want justice," Lorelia said. "Justice for those the Volaris killed. Justice for all the innocents whose lives they've stolen. Justice for *my son*." She cocked her head to the side, and behind her, her men unsheathed their blades. "Now. Are you going to be a problem?"

"I . . . I . . ." Marlo looked to me, breath ragged, despairing. Then he glanced at Garrus, who was shaking his head, pleading with his eyes, begging Marlo not to do the stupid thing. I remembered Zell on the steps of the city, so long ago, and how I'd looked at him.

"No," Marlo said quietly. "There's no problem. Take them away."

I breathed in deep as Lorelia's men grabbed me, as they bound my wrists, as they hoisted Ellarion's prone form up, as they dragged us all out of the canteen. Mercer watched us go, lips still twisted in a hateful sneer. And in a weird way, I was relieved. Not relieved that I was captured, obviously. Not relieved Mercer still breathed. But relieved to know the truth, at last. To know I could trust my mind, to know the world really was what I'd been most deeply afraid it would be. Because there was no escape from my father, from my past, from my destiny. Even here, in the city of his enemy, behind the great walls and surrounded by mages sworn to protect me, he'd found a way to get in, to hurt me, to capture me. All roads led back to my father. And they always would. One way or another, this ended with him.

As the guards jerked me up the stairwell, I looked back over my shoulder one last time at Marlo. My eyes met his.

Then he turned away, ashamed.

TWENTY-FOUR

THEY THREW ME INTO MY ROOM, TIED MY HANDS BEHIND my back with thick rope, and locked the door. I'm guessing they did the same thing to my friends. With no clocks and the whole underground thing, I had no way to know how much time had passed. Given how bored I got, I'm pretty sure it was somewhere between three hours and a million years. I paced around. I flopped on the bed. I attempted, unsuccessfully, to open the window with my feet. I drifted off into a weird contemplative state where I tried to simultaneously figure out exactly what was going to happen next and to also shut every thought out of my head.

A firm knock on the door jerked me out of it. "Uh, come in?" I sat upright in my bed. "I mean, I'm a prisoner, so I don't think I have much of a choice?"

The door swung open. I don't know who I was expecting. Lorelia? Marlo, maybe? But the face I saw then, glaring at me from the hallway's darkness, made me gasp and shift back, sliding up against the room's wall.

Miles Hampstedt, Lord of House Hampstedt, former friend, current betrayer, strode into my room. His face hadn't changed: same soft pale cheeks, big gray eyes, tightly pinched pale lips. But when he walked, the way he walked, it was like he was a whole different person. Gone was the awkward, fumbling walk of the doughy nerd who'd pined for me all those years. When Miles walked now, he walked confidently, assertively, the walk of a man who expects people to get the hell out of his way. He was wearing the uniform of a Western general, a long gray coat that swished behind him like a cape, clasped together at the chest with little silver chains. He had long gloves on his hands, and tall boots, and his messy blond hair was tied back in a ponytail, leaving just a few curls dangling along the side of his face, framing a thin pale scar that ran down the length of his cheek. He walked over, arms folded behind his back, and I could barely recognize the shy boy I'd known for most of my life.

I don't know what had happened to him these past six months. But somewhere along the way, Miles had become a *man*.

"Miles," I breathed, looking around the room for something, anything, I could use as a weapon. I don't know why I was so scared of him. This was Miles. *Miles.*

"Tilla," he said, and when he smiled, there was a real warmth to it. "We have to stop meeting like this."

Okay, even in my fear, I felt a pang of irritation. "Nice line." I rolled my eyes. "How long were you working on it?"

"I came up with it this morning, when I learned they'd captured you," he admitted, with a sheepish shrug. "Just seemed like a way to make this less awkward."

"Oh, I'm pretty sure it's going to be awkward no matter what," I said. Miles strode over, grabbed a chair, and took a seat alongside my bed. My skin crawled at the sight of him, but I fought back the urge to slide away, to show him any fear. Instead, my gaze fell on a golden pin on his chest, a shining hawk, its talons opens, its eyes little bloody rubies. "What happened there? The Hampstedt owl wasn't badass enough?"

"Hmm? Oh, you mean the Bloodhawk." Miles idly poked at the pin. "I'm not sure when the men started calling me that. Around the Battle of Bridgetown, I think. When I got this." He ran a finger down the scar on his cheek. It was genuinely creepy how different he seemed, how assured, how wounded. The boy I'd traveled with, the one who couldn't believe he'd knocked out a mercenary with a chair leg, was gone. This was a warrior who'd fought, who'd killed, who'd seen the madness of a battlefield firsthand. "Your father said I should make it my sigil. That it would help command respect."

My father. Those words set off a whirlwind of emotions that I was totally unprepared to deal with. Even weirder, though, was how much they put Miles's new demeanor into context. Because that was whom he reminded me of, with that stiff walk, that confident air, that sense of quiet, lurking power. My father hadn't just taken Miles under his wing. He'd reshaped him in his own image.

That was too creepy to think about. "What are you doing here, Miles? How did you even get here?"

"That's a long, boring story, involving a whole lot of bribes, a trip down the Adelphus, and three days spent hidden in a shipping crate." He gestured around him. "It's so funny, right? You and Jax, you were always obsessed with those tunnels.

And here we are, in the greatest tunnels of all. Sometimes, it really feels like time moves in circles."

I had *so* little patience for his philosophizing. "What is this all about? What are you after?"

"What am I after?" he asked, incredulous. "I'm after freedom, Tilla. Not just for the West but for all the people of Noveris. Your father and I, we're going to liberate this Kingdom. We're going to end the tyranny of the Volaris, once and for all." He inched his chair toward me, uncomfortably close. "And we couldn't have done it without you."

I knew he was just fishing, but I couldn't avoid the bait. "What are you talking about?"

"It occurred to me after the incident at Pioneer's Pass. You remember. When you killed my mother?" Something flickered in his eyes, something angry and hateful. "Your father and I, we retreated back toward the coast. And the whole time, there was just one question I couldn't wrap my mind around. I'd seen Razz's body, seen the soldiers Lyriana had tossed about. I knew she'd used magic. But I also knew with absolute certainty that we'd taken her Rings.

"So how had she done it? It didn't make any sense." He shook his head, ringlets bouncing. How many times had he told this monologue to the mirror? "There was only one explanation. The mages' power, their magic, wasn't in the Rings. It came from somewhere else. But where? I made figuring that out my mission. And it took a while. It took study and experimentation and dissection. So much dissection. But finally, I got it." He reached into his coat and took something out, a small glass tube nestled in some kind of metal contraption. A syringe, I realized, with a little hollow tube on one end and a plunger on the other. And in that vial, swirling around, thick and crimson was . . .

"Blood," I whispered. "Mage blood."

"Technically speaking, it's a solution that's eighty percent mage blood, distilled with meyberries, Orlesian ash, and a few other chemical compounds. Took me a while to get the balance right." Miles twirled the vial in his fingers, spinning it like a coin. The blood inside sloshed around, a lush red flecked with hundreds of tiny golden specks like stars in the sky. "Injected directly into the bloodstream, this serum can turn anyone into a mage. And not just any mage, either. They're stronger, more powerful, skilled in ways even the Volaris haven't figured out. Bloodmages, we call them. And they've helped us turn the tide of the war." He shook his head wistfully. "Mother spent her life trying to find a way to destroy the mages. She never considered making her own."

"So you can make anyone a mage," I said. More and more of the pieces were sliding into place, though I was increasingly terrified of the picture they were forming. "Pretty Boy . . . Mercer . . ." I remembered Lorelia's arms, those purple bruises around red pinpricks. "Lorelia too."

Miles nodded. "She and Lord Kent go way back, all the way to her time in the West. She's been his best agent in the city for years. The whole Gray Priestess thing was her idea. Brilliant woman. And it couldn't have worked out better once we sent her the serum. It gave her the power she needed, and it let her cement her hold over these cultist saps."

"How about you, huh?" I remembered him sitting with Lyriana, asking sheepishly if he'd be able to learn magic, still just a shy timid boy. "Are you a mage now, too?"

"There are costs to the serum," Miles replied. "Once you take it, you become dependent. Miss even a single dose, and you go through withdrawal worse than a grief-weeder going cold turkey." He shrugged. "Some take that trade. Me, I prefer keeping my options open."

"There's nothing you haven't thought of," I spat. "And what about Markiska, huh? Was killing her part of your plan too?"

"That was . . ." Miles began, and stopped himself. "Ah. No. The last time I told you my great plan, you broke free and ruined the whole thing. I'm not going to make that mistake twice." He stood up, turning away. "Soon enough, King Leopold will be dead. The people of this city will be free. And maybe then you'll finally understand why you tied your wagon to the wrong horse. Maybe then you'll see what we—what I—am capable of."

"Is that why you're here, Miles? In my room? To brag about what you're capable of?"

There it was again, that seething anger behind his smile, that snarling hissing beast inside of him. I'd seen it once before, on the day he betrayed us, when he'd towered over me, spitting mad, raging about how I'd slept with Zell. "No," he said, and then forced it down, that real self, hiding it behind an amused shrug. "I came here because . . . I wanted to see you again."

"Seriously?"

"I have it all now, Tilla," he said. "Power, respect, armies at my command, a whole Province that sees me as a hero. And the girls, wow. The girls." He tried to act cool but looked at me out of the side of his eyes for a reaction, checking to see if

I was jealous, and I have never ever wanted to punch someone more. "There's a part of me that wants to give up on you. To punish you for what you did to Mother, to see you tried like the traitor you are. But I can't do that. Because despite everything that's happened, I still think about you. I still miss you. I still . . . I still want you by my side."

Unbelievable. "You son of a bitch, Miles," I said, thinking of his mother's head crushed under the rubble, and regretting nothing. "Jax is dead. You know that, right? Jax is dead because of you."

"No. No!" he yelled, wagging a gloved finger in my face. "I had nothing to do with that. That was all Razz. . . ."

"Bullshit!" I yelled back. "You betrayed us. You're the reason we were locked up in that tower. If you hadn't thrown your little jealous tantrum, all five of us would've made it safely to the Capital. We'd all be here together, just like we were supposed to. But no. You put yourself first. You sold us out. And because of your little tantrum, Jax is dead and gone and never coming back." I blinked away my tears. "You can talk all you want about freedom and justice, throw my father's words back at me. But I know you, Miles. I know who you really are. Under that General's robe and that fancy pin, you're a selfish, pathetic coward. And someday, someday you'll pay for it. You'll pay for what you've done. You get what I'm saying, Miles?" I wanted to hurt him so badly, to make him feel all the pain I did, to break his heart again and again and again. "I'll kill you like I killed your mother."

Miles's hand shot out, grabbing my cheeks and pinching my face painfully. "Don't. You. Talk. About. Her," he hissed, and there they were, the tears in his eyes. Good. Good! He slammed my head back against the wall, digging his fingers into my face, and I felt his hot breath on me as he panted, saw the rage, the hunger in his gaze. "Say you're sorry," he hissed. "Say it. Say it!"

"Fuck you," I said, and spat in his face.

With a petulant growl, he clenched his free hand into a fist and wound it back up, but he never got the chance to strike because a shape suddenly appeared behind him, a vaguely man-size shape, and it smashed something thick and wooden across the back of his head. Miles lurched forward, tumbling onto the floor in an unconscious heap, and standing behind him, club in his hands, was Marlo.

I've never been happier to see anyone in my life.

"Marlo!" I gasped. "Are you . . . rescuing me?"

"Yeah, I guess I am," he said, and pulled a flimsy-looking dagger out of his cloak. I held out my hands, which tingled like they were full of needles, and he began sawing at the rope.

"Thanks," I said, glancing at Miles's prone form. I don't know what would have happened if Marlo hadn't shown up, but I doubt it would have been good. "How did you get in? Aren't the guards outside the door?"

"Not anymore," Marlo said. "I brought some beer up for them an hour ago. Laced it with poppydraught from the apothecary's. They're knocked out so cold, they'd sleep through a hurricane."

"Huh," I said, and okay, that was actually kind of impressive. A lot more impressive than Marlo's attempts to cut through my ropes. "The others . . . Zell, Lyriana, Ellarion?"

"Already freed 'em," Marlo said, his tongue sticking out over his lip as he concentrated. "Even gave them a few Rings

I stole from the armory. When I get you out of here, we'll throw them a signal, and they'll take care of the squad of guards outside."

He'd really thought of everything. Which raised plenty of other questions. "Um, not to look a gift rescue in the mouth, but . . . why are you doing this?"

"Because I'm an idiot," Marlo replied. "An idiot who actually believed in this faith, who trusted the Gray Priestess, who swallowed her bullshit. I joined this cult because I believed in a better world. A fairer world. I'd fight for that. I'd die for that." His brow furrowed, and he sawed more intensely, making me more than a little worried about getting my hands cut. "But that's not what this place has become. Not what *she's* turned us into." He shook his head angrily. "You were right, Tilla. Screw taking sides. I'd rather die a free man than live as someone's pawn."

As dire as the situation seemed, it warmed my heart to hear Marlo back me up. Decent people were still out there. A few of them, anyway. "So you didn't know? About Lorelia working with my father?"

"No. It was a secret to all but the most senior members of the Disciples. Even Garrus only found out a week ago, when they brought him in because they needed more muscle." Emotions danced across Marlo's face: hurt, betrayal, and sorrow. "He says their magic is proof. The Titans have blessed the Westerners as they blessed the Priestess. He says they want us to go to war."

"It's a lie," I replied. "All of it. Miles has this serum that can turn anyone into a mage. Lorelia's just . . . She's just manipulating you."

"I know," Marlo said, but the heartbreak in his voice said he desperately wished it wasn't so. "There's more, though. Something's going to happen tonight. Something big. Garrus didn't know the details, just that it involved kidnapped children and the Ascendance Day Masquerade. He said it would change everything."

"Miles mentioned killing the King," I mused. "Wait, what was that about kidnapped children?"

Marlo jerked the dagger, cutting through one of the cords and nicking my outer wrist. "I don't know the details. Just that the plot involves kidnapping the children of a bunch of powerful nobles. Then they force the nobles to go along with their plan, if they ever want to see their kids alive again."

That rang a bell. "The Inquisitor said Jonah Welarus had gone missing," I said, and then I remembered the last time I'd seen Jonah, at the riot in Mercanto Plaza, how he'd been there one second and then gone the next. "The Festival. That's why they caused all that chaos. They were kidnapping their targets." The more organized this all seemed, the scarier it was. "Marlo, who did they kidnap?"

"Garrus didn't know," he said. "Just that they'd already been taken. And they killed a girl, someone at the University, I think. To make sure the nobles took them seriously."

My gut tightened into a ball of dread. I felt sick. "Markiska." Because that was it, wasn't it, the truth, so horrible and mundane all at once, the kind of terrible, calculating detail my father excelled at. When you wrote it down on paper, it all seemed so simple. Send a few agents into the city to give powers to the Ragged Disciples. Use those Disciples to kidnap the kids of some powerful nobles. Blackmail those nobles into doing whatever you wanted. But the plan would fall apart if the nobles doubted you, if they ran instead to the Inquisitor, if they called your bluff. You had to make sure they knew you were serious. So what better way to prove it than to kill a noble's kid? And not just any kid, either, but the daughter of a powerful Eastern Baron, murdered right in her own dorm room. You'd need proof, of course. Like the pearls from a distinctive bracelet, one she always wore, sent in an envelope along with a threat.

After that, those nobles would know you meant business. And they'd do whatever you told them.

The last two weeks I'd been obsessed with finding out the truth about what happened to Markiska. But now that I knew, it was crushing, devastating, so much worse than I'd ever imagined. Markiska's death had nothing to do with Darryn Vale after all, nothing to do with her plot to disrupt his engagement, nothing to do with her as a person. She'd just been a pawn, nothing more, a detail to check off the list, a means to an even bloodier end. She'd been killed like her life hadn't mattered, an afterthought to make my father's plan work. She'd been killed like she was nothing.

After Jax's death, I'd thought I hated my father and Miles. But it had been a cold hate, a hate tempered by fond memories and the hope, with my father at least, that things might somehow, someday work out. Now that hate burned, burned so hot I dug my nails into my palms just to feel pain, so hot I felt ready to explode. They'd killed a girl, a wonderful, kind, free-spirited girl, a girl who was one of my only friends, just to prove a point. I hated them *so much*.

Marlo's dagger cut through the last cord, and I jerked my

hands free with a grunt. "Are you okay?" he asked. "You look kind of . . . murderous."

"That girl they killed was my friend," I said, and it took real effort to get the words out. "They'll pay. My father. Miles. Mercer. Every last one of them."

"Okay. Yeah. Sure. But for now, let's focus on getting out of here. I told your friends that I'd light a red Luminae from the roof when we were ready. They should all be waiting."

"And Garrus? Is he with them, too?"

Marlo's eyes dropped. "No," he said, and his voice could barely hide the heartache. "Garrus is . . . loyal to Lorelia. He'd follow her to the end."

"Oh," I said, and somehow, seeing his pain calmed my burning anger. I wasn't the only one who hurt, the only one who'd lost someone. My father was like a plague, a pall of horror cast over the entire Kingdom. We all suffered for his ambition. "I'm sorry."

"He's sleeping off his own mug of poppy beer as we speak. I left him a note. I hope someday he understands." Marlo took my hand. "Now come on. We've got to g—"

A thunderous explosion cut him off mid-sentence, shuddering the whole building like we'd been hit by an earthquake. Marlo and I flew to the side, and the entire wall on the room's far side blasted apart, showering us with chunks of wood and mortar. I hit the ground, hard, and scrambled up to my feet, coughing through the clouds of dust and smoke. I could hear sounds coming from outside, men screaming and blades clanging and that ever-present crackle of magic. My shirt pulled up over my mouth, I pressed forward with Marlo, to the gaping hole in my room's wall.

The courtyard outside the sanctum was a mess. The bodies of black-cloaked cultists lay everywhere, along with a few armored pale men I'm pretty sure were Westerners. Little fires smoldered, and broken chunks of adjacent buildings littered the ground. I squinted down through the smoke and could make out the shapes of my friends in the middle of the courtyard, Lyriana and Ellarion and Zell, standing in a tight circle, taking out the last of the men who'd been stationed to guard us. One rushed Zell with an ax, only to be grabbed and hurled into a wall; Ellarion flicked his hand toward a nearby rooftop, taking out an archer with a perfectly thrown lance of ice.

"You were supposed to wait for my signal!" Marlo bellowed.

"Obviously that didn't work out!" Ellarion yelled back. "Now come on! We need to get out of here before the reinforcements arrive!"

"Jump!" Lyriana shouted, gesturing to make it clear that yes, she was talking to us, telling us to jump out of a third-story room into an urban battlefield.

I shot one glance at Miles, still passed out on the floor, and tried to think of a way we could take him with us as a hostage or something. But there was no time, not a second to waste, not with the screams coming from below and the thunder of footsteps all around. Even as Marlo hesitated, I grabbed his hand and jerked him out, pulling him through the hole in the wall. We plunged down for a terrifying moment, and then Lyriana flicked her palms, raising them up to the sky. Her Rings throbbed white, and a gust of Lift caught us, slowing our fall like we'd just landed on an invisible cloud. Lyriana twisted her hands now, reeling us in as if on a fishing line, and we gracefully floated to the ground next to her.

"That . . . that was . . . We were . . ." Marlo stammered.

"Save the amazement for later," Lyriana barked. "Where do we go now?"

"Uh . . . the northeast wall of the chamber! There's a path there leading out!"

I was going to ask *out where,* but a metal bolt whistled by me and struck a pillar just a few feet away. I spun around to see another group of cultists charging toward us with crossbows in their hands, and decided that *just out* was good enough for now. Following Marlo's lead, I took off in a sprint, flanked by Ellarion and Lyriana. Zell ran up ahead, so I could only see his back.

Alarms sounded, clanging bells and tooting horns. We sprinted through a marketplace, hurtling between the stands. All around us, people were pointing and shouting, throwing themselves out of the way. Faces watched from the windows, terrified and furious. I almost wanted to laugh: just a day ago, I'd been fleeing through the streets above to get to the Undercity, and now I was fleeing the Undercity. Was my goal to get *everyone* in the Kingdom after my head?

A pair of Disciples, armed with spiked clubs, popped out around the corner in front of us, but Zell took them out before they could even yell *halt,* dropping one with a spinning elbow to the skull and smashing the other's face into the side of a building. "How much farther?" he grunted.

"Just a little more . . ." Marlo gasped for breath. Our pursuers were closing in on us, their shouts louder and nearer, and there was something else, the sizzle of lightning, the thunder of rumbling stone. The bloodmages. They were on the hunt.

"There!" Marlo yelled, as we burst out of the cluster of buildings. About fifty feet of road stretched out from us to the wall of the massive chamber that housed the Undercity, and a pair of heavy doors that were our only chance at getting out of here. But they weren't unguarded. No, that would be too easy. At least a dozen cultists blocked the doors, hidden behind wooden barricades, a few even up in makeshift towers. They drew their bows at the sight of us, their commander shouting the kill order, and I winced as I braced for impact. . . .

Ellarion didn't wince, though. He jumped forward, twirling through the air in a beautiful sideways pirouette, and when he landed he threw both hands out toward the men, fists clenched and wrists curling. The air around him sizzled, shimmering like a heatwave, little sparks flickering all around him like fireflies. He let out a roar, his voice the grinding of ancient massive gears, and then fire scorched out of him, like a demon expelled, a massive ball of flame the size of a boulder, a miniature sun.

And Lyriana was up now, bounding over him with a quick jump and throwing out her own hands, her fingers contorting in intricate forms, blindingly fast like the legs of a spider. She shot out a blast of force, a Lift, and the fireball burst apart, shattering into a dozen perfect meteors of flame, each guided toward an archer with perfect precision. The missiles screamed through the air and hit their marks, bursting apart in rivulets of red and orange. Men screamed. Barricades burst. Towers fell. And that whole line of defense was wiped out.

"Remember when I scolded you for keeping up your magic?" Ellarion panted. "I take it all back."

"Duly noted," Lyriana replied, and we kept running.

The doors in front of us were just like the ones we'd come in through originally, massive stone slabs decorated with reliefs of the Titans. Lyriana and Ellarion blew them open together, each throwing a blast of Lift that sent them shuddering wide. Behind them lay another stone shaft like the one we'd come in through, leading down into darkness and who knows what else. As I crossed the threshold, I felt relief, not just at the freedom, but at the familiarity. I think some part of me felt at home here, hiding in dark passages, running underground. You could put me in Lightspire, dress me in a fancy gown, and send me to classes, but I'd always be Tilla of the tunnels.

"Stop!" a man roared like a thunderclap. I glanced back to see Mercer Stone sprinting out of the city, flanked by a group of other Western men. Some I recognized as my father's elite knights, while others were unfamiliar. But the air around them pulsed and crackled, and their hands glowed with magical light. How many bloodmages were there? How many had gotten into the city?

Mercer let out another roar and pulled back his fists, gearing up to send the mother of all lightning bolts our way. But Ellarion moved first, dropping to his knees and jerking his clawed hands upward, like he was scooping up handfuls of invisible dirt. The stone floor in front of us rumbled and twisted, and then massive columns burst up out of it, thick stalagmites that barricaded the doorway. I heard lightning sizzle and strike the stone, but the stone held strong.

Ellarion, though, fell back grimacing, his forehead slick with sweat, his breath ragged. He opened and closed his fists, hissing in pain like an old man with arthritis. "Cousin!" Lyriana said, running over to support him.

"It's fine," he said, though it very clearly wasn't. "Never been good at . . . stone magic. Hurts like hell."

Zell turned to Marlo. "Where do we go now?"

"I . . . I don't know . . . I hadn't thought that far ahead," Marlo said. "There are some forbidden tunnels up there. We could probably lose them inside."

"Didn't you say those tunnels were full of 'all kinds of scary shit'?" I asked, and then I heard bellowing from the other side of the stone barriers, and the surge of magic. The columns buckled, little chunks breaking off and hurtling our way. They wouldn't hold too long. "All right. Scary shit it is."

We took off running again, following Marlo's lead, though exhaustion was setting in. My side burned with a runner's stitch, Marlo looked like he was ready to pass out, and Ellarion was still wincing, his hands trembling as the veins on them bulged with tension. Marlo led us down the shaft, then swung a hard right through a narrow passage, then a left, then another right. There were no more Luminae here, so Lyriana threw up some orbs of Light to float after us like fireflies.

"How much farther?" I panted, even as the cries of the pursuers echoed after us.

"I don't know," Marlo replied. "I've never been down this far! I just know that . . . you're not supposed to . . ."

"Stop," Ellarion cut in. He froze in place and turned back to us, his odd expression illuminated in the wobbling glow of the Light orb. "Do you feel that, cousin?"

"Huh," Lyriana said, the same flummoxed look on her face. "Yeah, I . . . What *is* that?"

I didn't feel a damn thing. "What are you talking about?"

"There's magic in the air," Ellarion said. "But not like any magic I've ever felt. It's like . . . singing . . . in my head . . . calling out . . . ancient and strange. . . ." He turned to the stone wall next to him, and ran his hand along it, almost caressing the surface. "It's coming from here."

And no sooner had he finished the sentence than the wall lit up, a glowing blue halo around his hand. He jerked back, surprised, and the light spread outward, pulsing through streaks in the stone like blood through a vein, before arching around down to the floor under our feet. The lights spread out, snaked around us, and then branched back together, forming a clear illuminated rectangle underneath our group.

"Uh, guys?" I said, "Maybe . . . we should move?"

But before we could, the blue light flared, so bright it was blinding, and then the ground under our feet just vanished into dust. We all screamed as we fell down into the darkness, limbs flailing, and hit the sleek surface of an angled ramp. I instinctively clung to it, digging in my nails, but the surface was perfectly polished, so I just slid, down, down, down. Above me, the hole we'd fallen through sealed itself back up, like a mouth closing shut after swallowing us.

The ramp ended. I fell, weightless for a second, before slamming my butt on a hard floor. The others tumbled down around me, and we all sort of sprawled out in a heap. It wasn't the most graceful way to escape our pursuers, but I'd take it.

Ellarion was the first to speak. "Where are we?" he asked, and I dared to look around. We were in a wide chamber, maybe the size of the Great Hall at Castle Waverly, with a high stone ceiling inlaid with complex geometric patterns. It was bright, even though I couldn't actually see any light sources, the whole room was illuminated with an eerie blue glow. The center of the room, where we'd landed, was empty, but the walls were all lined with rows of heavy stone chairs. And sitting in them . . .

My breath caught in my throat. Sitting in the chairs were *people*. No. Not people. The figures in the chairs were bigger than people, maybe nine feet tall, with broad smooth torsos and wide seven-fingered hands. They sat nude, their skin as white as snow, and no genitals as far as I could tell. Their heads were bald like massive eggs, and they all had the same exact face: wide ice-blue eyes, bony ridged noses, and thin orange lips twisted in serene, haunting smiles.

Titans.

We were surrounded by Titans.

I stumbled away, but they were all around us, unmoving, like statues made of alabaster flesh, staring at us with those gaping, friendly eyes. I wanted to scream, but what came out wasn't sound but something else, a choking, hacking gurgle. Next to me, Marlo fell onto his back, gasping, and Zell staggered around, barely able to stand up. Something was wrong with me, with all of us. I felt like I was drunk, the kind of drunk where the whole world is spinning and you're just begging for it all to end. I lurched forward and fell onto the ground, catching myself with my hands, but the ground wasn't the ground anymore but skin, covered in thin bristly hairs, that twitched at my touch. Noises flooded my ears, the buzzing of insects, the screaming of children, and singing, a distant choir, voices intertwined in a haunting foreign melody. I pulled away, terrified, and now something was happening to my hands: the skin on them rippled and twisted, like there was something crawling underneath my palms, pushing to tear out.

"No no no," I moaned, and beside me Ellarion was hunched against a wall, staring in horror at his hands, which kept bursting into flame. Marlo was next to him, curled up into a fetal ball, wailing, and Zell sat on his knees, whispering, "She's dead, she's dead," over and over again. Lyriana alone seemed to be holding it together, though big golden tears ran down her cheeks; she twisted her hands and flared her fingers, like she was desperately trying to work some magic, but she couldn't stop shaking.

I tried to walk toward her, but a fog had crept in, thick and gray, starting at the edges of my vision but expanding with every step. My whole body was tingling, electric pins and needles, and my stomach lurched. I'd never wanted anything as badly as I wanted this feeling to end. The fog was thick now, so thick I couldn't even see the walls of the room or the terrifying grins of the Titans. I pushed through that fog, step after step, toward the space where Lyriana had been. I could see her silhouette, just barely. "Lyriana!" I called, but as I stepped closer, I realized it wasn't her, not anymore. It was a man, tall, with messy hair and broad shoulders, a pale man in a Western tunic.

He turned to me, and my heart stopped.

"Hey, Sis," Jax said.

And here's the thing. I *knew* it wasn't Jax. I had enough of my wits to know something was messing with our heads, that we were seeing things, that this was a hallucination or a vision or something. But I didn't care. In that second, I was just so happy to see him again, so happy to see his big smile and his freckled nose and his dumb floppy hair, that I forced myself not to question it. It was Jax, Jax, damn it, and I'd take another minute with him any way I could.

"Jax," I said, my eyes stinging, my knees weak. "What . . . what is this place? What's happening?"

He shrugged. "How in the frozen hell would I know?"

"Because you're . . . I mean, we're . . ." I stepped forward and reached out a hand, and I was sure it would push through him, but no, I felt his chest, real as the day he'd been alive. That was enough, enough to break me, to send the tears gushing like waterfalls. I lunged and grabbed him in a hug, buried my face into his chest, clutched him in the tightest pincher grip.

"Hey, take it easy, Sis," Jax laughed. "Squeeze any tighter and you'll break me in half."

"I'm sorry," I said, pulling away, and any doubts I had that he was real were replaced by the overwhelming certainty that he *was* real, because he had to be. "How are you here? I mean, you were . . ."

"Dead?" He grinned, in that way that only Jax could grin about being dead. "Yeah, I don't know the metaphysics of it. Magic's tricky that way, right?" He cocked his head to the side, sizing me up. "Wow. Look at you. A real Lightspire gal."

I glanced down to realize that I was now wearing a dress, the blue gown I'd worn to Darryn Vale's party, which I was almost certain I hadn't been wearing a second ago. Again: didn't care. "Oh, this? It's just something Lyriana gave me."

"Naw, don't be modest." He grinned and stepped closer, and I don't know why but something in his smile set me on edge. "This is what you always wanted, isn't it? How many afternoons did I spend listening to you ramble about some pretty dress you wanted to wear, some handsome young Lord you wanted to romance? Of course, you were still thinking small then, still thinking like a lowly backwater Westerner. And look at you now! Living in Lightspire! Best friends with the Princess! Dating an amazing guy! It's everything you ever wanted!" He cocked his head to the side. "So why are you trying so hard to screw it all up?"

"What?"

"I mean, you had it all!" Jax threw his hands out wide. "And all you had to do was sit back and accept it. So your roommate got killed. Who cares? People die all the time, eh?" He rapped his knuckles on his chest. "But no. You had to do the same shit you always do, sticking your nose where it doesn't belong, breaking the rules, getting into trouble. And look where it got you! Hiding out in some underground vault, hunted, scared, with literally everyone in the city wanting you dead. Classic Tilla, huh? Throwing away every good thing you've ever had. Why can't you just do the smart, sensible thing for once? Why can't you look after yourself? Why can't you just *be happy*?"

"No," I argued, but those words hurt so much coming out of his mouth. "Jax, you know that's not true. . . ."

"Oh, but it is true." He stepped toward me, but *stepped* wasn't the right word; it was more of a flicker, a ghostly glide. "And you know what? If it was just your own life you were screwing up, that wouldn't be so bad. But like always, you've dragged your friends down into hell with you. Lyriana, Zell, Ellarion, even poor Marlo . . . all of their lives ruined because you just couldn't accept the great hand you'd been dealt. You're going to get them all killed, you know." He flickered toward me again, and now his face was pale, sunken, the way he'd looked when he died, and the hilt of Razz's dagger jutted out of his blood-soaked chest, and I crumpled down onto the floor, breath trapped in my throat. "Just like you got me killed."

"No," I begged, and this was just too much, too cruel. I couldn't see him like this again, the way he'd lain on that tower floor, the way he'd always be. "Please, no, please . . ."

His gaunt face grinned, blood dripping out between his teeth. "Hey. Sis. Wanna see a cool trick?"

Then he opened his mouth wide and something burst out like a javelin, a spindly long finger with five barbed knuckles and a long dirty nail. A skarrling's leg. Now I screamed and scrambled back, but more and more legs were bursting out of his mouth, shredding open his face like it was tissue paper, and his body writhed and trembled, and the ground beneath me bristled with skarrling teeth, and then—

A hand, Lyriana's hand, shot out of the fog next to me. "Tilla!" she screamed.

I grabbed it, instinctively, and as soon as my skin touched hers, it all melted away. The fog, the ground, the drunken feeling, and that horrible Jax-thing vanished, like they'd never been there. There was just Lyriana, standing in front of me, sweat streaking down her determined face as her free hand flitted with precise gestures. I gasped for air, clutching her close, like a drowning man to the side of a boat. "I . . . It was . . . I . . ." I stammered. "What's happening?"

"Raw magic," she choked out, like each word took a tremendous amount of concentration. "Too much. In the air. I'm working a Null art to protect us but . . ." She grunted and strained, brow furrowed. "Can't keep it up . . ."

I glanced around, taking in the room afresh. It looked the same as when I'd first fallen in, with the high ceiling and geometric walls, but it was also different. Where it had been impeccably clean when we'd landed, it was dusty and old now, covered in spiderwebs, the walls crumbling and the reliefs chipped. A few skeletons lay on the ground around us, unlucky explorers who'd gotten trapped in this place. And the Titans . . .

The Titans were still around us, sitting in their thrones. But they'd changed too. Their alabaster skin was a rotten gray, clinging tight to their frames like dried jerky. Several had patchy holes in their chests, exposing strange, porous bones. Their faces weren't beautiful anymore, but gaunt mummified husks, eye sockets empty, lips rotted away to expose toothless brown gums. These were corpses, I realized, and really disgusting ones at that.

"Tilla," Lyriana said, snapping me back into focus. "The others. We have to help them. Now."

She was right. Ellarion, Zell, and Marlo were still trapped in their nightmares, shaking and moaning and sobbing. We made our way to them one by one, and at Lyriana's touch, they all snapped out of it, just as I had; Ellarion staggered to his feet and joined Lyriana in casting whatever it was that was keeping us safe, while Zell just looked at me with wordless, teary-eyed relief. When all five of us were cleared, we pushed through the room in silence, huddled up around Lyriana like she was a fire in a snowstorm, and made our way to the open door at the far end. And when we'd all pushed through it into the dark hallway beyond, Ellarion spun around and jerked his hand through the air in a harsh horizontal swipe, making pillars of stone shoot out of the side of the doorway and seal the chamber away.

Lyriana collapsed, exhausted, and Marlo slumped against the wall with a moan. Zell turned to me, and he didn't need to say a word. I saw the gratitude, the pain.

"What just happened?" Marlo sniffled. "What in the frozen hell was that place?"

"A crypt," Ellarion rasped back, opening and closing his fists with a grimace. "When men die, we bury them in fancy coffins and build statues of how glorious they were. Turns out the Titans did the same, except with magic, preserving their appearance, lingering long after they were gone." He shook his head, hair swaying. "But that magic went rotten, turned wild and loose, like a poisonous gas. It got into our heads. Made us see . . ." He paused. "Nightmares."

"Titans didn't build crypts," Lyriana said in a weak voice, still hunched on her knees on the floor. "They were immortal. They Ascended into the heavens."

"Clearly, the scripture leaves something to be desired," Ellarion replied.

Lyriana wasn't taking it well. "But . . . if that part was wrong . . . what else is wrong? What *were* those things in there? Ellarion, what have we been worshipping all this time?"

"Figure that out another day," Zell said, unusually harsh, but given what we'd been through, understandable. "Right now, we need to get as far from that room as possible."

"I agree," Ellarion said, and he knelt down to help Lyriana up to her feet. "Let's get the hell out of here."

TWENTY-FIVE

WE WANDERED THROUGH THE HALLWAYS FOR ABOUT HALF an hour before finding our first bit of good luck in days: a massive carving in one of the walls that seemed to be a map of this part of the tunnel system. It didn't make sense to me, but Zell understood it, and was able to memorize it well enough to navigate us up and out of there. After an eternity of walking and a Lift from Lyriana up a seemingly endless shaft, we found ourselves walking in the crumbling pathways of a functional Lightspire sewer system, before emerging up, through a drain, into a run-down little corner of the Moldmarrow district.

It was midday when we came out, and I can't tell you how good it was to feel that hot summer sun on my skin again. Tilla of the tunnels be damned, I was ready to pretty much never go underground again. I might've basked more and done a twirl in the street, but Ellarion reminded me that the Inquisitor's eyes were everywhere, and we were still, you know, wanted fugitives. So we skulked around until we found an abandoned-looking house, and Zell picked the lock to get us in. We sprawled inside an empty room, stretching out on the wooden floor, while Marlo filled everyone in on what he'd told me.

"So let me get this straight." Ellarion rubbed the bridge of his nose with his hand. "The Ragged Disciples are working with the Westerners to try to kill the King during the Ascendance Day Masquerade. They've got an unknown number of soldiers and . . . bloodmages . . . in the city, and they've used them to kidnap an unknown number of noble children, whom they're holding hostage to blackmail their unknown parents into participating in this unknown plot. That about the speed of it?"

"That's all I know, yeah." Marlo nodded.

"We have to warn my father," Lyriana said. She still looked rattled and exhausted, slumped against one of the building's shaky walls. "We can go straight to the Godsblade and tell him everything we know. There's enough time to cancel the masquerade and try to stop this plan."

"If we do that, the children they've kidnapped are dead," Zell said coldly.

"And let's not forget the other vulture on our shoulder," Ellarion chimed in. "Inquisitor Harkness was already prepared to send us to the torture chambers before a dozen of his men died in our escape. If we walk into the Godsblade, we're going straight to the Black Cells, no matter how convincing our story is. And then we're not helping anyone."

"So what do we do, then?" Lyriana demanded. "This isn't just about saving my father's life. If he dies, the Kingdom will plunge into chaos. I don't know what else Lord Kent has planned, but . . ."

"But I'm guessing it ends with all of our bodies hurled into a mass grave," I finished.

"We could probably get into the masquerade," Ellarion mused. "We'll be disguised, and I can get us into the Godsblade. We can keep an eye on the King and keep him safe."

"Safe from what?" I asked. "I mean, we don't know if there's an assassin with a dagger, or a bloodmage hiding in the rafters, or what. We don't know anything."

"We know *something*," Ellarion countered. "We know they're blackmailing Molari Vale, and they *were* blackmailing Captain Welarus. That's at least two of the nobles accounted for."

"Okay, but . . . what does that tell us?"

He sighed. "Not enough."

"What if *we* saved all the kidnapped kids?" Zell offered. He rose to his feet and paced around the room, and I could practically see the tactical gears in his head spinning. "Let's say we rescued them first. Then we'd know they were safe. We could get to their parents first and find out what they'd been blackmailed to do. Then we'd know the plot, and we could protect the King."

Ellarion nodded, considering it. "It could work . . . but we have no idea where they're keeping them. For all we know, they're probably back in that Undercity."

"No," Marlo said. "The Disciples communicate by Whispers, which don't go underground. They'd want the kidnapped kids somewhere accessible, somewhere they could easily keep in touch with their command and act if they had to. . . ." He nodded to himself. "There's a warehouse on the docks in Rustwater that the Disciples use to store our most valuable contraband. Garrus mentioned working some shifts there the other night, but he wouldn't tell me what he was guarding."

"We split into two groups, then," Zell went on. "One team gets to the warehouse and saves the kids. The other gets to the masquerade and watches over the King, using the information from the first group to stop the plot."

"Yeah, but how are we going to communicate?" I asked.

"I can handle that," Lyriana said, and when we turned to look at her, she waggled her fingers. "Magic."

Marlo shook his head. "Look, it's a nice plan. But you're all forgetting something. This warehouse isn't just going to be sitting there unguarded. They're going to have men on it. A lot of them. Ragged Disciples, Westerners, maybe even some of those bloodmages. All five of us together couldn't take it, much less if we split off into groups."

"We could try?"

"We'd get killed."

A silence settled over the room, and Ellarion turned away with a growl. I slumped against a wall, rested my head in my hands, and closed my eyes. I was so tired, so damn tired. All I wanted was to curl up in a ball and be away from all of this, from the running and the fear and the violence, from a world where I couldn't bear to look Zell in the eyes. The words of Jax, well, that Jax-thing, hung heavy over me. *Why can't you just be happy?*

And as much as I didn't want to, my mind tumbled down that long messy road of what-ifs. What if we'd never snuck out to that beach, back in Castle Waverly? What if I'd taken my father up on his offer? Would I be happy then? The daughter of the Lord of the West, standing with him where Miles was now? Jax would still be alive, for one thing, and Miles never would have discovered the secret of the bloodmages, so this disaster wouldn't be happening. Was this whole thing really my fault? Did I really bring loss and pain onto everyone who loved me? What did Galen say to me, way back in the Godsblade? That death followed me like a shadow?

Galen . . .

Shit! Galen!

I shot up like a bolt. "Marlo, the Inquisitor isn't looking for you. Could you get to a Whisper Roost and send a message to someone in the Godsblade? Lord Galen Reza?"

"Probably, yeah," Marlo said. "Why? Who's he?"

"Someone who owes me a favor," I said. "And probably our only shot at pulling this off."

"What do I tell him?"

"Just leave that to me."

The rest of the day passed in a slog of waiting. We waited for Marlo to send a Whisper, and then waited longer for a reply. We threw out more plans, but none of them really made sense. Marlo bought us a bottle of wine and some spiced meat pies, but my stomach was too unsettled to eat or drink. At one point, I fell asleep and dreamed of being a little girl again, splashing with Jax in a sparkling Western brook, my father watching us with loving pride.

The knock came right around sunset. We all perked up, defensively. Zell slid into a fighting crouch, and Ellarion and Lyriana flexed their fingers. Cautiously, I crept to the door and pulled it open.

Galen Reza stood outside, flanked by a dozen of his men. They wore heavy cloaks to hide their faces, but I could see the shapes of swords underneath. The others tensed up behind me, and my stomach twisted into a knot. What if I'd misjudged him, and he just had us all arrested now? Was our Westerner bond really that strong?

Galen stepped into the house, gestured to his men to keep watch, and closed the door behind him. He looked around the room, at our charged, combative poses, then let out a weary sigh. "Someday, you're going to have to explain to me how you keep getting yourself into these situations."

"Believe me, I'd like to know," I said, and I could feel myself relaxing, just a little. "I'm so glad you came."

"Don't thank me yet," Galen said, eyes flitting between Zell and Ellarion. "You're the most wanted fugitives in the entire Kingdom. I've never seen Harkness so livid. He's got every man he has out there right now, tearing the city apart to find you." His gaze stopped on me. "According to him, you're all a bunch of cultist traitors and Western spies."

"But you don't believe him."

"I know you'd sooner hurl yourself off the top of the Godsblade than work for your father," Galen replied. "Everything else I'm unsure of. You've got ten minutes for this to make sense. Start talking."

We caught him up on everything as quickly as we could, though it must have sounded like a confusing jumble. I watched his expression change from skeptical to alarmed to horrified. When we were all done, including his part in Zell's proposed plan, he just stared at us. "What you're asking me to do... keeping this from the King and the Inquisitor . . . is treason."

"I think you committed treason the minute you showed up here," Ellarion unhelpfully added.

"It can work, Lord Reza," Lyriana pleaded. "With you and your men, we can rescue the kidnapped children and prevent the assassination attempt. We'll stop Lord Kent and his bloodmages."

"Bloodmages," Galen repeated, lip curled in disgust. "It's sickening. Stealing our magic, our culture, just to turn it against us." He shook his head. "It explains so much, though. The sudden turn of the war. The victory at Bridgetown. The rumors we'd heard that just didn't make sense." He turned to me. "How many of these bloodmages did Miles tell you he had out there?"

"I don't know. He made it seem like . . . like maybe a lot."

"Titans' Breath . . ." Galen turned away. "Last night, the King agreed to my request for more help with the war, maybe because he's been so grief-stricken over the idea that you're all Western traitors. Four companies set out this morning. Nearly the entire royal army. And they have no idea what they're riding into."

"We'll still have time," Lyriana said. "After we stop the plot tonight, my father will send word to the generals. He'll turn them back before they reach the West."

"If he's still alive to give the order," Galen said.

"Will you help us or not?"

"I shouldn't," Galen replied. "I should go straight to the King with this. But the fact of the matter is, it's his poor judgment and reliance on Harkness that's let it get to this point to begin with. They made this mess. And I don't trust them to fix it." He paced for a moment, thinking it over, and I knew I should give him space, but we weren't exactly made of time. Finally, he nodded. "Suppose we do this your way. Rescue the kids. Save the King. After that, we'll come clean, tell him the whole story, and stay on the up-and-up. No more plots, no more sneaking around, no more conspiracies. Agreed?"

"Agreed," I said, and I meant it. All I wanted was for this to be over.

"All right, then," he said, and opened his coat, revealing the two forked daggers sheathed at his hips. "Let's go save these kids."

We'd finalized the plan while waiting. Galen and his men, accompanied by Zell, would do the rescue operation. Meanwhile, Marlo, Lyriana, Ellarion, and I would sneak into the Ascendance Day Masquerade to protect the King. We all prepared in our own ways. Ellarion practiced his arts, flickers of fire curling around his fingers, while Zell walked through some stealthy khel zhan forms. Marlo paced anxiously. I took a lot of deep breaths. And Lyriana gathered a few small round pebbles from the road outside, laid them out on a table, and begin waving her hands over them as they flickered with tiny sparks of magic.

When she was done, she called me, Galen, Zell, and Ellarion over. The stones still looked mostly like little stones, though they did glow with a strange purple light. "It took longer than I would've liked, but these should do the trick," she said.

"What trick?" I asked, and even Ellarion looked confused. "Am I missing something?"

"They're called Talking Stones. An ancient art from the days of the first Volaris Kings, lost to time. I found a scroll about it in the Library and have been trying to re-create it ever since." She picked one up and nestled it in her ear, which, gross. "I know it seems strange, but so long as we're within, say, ten miles of each other, the magic should hold. Press down on the hinge of your jaw when you talk, right by your ear, and all of us will hear what you have to say."

"Seriously?" Ellarion picked up a stone and examined it. "I've never even heard of magic like this."

"What part of 'lost to time' don't you get?" Lyriana smiled, which just made me realize how long it had been since I'd seen her do that. "Seriously. It works."

"Okay, but, we have to put street rocks in our ears?" I asked, and everyone just stared at me. "Fine. I'll do it. But I don't like it."

We nestled the stones into our ears and tested it out, with Zell stepping outside and closing the door. A moment later, my ear tingled, like there was something warm and wriggling inside, and I heard Zell's voice, loud and clear, as if he were standing right next to me. I jumped a little, and Ellarion beamed at Lyriana with pride.

Night had fallen by this point, bathing us all in that wan blue you only saw under the constant glow of the Godsblade. The masquerade would start in just under an hour. So there was nothing left to do but get going. We gathered together outside the house, huddling together in a circle for one last moment together, hands clasped, heads bowed. Lyriana offered a prayer that we would succeed in our mission, that we would all make it back safely; she hesitated a little when it got to praising the Titans, but she kept going. I thanked Galen for his help, and hugged Marlo, which seemed to catch him by surprise. And then, as he, Lyriana, and Ellarion took off toward the Golden Circle, and Galen and his men took off toward the docks, I found myself alone in the empty courtyard with Zell.

"Tilla," he said, and he still couldn't quite look at me. We were just a foot apart, but it felt like a mile. The weight of our last conversation on the rooftop hung suffocatingly over us, but even heavier than that was the weight of why we were parting. Because even if neither of us was saying it, even if neither of us *dared* say it, the fact is that there was no reason to assume this plan would work. Zell could die trying to rescue the kidnapped kids. I could be captured at the masquerade. There was a chance, a terrifyingly plausible chance, that this would be the last time we talked.

And I had no idea what to say.

"Zell, I . . . I just . . ." I tried, but the words didn't come. I wasn't ready to forgive him, not all the way, because I still felt so hurt by everything he'd kept from me, and because I still felt so much guilt over what I'd kept from him. Yet I wasn't ready to let him go, either, to accept the idea that we might part forever on this horrible, uncertain note. I wanted more time, more time to think, more time to breathe, more time to understand what I really wanted and how I really felt. But time was the one thing we didn't have.

"Be safe, Tilla," he said.

"You too."

Zell's eyes met mine for possibly the last time. Then he pulled away and walked off, joining Galen and his men, and leaving me cold and alone.

TWENTY-SIX

LYRIANA, ELLARION, MARLO, AND I HAD ONE LAST STOP TO make along the way. The Ascendance Day Masquerade was the Heartland's most important social event of the year, an impossibly opulent gathering in the massive ballroom on the Godsblade's first floor. Lords and ladies rode in from all over the Province, traveling for days just for one decadent ball with the city's elites. They wore their finest clothes, ate the fanciest food, and did that intricate twirling dancing. The good news was, they all wore long gowns and elegant masks, which meant we could easily get in disguised. The bad news was, we had to get long gowns and elegant masks.

That meant a detour to Madame Coravant's Boutique, a high-end seamstress not too far from the University. We cut our way there through narrow alleys and cluttered side streets, wearing hooded robes Marlo had swiped to hide our faces from any Sentinels swooping overhead. We were only a few hours away from midnight, the full round moon barely shining through a heavy veil of dense black clouds. Normally, this was the time of evening when the city would settle down, when folks would return to their homes, when the bustling sounds of the streets would settle into the evening's dull hum. But tonight was Ascendance Day, which meant the entire city was alive and rowdy in joyous celebration. Music sounded at every corner, the strumming of lutes and guitars, the harmony of choirs. Town squares and marketplaces were packed with masked partygoers, twirling with laughter and dancing coordinated jigs. Every tavern we passed was overflowing, the buildings shaking with laughter and spilling drunks out onto the street. Children threw firecrackers, vendors hawked pastries, and every now and again, a massive burst of magical light would streak through the sky, sparking ribbons of gold and purple that blasted from the heights of the Godsblade and circled the city like playful doves.

Given the stakes of everything going on, it would've been petty to complain about the fact that I didn't get to enjoy my first Ascendance Day. But I'd be lying if I said part of me wasn't a little pissed.

Madame Coravant's was closed, of course, because no one would buy their dress on the actual day of the masquerade. So we made our way to the shop's back door, which Ellarion unlocked with an effortless twirl of his fingers. Our plan involved Marlo being a lookout, so he stayed outside, while the two royals and I hurried into the darkened store, pacing together amid the rows of gorgeous hanging dresses and blank-faced mannequins.

"Is there really no other way to get our disguises?" Lyriana nervously glanced around. "Do we really have to steal them?"

"The entire fate of the Kingdom depends on us getting into that hall, and you're worried about a little petty theft?" Ellarion said, and even though I mostly agreed with him, I'd hardly call this theft petty; any one of these dresses probably cost more than the average person in this city made in their lives. "Now hurry up and grab something. We don't have much time."

Ellarion's disguise was the easiest. He grabbed a long black frock coat that buttoned halfway up his chest, with sparkling silver spirals embroidered along the shoulders, ruffled sleeves, and a billowing frilled collar that spilled out like a cresting wave. He pulled his messy hair back into a bun and slipped on a mask of what I think was supposed to be a sexy demon, the face a sleek shimmering red, with full lips curled into a smirk, and four tiny little horns jutting out of the forehead. Lyriana, on the other hand, would have probably spent hours browsing if we hadn't hurried her along, but what she ended up grabbing was, of course, stunning: a red-and-gold gown with a tall collar made of shimmering peacock feathers, bare arms, and a billowing layered skirt that led to a long, lacy train. She topped it off with an Eastern-style half mask, the eyes painted with long multicolored lashes, the edges studded with tiny round rubies.

My disguise was the hardest, because my pale skin would stand out immediately on the ballroom floor. We needed a dress that covered pretty much everything, which was surprisingly rare. We found the best option at the very back of the shop, a slick purple gown with a high rounded collar, full-length sleeves, and a front that laced up all the way with a web of glittering silk strands. For my mask, I went with what

I think was supposed to be a raven, a full-face mask as black as nightglass, with feathers around the sides, a slight hooked beak, and a veil of sheer silk that flowed down to my shoulder blades.

I stepped out of the changing room, and Lyriana clapped, while Ellarion nodded in approval. "Would it be inappropriate to say you look stunning?"

Lyriana elbowed him in the side. "You just can't turn it off, can you?"

He shrugged. "It's a real problem."

I was about to say something mocking back when I felt a buzz in my ear, that soft tingling warmth. Zell's voice came through, even though he was halfway across the city. "We're at the warehouse," he said in a tense whisper. "Heavy guard duty. Lot of Westerners. Galen's going to try to draw them out to the front so I can get in through a side entrance. Getting into position, maybe twenty minutes to go. How's your side?"

Lyriana, Ellarion, and I all stared at each other, so I reached up and awkwardly pressed the side of my ear. "We're, uh, almost ready. Just getting into our costumes," I said, and boy, did that ever sound frivolous compared to what Zell was up to. "We're leaving for the Godsblade now."

"Good," Zell said, and it was painful hearing him but knowing he was so far away. "Going quiet now. I'll let you know when we're in."

The buzzing feeling vanished, leaving us only with the silence in the room. "Well." Ellarion cleared his throat. "Let's get moving."

Getting into the Godsblade was its whole own challenge. There was no way we'd get in the front, with the rest of the guests; rows of armed Watchmen lined the steps outside the tower, making every person who entered take off their mask and show their passport. But there were other ways in, ways that only people who'd lived in the tower their whole lives would know. Ellarion led us down a twisted maze of streets to a hulking wall at the back of the building. "There's a small courtyard on the other side," he said, "and a door that leads directly to the kitchens. My guess is there'll be five, maybe six Watchmen keeping guard. We take them fast and quiet, and get in before anyone realizes what's happened. You with me?"

"Sure," I said, and Lyriana nodded, looking a lot more confident than I felt. I inhaled deeply as she Lifted the four of us over the fence, and I clenched my hands into fists, readying for the fight to come as we descended into a tiny, walled-off courtyard. . . .

But there weren't five or six Watchmen waiting for us. There was just one, a young man with big brown eyes and a mess of patchy fuzz that was maybe supposed to be a beard. He gawked at us with surprise, which gave Ellarion enough time to throw out a gust of wind that hurled him into a wall and left him reeling. Ellarion crossed the distance to him in a few leaps, kicked his sword out of his hand, and pressed him to the ground with a knee to the chest. "Make a noise and you're dead," he hissed.

"Please don't hurt me!" the Watchman begged, so pathetic you'd think this was his first day on the job. *Was* it his first day on the job? "I'll do anything you say!"

"Where are the other Watchmen? How many are there in the servants' halls?"

"None!" the boy gasped, pushing ineffectually against

Ellarion's knee. "It's just me! Everyone else is stationed at the front or patrolling the Iron Circle!"

Ellarion glanced back at us, uneasily. He'd based his estimates off what he'd seen on previous years, and he'd been expecting security to be tighter this year, given the situation. It didn't make any sense. Why would they have *fewer* guards protecting the building? Ellarion turned back to the Watchman, jerking him up by the collar. "What's going on here? Whose orders are you following?"

"Captain Welarus!" he stammered. "He drew up all the plans last week, before he . . . before that Zitochi . . ." His eyes went wide with sudden understanding. "Wait a minute. You guys are with him! You're the fugi—"

"Sleep," Ellarion said, running his hand along the young Watchman's face. The boy's eyes rolled back into his head, and his head hit the grass with a thump. Ellarion turned back to us, brow furrowed in alarm. "You thinking what I'm thinking?"

"We know they kidnapped Jonah Welarus," I said. "They must have made the Captain change the orders . . ."

"Leaving the Godsblade more vulnerable than ever," Lyriana finished. "I don't like this at all."

"Me neither," Ellarion said, and strode toward the door. He turned back to Marlo, who was still staring at the unconscious Watchman with a look of awed disbelief. "Marlo. You stay out here and keep a lookout. Stall anyone who's coming in. Knock 'em out if you have to."

"Of course," Marlo said, cracking his knuckles, though I doubted he'd ever punched anyone in his life. Still, he was the only man we could spare for it, and a part of me was happy he'd be out of harm's way.

Ellarion led us into the building, pacing through a kitchen stacked with dishes to the wide, domed hallways of the Godsblade. The shimmersteel floor lit up with golden halos around our feet, and circles of blue and gold light danced on the walls at our side. I could hear music, the elegant harmonies of a fancy orchestra, and the gentle bubbling of voices in refined conversation. This part of the building was mostly empty, save the occasional cluster of hustling servants, and no one paid us any mind. We'd crossed the threshold; now we were just masked guests, same as any others.

Ellarion led us around a heavy pillar, and then we were there, in the grand ballroom, looking out at the fanciest, most amazing party I'd ever seen in my life. The ballroom was an enormous round chamber, taking up most of the Godsblade's first floor, with a high domed ceiling and tall semi-translucent windows along the walls. Normally it was empty, but it was packed now with at least two hundred people, all wearing gorgeous gowns, elegant suits, and a dazzling variety of masks. Wine poured in gently rushing fountains, surrounded by plates of cheese and bread that hovered with some unseen magic. Decorations lined the walls and the pillars: garlands of flowers of every color, boughs of redwood and bonetree, twirling hourglasses filled with a sparkling red sand. Panes of glass hung on thin wires from the ceiling, with moving images magically projected onto them by a group of Maids on a raised platform: the Titans Ascending to the heavens in a glow of light, the old Volaris Kings discovering their Rings, King Leopold looking bold and majestic.

An orchestra made up of at least thirty people sat on chairs at the dance floor's far end, playing maybe the most beautiful song I'd ever heard. Some folks loitered around the edges of the room with their masks off, getting food or drink, but most were on the floor itself. I'd seen the Lightspire nobles dance, even had Lyriana attempt to teach me how, but it was still a thing to behold. More than a hundred of them were out there, men, women, and children, moving in perfect synchronicity with the beat in measured, symmetrical strides. With one hand raised in the air, they stepped and twirled, slid and spun, gliding as individuals in three outer rings before coming together as couples in a wide circle in the middle. It was so neatly structured, with such refined elegant movements, it felt like looking at the inner workings of a grand clock, each little gear perfectly synchronized with the others.

But we weren't here to gawk at the dancers (or to eat one of those giant green peppers stuffed with spiced beef, tempting as they looked). We were here to protect the King. He was at the other end of the room, opposite the band, on an elevated stage framed by flowering stalks of elderbloom. King Leopold sat on a dazzling shimmersteel throne, wearing a flowing robe that changed colors in the light, and a mask of a stag with enormous golden horns. Queen Augusta stood next to him, a vision of beauty in red, with a tiny half mask that showed off her stunning jawline. Princess Aurelia was up there too, standing awkwardly in the back, her beautiful black hair spilling out from her simple butterfly mask.

And surrounding all of them on the stage were Shadows of Fel, their bald faces unmasked, their dusky gray robes a sharp contrast to the opulence all around them. Inquisitor Harkness was up there too, wearing a simple gray suit and a featureless black mask, squinting out at the room with beady eyes. A chill ran up my spine. He couldn't recognize me, not in my disguise. Could he?

"Shadows on the royal stage," Lyriana whispered.

"The whole world's gone to hell," Ellarion replied.

I was about to ask what the plan was, but then my ear tingled again, and there was Zell's voice. He was hoarser now, panting a little, and I could hear other sounds behind him, voices shouting and the clang of metal. "We're in," he said. "Galen cleared a path to the cells. I got the first one open." I heard the sound of cloth being ripped, and then terrified voices yelping. "Two boys here. Jonah Welarus and Darryn Vale."

So we were right. Welarus and Molari were being extorted. "Are they safe?" I asked.

"Little bruised, but alive," Zell replied. "We're moving to the next cell. I'll get back to you when it's open."

My ear went silent. I turned to Ellarion, who was already scanning the crowd. "We need to get to Molari and find out what they made him do."

"How do we find him? I mean, isn't everyone wearing masks?"

"You can still sort of recognize his general shape," Lyriana said. "Plus, Molari always wears the same mask every year, this gold representation of his grandfather."

I was about to ask how I was supposed to know that, but Ellarion was already off, pacing toward the stairs to the balcony. He reached up to touch his jaw, and I heard his voice echoing in my ear: "Spread out. Search the floor. I'll get the high ground."

Lyriana moved away from me, rushing toward the other

side of the dance floor, which I guess left this half of the room to me. I pushed my way through the crowd, trying to be as inconspicuous as possible, but I still nearly tromped over a little boy hiding in his mother's skirt. This plan was seeming more and more dubious by the second, and I swear I felt the heat of the Inquisitor's gaze on me, the roving eyes of all those Shadows. Even fully disguised, I stood out like a sore thumb.

"There!" Ellarion said in my ear. "To your right, Tilla!"

I swiveled to the right and yup, there he was on the dance floor, Molari Vale in the flesh. His heavy frame was draped in a lush black suit, and he moved with a surprising deftness, gliding lithely on his feet like a man half his age. His mask was legitimately terrifying, a reflective solid-gold visage of an old man's weathered face, with haunted eyes that screamed *kill me now.* "I see him!" I said, pressing down on my jawbone as subtly as I could. "What do I do?"

"Go to him! Tell him Darryn is safe and find out what his part in the plan is!"

"Go to him?" I repeated, because even though he was only fifteen feet away, it was fifteen feet of bustling dance floor, at the innermost circle of single dancers. "How am I supposed to do that?"

"You dance!" Lyriana said, a little more forcefully than I would've expected. "I taught you how, didn't I? All you have to do is cross to him and link arms, and then you'll be able to talk."

"You don't understand. I'm going to screw this up and get caught," I protested. The rings of dancers spun before me like the blades of a circular saw. I'd never been good at dancing, not even back at Castle Waverly, and the dancing there was worlds simpler than the intricate movements I was seeing here. My dress felt hot, unbearably hot, and I was sweating in my mask. "Maybe I wait until he—"

"Tilla! We don't have time!" Ellarion growled. "We've got maybe a few minutes until they catch us. Now get on that floor and talk to him!"

"Okay! Fine!" I replied in the loudest whisper imaginable, and stepped forward to the edge of the floor.

I thought of Zell, out there in that warehouse. Hands bloodied. Breath ragged. Putting his life on the line.

With a deep intake, I took that first step onto the floor, and was immediately swept up in the movement. Like a driftwood husk tossed into a raging sea, I was carried along by the floor's current, moving with the motions of the dancing wave alongside me. I raised my gloved right hand, pinkie folded down, and focused on my feet. My brain spun trying to remember the motions Lyriana had taught me: step, step, back, pivot, gentle slide? Or was it slide then pivot? I tried the first and drifted immediately out of sequence, nearly pushing over an older woman in a hooped gown. She shot an icy glare at me, and my heart stopped, sure that this was the moment I'd be exposed, that the music would stop, that the Inquisitor would yell "TRAITOR" and this whole plan would come crumbling down.

But the woman just turned away, and the dancing went on, so I tried to keep going and not trip over my dress. I was closer to Molari now, maybe halfway there, but the struggle was in crossing that distance without standing out. A young girl stepped in front of me, maybe twelve or thirteen, and she was just slow enough at the movements that I could mimic what she was doing. Copying her (and hoping she didn't notice), I took a step forward, then a slight slide to the side, then a twirl and a bow, all in sync with the music. I couldn't believe it, but I think I actually pulled that part off. We did it again, then a third time, now with a pivot in the middle, and for one moment, one fleeting tiny moment, I actually felt the music, felt the rhythm, felt natural. My heart swelled with pride. I might've been born a bastard daughter in a backwater Province, but in that second, I was ballroom dancing at the heart of the Kingdom, and I was actually fitting in.

Then I was right behind Molari, and there was no time for pride. I reached out and took his shoulder, much less gracefully than I could have, and he spun back into me, wrapping a thick hand around my waist to pull me in close. I threw my arms around his neck, which was never a thing I thought I'd do. We slid gracefully into the inner circle, where the couples were, and rotated in slow harmony. I couldn't see his face through his mask, but I could feel the discomfort in his body, and hear the ruffled tone in his voice, half-annoyed, half-perplexed. "Pardon me, my lady. I don't believe I've had the pleasure. . . ."

I had no time for pleasantries. I leaned in close, whispering right in his ear, and pressing down on my jaw so the others could hear it, too. "Oh yes you have. Tilla the Westerner. The one you testified against. Remember me?"

I felt his entire body stiffen. He was terrified. Good. "What do you want?" he whispered, as we kept turning on the dance floor.

"Listen to me very closely. There's a rescue operation happening right now. We've already freed your son."

"Darryn is safe?" Molari gasped, and stumbled back, nearly pushing out of the circle. I actually had to pull him back to me to keep up our dance. "How?"

"Later. Right now, you need to tell me what they made you do. What's your part of their plan?"

"What they . . . what they made me . . ." he repeated, obviously trying to strategize and coming up blank. I squeezed tight, pressing down hard on the folds on the back of his neck, and he let out a barely audible hiss. "Cargo shipments. A dozen freight crates coming into the city from somewhere north, containing who knows what. Delivered to a number of warehouses all over the city. The people who took Darryn, they made me authorize the containers onto my ships, and sign off that they were carrying my grain. Normally, there'd be an inspection, but well, the Vale name carries certain perks."

"That's it?" I said, but even as I did, I remembered what Miles had said back in the Undercity, about how he'd gotten into the city in a shipping container.

"That's all, I swear!" Molari insisted, and we were almost to the edge of the inner circle now. "Now, please! Don't hurt my son!"

"Stay quiet, and I won't," I replied, trying to make my voice as low and sinister as possible. We split off, gliding through the dancers toward the edges of the floor. Molari took off toward the bathrooms in a halting shuffle, and I paced into the crowd. "You catch that? I think the containers are how they're getting into the city."

"You could fit thirty men into one of those grain crates," Ellarion replied, and I could see him up on the balcony, hands clenching the railing. "Multiplied by a dozen . . . that's an army."

"Titans' Breath," Galen's voice said, joining the conversation. He sounded like he was outside somewhere, a river rushing behind him. "How many of them are bloodmages?"

"I don't know."

Then Zell's voice cut in, and it was still so weird that we were all talking like this. "Second door open. There's a girl in here. Says her name is Sera Povor. Know who that is?"

"Daughter of Sebastian Povor, leader of the Hands of Servo," Ellarion said. "One of the most powerful mages in the city. Who *haven't* they compromised?"

"I see him," Lyriana chimed in. "Near the wine, on my side. I'll go talk to him."

"Only one door left," Zell followed up. The sounds of fighting around him seemed louder, and I heard what I'm pretty sure was an agonized scream. "I'll get back to you when we've got it."

I scanned the room until I saw Lyriana, on the far side, making her way to a refreshment table. I immediately knew who she was going for, an older man with graying hair sitting on his own on a footstool, his mask up on his forehead, drinking with shaking hands what I'm sure wasn't his first glass of wine. Lyriana slid up next to him and leaned over, whispering. I saw him tense up, just the way Molari had, and then I saw his eyes go wide with relief. He actually dropped his goblet, but Lyriana caught it, preventing a noisy scene. He said something back to her, and then she stood up, pressing her jawbone so we could hear. "This isn't good."

"What isn't?"

"They made him sneak into the grand mechanism of the Central Gate," Lyriana said. "After they closed it for the night, he sabotaged it, broke the gears with his magic. That Gate's effectively locked shut."

"There are other gates, though," I said, thinking of the King's Gate I'd entered through, those six impossibly long months ago.

"True, but those are only a carriage in width. The army of mages that left this morning . . . they can't get back in. We've been cut off from any help."

I could feel my pulse quicken, my chest tighten. I felt the way I had on that beach back in the West, when my father had met with Rolan Volaris, when Lady Hampstedt brought out her chest of mage-killer bombs. Something bad was going to happen. Something really bad. And we were running out of time to stop it.

"And now . . . what I know you've all been waiting for . . . the Celestial Rejoice!" the conductor of the orchestra boomed, and the room rumbled with excitement. Everyone got on their feet, clapping, and the children in the room let out whoops of excitement. The timing couldn't have been worse; before, at least, we could see through the room, but now the crowd was thick and pressed together. The conductor waved his hands dramatically, and the orchestra broke into a fast, lively song, strings strumming wildly and drums thundering. This was obviously a dance everyone knew; the entire room moved as one, spinning, hopping, raising both hands up to double-clap on key beats. Jets of smoke and light billowed out from the walls, and the panes above flashed different colors, a flickering rainbow. On the stage, King Leopold rose to his feet, arms outstretched, while Queen Augusta and Princess Aurelia bowed their heads.

"Last door open," Zell's voice said, and it was hard to hear him now over the din. "Young boy. Name's Kevyn Tobaris."

"Kevyn Tobaris?" Lyriana repeated in confusion. "He's the son of Margalyn Tobaris, a friend of my mother's . . . but she has no real power. She's just a noblewoman. . . ."

"She's your mother's friend, which is its own power," Ellarion said. "There! I see her! Center of the room! With the skull mask!"

I stood up on my tippy toes, trying to see above the dancing throng, and I caught a glance of her, I think, a tall woman with a lean figure, her mask a polished ivory skull, pushing her way through the crowd toward the stage. Maybe it was just paranoia, but it seemed like she was moving with a purpose, the only person on the floor who didn't give a shit about dancing.

Lyriana clearly thought the same thing. "It's her!" she shouted in my ear. "She's the assassin! Tilla, you have to stop her!"

"I'm trying!" I yelled back. The tempo of the song quickened, and everyone started dancing faster, twirling around doing little hops as they clapped. I could only catch glimpses of Margalyn through the bustle, shoving toward the stage with a driven aggression, weaving her lean frame between dancers and refusing to let up. I pushed after her, but it was harder and harder to keep up appearances with this wild dancing mob. All I wanted to do was move, but I ended up dodging a whirling elbow and shoving some old guy who was in my way. At this point, I barely cared about getting caught. I just knew I had to stop her, no matter the cost.

In front of me, Margalyn had left the throng and was crossing those few precious empty feet toward the stage, her gaze locked on the King, her hands pulling out of her pockets. I jostled through the last of the group, into the open air, and I could see the Shadows on the stage stiffen, see the Inquisitor lunge to his feet. It was now or never. I had to act.

So I dove forward, grabbed Margalyn by the waist, and tackled her down to the floor.

We hit the shimmersteel with a hard thud. Margalyn let out a pained scream as the side of her head hit the ground and her mask flew off, sliding across the floor. The orchestra stopped instantly, and the room seemed to pretty much gasp all at once, every single eye on us. Onstage, the Shadows moved as one, shielding the royal family with their bodies. At the fringes of the chamber, two dozen guards drew their blades. But I just held strong, pressing Margalyn down, keeping her from the stage, from the King.

"What is the meaning of this?" the Inquisitor roared. Next to him, several Shadows raised their hands, and smoky tendrils of darkness emerged from their bodies, curling around them like snakes.

The jig was up, I guess, so there was nothing left to do but play it straight. I stood up, keeping a foot on Margalyn's back, and in one fluid motion tore my mask off and raised my hands up over my head. King Leopold and Queen Augusta staggered away like I was a lioness rearing up in front of them. And the Inquisitor stared at me with more hatred than I would've ever thought one person could be capable of. "You . . ."

"Listen to me, King Leopold!" I yelled, because what did

I have to lose? "The Ragged Disciples are working with my father to try to assassinate you tonight! They've kidnapped the children of several nobles to blackmail them as part of this plot. They've got Western men in the city, dozens of them, and any second now, they're going to strike!"

"It's true, Father!" Lyriana said. She was next to me now, having pushed her way through the crowd, and she took off her mask and shook out her hair. "All we're trying to do is save your life."

Seeing there was no point left in hiding, Ellarion hopped over the balcony, using just a tiny gust of Lift to carry himself gracefully down to our side. "Your Majesty," he said with a bow. "You're in grave danger. You have to listen to us now."

A nervous murmur ran through the room. I saw Queen Augusta blanch at the sight of her daughter, and Princess Aurelia just stood there, stunned. One of the Shadows tried to hold King Leopold back, but he shoved past him, moving toward the stage's edge. "What are you talking about?"

"Your Majesty, this is preposterous," Inquisitor Harkness said, stepping before him. "She's attempting to deceive you. . . ."

"She speaks truth!" Margalyn cried out from beneath me. "They have my boy! They'll kill him if I don't do what they say!"

"What?" Inquisitor Harkness asked, and was that actual surprise?

I raised my foot off Margalyn because I figured she didn't pose a threat anymore. "He's fine now," I said. "Don't worry. My friends saved him. Whatever they told you to do, you don't have to do it. You don't have to hurt anyone."

Margalyn stood up, dusting herself off, and I felt a little bad about having tackled an older lady. "You don't understand," she sobbed. "I wasn't going to the stage to hurt the King. I was trying to *warn* him. The people who took my son, they . . . they said all I had to do was make sure the royal family was in the room when the Celestial Rejoice ended."

What, now?

"That's it?" I asked. "Then . . . where's the assassin?"

My ear tingled again, and Zell's voice came through. "Tilla. I was wrong. There's another cell. This one's the most heavily guarded."

My stomach tightened into a terrible knot. We'd missed something after all, something really important. "What happens when the Celestial Rejoice ends?" King Leopold demanded. Another murmur ran through the room, this one louder and more urgent. A few people started moving toward the doors.

"No one move!" Inquisitor Harkness roared, his voice thundering as it echoed off the chamber's walls. "Bar the doors! Now!"

The guards looked around, reluctantly, and then followed the order, stepping back to block the entryways. A few guests voiced their protest, and one even pushed against them, but most just crowded toward the center of the floor, huddling together, staring at the stage for guidance.

"We're opening the cell now," Zell said in my ear. I felt weak, light-headed. I wanted to run, to hide, but there was nowhere to go.

"Your Majesty," Inquisitor Harkness oozed. "This is a plot

to ruin your reputation and pave the way for insurgency. You must not listen to these lies. . . ."

I looked to Lyriana, to Ellarion, for help, but they looked just as confused as I was. What had we missed? *What had we missed?*

"There's someone in here. It's . . . it's . . ." Zell said, and then, even through the Talking Stone, I heard the shock in his voice. "It's Princess Aurelia."

But that couldn't be possible. Princess Aurelia was on the stage, right in front of me, standing right behind her mother and father. Lyriana and Ellarion stepped back, horrified . . . and the air around "Aurelia" began to waver, to tremble, to shimmer like the space above stone on a hot day.

Oh no.

Oh no no no no.

Harkness turned to Aurelia, the one on the stage, but she wasn't Aurelia anymore, but a blinding refraction of light, a maze of reflections on a dozen invisible mirrors. The King and Queen jerked away from it, while the Shadows looked to one another, their tendrils tensed and writhing. That impossible shape twisted and contorted, and then the effect vanished in a rush, and Aurelia vanished with it. Hunched over in her place on the stage, just a few feet behind the King, was Lorelia, the Gray Priestess. She straightened up, unfolding like a switchblade. Her hair was wild and tangled, and she wore a frayed gray dress that looked more like a funeral shroud, tied around her waist with an oddly thick leather belt. Her purple eyes glowed with an impossible burn. She was a vision of rage, of righteous fury.

"How?" King Leopold stammered, all the blood drained from his face. "Who?"

But Lorelia had no interest in his questions. She reached down to that thick belt, and now I could see there was something attached to it, a pair of round leather disks with glass cases. And inside of each of those glass cases was a chunk of Heartstone, the gem from a mage's ring, flickering and burning with a chaotic internal fire, a hurricane trapped behind ice.

Mage-killers.

My breath stopped. My whole body froze.

We were all going to die.

"This is for my son," Lorelia said, and flicked the button on the side of the mage-killers. "For Petrello!"

The gems inside cracked and sparked.

And then they burst.

TWENTY-SEVEN

THAT MOMENT LASTED FOREVER.

Next to me, Lyriana screamed. I staggered back. The Shadows pounced. The Inquisitor bellowed. King Leopold dove away. Queen Augusta screamed.

And Ellarion threw up both his hands, palms out, fingers spread wide, howling in concentration. A viscous purple membrane instantly rippled out of his palms, like water floating in the air, sparkling purple water lit up with tiny stars. A Shield. It curled around him, around Lyriana and me, wrapping around us like a translucent shell, sealing together at our backs like a drop of dew on a blade of grass. Sweat streaking down his face, hands trembling, Ellarion sealed the three of us in a bubble of pure magic.

Just as Lorelia exploded.

One second she was there. The next she was gone, replaced only by a column of orange-and-scarlet fire, a roaring wall of flame that swallowed everyone on the stage in one massive burst. It surged past them, toward us, and I could hear the other guests scream for just one second before being cut off. That column of fire hit Ellarion's Shield, and I winced, bracing for death. The purple membrane buckled at the impact, shuddering and quaking, tiny bubbles rippling through it like blisters. But it held, at least it held then, as Ellarion gritted his teeth and let out a primal grunt, putting every ounce of energy he had into keeping it up. The fire roared around us, like we were a boulder in a river's path, but it didn't stop for anyone else. So I watched from that safe little pocket, hand clenched over my mouth, as the wall of flame tore through the rest of the room, consuming everyone and everything, men, women, and children, alive one moment and gone the next.

Then it had passed, blasting out through the Godsblade's cavernous front doors, and not a moment too soon because there were a few loud pops from Ellarion's direction, and he crumpled, exhausted, to his knees. That purple Shield vanished, but the wall of fire was gone too. I felt the heat of the room all at once, the air dense and suffocatingly hot, the smell of burning overwhelming. It had happened fast, so fast, my mind had barely processed it. But now I saw just what Lorelia had done.

The beautiful ballroom was a charred ruin. The walls were black, the shimmersteel warped and distorted. And the people, all the people who'd been in the room, the happy dancers, the joyous families, they were all gone. A fine layer of gray ash covered the entire floor, specked only with occasional flakes of brittle bone or blackened jewels. They were dead, all of them. Molari Vale. Inquisitor Harkness. Margalyn. That little girl I'd danced with. And on the stage . . .

"Mama? Papa?" Lyriana asked, her voice trembling, the smallest and weakest I'd ever heard her. But there was nothing left to answer, only the hollow-eyed remnants of her father's mask, staring at us from a pile of ash.

On his knees, Ellarion let out a choked wail of pure agony. Lyriana and I spun to him, and I had to fight back another scream. Those pops I'd heard had been his Rings bursting, overheating from the strain of keeping up the Shield. Tears streaked down his cheeks as he held up what was left of his hands. His left was a twisted husk of flesh, fingers fused together in a blistered claw. His right was completely gone, blown off at the wrist, just a seared stump with a jag of bone sticking out. Ellarion, cool unflappable Ellarion, looked up at me, utterly terrified.

"Help," he begged.

That was enough to move Lyriana, to pull her away from the sight of her parents' remains. She sprinted toward him, tearing off strips of her dress to wrap around his wounds, and whispered under her breath as her own Rings glowed green. He collapsed into her, barely conscious, and she cradled his shivering form in her lap.

"What do I do?" I asked, my voice a thousand miles away. "How can I . . ."

"Go get help!" Lyriana yelled, not looking up from her cousin's trembling form. I staggered toward the entryway, but as I made it to the doors, though, I saw that it wasn't much better. The blast had shot out onto the street, far enough to blacken the walls of the nearby houses. The steps of the Godsblade were scorched, littered with corpses: smallfolk who had gathered up just for a peek at the masquerade, and the Watchmen who'd protected it, cooked alive in their armor. In the distance, I could see a few survivors huddling up, terrified faces staring at me from broken windows.

A blast went up, this one farther away, from the far side of the city. I gasped and lurched back as a blossom of flame shot up over the cityscape, from the Market District, I think. Then another one went off, from the army barracks, and another from the University, and another from the Kaius Kovernum. The whole city was exploding, bomb after bomb going off, like flickers of lightning in the mass of a storm. The ground shook with each one, and now it seemed like the night itself was screaming.

The enormity of it all hit me. This was my father's final move, his play for all the marbles. This had never just been about killing King Leopold. This was him killing *everyone*, the entire leadership of the Kingdom of Noveris, in one fell swoop. Every noble, every aristocrat, every priest, and every scholar, wiped out in a single brutal cull. He didn't need to win on the battlefield, not if he could steal the throne while the soldiers were on the march. Even the biggest snake was only as vicious as its head, and tonight, that head had been severed.

The Central Gate hadn't been barred to keep the army out. It had been barred to trap us all in.

My ear tingled, and I suddenly remembered the other half of our group. "Tilla!" Zell yelled, his voice barely audible over the city's roar. "What's happening? Are you okay?"

"I'm . . . I'm alive. Lyriana and Ellarion too. But everyone else . . ." I said, and the words felt impossible to get out. "They're dead, Zell. All of them. They killed everyone."

"The King . . . ?" Galen's voice asked, and my silence was the answer. "No. No!"

"What do we do?" I looked around, feeling so small and so lost. Behind me, Lyriana was still cradling Ellarion on the charred ballroom floor, whispering intently as she tried to stem the blood oozing out of his right stump. In front of me, columns of smoke reached out from all over the city, like the tendrils that had flanked those doomed Shadows of Fel. The clouds rumbled overhead, and I felt the first droplets of rain strike me, a hot summer rain on a dark bloody night. Screams and wails still cut through the air, but I heard other sounds too now, more worrying sounds: the crackle of ice and the sizzle of lightning, the clang of blades striking together. The massacre wasn't done. It was just getting started.

"We need to fight," Galen tried. "Regroup somewhere, marshal with the City Watch, contact the army, and—"

"No," Zell cut in. His voice was hard and cold, the edge of a blade. "The battle is over. The city is lost. All we can do is flee with our lives."

I could hear Galen breathing hard, struggling with the inescapable truth of it, before letting out a heartbreaking sigh. "Okay. Listen close. We're safe for now, but there's fighting all around us. The Westerners are blocking all the roads and rounding people up. It's only a matter of time before they get to us."

"So how do we get out?"

"The river," Zell said. "They can block the roads and lock the gates, but they can't stop the river from flowing. Not right away."

"Yes. Yes," Galen replied. "We're not far from the

waterfront. We can commandeer a ship, get these kids and the rest of my men on board, and sail off down the Adelphus."

"What about Tilla and the others?" Zell demanded.

"The Royal Canal runs by the Godsblade. Tilla, do you know how to get to the Selvarus Docks?" Galen asked.

"Yeah," I replied. The Royal Canal was a narrow rift of water that ran through the heart of the city, frequented by traveling barges that peddled their goods on a series of little piers. I'd been there a few times with Markiska, picking up dyes and silks from Eastern merchants. The Selvarus Docks were a short run from the Godsblade, maybe twenty minutes if we cut through alleys. "I can get us there."

"Then that's our best bet." There was another explosion, and I couldn't tell if I was hearing it for real or through the Talking Stone. "We have to move now. I'll talk again when we're closer."

"Okay," I said, though nothing seemed even remotely okay about this situation. "And listen . . . if we don't make it . . . If we're not there when you come by . . . keep going. Don't wait for us. Just sail on and get out of here while you can." I looked out at those scorched steps, at the mangled bodies. "Too many people have died already."

There was no reply, so I had to assume they'd heard it. I turned to the ballroom, still fighting back horror at the carnage in front of me. Lyriana had gotten Ellarion stable; both his hands were wrapped up in cloth, the bleeding stopped, and he looked at least halfway conscious. "Did you hear the plan?" I asked them.

"I heard," Lyriana said quietly. "To flee the city. To abandon it to these murderers."

"The Heartstone," Ellarion choked out, every syllable a labor. "We have to protect the Heartstone. If they take it . . . they take everything."

I understood their reluctance, but I also had no time for this. "I know it's not easy, but we don't have a choice. There's no way we can fight, not in the shape we're in. We have to run."

Lyriana looked up, startled, and I wondered if what I'd said was somehow surprising. Then I realized she was looking past me. "Do you hear that? Footsteps?"

She was right. There were footsteps coming our way, getting louder and louder, thundering over the screams and the explosions. I spun to look back out the door, and there they were, just coming up on the bottom of the steps, at least a dozen men in glinting helmets. Westerners.

"Shit!" I yelled at Lyriana, because they'd be up here any second. "Hide!"

I sprinted toward her, and together we helped Ellarion to his feet, his arms around our shoulders, his head drooping as we hurried along. We didn't have time to make it across the room to the back door, and the side exit near us was blocked, so we took the only option left, sliding down behind the blackened husk of a fountain that just barely hid us. Lyriana clasped a hand over Ellarion's mouth, stifling his moans, and it took every ounce of strength I had to fight the tremors going through me, the overwhelming urge to just get up and run.

Through the reflection on a pillar in front of me, I could see the men as they marched in. They were soldiers, all right, Westerners, their armor gold and red. They walked forward, blades drawn, presumably ready to kill any survivors they encountered. My whole body tensed up as one stomped my way, but then stopped just a few feet short and turned his back. All of them went rigid, at attention, hands folded together at their waist. It was a Western salute, the way our soldiers greeted their Lord. Which meant . . .

Three more men walked into the room, moving far more deliberately than their vanguard. On the left was Mercer Stone, who I'd really hoped had died down in the catacombs. His brown leather armor was dotted in specks of blood, and little bursts of lightning flickered around his hands like fireflies. On the right was Miles, General Miles "the Bloodhawk" Hampstedt, and it was unnerving how natural he looked with a sword sheathed at his side. *I should have killed him*, I thought, *back in the Undercity. If I'd just acted a little faster . . .*

But I lost that train of thought as soon as I made out the third man, the one in the middle. It was my father, Lord Elric Kent himself. He looked grander and more impressive than I'd ever seen him, wearing a gleaming silver breastplate decorated with an ornate image of an eagle in flight. Jewel-handled daggers sat at his hips, and a long red cape fluttered after him. The war had aged him, just like it had aged Miles; the lines in his forehead were thicker, and his hair, still hanging around his shoulders, had streaks of gray. His neat goatee was a full beard now, cut down to a sharp point below his chin. And most noticeable of all were his green eyes, the eyes that looked so much like mine, the eyes that I had always thought were the link between us. Where before they'd been sparkling, full of cunning and hidden depths, they were bloodshot and exhausted now, the kind of eyes that looked like all they wanted was rest.

I clenched my hands into fists so tight my nails cut into my palms. This was my father. *My father.* In the same room as me again, after everything that had happened. My father, the man responsible for this mass murder, for Markiska, for Jax. For the first time, I didn't feel any conflict, no pangs of regret or childhood yearning. I only felt two things.

Fear.

And hate.

The three men strolled into the center of the room in silence, the weight of the moment heavy even on them. Mercer kicked a goblet out of his way, knocking it through the ash, while Miles gaped up at the domed ceiling in wonder. "By the Old Kings, it's beautiful. It's so much more beautiful than I'd imagined."

"That it is," my father said. "And now it's ours."

Miles turned back to him, and even from here I could see the worship on his face. He'd always wanted a father of his own. Looks like mine did the trick. "You did it. You really did it. The West is free. The Volaris are dead. The kingdom is yours, Lord Kent." He stopped, then bowed his head. "I mean . . . King Kent. Your Majesty."

King Kent. *King* Kent. It felt so wrong, so impossible, and yet at the same time, inevitable, like this was what my father had wanted all along, the only outcome of the journey he'd been on his entire life. "I couldn't have done it without you, Lord Hampstedt," my father said, but there was something odd in his voice, a hesitancy belying the show of respect. "Your bloodmages made this possible."

Next to me, on the floor, Ellarion twisted, and Lyriana clenched her hand more tightly over his mouth. Her eyes met mine, and they were burning, hot flickers of golden rage, the signs of her passion overwhelming her restraint. I reached out to squeeze her shoulder and keep her calm; Heartmagic or not, we couldn't clear this room.

"I wish my mother were here." Miles's voice choked up a little bit. "I wish she could see this."

"She's gazing down on us from the Hall of the Old Kings," my father replied. "All our ancestors are. Your mother . . . my father . . . every Westerner who ever fought and died, every Westerner who ever dreamed of freedom, is looking at us right here, right now, their hearts filled with pride."

Miles let out a little chuckle. "Already giving speeches like a King."

"I suppose it comes with the territory."

"Your Majesty!" a voice shouted, and I still couldn't handle someone calling my father that. A soldier ran out from the bathrooms on the far side of the room, dragging a man behind him, a bulky man in an elegant suit. Molari Vale. He'd managed to hide out during the explosion. He let out a moan as the soldier shoved him forward, throwing him down on his hands and knees before the three men.

"What have we here?" my father asked.

"Awfully big for a rat." Mercer grinned.

"My Lords. My King," Molari begged, still keeping his head down low. He was panting, trembling, and his voice came in hoarse gasps. "I pledge to you my life and the full, ample resources of House Vale. I swear, I shall serve you loyally and faithfully. That's a promise."

"The same promise you made the last King? The one you betrayed?" Miles shook his head, and the irony of Miles calling anyone else a traitor was enough to make *me* explode with Heartmagic. He turned to Mercer and shrugged. "Kill him."

"No!" my father yelled, but it was too late. Mercer Stone flicked his hand idly toward Molari, and what looked like a blade of lightning shot out, hissing through the air, burrowing straight into Molari's forehead and bursting out the back of his skull. Molari let out a single weak gurgle, eyes rolling up into his head, then keeled over, dead.

"Damn it, Miles!" my father roared, grabbing him by the collar and jerking him forward. "He could have been useful!"

"He would've betrayed us the first chance he got!" Miles protested, thrashing about, and any dignity he'd gained with his cloak and his cool scar was gone. There was the Miles I knew, the impudent entitled child, wriggling to get out of someone bigger's grasp.

"You don't get to decide that!" my father bellowed.

Mercer Stone stepped forward, and I was sure he was going to slap Miles or something. But instead he reached out and grabbed my father, putting one firm hand on his shoulder. "Your Majesty," he growled, and it wasn't deferential.

It was a *threat.*

My father glanced back at him, just a little startled. But then he nodded and let Miles go, and with a nod, Mercer released his grip. Miles pulled away, dusting himself off, lip curled with petty indignation. I could barely believe what had just happened, but it explained that weird tension in the air, the power imbalance. My father was, unquestionably, the King . . .

But the bloodmages answered to Miles.

Was there any thought more terrifying?

My father turned away, his mouth a hard angry line. Even now, at his moment of greatest triumph, he was still trapped, still plotting for freedom. My father was like a shark, always moving, always scheming. Never happy.

There was a soft ding from the side of the hall. All eyes flicked there, to an aravin that had just arrived from somewhere up high, an aravin that was practically trembling with charged magic.

"Down!" Mercer screamed, hurling himself in front of my father and Miles. The aravin's doors slid open and a surge of energy blasted through the room, a wave of magic so raw and furious it felt like a wave of needles tingling through my body. The earth trembled and I smelled frost and dirt and the salt of the surging sea. Then columns of jagged ice burst out of the floor of the ballroom, surging up like a wall between my father and me, and crushing one Western soldier directly into the ceiling. I could see Hands of Servo in the aravin, four of them, including the one who'd testified against me at my trial. They stood in a row, hands whirling in dizzying circles as icicles blasted out of them and hurtled like spears into the Western soldiers.

We wouldn't get a better opportunity than this. "Run!" I yelled, and lunged to my feet, pulling Lyriana up with me. Ellarion lurched after us, awake enough to know we had to move. Behind us, the bloodmages were fighting back, throwing up strange Shields of pulsing light, and sending blasts of fire back into the aravin. Mercer whipped his arm around, shooting out another of those lightning blades, and a Hand shrieked as it hit him. Miles scampered back, throwing himself behind a pillar.

And across the chaos and violence and the scorching heat, my father still stood strong, unflinching. His eyes met mine just as I reached the door, and they widened with surprise.

"Tillandra?" he asked.

Then we were gone, sprinting through the halls, leaving the battle in the ballroom. We burst into the courtyard at the back of the building where we'd left the sleeping Watchman. Marlo was still standing there (and thank the Old Kings he was okay), but his jaw hung open, his whole body shaking. "What . . . What is . . . What . . ." he stammered, and I could see behind him the unfurling smokestacks of even more explosions.

"We'll explain later! Now we have to move," Lyriana commanded. She didn't bother Lifting us gracefully over the wall this time; she just threw out both her hands and a blast of raw force smashed through the wall, sending its bricks hurtling out into the street. On a normal night, that would've turned every head and brought the Watch tearing down on us, but this was most certainly not a normal night.

But standing in the street, just through the hole she'd blown, were a trio of Ragged Disciples, black-robed, black-masked. Because of course, when could I ever catch a lucky break? Two lanky Disciples wielded swords, while the big one in the middle held a huge wooden club. They swiveled to us in surprise, and I dropped low into a combat stance. Next to me, Lyriana hissed and scrunched up her hands, gearing for a fight.

The big Disciple beat us to it. He swung his club in a wide arc that smashed his buddy on the left in the face, knocking him clear across the street. The other Disciple turned to him, stunned, just in time to catch a fist to the jaw.

His mask shattered, and he dropped like a stone. The big Disciple turned back to us and ripped off his mask, revealing a familiar stubbled face with a dimpled chin.

"Garrus?" Marlo's voice trembled. Even here, with everything that happened, he looked like he couldn't believe his luck. "You . . . you saved us? You came looking for me?"

Garrus bounded forward, grabbing Marlo in a massive hug that lifted him clean off his feet. "Of course I did," he said, and the big guy's eyes were glistening with tears. "I love you, you idiot."

Marlo leaned forward, pressing his forehead to Garrus's, speechless for once. Then a blast sounded from the Godsblade behind us, a scream, the thunder of footsteps. "Selvarus Docks," I said to Garrus, and he nodded, sliding an arm around Ellarion to help him stand. The tender reunion was over. We had to run.

We rushed out through the hole Lyriana had blown and took off through the city, but by now, the entire Golden Circle had become a war zone. Rooftops burned all around us, and the sky was barely visible through the columns of dark smoke. It was raining harder, those thick heavy droplets they got out here, but I doubted it would do anything to put out the fires. A family ran by, parents dragging along sobbing children, while two men grappled on the floor of an alley nearby. An unseen figure in a house frantically boarded up the windows, while a pair of women sat on a rooftop nearby, waving their arms and begging for help. Shattered Luminae lay on the ground, their blue and yellow embers glowing in the broken cobblestone. A spiral of green fire shrieked across the sky and plunged into the side of the Godsblade, sending rivulets of flame raining down. And worst of all was the noise, so loud and overpowering it made the ground tremble: screams and wails, swords striking, stone crumbling, the sizzle of flame and the smashing of earth. It was like the entire city was alive, a gigantic animal thrashing in agony.

"No," Lyriana moaned, "no!" and I couldn't imagine what this was like for her, to see her city, her home, so devastated. Looking at the despair on her face, I knew the heartbreak of this night would never leave her; it would be a forever-wound, a scar on her life, the moment when it all changed. I hurt for her, hurt so badly, but I also knew that if we were ever going to have a life at all, we had to move.

We kept running through broken streets and crowded alleyways, pushing through the city toward the Royal Canal. My side ached, my feet throbbed, and my wet hair clung to my face like a mop. Ellarion was pushing on with us, even though his eyes looked sunken, and his breath came in hard gasps. His mangled hands hung limp at his sides, enveloped in glowing light and wrapped in makeshift bandages. He looked like a walking corpse, animated just enough to keep moving, ready to collapse onto Garrus at any second.

We cleared an alleyway and burst into a crowded courtyard. If what I'd seen before was the fringes of the battle, this was the raging inferno. Men fought all around us, a frantic melee of bloodied faces and clanging blades. It was hard to read the chaos, but it looked like a group of City Watchmen was fighting against a mob of Disciples, their polished swords clanging against the cultists' axes and clubs. One Watchman got in a lucky blow, cleaving a cultist's head open, only to catch a dagger in the side. Another turned to help him and was brought down with an ax to the neck.

A door swung open at the courtyard's far end and a Heartlander woman stepped out, her hair pulled back in a bun, her teeth gritted with determination. She raised her hands and the Rings on her hands pulsed white and turquoise as the air crackled with magic. Dazzling lights flickered in the faces of the cultists, like a dozen little firecrackers bursting right in their eyes. She was a Maid of Alleja, so not exactly a hardened warrior, but her magic was working; the cultists staggered back, blinded. Then one pulled back his hood, and I saw pale skin, blond hair, and wide eyes pulsing with green veins. A Westerner. A bloodmage. He flared out his hands, and tiny iron balls shot out of his sleeves, hurtling through the air at a blistering speed and punching several holes clean through the woman, like she was made of paper.

"No!" Lyriana screamed, and raised up her own hand, Lifting the bloodmage and sending him flying into the corner of the nearest building. He hit it with a hard crunch, leaving a long bloody smear on the wall. The City Watch rushed forward, and the fight resumed, a blur of sparking metal, a clash of colliding bodies. I could see the agony on Lyriana's face, the desire, the *need*, to help . . . but next to her, Ellarion let out a gasp, and I could see blood blossoming out around his bandages, dripping from his wrists. Our eyes met, and Lyriana knew as well as I did there was no stopping now.

The Royal Canal wasn't far from the courtyard, just a few more alleys and a shortcut through a closed marketplace. We were making good time, I think, close to what I'd predicted. We might actually make it out of here.

If Galen had actually gotten the boat, that is. If the river wasn't blocked off. If he and Zell were even still alive.

We rounded a corner to a long stone flight of stairs, flanked on both sides by tall buildings. The Royal Canal was just on the other side of this hill, just up these stairs. I don't think I'd ever felt so exhausted, but I pushed on, forcing my feet to keep running. Step after step vanished under my feet, and I could hear the rushing of the canal now and the crashing of ships in the rocking surf. My ear tingled, and there was Galen's voice, just barely. "Tilla!" he yelled. "We got the boat! We're almost to the docks! You en route?"

"We're coming!" I shouted back. Garrus was almost at the top of the stairs, Ellarion slung over his shoulder, and Lyriana and Marlo were just a few steps behind him. "We'll be there in one m—"

I never got to finish that sentence because there was an earth-shuddering blast from somewhere at the base of the stairs, and then a bolt of lightning hit the steps just in front of me. They exploded in a burst of brick and light, but I didn't really see that because I was airborne, hurled back down. The world spun wild, and then I felt sharp bruising pain as I hit the stone with my shoulder and tumbled down at least a half dozen steps before coming to a stop. My ears rang with a dull thunder, and I tasted a mouthful of blood. Gasping, panting, I pulled myself up onto my hands. I was most of the way back down, my arm throbbing, my vision blurry. Above me, a jagged crater the size of a grapefruit smoldered where I'd been standing. Lyriana and Marlo were sprawled out just past it, staggering to their feet. And behind me . . .

Mercer Stone paced toward us from the alleyway, his

face contorted into a furious scowl. Flanking him were a half dozen Western soldiers, brandishing spears and swords, faces hidden behind silver helms. Lightning danced around Mercer, ribbons of flickering yellow that swam around his body like eels. He had a long gash in his forehead, and what I'm pretty sure was a shard of glass sticking out, but he didn't look like he even felt pain at this point, just hot, murderous rage. Was this how he'd looked before he'd killed Markiska? Was his hideous face the last thing she'd seen?

At the sight of me scrambling, his mouth curled into a yellow-toothed sneer. "Kill them now," he growled.

I tried to stand again, but my legs were too weak still, my head still swimming, so I fell onto my back. The soldiers rushed forward, charging up the steps. I tried to stand again, managing to make it up to my haunches, but I was too slow, too late. The fastest soldier, a lean man with a dented helmet, was almost up to me, and he geared up for the strike, pulling back his spear. I braced for the end.

A shadow moved, plunging down from a rooftop like a hawk going for the kill. It slammed into the soldier and drove him to the ground, hard, and then I saw it was a man, a man with short black hair and a City Watch uniform, wielding a short sword in each hand.

Zell. By the Old Kings, it was Zell!

With cold precision, he jabbed one of the swords into the gap in the armor under the soldier's armpit, driving it in and out with a misty red spray. The other soldiers stopped in their tracks, startled, and Zell rose to his feet, kicking the man's twitching body aside. He stood strong and tall between me and the mob, holding his two swords out at his sides as droplets of blood trickled down the blades. Lit up by the flickering flames, he was terrifying, unstoppable, a vision of death itself. Even Mercer looked stunned.

My stomach plunged, and my heart thundered, because I knew damn well what he was doing. He was making himself a line, a wall, staying back to fight so the rest of us could flee. "No," I said, "no, Zell, no . . ."

Then he turned back to me, just a little, so I could see his profile. His wet hair was matted down with the rain, and a thin cut slit open his cheek. But his eyes were still somehow so soft, so brown, so beautiful. They were the tender eyes I'd looked into so many nights across a pillow, the eyes that had sparkled when he'd said he loved me, the eyes that had first charmed me at that Bastard Table, so many lifetimes ago. After everything we'd been through, everything we'd done, they were still the same eyes that I loved, that I'd always love.

"Go," he whispered, but his eyes said so much more.

I'm sorry, they said.

I choose this, they said.

I love you, they said.

Good-bye.

Then one of the soldiers let out a war cry and rushed him, slicing toward his chest in a dazzling horizontal slash. Zell blocked it with one of his swords and swung around, striking him in the base of the skull with the pommel of the other, even as two more soldiers charged his way, as Mercer spread his arms out and surged with magic. A hand grabbed me, jerking me up to my feet, and I found myself staring into Lyriana's exhausted face. "We have to go," she choked out. "We have to run now."

"No . . ." I said, but I was moving, pulled along the steps toward the crest, toward freedom, toward safety. Garrus was already up there with Ellarion, gazing out the other way. "The boat's here," he called. "But soldiers are closing in fast. They can't stay long."

"I'm sorry," Lyriana said, her cheeks wet with tears or rain or both. "But we *have* to go." I felt weightless, floating, as she pulled me up, each step a mile separating me from Zell. I heard blades clash and voices howl, heard a man yell and a body hit the ground. We were almost to the top now, almost to Ellarion, almost to the boat. The air behind me sizzled, and I heard Zell's voice crying out in pain, a sound that felt like it was reaching deep into me and crushing my heart.

I looked. I had to look. I couldn't not. And I saw Mercer Stone raise up his hands, lift Zell into the air like he was a doll, and smash him hard into the stone courtyard behind him. I heard Zell scream as his arm shattered against the stone, and I heard the awful smack of his head hitting the ground. His swords clattered out of his hands. He coughed blood and rolled onto his side. Mercer turned his back to me, spreading his arms wide, a ripple of lightning forming around him for a killing blow.

And I stopped running.

Lyriana pulled me again, but I jerked my arm out of hers. In that moment, in the devastated city, surrounded by flame and ruin and death, I felt suddenly overwhelmingly calm. It was like time had stopped, like all the fear and anxiety and panic bled out of me in a rush. It was the calm that came with certainty, the calm that came from being freed from worrying about what to do, the calm of transcending choice.

For the last six months I'd lived in a perpetual state of uncertainty, trying to be someone I wasn't, trying to force myself to be hidden, to be silent, to be still. For the last six months, I'd tried to be the girl who would choose safety, the girl who would keep walking, the girl who would settle, the girl who would be happy.

But that wasn't me. That would never be me. I was Tilla of the tunnels, Tilla the traitor, Tilla the exile, Tilla the bastard. I was the girl who chose rebellion, the girl who loved a Zitochi warrior, the girl who risked it all to avenge her friend. I was reckless, and I was foolish, and I'd probably never be safe. But I was *me*.

And I wasn't about to let Zell die alone.

I sprinted down the rain-slick stairs, ignoring Lyriana's cry. There were two soldiers left alive, but they had their backs turned to me, taking in the spectacle of Zell struggling to stand as Mercer readied the blast that would finish him off. Running hard, I pulled a sword off one of the corpses, a light blade just longer than my forearm with a sturdy wooden handle. The soldiers didn't hear me approach, not over the roar of the city and the pounding of the rain, and that was the lucky break I needed. I slammed into the first one, cleaving open the side of his torso as I sent him stumbling down the steps. The second one spun around to see me, swinging a hefty ax in a wide arc. But he was slow, too slow, and my body still knew the khel zhan. I weaved to the side, dodging his blow, and whirled around like a blur, slitting open his throat with the very tip of my sword. He jerked to the side, wheezing, his life shooting out of him in a crimson spray.

That just left Mercer, his back still turned, his eyes still trained on his prey. He pulled back his hand, those lightning eels curling into a ball of flame in his palm, but he never got the chance to shoot it because I ran right up to him and stabbed him in the back, jamming my sword up to the hilt into the base of his spine, so the crimson blade burst out of his stomach like a nail driven through a board.

Mercer gasped in pain and lurched forward, but he didn't fall. My blade slipped out of my hands and he turned his head back to see me, blood trickling out between his teeth, his eyes throbbing so hard they looked ready to burst out of their sockets. "Die," he said, and turned that hand full of lightning to me. . . .

Then Zell moved. In one fluid motion, he sprang forward, grabbed one of his swords, and plunged it down into Mercer's chest, so the blade ripped out of his back just a few inches from my face. Mercer let out another sound, this one more of a gurgle, and the lightning around him flickered and then vanished, the veins in his eyes receding into the white. He stood there like that, my sword in his back, Zell's sword in his chest, then he crumpled to his side and lay still.

Zell and I stared at each other, both of us panting, our faces slick with blood and rain, surrounded by the bodies of the men we'd killed. Then he stepped forward and then I did, and he pulled me into his arms and held me, and there it was, the strength, the warmth, the safety. This was right. This was what mattered. We'd both made terrible mistakes, but right then it didn't matter anymore, because we had each other, because we were both alive, because I could still breathe in that smell of frost and feel his warm cheek pressed to my forehead. This was better than all the fancy dresses and decadent balls, better than kissing a thousand mages, better than safety, better than happiness. The world was a storm, but together, we were a port of calm. Together, we could do this.

"Come on!" Lyriana yelled.

I took Zell's hand, felt his skin against mine, felt our fingers lace as one.

And together again, we ran.

TWENTY-EIGHT

THE BOAT WAS A MIDSIZE MERCHANTS' SHIP, A STURDY THING with a tall mast and a golden figurehead of a mermaid. It floated along the gentle currents of the Adelphus, far enough from Lightspire that we could only see the blackened walls, the towering Godsblade, and the hundreds of columns of smoke reaching up into the sky. Morning was breaking out to the east, the first rays of sunlight painting the sky a rosy pink, even as the city burned. It was a new day, the first dawn of a new world, and the sunrise was almost mockingly beautiful.

I stood on the deck of the ship, my hand resting on the railing as we bobbed lightly along the river. Dozens of boats sailed around us, packed tight with the other people who'd made it out before the bloodmages had set the river at the city's exit ablaze with pillars of magical flame. We were a refugee fleet, an armada of exiles, united not in where we were going but only in the fact that we had fled. Looking out at those boats, I saw nobles and commoners alike, pressed together, staring at the smoldering city with haunted, tearstained eyes.

Streaks of sparkling light cut through the sky above us. Whispers dispatched to bring the news to the rest of the Kingdom. The walls of Lightspire still stood. And yet the great city had fallen all the same, destroyed from within, undone not by a great army but by love, by a mother's love for her son, by a father's love for his daughter. The Volaris dynasty was dead; King Elric Kent sat on the throne, and the whole continent was his to shape in his image.

I turned away from the city, from the other survivors, to look back at our own ship. Galen had let on anyone he could, so it was crowded like the others, but I could make out a few familiar faces. Darryn Vale sat with his feet dangling over the edge of the ship, sobbing into his hands. Marlo and Garrus stood together on the upper deck, arms around each other, gazing out at the city with faces etched with guilt. Princess Aurelia lay with her head in the lap of a sweet-looking older woman, who stroked her cheek with a weathered hand and promised her it would be okay.

The door to the lower decks swung open, and Lyriana stepped out. She'd cleaned herself up a little, washed away her tears and pulled her hair back into a ponytail, but nothing could wash away her devastated expression. "How is Ellarion?" I asked as she came over to me, even though I was terrified of how she'd reply.

"He'll live," she said. "There's two Sisters of Kaia tending to him down below. They've got him stable, and his wounds sealed off."

"But his hands . . ."

Lyriana looked down, silent, and that was answer enough.

A breeze blew over us, a chill and mournful wind that whistled through the sail and made us all shudder. I took Lyriana's hand and we walked together up a flight of stairs to the helm of the ship. Zell and Galen were there, helping the navigator and looking at an elegantly drawn map spread out over a nearby table.

"We'll make port in Ashelos tomorrow," Galen said. "I know the steward there, and he won't take this coup kindly. He'll shelter us, at least until Kent's men come looking."

"And then?" Zell asked.

"Then . . ." Galen repeated, and let out a long defeated sigh. I'd never seen him like this, never imagined he could even be like this. "Then I don't know. We run and hide, and run some more, run until they catch us and mount our heads on pikes?"

"Galen . . ." Lyriana said, but he waved her off.

"What can we do? We've lost. They've won. That's all there is."

"No," I said, and every head turned toward me. Everyone around me, every last person, was seized with despair and hopelessness, acting like the only option left was to embrace the inevitable death. I got that. What had happened, what my father had done, was unimaginable. But I still felt that calm I'd felt on those stairs, still felt that certainty that came from having only one option. My father had taken choice from us. And in its own way, that was a blessing.

"No?" Galen asked.

"No," I repeated. "They've won today, yeah. The battle is theirs. But the war? That's just getting started." I could see more people turning my way, a small crowd forming, and

I felt a weird feeling of disconnect, like I was an old woman looking back at my life, reliving this memory. *This was important*, I knew. *This was the moment it all changed.* "My father and Miles barely see eye to eye. The bloodmages act tough, but I've seen them beaten. There's a whole Kingdom's worth of people who won't bow down. And we've got something my father doesn't."

"What's that?" Lyriana asked.

"Nothing to lose," I replied. Zell nodded, and I saw the smile in his eyes, the determined look he always got when he was gearing up for a fight. "You all got used to being on top, to being in charge. Well, guess what? You're rebels now. You're fighters. And if there's one thing we've learned today, it's that a band of determined rebels can take down even the mightiest Kingdom." I saw heads nod in the crowd, heard the murmurs of approval. "The old world is dead. This is our chance to make something new, something better, to break the cycles of history and find our own path. This right here? This is the beginning of the resistance."

"You're damn right," Galen said, and slammed a hand on the wheel, alive again, driven. "To the survivors!" he shouted, his voice carrying over the water to the other ships. "To the resistance!"

Voices rose up around us, shouts of agreement, fists raised in the air. Galen shouted again, rallying the crowd, and I felt Zell's arm slide around my waist, hold me close with pride and love and resolve. On the other side of me, Lyriana squeezed my hand tight, and we stood there like that, together again, as our ship carried us south. I didn't know what the future would hold. I didn't know how this would all end. But I knew what I would do, what I had to do, and that was enough.

I would resist. I would bleed. I would struggle and I would kill and I would bring down my father and Miles, tear down their Kingdom, and make them pay for everyone they'd killed, for the King and the Queen, for Markiska, for Jax. I'd lead the way to a better future.

And I would fight until my last dying breath.

ACKNOWLEDGMENTS

Everyone in publishing tells you that your second book will be the hardest one you've ever written. I can now definitively confirm that's true. This book was an absolute labor of blood, sweat, tears, and whiskey, and I never would've made it through without my incredible support network.

Thanks, first of all, to the truly amazing team at Hyperion. You guys were always there for me, whether it was talking me through a frantic phone call of the debut jitters or sharing the excitement of launch. Thanks to my editor, Laura Schreiber, who remains an absolute legend, and helped me untangle this story's many complicated threads. I've never been so happy to see an e-mail with editorial notes in my life. Thanks as well to Cassie McGinty, a publicity wizard who set up a phenomenal launch and showed me the ropes of touring, and was always there with a cheerful answer and some great advice. And thanks to Mary Mudd, Tyler Nevins, Levente Szabo, Sara Liebling, Guy Cunningham, Dina Sherman, Kevin Pearl, and everyone else on Team Bastard.

To my champion and one-of-a-kind agent, Sara Crowe, who kicked ass every step of the way. Here's to this one and many more.

To my debut group, for the encouragement and advice and solidarity in riding out this year. We entered doe-eyed idealists; we walked out hardened warriors. Special shout-outs to Jilly Gagnon, Stephanie Garber, Emily Bain Murphy, Nic Stone, S. Jae-Jones, Ashley Poston, Scott Reintgen, and Misa Sugiura.

One of the joys of having a book out is getting to meet other published authors, to learn from those who've come before and try not to fanboy too hard at your heroes. Huge thanks to Dhonielle Clayton, Roshani Chokshi, Dahlia Adler, Parker Peevyhouse, Randy Ribay, Kelly Loy Gilbert, Jessica Taylor, and Tara Sim.

And then there are all the friends I couldn't have done this without, whose companionship got me through the roughest stretches:

The Wednesday Nite D&D Crew, for providing the best writing environment I could ask for: Owen Javellana, Chelsa Lauderdale, Eric Dean, Jennifer Young, Keyan Mohsenin, and Jessica Yang.

The Bullmoose Party, for always being there with a laugh, and for never letting go of my bad horsemath: Michelle and Geoff Corbett, Owen and Nikki Wiles, Brendan Berg, Brian Resler, and Christian Rose.

The Boardgame Boyz, because sometimes you just gotta drink some beers and roll some dice: Sean McKenzie, Geoff Lundie, and Brendan Boland.

To my family for their endless support: Ann and Simon, Yakov, Yulya, Marina and Daniel. Love you all.

And finally to Sarah and Alex, my heart and soul. It's all for you.

ZITOCHI
TUNDRA

ZHAL KORSO

BORDERLANDS

WESTERN PROVINCE

DOLAN ESTATE

CASTLE WAVERLY

BRIDGETOWN

SKARRLING CAVE

FROSTKISS MOUNTAINS

PORT HAMMIL

PORT LORRENT

MARKSON RIVER

THE NEST

SWAMPLANDS

ENDLESS OCEAN

TO K'OLALI ISLES

the KINGDOM of NOVERIS